THE JOSHUA STONE

THE JOSHUA STONE

JAMES BARNEY

wm
WILLIAM MORROW
An Imprint of HarperCollins*Publishers*

THE JOSHUA STONE. Copyright © 2013 by James Barney. All rights reserved. Printed in the United States of America. No part of this book may be used or reproduced in any manner whatsoever without written permission except in the case of brief quotations embodied in critical articles and reviews. For information address HarperCollins Publishers, 10 East 53rd Street, New York, NY 10022.

HarperCollins books may be purchased for educational, business, or sales promotional use. For information please write: Special Markets Department, HarperCollins Publishers, 10 East 53rd Street, New York, NY 10022.

FIRST EDITION

The mosaic piece of art on page 345 was created by Creative Commons. Used with permission.

Library of Congress Cataloging-in-Publication Data has been applied for.

ISBN 978-0-06-202139-7

13 14 15 16 17   OV/RRD   10 9 8 7 6 5 4 3 2 1

To my parents,
Captain William C. Barney, USN (ret.),
and Edna Barney

Thank you for all your love and support, and
congratulations on your 50th wedding anniversary

THE JOSHUA STONE

PROLOGUE

THURMOND, WEST VIRGINIA
October 5, 1959

IT was time. Dr. Franz Holzberg stood at the security desk of the Thurmond National Laboratory and waited patiently for the guard to buzz him through the heavy steel door that provided access to the lab. *Funny*, he thought as he waited. *They don't even know what they're guarding.* He shook his head and considered that thought for a moment.

If they only knew . . .

A second later, the door opened with a loud buzz, and Holzberg stepped into a steel enclosure about five feet square and seven feet tall. He turned to face the guard and pulled a chain-link safety gate across the opening.

"Ready?" asked the guard.

Holzberg nodded, and the compartment in which he stood suddenly lurched downward and began its long descent toward the laboratory spaces, nine hundred feet below the ground.

Two minutes later, the elevator shuddered to a halt, and Dr. Holzberg exited into a wide, empty passageway, about twenty feet across and two hundred feet long. The cracked, concrete floor was sparsely illuminated by overhead industrial lighting. A pair of rusty trolley rails ran down the middle of the corridor—a remnant of the mining operations that had once taken place there decades earlier.

Holzberg took a deep breath and savored the pungent smell of sulfur and stagnant water. After three long years of working on this project, he actually felt more at home underground than in the charmless cinder-block rambler that the government had provided for him "up top," in Thurmond.

He started off toward the laboratory at the end of the corridor, his footsteps echoing loudly throughout the vast space. As he walked, the protocol for Experiment TNL-213 streamed through his mind for the thousandth time. *Today is the day*, he reminded himself, allowing just the faintest of smiles. Today, God would heed *his* command. *Just as God heeded Joshua's command at Gibeon.*

Holzberg passed through the laboratory's heavy security door and entered a long, rectangular room resembling a tunnel, with unpainted cement walls, ceiling, and floor. The middle of the room was dominated by a large pool of water, twenty by thirty feet across and thirty feet deep, with a steel catwalk extending across it. A sturdy steel railing circumscribed the edge of the pool. Overhead, four long rows of incandescent bulbs illuminated the entire room with bright, white light. High up on the walls, thick, multicolored bundles of wires and cables snaked like garlands across sturdy brackets, with smaller bundles dropping down at uneven intervals to various lab equipment and workstations around the room.

Holzberg spotted four technicians in white lab coats

busily preparing the lab for the upcoming experiment. He acknowledged them with a nod and then quickly made his way to an elevated control room overlooking the pool. He entered without knocking and greeted the room's sole occupant, a bespectacled man in a white lab coat. "Good morning, Irwin," said Holzberg in a thick German accent. "How are the modifications coming along?"

Dr. Irwin Michelson swiveled on his stool. He was a wiry man in his midthirties, with disheveled black hair and a two-day-old beard. He pushed his glasses up on his nose. "They're done," he said.

"Done? You've tested it?"

"We changed out the power supply, like you suggested, and increased the cooling flow to two hundred gallons per minute. We tested it last night and were able to generate a ninety tesla pulse for twenty-five seconds with no overheating. We probably could go higher if we needed to."

"Good. And the sensors and transducers?"

"All set."

Holzberg nodded appreciatively to his tireless assistant. "*Sehr gut*. Then let's proceed."

It took nearly three hours for Holzberg, Michelson, and their team of four technicians to complete the exhaustive checklist for TNL-213. This experiment had taken three years to plan and had required millions of dollars in upgrades and modifications to the lab.

Nothing would be left to chance today.

By early afternoon they'd finished their thorough inspection of the equipment. They'd checked, double-checked, and triple-checked each of the hundreds of valves, levers, and switches associated with the lab's "swimming pool" test rig. Everything was positioned according to a detailed test protocol that Dr. Holzberg carried in a thick binder prominently marked TOP SECRET—WINTER SOLSTICE.

Michelson knelt on the steel catwalk that bridged the 160,000-gallon pool of water and carefully inspected a rectangular steel chamber that was suspended above the water by four thick cables. Numerous electrical sensors were welded to the exterior of this chamber, and a rainbow of waterproof wires radiated out from it, coiling upward toward a thick, retractable wiring harness above the catwalk.

"Transducers are secure," Michelson said over his shoulder.

"Good," said Holzberg from the railing. He made a checkmark in his notebook and read the next step of the protocol aloud. "Mount the seed."

Michelson stood and turned slowly to face his mentor. "So it's time?"

Holzberg nodded.

Michelson dragged a hand over his unshaven face and cracked a smile. "God, this . . . this is incredible." He was barely able to contain his excitement. "This'll give us a whole new understanding of the universe."

"Perhaps," said Holzberg.

"Right, perhaps. And *perhaps* the Nobel Prize, too."

"No," said Holzberg firmly, his expression suddenly turning dark.

"But . . . if this works, we could publish our findings. By then the government—"

"Irwin, *no*. We've had this discussion before."

Michelson sighed and looked deflated. "Right, I know. Not until the world is ready."

Holzberg inched closer to his protégé. "Irwin, this is a responsibility you must accept. Einstein *himself* was confounded by this material."

"Einstein was overrated," Michelson mumbled.

"Perhaps. But that does not change the fact that we have been entrusted with something very special here. We must study and solve it. Until we do, it is simply too dangerous to expose to the world. *That* is our burden. Do you understand?"

Michelson nodded sheepishly.

Holzberg patted his younger colleague's shoulder. "Good. Now, let's get the seed."

The two men made their way to the far end of the room, where a circular vault was mounted flush with the cement wall. The vault door was protected by a bank-grade, dual-combination lock with twin tumblers. "Ready?" Holzberg asked.

Michelson nodded.

One after the other, the two men turned the pair of dials on the vault door four times each, alternating clockwise and counterclockwise. When the last of the eight numbers had been entered, Michelson pulled down hard on the heavy handle in the center of the door, and the vault opened with a metallic *ka-chunk*. He swung the door open slowly, and, as he did, the vault's lights flickered, illuminating the interior with an ethereal blue light.

There was only one object in the vault: a clear glass cylinder about eight inches high and four inches in diameter housing an irregular black clump about the size of a golf ball. "The seed," Holzberg whispered as he reached inside and retrieved the cylinder, cradling it carefully in both hands. He held it up to the light and peered inside. "Your secrets unfold today."

Thirty minutes later, with the seed securely mounted in its special test chamber, and the chamber lowered deep into the pool, the two scientists returned to the control room for their final preparations.

"Transducer twenty-one?" said Holzberg, reading aloud from the test protocol.

Michelson pressed a button on the complex control panel and verified that transducer 21 was providing an appropriate signal. "Check."

"Transducer twenty-two?"

Michelson repeated the procedure for transducer 22. "Check."

"That's it then," said Holzberg, turning to a new page in his notebook. "We're ready." He checked his watch, which indicated 4:15 P.M. Then he picked up a microphone that was attached to the control panel by a long wire. "Gentlemen," he announced over the lab's PA system. "We are ready to commence experiment 213. Please take your positions."

In the lab space below, the four technicians quickly took up positions at their various workstations. One after another, they gave the thumbs-up signal that they were ready.

"Energize the steady-field magnet," announced Holzberg.

A loud, steady hum suddenly filled the lab, followed by the sound of rotating equipment slowly whirring to life. Several seconds later, Michelson quietly reported over his shoulder that the steady-field magnet was energized and warming up.

"Remember," Holzberg said, "bring it up slowly."

Michelson nodded. "We're at thirteen teslas and rising," he said, his attention focused on a circular dial on the control panel.

"And the cooling water outlet temperature?"

Michelson glanced at another gauge. "Sixty-two degrees."

Eight minutes later, Michelson announced they were at 25 teslas, the peak field for the steady-field magnet. "Outlet temperature's creeping up slightly," he added with a hint of caution.

"What about delta T?"

Michelson pushed a button and read from a gauge on his panel. "Nothing yet. Zero point zero."

Holzberg pressed the microphone button and announced to the lab, "Prepare to energize the pulse magnet."

There was a flurry of activity in the lab space below as the technicians quickly went about opening valves, flipping switches, and starting various pumps and other equipment. Eventually, all four gave the thumbs-up signal.

"Ready," reported Michelson.

Holzberg swallowed hard. *This was it.* He paused for a moment before giving the final command. "Energize it now."

Michelson pulled down on an electrical breaker until it clicked loudly into place. A deep buzzing sound immediately permeated the entire laboratory. The overhead lights dimmed momentarily and then slowly returned to their original intensity. "Energized," he reported nervously.

"Bring it up slowly."

"Total field is twenty-seven point three teslas." Michelson was slowly turning a large knob in the center of the control panel.

"Outlet temperature?"

"Seventy-eight degrees."

"Keep going."

Michelson continued turning the knob slowly until the magnetic-field strength had reached 70 teslas. There he paused and quickly checked his instruments. "Outlet temperature is one hundred twenty-two degrees and rising," he said nervously. "We don't have much more room."

"Any delta T?"

Michelson checked again and shook his head. "No. Still zero point zero."

"Keep going," said Holzberg.

Michelson nodded and again twisted the dial clockwise. He read out the magnetic-field strengths as he went. "Seventy-six point four. Seventy-eight point zero. Eighty point two . . ."

"Temperatures, Irwin."

Michelson quickly turned his attention to the outlet temperature gauge. "One hundred *forty-five* degrees and rising."

"Keep going," Holzberg said.

"Eighty-one teslas," said Michelson nervously. "Eighty-two. Eighty-three." His voice cracked slightly. "Uh . . . we're getting close to the outlet limit."

"Any delta T yet?"

Michelson quickly checked. "No. Zero point zero."

"We need a higher field." Holzberg touched Michelson's shoulder and nodded emphatically for him to continue.

Michelson's voice grew increasingly nervous as he continued reporting the rising magnetic-flux levels. "Eighty-seven point three. Eighty-eight point four. Eighty-nine point six . . . *ninety point one.*"

Suddenly, there was a loud beep, and an amber light began flashing on the control panel.

"Outlet temperature alarm," Michelson reported. "One hundred seventy-five degrees and still rising. Should I bring it back down?"

"*No,*" said Holzberg firmly. "We need a higher field."

Michelson started to protest, but Holzberg cut him off. "Irwin, the flux levels!"

Michelson snapped his attention back to the control panel. "Ninety-three point one . . . ninety-four point four . . . *shit.*"

Another shrill alarm sounded on the panel.

"Core temperature alarm!" Michelson shouted above the noise. "We've got to shut it down!" He began turning the knob counterclockwise.

"No!" Holzberg barked, grabbing his arm. "Check the delta T."

Michelson wiped his brow and checked. "Delta T is . . . zero point *one* seconds."

"My God," Holzberg whispered. "It's working!"

"Zero point two seconds," Michelson reported, still holding down the button. "Zero point three . . . zero point four."

"Bring it up just a bit more," said Holzberg over the constant noise of the two alarms.

"But—"

"Do it!" Holzberg snapped.

Michelson swallowed hard and slowly tweaked the knob clockwise to increase the power to the pulse magnet. "We're gonna lift a relief valve."

"What's the reading?"

Michelson pushed the delta T button. "*Whoa* . . ."

"What is it?"

"Ten point five seconds. That's incredible." He continued holding the button down. "Fourteen seconds . . . twenty . . . thirty . . . *fifty* . . ."

"We've done it!" Holzberg exclaimed, patting Michelson on the back. "Okay, you can bring it back down now."

Michelson quickly began twisting the knob counterclockwise. After several seconds, however, he suddenly looked confused.

"What is it?"

"Outlet temperature's . . . still going up." Michelson quickly pushed the button for delta T again. "Holy shit."

Holzberg leaned in close and observed that the dial for

delta T was now spinning rapidly clockwise. An odometer-style counter below the dial indicated that the accumulated value was now at *500 seconds . . . 600 seconds . . . 700 seconds. . . . * The dial was spinning faster and faster.

"Shut it down!" Holzberg bellowed.

"I am. Look!" Michelson showed that he had already twisted the knob for the pulse magnet all the way to the left.

"Cut the power!"

At that moment, a thunderous scream erupted in the lab space below, and thick plumes of steam instantly billowed up from the pool. The technicians could be heard screaming emphatically to each other.

"Relief valves are lifting!" Michelson yelled over the cacophony.

Holzberg was just about to say something when suddenly there was a blinding flash of white light below. Instinctively, he shielded his eyes.

"My God," Michelson shouted. "Look at that!"

Holzberg uncovered his eyes and gazed in awe at the spectacle now occurring in the lab below him. A brilliant aura of light was hovering directly above the reactor pool, swirling in undulating patterns of blue, green, red, and yellow. The aura lasted for several seconds before giving way to a violent, blinding column of light that shot suddenly out of the pool, straight to the ceiling.

Holzberg again shielded his eyes.

A split second later, there was a loud *whoosh* and the entire lab filled with blinding white light. The control room windows shattered instantly, and Dr. Holzberg hit the floor.

The blinding light and whooshing sound subsided after several seconds, leaving in their place a terrifying jumble of alarm sirens and horns and the panicked shouts of the technicians below. Holzberg groped on hands and knees through the broken glass until he found the prone body of Dr. Michelson, who was either unconscious or dead.

"Irwin!" said Dr. Holzberg.

There was no response.

With effort, Holzberg pulled himself to his feet and gazed in utter disbelief at the chaos unfolding below him.

"*Mein Gott*," he whispered. "What have we done?"

A second later, a man in a black leather coat suddenly appeared in the lab space below, seemingly from nowhere. *Who is that?* Holzberg wondered, utterly confused. *And why does he look familiar?*

PART ONE

Then Joshua spoke to the Lord in the day when the Lord delivered up the Amorites before the children of Israel, and he said in the sight of Israel:

"Sun, stand still over Gibeon;

And Moon, in the Valley of Aijalon."

So the sun stood still,

And the moon stopped,

Till the people had revenge

Upon their enemies.

Is this not written in the Book of Jasher? So the sun stood still in the midst of heaven, and did not hasten to go down for about a whole day. And there has been no day like that, before it or after it, that the Lord heeded the voice of a man; for the Lord fought for Israel.

HOLY BIBLE, the book of Joshua 10:12–14

1

THELMA SCOTT grimaced as she wiped off the Formica counter of the Fire Creek Diner, known to everyone in town as "Thelma's." She stopped for a moment and slowly wiggled all of her fingers, taking note of the increased pain in her joints. "Gonna rain," she mumbled. She prided herself on being able to predict the weather better than anyone on TV, and it was definitely going to rain today. She could *feel* it.

Outside, the morning sun was just cresting over Beury's Ridge, nine miles away. Yet this did virtually nothing to brighten the hardscrabble town of Fire Creek, which was nestled deep in the valley below the ridge. At this hour, the tiny town was still enveloped in an opaque blanket of autumn fog that had filled the New River Gorge Valley overnight. Thelma peered through the diner's front window and observed the swirling mist outside, thicker than normal for this time of year. *Yep, rain within the hour*, she predicted.

Instinctively, Thelma glanced at the old clock on the

wall, which read 6:05. Then, as she did every morning, she stepped onto a chair and tweaked the big hand forward three minutes. *Always three minutes. Every day.*

She started a pot of coffee and fired up the diner's antique O'Keefe & Merritt gas griddle. The morning crowd would be here soon, although "crowd" wasn't quite the right word. The old codgers Tommy Ellis, Frank Rutter, and Joe McMahon would be here for their buckwheat pancakes, toast and butter, and double-thick sliced bacon. They'd sit in their regular booth and swap war stories, mining stories, and political bluster for hours until one of them would finally stand up, scratch his belly, and say, "Well, someone's got to get some dang work done around here." Joe's wife would sit at the counter the entire time, chain-smoking Marlboro Lights and chatting with Thelma about the latest hardship to befall some member of the McMahon clan. Then, with luck, several of the younger men in town (and there were very few of those) would stop by on their way to Fayetteville or Beckley for their mining jobs. They usually just picked up coffee to go.

That was the extent of the morning crowd at Thelma's.

It was amazing to her how much things had changed around here. Fire Creek had never been a big town. Even when she was younger and the town was in its heyday in the 1940s, the population was never more than five thousand. But it was *bustling* back then. The New River Coal Company was still in business in those days, extracting bituminous coal from the Fire Creek vein at full capacity. The massive coke ovens on the outskirts of town burned twenty-four hours a day, converting the sulfur-rich Fire Creek coal into valuable coke for the steel industry. Thelma remembered how the entire town felt such a sense of pride about their contribution to the war effort. The coke from Fire Creek was used to make Pittsburgh steel, which, in turn, was used to make tanks, ships, and guns. Back then, the foursquare houses in town were all freshly painted, and American flags flew from nearly every porch.

That all changed, however, in 1955, when the federal government came to town.

Thelma checked the refrigerator to ensure she had all the supplies she needed for lunch: hamburger patties, hot dogs, cold cuts, potato and macaroni salads, coleslaw, and soft drinks. It was Friday, which meant the "ghost hunters" would soon be arriving.

Thelma had first noticed them about five years ago: small groups of tourists arriving sporadically in cars and vans, mostly on weekends. Apparently, someone on the Internet had popularized the idea of taking self-guided "ghost town" tours along the New River Gorge. And, for some reason, they had included Fire Creek on their map of West Virginia ghost towns, although Thelma could never figure out why. *People still lived here. How could it be a ghost town?* Granted, the town's population was less than four hundred and dwindling by the year. But it wasn't a ghost town.

At least, not yet.

Thelma poured herself a cup of coffee and was just about to click on the TV when there was a loud knock on the front door of the diner. It was a repetitive, insistent knock that rattled the metal OPEN/CLOSED sign hanging on the doorknob. She squinted to make out the features of the person standing in the fog outside the glass door, but all she could tell was that it was a man. He was hunched over slightly and . . . wearing a hat. "We're closed," she yelled to him, still puzzling over the hat. It looked like a fedora, and the only person she knew who wore a fedora these days was Frank Rutter. But that wasn't Frank. . . .

The man knocked again—several loud raps on the glass. "Please," he said in a muffled voice. "I need help."

Thelma inched toward the door, her pulse quickening. A few years ago, one of the McMahon boys had come into the diner late at night, brandishing a gun and demanding money. The poor kid was addicted to OxyContin and was desperate for a fix. Thelma would never forget how he apologized and actually cried as he robbed her. He was later arrested for armed robbery and put in jail, where he still was today. That experience had shattered Thelma's sense of security and made her very hesitant to open her door to strangers, especially in the dark.

The man outside knocked again and pleaded through the glass door, "Please. I need a doctor."

"Oh my word," Thelma gasped, rushing to the door. She could now see that it was an elderly, white-bearded man, and he was hunched over, holding his stomach. His white shirt was soaked through with blood. *Danger be damned*, she thought. She was not going to let this poor old man die outside her front door. She unlocked the door and flung it open.

The wounded man stumbled into the diner and immediately dropped to his knees beside the lunch counter. He had his hands clutched to his bloody stomach, and he was wincing in pain.

"Lord in heaven!" Thelma said. She put her hand on the man's back, momentarily unsure about what to do. His head was down, so she couldn't fully see his face. *But something about him was familiar.* "I'll call 911," she said, rushing toward the phone behind the counter.

"*Vaht?* No." The bearded man spoke with a heavy German accent. He looked up and seemed genuinely confused. "I need a *doctor*."

What the heck does he think I'm doing? Thelma quickly

punched 911 into the phone. As she waited for the operator, she tried to place the man's voice. *Where had she heard
that accent before?* A moment later, the emergency operator
picked up, and Thelma explained the situation to him and
gave the address of her diner. "Yes," she repeated before
hanging up. "Fire Creek. East of Mount Hope, at the end of
Route 26."

Thelma returned to the diner floor to comfort the
injured man, who was now lying in the fetal position, panting in short breaths. "It's gonna be a while, honey," she
said soothingly. "They're coming all the way from Beckley.
Could be twenty-five minutes or more."

The old man groaned at that news, and Thelma's heart
sank. What could she do? She didn't know the first thing
about treating wounds. The man was panting in shallow breaths and appeared to be going into shock. Thelma
decided the only thing she could do was keep him awake
and alert. "What happened to you, sweetie?" she asked.

The man convulsed in pain and said nothing.

Thelma leaned over and got a full view of the man's
bloody abdomen. She quickly recoiled and cupped her
mouth with her hands. "My God," she whispered. *It must
have been one of those drug gangs.* The backwoods in Fayette County were notorious for concealing marijuana
farms and trailer-home meth kitchens. Those people were
truly crazy.

But this man didn't seem like the type to be involved
with drugs. "You visiting from somewhere?" she asked.
It was the only thing she could think of given his foreign
accent and odd attire. He wore a white dress shirt—soaked
with blood in the front—a black necktie, gray wool pants
with suspenders, a matching gray jacket, and black dress
shoes, thoroughly caked with mud. His fedora lay on the
floor, near his head.

The wounded man did not respond to Thelma's question. His breathing was getting more sporadic now, almost spastic.

"Oh dear," Thelma whispered. *He ain't gonna make it.* She started off toward the phone again. "I'll call Hiram Johnson. He was a medic in the army."

"No," groaned the man, drawing his knees up closer to his chest. "Call . . . Dr. . . . Reynolds." He sucked in several shallow breaths before continuing. "Princeton 572."

Thelma stopped short and turned around slowly. A strange feeling suddenly emerged from the pit of her stomach. "Where'd you say you was from?"

"Thurmond," the man grunted.

Well, Thelma knew that was a lie. Thurmond really *was* a ghost town. *Nobody has lived there since . . .*

Then suddenly it hit her. She now realized where she'd heard this man's voice before. She stepped slowly toward his contorted body, her eyebrows scrunched in confusion. "Who *are* you?" she asked.

The man didn't answer. He was losing consciousness. Thelma stooped down and lightly slapped him on the cheek several times. "C'mon now," she said. "Don't go nowhere." With her thumb and forefinger, she lifted one of the man's eyelids, revealing a glassy, dilated pupil. She had no idea what she was looking for, but she'd seen people do this on TV. She grabbed the man's bearded jaw firmly with one hand and gently shook his head back and forth.

The man came to and coughed meekly.

"That's it, honey," Thelma said. "Stay with me, now. Help is on the way."

The man stared up at her blankly.

"Now, tell me where you came from *exactly*."

The man whispered something indecipherable.

"Huh?"

"Thurmond . . . National . . . L—" The word "laboratory" never made it past his lips before his eyes rolled back into his head and his body went completely limp.

But Thelma had heard enough. Her eyes widened as she stood and slowly backed away from the bleeding man. "Not possible," she whispered, shaking her head in disbelief. "Not possible."

2

KILL ME now," whispered Mike Califano to the attractive blonde next to him. They were seated in the third row of Training Room D at the Department of Energy's headquarters on Independence Avenue. The lecturer at the front of the room was droning on for the third straight hour about security breaches at the nation's sixty-five civilian nuclear power plants. *Hypothetical* breaches, that is. The type of "what-if" scenarios that only a roomful of pencil-pushing DOE security analysts could manage to dream up and get excited about.

But Califano was not excited. The lecturer at the front of the room was Roger Hutton, an insufferable know-it-all prick who had recently been promoted ahead of him. At the moment, Hutton was talking about the possibility of terrorists tunneling their way into the Savannah River nuclear facility in South Carolina, and he had dozens of classified diagrams and topographical maps to prove his theory.

Bullshit, Califano thought, shaking his head just as much as he thought he could get away with. He'd seen the real thing enough to know that none of these exotic scenarios was even remotely plausible. The *real* threat was—and always had been—the risk of an inside job, a saboteur who could be placed inside one of these plants and then wreak havoc upon receiving orders from the outside. Califano knew that once two or three such agents were in place at a nuclear facility, no amount of pencil-pushing analysts or high-tech security measures could stop an enemy intent on creating mayhem. And here was Hutton, blathering on about *tunnels*.

C'mon, man, Califano thought. He quickly scanned the audience and was surprised to see that nearly everyone was still diligently taking notes. These were men and women from the FBI, the CIA, the DIA, and other government agencies, who had all been sent to the Department of Energy for two days of training about the nation's energy infrastructure and how to protect it from terrorism and other threats.

Califano crossed his arms and sighed, prompting a disapproving glance from the blonde next to him. She held his gaze for a moment before returning her attention to the lecture. But Califano kept his eyes fixed on her after she looked away. *Why doesn't she have a training booklet?* he wondered. *And why wasn't she here this morning?* He was still mulling these questions over when his cell phone suddenly buzzed in his pocket, eliciting another scornful look from his blond neighbor. Califano retrieved his phone discreetly and glanced down at the incoming secure text message. It read: SCIF, ASAP.

That could be only one person.

Califano immediately rose, gathered his training materials, and began making his way—disruptively—to the center aisle that led to the exit door at the back of the room.

Roger Hutton stopped his lecture in midsentence with a look of disbelief on his face.

After a long, awkward interruption, Califano finally reached the center aisle, where he momentarily paused and met Hutton's incredulous stare. "Oh, sorry," he said with a shrug. "Gotta take a leak."

The room erupted with laughter.

Califano turned to leave but suddenly stopped short, as if he'd forgotten something. "Oh yeah," he said, turning back to face Hutton. Every eyeball in the room was now on Califano. "You know, there's an important feature you forgot to mention on that map." He pointed to the topographical survey map of the Savannah River that was currently being displayed on the large screen at the front of the room.

"What's that?" asked Hutton with unveiled contempt.

"Got a pen?"

Hutton rolled his eyes and reluctantly retrieved a pen and paper from below the podium.

A moment later, Califano rattled off a long set of lat/long coordinates from memory, without the slightest bit of hesitation or appearance of mental effort. "Take a look at 33.33384 north and 81.73780 west." He paused to let Hutton scribble down those coordinates. "There's something important that everyone should see." Califano gave a perfunctory nod, then turned and headed quickly to the exit.

Once Califano had slipped through the exit door at the back of the room, he immediately spun and caught the door just before it closed. He crouched low and peeked through the remaining crack at Hutton, who was still standing at the podium. "Come on, you tool," Califano whispered to himself. He knew Hutton wouldn't be able to resist checking the coordinates he'd just given him, if only to try to show him up. As he watched, he saw Hutton typing the coordinates into his laptop computer at the podium. "That's it," Califano whispered.

Seconds later, the large screen at the front of the room suddenly zoomed in on the precise coordinates Califano had just provided. In the center of the screen, large enough for the entire audience to see, were two words that Califano himself had electronically added to the map late last night, after hacking into Hutton's presentation materials: BITE ME.

The audience roared with laugher.

With that, Califano turned and walked away with a satisfied grin. *His work here was done.*

The SCIF at the Department of Energy was located deep beneath the iconic James V. Forrestal Building at L'Enfant Plaza, which many considered to be one of the ugliest buildings in Washington, D.C. "An elephant teetering on giraffe legs," was how the *Washington Post* had described the building when it opened in 1968. Indeed, the Forrestal Building was a particularly unflattering example of "Brutalist" architecture, a style that had swept through Washington, D.C., in the late sixties and early seventies. The fact that the building was named for a former secretary of defense who committed suicide by jumping from the sixteenth floor of Bethesda Naval Hospital only added to its melancholia.

Califano exited the elevator at the B–3 level and made his way to a gray metal door marked SCIF, which stood for Special Compartmented Information Facility. He pressed his key fob against a sensor beside the door, and the door clicked open automatically. He entered and allowed the door to swing shut behind him with a clank. "How ya doing?" he said to the guard at the front desk.

The guard nodded without altering his steely expression. "Empty your pockets."

Califano complied, placing his wallet, cell phone, keys, and loose change in a small plastic bin on the table. The guard put the bin high up on a shelf behind him. "You can pick those up when you leave. If you need to take notes, use the pen and paper provided in the reading room, and leave your notes in the safe."

"Right," said Califano. After nearly eight years at the DOE, he knew the SCIF procedures cold.

"Arms up," said the guard.

Califano spread his arms as the guard waved a metal-detecting wand all around his body. "Admiral Armstrong's waiting for you in reading room four."

Califano thanked the guard and made his way down a short hallway to reading room 4. He knocked twice and entered.

The reading room was about ten feet square, with bare white walls and a small table and four chairs in the center. There was a heavy-duty, security-grade filing cabinet pressed against one wall. Sitting at the table was a well-dressed man in his late sixties, with silver hair and a distinguished, weathered face. "Have a seat," said Vice Admiral Robert Armstrong, deputy director of the National Security Agency.

Califano seated himself at the opposite side of the table.

"Michael," said Armstrong. "You've been at DOE seven years."

"Almost eight."

Armstrong nodded. "Right, almost eight. A bit longer than we expected, to be sure. And I know you're eager to move on to another assignment. But I wanted to let you know you've done a terrific job here."

Califano shrugged. "Just routine stuff."

"Nonsense. You've given us valuable insights into the

foreign infiltration of our national labs, scientific espionage, technological intelligence that we simply could not have obtained through . . . *normal* channels. Nothing routine about it."

"Am I getting a promotion?" asked Califano with a wry smile. He knew the answer was no.

"Sorry, Michael. A promotion would invite scrutiny. There would be fresh questions about your, uh . . . background."

Califano nodded knowingly. His "background," as the admiral had so quaintly put it, should have automatically disqualified him for this job. Indeed, as Califano well knew, he was lucky to have *any* job, let alone a job with an SCI security clearance and a direct line to the deputy director of the NSA. And he owed all of this to Admiral Armstrong.

"Besides," Armstrong added, "you'd spend all your time supervising others, writing personnel evaluations, pushing paperwork. You don't want to do all that stuff, do you?"

Califano shook his head emphatically. He hated bureaucracy with a passion.

"Trust me. You're most valuable to us where you are right now, an assistant security auditor with no subordinates. Totally below the radar."

"But I'm getting a little old for this position, aren't I?" In fact, at thirty-four, Califano was already the second-oldest assistant auditor in the department, and the *only* one who'd held that position for seven straight years.

Armstrong seemed amused by this question. "Hmm, let's see, Michael. You're insubordinate and openly disrespectful to your supervisors. You keep bizarre hours, and you're chronically late with your audit reports. Hell, you can't even be bothered to follow the department's dress code."

"What? I'm wearing a blazer."

"Yeah, over faded jeans and tennis shoes. Definitely not authorized. Plus your hair's too long."

"There's no regulation on hair. I checked."

"My point is, Michael, I don't think *anyone* around here is surprised that you haven't been promoted in nearly eight years."

Califano smirked. "Yeah, I guess not."

Armstrong reached across the table and patted Califano's arm. "You're a good man, Michael. An asset to this department and the NSA. The best scientific intelligence analyst we've ever had. Stick with us a little longer, and I promise I'll get you that transfer you've been asking for."

Califano nodded his unspoken appreciation.

Then Armstrong straightened in his chair, his expression suddenly turning grave. "But right now, I need your help on something very serious."

Califano leaned forward, intrigued. *Anything to get him out of Hutton's training.*

"There's been some activity in one of your programs. We don't understand what it means, and we need your help figuring it out. I'm afraid there's not much time."

"Which program?" Califano was already mentally organizing a list in his head of more than fifty top-secret research programs that he routinely monitored, flagging in his mind the most likely candidates for having recent and unusual activity.

"Winter Solstice."

The thin program file for Winter Solstice instantly appeared in Califano's photographic memory. "But that program is—"

"Dormant, I know."

"No, not just dormant. I mean, it hasn't had activity since . . ." His brain searched for the correct date.

Armstrong beat him to it. "Since 1959."

"Right. So why would there suddenly be activity in that program *now*?"

Armstrong checked his watch and pushed back from the table. "I'll explain it on the way."

"On the way where?"

Armstrong pointed straight up. "The roof."

3

THE ROTORS of the Bell 407 helicopter were already spinning when Califano and Armstrong reached the rooftop helipad of the Forrestal Building.

"Keep your head down," Armstrong yelled over the rotor wash.

This warning was unnecessary, however. Califano knew his way around helicopters from his frequent trips to secret DOE laboratories all around the United States. As they approached the rear door of the helicopter, a hand suddenly reached out from the passenger compartment to help Admiral Armstrong into the chopper. Califano climbed in after the admiral and situated himself in one of the two leather seats that faced forward. It was only after he had buckled himself into his seat that he took a good look at the third person in the passenger cabin, who was now sitting directly across from him. It was the blond woman from the training room. And now it suddenly made sense why she'd appeared from out of nowhere this afternoon and with no training booklet.

Admiral Armstrong quickly performed an introduction, shouting above the rising rotor noise. "Michael, this is Ana Thorne of the CIA. She's going to be helping us with this matter."

Califano extended his hand. "Nice to meet you."

Thorne grasped Califano's hand firmly and leaned in close to him. "Nice to meet you, too . . . *again*."

Califano cracked a smile. "You were stalking me this afternoon."

"Just gathering intel," Thorne said with a shrug. "Wanted to see you in your natural state."

"Well," said Califano, still holding her hand. "What'd you think?" By now, the rotor noise had reached a high, steady pitch, and the chopper was shuddering in undulating waves of resonant frequencies as it prepared to lift off.

Thorne shouted into Califano's ear, "You're cynical. And you tend to telegraph your emotions. Those are dangerous liabilities in the field." What she didn't tell him was the rest of her assessment: *tall, reasonably athletic, good-looking in a dot-com-millionaire-nerd sort of way, and confident. Perhaps too confident. Likes to challenge authority, which could be a problem.*

A moment later, the chopper lifted off from the roof.

Califano released Thorne's hand and sat back in his seat as the chopper rose high above the DOE headquarters, nosed down about twenty degrees, and banked left toward the Washington Monument and the Tidal Basin. His eyes were still fixed, however, on the female CIA officer across from him. She had shoulder-length blond hair; smooth, pale skin; light green eyes; and the calm demeanor of a predator. She looked to be in her early thirties. Fit and serious and . . . *What was that?* Califano caught a glimpse of the woman's right ear through a break in her hair. The helix and lobe of the ear appeared to be badly scarred, as was the surrounding skin of her upper neck.

Almost as if she could read his mind, Thorne quickly turned her head away and adjusted her hair. Her lips tightened as she stared out the window of the chopper.

Crap. Had he been leering? Telegraphing his thoughts again, as she'd predicted? Califano considered apologizing to her, but he realized that would only make matters worse. Instead, he put her out of his mind altogether and turned to Admiral Armstrong. "Where are we going, sir?" he shouted.

Armstrong cupped a hand to his ear.

Califano shouted the question again: "Where are we going?"

"To see our patient," Armstrong replied.

The helicopter flew northwest along the Potomac River at a remarkably low altitude. *No doubt some special clearance was needed for this flight plan*, Califano thought. He watched as the Memorial Bridge, the Roosevelt Bridge, and then the Key Bridge glided gracefully beneath them as they made their way out of the nation's capital. Soon, the river itself changed from a greenish-brown ribbon of glass to a tumultuous tumble of gray rocks and whitewater as they cleared the Chain Bridge and flew low over a portion of the Potomac River famous for its deadly rapids. Two minutes later, the chopper banked hard left and soared low above the dense canopy of the George Washington National Forest, already resplendent with autumn colors.

Califano knew exactly where they were, so he was not surprised when the dense forest suddenly gave way to a massive complex of office buildings flanked on three sides by twenty acres of sprawling parking lots. The headquarters of the Central Intelligence Agency. "Nice place you got here," he shouted to Ana Thorne.

"We make do," she replied.

The Bell 407 hovered for a minute, awaiting clearance to land. Then it descended gracefully onto a square patch of manicured grass on the east side of the main building, about a hundred feet from the white hemispherical CIA auditorium known as "The Bubble."

The three passengers disembarked from the helicopter and were immediately greeted by a large, bespectacled man with reddish hair and fleshy features. He wore a blue V-neck sweater, white shirt, and striped tie with khaki slacks.

Admiral Armstrong shook the man's hand and then gestured toward Califano. "Bill, this is Michael Califano, our very best scientific intelligence analyst. Michael, meet Dr. Bill McCreary, director of, uh . . . *what* are you calling your program these days?"

"Disruptive Technology Analysis and Intervention," said McCreary. "DTAI for short." He extended his hand to Califano.

"How you doing?" said Califano, shaking the man's hand.

"So how's our patient?" Armstrong asked.

"Not well, I'm afraid," said McCreary. "Touch and go at this point."

"Then let's go see him."

The Medical Intelligence Unit at Langley was housed in building 3 and consisted of an isolated corridor of four large "examination" rooms, each crammed with computers and scientific equipment. *Not all of it strictly "medical" in nature*, Califano guessed. Each examination room was fitted with a large two-way mirror.

The four of them entered a darkened viewing room overlooking examination room 2. Califano found himself looking down upon an elderly man secured to a hospital bed by several parachute-grade nylon straps. His abdomen was heavily bandaged. Two armed guards stood nearby as a medical technician tweaked knobs on what appeared to be an anesthesia machine. The patient was writhing beneath the straps, groaning and muttering nonsensical phrases. *"Mein Gott!"* he said in German several times. Then, switching to English, he mumbled something about "murder of science." The medical technician quickly adjusted a knob on the anesthesia machine, and the old man seemed to relax a bit. After a minute or two, he stopped talking altogether and gave up his struggle against the restraints. As he drifted into a drug-induced stupor, he uttered one last phrase, which was clearly audible over the speakers mounted in the ceiling of the observation room: *"Es gibt noch Zehn mehr."*

All four of them looked at each other and shrugged. "What's he on?" Armstrong asked.

"At the moment," said McCreary, "a mixture of amobarbital and morphine. But we've tried different drugs, different dosages, and different combinations over the past several hours. Trust me, if he had something meaningful to say, he would have said it already. I'm afraid he's entered an advanced stage of delirium."

"Caused by his wounds?" asked Armstrong.

McCreary shook his head. "Not entirely. According to our medical team, the wound to his abdomen was caused by a small-caliber, high-velocity bullet, which passed through his stomach and nicked his pancreas before exiting the left side of his lower back. A lot of internal damage, plus the onset of infection, which is typical for this type of injury when it isn't treated right away. But according to our medical folks, none of that is the proximal cause of the psychological symptoms we're seeing. These symptoms are more consistent with dementia, which is normally associated with old age."

"How old *is* he?" Armstrong asked.

Califano was wondering the same thing. The man strapped to the bed looked ancient. He had long, wild, white hair and a white beard with a mustache to match. He looked like a crazed, skinny Santa Claus. His blue eyes were hazy and sunk deep into his face, rimmed by several layers of dark bags. His fingers were crooked and bony. *And his fingernails . . .*

"Doc, what's up with his fingernails?" asked Califano. The man's fingernails were long and curly, like frozen snakes. It reminded Califano of a picture he'd once seen in the *Guinness World Records* of a man with the world's longest fingernails.

"We're not sure. His hair and fingernails have been growing at a rapid rate ever since he arrived. A very unusual phenomenon that we're still trying to figure out. We think he may be suffering from some form of Hutchinson-Gilford syndrome, also known as progeria or rapid aging."

"Do you know the cause?" asked Armstrong.

McCreary shrugged. "No. In fact, there's no recorded case of an adult onset of this disease. It's an extremely rare birth defect, always associated with newborns. Typically the afflicted children don't live past ten or twelve."

They all looked down at the bizarre man strapped to the bed, whose body was now completely limp.

"All right, hold on," said Califano, shaking his head. If there was one thing he hated, it was not being in full command of the facts. And when there was a puzzle to be solved, his brain craved resolution like a junkie craved drugs. "Can we just back up a bit here a bit?" He looked at Admiral Armstrong with raised eyebrows, as if to say, *May I?*

Armstrong nodded that he could proceed.

"All right," said Califano. "Can someone please tell me how any of this relates to Winter Solstice?"

There was a moment of awkward silence as the other three exchanged glances. Finally, Dr. McCreary spoke up. "Yeah, I think I can explain that."

4

THURMOND, WEST VIRGINIA

MALACHI STOOD in the cold drizzle, the collar of his black leather coat upturned. *Where were they?* His contacts were supposed to be waiting for him at this very spot. He was sure of it. A man and a woman in a car. He couldn't remember their names or faces, or the make of their vehicle, but he was sure they were supposed to be waiting for him here, flashing their lights to signal him. After all, they'd rehearsed this.

Hadn't they?

The truth was that he could no longer be sure. His memory at this point was a tangled mess. He was oddly self-aware that he was suffering from some sort of delirium—a general sense of disorientation about time, place, and person. The rational part of his brain was able to identify these symptoms precisely, yet this did nothing to bring back his memories or straighten out the confusing jumble of thoughts and images in his mind. Random recollections had been trickling into his brain for hours, in no particular order and with no apparent logic or motif. As he stood motionless in the cold mountain rain, he could not remember exactly how he'd gotten there, or why. Nor could he remember his real name. "Malachi" was a code name; he knew that. But it was the only name he could remember.

Perhaps this isn't the right spot after all, he thought. He scanned the muddy road that ran parallel to the railroad tracks and saw nothing in either direction. Then, as he'd done for the past hour, he studied the abandoned building on the other side of the tracks, scrutinizing every detail, hoping for a clue that might trigger some useful memory. The building's crumbling brick facade was badly discolored with moss, climbing vines, and indecipherable squiggles of graffiti. A faded sign at the top of the building read THUR-MOND in large black-on-white letters.

Malachi slowly shook his head. *This was all wrong.* To begin with, why was it light outside?

He struggled once again to piece together the chain of events that had led him to this abandoned coal station along the New River Railroad Line. He'd entered the lab around 10:30 P.M., although it might have been a little later. *Time*—he lingered on that thought for a moment. *Something about the time.*

A new memory was now hovering just beyond his mental grasp, tantalizingly close yet still too vague to visualize. Slowly, bits and pieces came into focus. There had been a struggle. Shots were fired. There was blood. *Lots of blood.* He now remembered walking through the mine shaft alone. Which would explain the portable carbide lantern that now rested by his feet. His mind continued processing these new facts, moving mental puzzle pieces around to make room for the new information. Traversing the mine would have taken some time, which might have thrown the whole schedule off.

Still, that did not account for the daylight. *How long had he walked?* It should have taken only an hour to get here from the lab. He'd rehearsed it many times, practicing for this very rendezvous. He must have gotten lost. He checked the dial of his Omega automatic, which appeared to be working just fine. It read 1:55 A.M. *Strange*, he thought. It should be the middle of the night right now. Instead, it appeared to be late afternoon. Somehow, he'd lost nearly an entire day.

Frustrated and confused, Malachi reached into the inner pocket of his leather coat for his cigarettes. As he did, his fingernails snagged raggedly on the lip of his coat pocket. He cursed and looked down at his grotesquely long fingernails. Then, for the third time in as many hours, he carefully retrieved his pocketknife and proceeded to trim all ten of them. After this, he sat down, removed his shoes and socks, and did the same for his overgrown toenails.

With this process complete and his shoes back on, Malachi slipped the pack of Chesterfields out of his pocket, shook one cigarette loose, and brought it to his lips. By now, the drizzle had increased to a light rain. He quickly cupped his hands and lit his cigarette, then looked across the tracks at the welcoming shelter of the railroad depot. Although the roof was partially caved in, it looked like there were still some dry areas inside. He quickly crossed the tracks, but stopped short when he reached an impenetrable thicket of thorny vines. He turned left and forged a new path through the wet undergrowth, making his way slowly around the corner of the building. After some time, he stopped and gazed up at the weathered advertisement painted across the entire west side of the building, which had been obscured from his previous vantage point.

Something about it was familiar.

At the top of the advertisement was a large circular seal with the words WEST VIRGINIA MAIL POUCH TOBACCO—FOR CHEWING AND SMOKING written around the circumference. In the center of the seal was a brown, irregular object—presumably a mail pouch—and the words TRADE MARK. Below the seal, the words MAIL POUCH were painted in gigantic, western-style yellow letters. What caught Malachi's eye, however, was a small addendum at the bottom of the sign, just below the letter *H* in POUCH. The addendum was painted in red, somewhat more crudely than the rest of the sign.

Malachi stepped closer and cleared away several strands of Virginia creeper that were partially obscuring the red lettering. Once the vine was cleared, he could now see the full message, which read:

$$\chi = E \cdot Z(U)$$

Something suddenly clicked in his brain. This appeared to be a mathematical equation of some sort, although he didn't immediately recognize it from his working knowledge of physics, chemistry, and mathematics. The more interesting question was why such an equation would be written *here*, on the side of an abandoned coal station in rural West Virginia. Only one logical explanation came to mind: *this message was meant for him.* As that realization sank in, a new thought began forming at the edge of his consciousness. Something about the first symbol in the equation, the small Greek letter chi.

The small chi was sometimes used in physics to denote a coordinate. For instance, it was used in Einstein's equations for the effect of gravity on a light beam. But Malachi knew this particular equation had nothing to do with gravity or light beams. *No, in this equation, chi meant something entirely different.* He remained motionless in front of the wall for several minutes, moving only to take occasional drags from his cigarette, which he kept skillfully cradled in one hand to avoid the rain. Finally, he took one last puff and tossed the butt to the ground. He now remembered the significance of the letter chi. It was something they had told him during his training. *He* was "chi." He was Mala . . . *chi*.

With this new perspective, Malachi considered the painted equation with renewed vigor. *What did it mean that he, Malachi, was equal to E·Z(U)?* In physics, the capitalized *E* most often stood for energy, although it could be used to denote other things, such as an electrical field. *But what about* Z? The only thing he could think of was the atomic number of an atom, usually written as Z. If that were the case, then "Z(U)" might be thought to represent the atomic number for uranium, which was 92. *Yet that made no sense.*

Malachi pushed the conflicting thought aside for a moment and focused all his attention on the small dot between the *E* and the *Z*, which usually denoted multiplication in mathematics. *Did that mean energy times 92? The energy of uranium, or perhaps the energy derived from splitting a uranium atom? Maybe it was referring to atomic energy in general.*

He was now thoroughly confused. This "equation" seemed to be nothing more than a meaningless assemblage of snippets from chemistry, physics, and mathematics. He was tempted to move on and seek shelter inside the depot, but he couldn't. This message had obviously been left for him, and he was determined to solve it. *It was the only thing he had.*

Something a colleague had once told him suddenly came to mind. "If a problem can't be solved mathematically, then it isn't a mathematical problem at all." Which meant that not everything in life was amenable to a mathematical resolution. There was a place—even in science—for inductive reasoning. Malachi looked with fresh eyes at the mysterious equation on the wall. In fact, the series of symbols *wasn't* a mathematical equation. How could it be, if one of the two equivalent expressions was a human being? A human being, with all his unique characteristics and idiosyncrasies, could never truly be "equal" to anything else. But if this wasn't a mathematical equation, then what *was* it?

Up until now, Malachi had closely analyzed each of the symbols in this expression except for one. Now, for the first time, he carefully considered the equals sign by itself, weighing its individual import. *Did "=" really mean "equals"? If not, what else could it mean?* His first hunch was that the symbol might be pictographical in nature.

In mathematics, two parallel lines or curves were usually denoted by equating them with the "||" symbol, an obvious pictographical representation of two parallel lines. The equals sign in modern mathematics was no different; it was literally a pictographical representation of two identical lines. Although few people outside of mathematics realized it, the equals sign was a fairly modern invention, dating only to the sixteenth century. In 1557, a Welsh doctor and mathematician named Robert Recorde published *The Whetstone of Witte*, in which he proposed the use of the pictographic symbol "=" in place of the more tedious expression "is equal to."

Malachi now had his answer. He turned and looked at the rusty railroad tracks behind him. At this particular location along the New River, the rails ran due east and west. *E and W. A pair of parallels. No two things could be more equal.* Malachi quickly returned his attention to the painted expression on the wall and marveled at its elegance—so simple, yet obscure enough to baffle anyone but him.

$\chi=E{\cdot}Z(U)$. *Malachi, walk east along the tracks for ninety-two paces.*

5

D R. BILL McCreary pointed down at the white-haired man strapped to the bed in examination room 2. "As far as we can tell," he explained to the group, "that man is Dr. Franz Holzberg."

Califano did a double take. "*The* Franz Holzberg? The famous physicist?"

McCreary nodded. "I believe so."

"But he died in—" Califano stopped short, realizing the import of what he was about to say.

"In 1959," said McCreary, finishing the sentence.

But Califano had already registered the coincidence and was now churning this information in his brain. *Holzberg died in 1959, the same year the Winter Solstice program abruptly went dormant.* "If I recall my history correctly," he said, "Dr. Holzberg died in Germany."

"Yep, that's how the press reported it at the time," said McCreary. "We've already given orders to exhume the body buried at his grave site in Limburg. Covertly, of course."

Califano wondered how the CIA went about "covertly" exhuming a buried body, but he decided he didn't want to know. "If Holzberg were still alive today," he said, "that would make him, what, ninety-six? Ninety-seven?"

"A hundred and three," McCreary said.

They all looked down at the old man strapped to the bed, with his tangled white hair and long, twisty fingernails. He certainly looked old, so 103 wasn't out of the question.

"Where'd you find him?" Califano asked.

Ana Thorne answered that question. "He wandered into a diner in Fire Creek, West Virginia, early this morning with a severe wound to his abdomen. He was incoherent and confused, but he indicated that he'd come from the Thurmond National Laboratory. That's what prompted the local police to notify the FBI, who notified us. We transported him here about seven hours ago from the trauma unit in Beckley."

"And who's 'we'?" Califano asked, looking back and forth between Thorne and Dr. McCreary.

Dr. McCreary finally spoke up. "Michael, I run the Office of Disruptive Technology here at the CIA. The program actually started at DARPA but was transferred here about six months ago. What I do here is similar to what you do at DOE, but on a larger scale. My team monitors thousands of scientific projects around the world, including government-funded research, academic research, and commercial projects. Like you, we look for trends, anomalies, unexpected events, and what are often called 'coincidences.' And like you, we have some very sophisticated computer modeling and data-mining programs at our disposal to help us spot these things."

Admiral Armstrong suddenly chimed in. "You know, Michael helped design some of those programs." There was a ring of pride in his voice, almost like a father boasting about his son.

"Oh, I know," said McCreary with a deferential nod to Califano. "And as a graduate student, too. Very impressive." He paused and cleared his throat. "Anyway, as I said, the difference between what you do and what we do is the scope and scale of the subject matter. You monitor sixteen national laboratories and a few hundred DOE-funded projects. The focus of my program is the entire spectrum of what we call 'dangerously disruptive technology,' so it cuts across all areas of science and technology, from chemistry to biotech to physics to information technology, genetics, communications, and everything in between."

"Dangerously disruptive technology," said Califano slowly, enunciating each word. "I'm curious. How do you define that?"

McCreary seemed a bit put off by the question, but he proceeded to answer it. "The official definition? It's technology that poses a clear and present threat to the national security interests of the United States."

"Yeah? How about the *unofficial* definition?"

McCreary bristled. "Let's just say I know it when I see it. It's things like human cloning, genetic engineering, cold fusion, and the like. We have the ability to model these technologies before they even exist, to observe their likely impact on our society, the health and safety of our citizens, the security of our country. If our models indicate that we should be concerned about an emerging area of research, we monitor it."

Califano was pretty sure they did more than just *monitor* it. After all, the title of their program included the word "intervention." But he decided to keep that observation to himself. "Okay," he said as he began perambulating around the darkened room. "Other than the fact that Franz Holzberg was apparently involved in this program, what else do we know about Winter Solstice? I can tell you that DOE's file on that program is pretty thin. It lists committee meeting dates, congressional authorization for the use of off-budget funds, and the initial procurement outlays for the construction of the Thurmond National Laboratory from 1955 through 1957. But there's absolutely nothing in there about the nature of the research or who was involved. How about you guys?"

"Unfortunately," said McCreary, "we don't have much more than that. The project was so secret, and so few people were involved, that I'm afraid the details may be lost forever." McCreary tilted his head toward the unconscious body of Franz Holzberg. "In fact, the last remnants may be locked up in that man's brain."

"Whoa, hold on a second," said Califano. He wasn't buying any of this. "Surely there must be some other information about this project. Thurmond cost tens of millions of dollars to build back in the fifties. That would be like *hundreds* of millions today. Somebody would have had to justify that expense to Congress. And by my calculation, the lab operated for at least two and a half years. There must be former employees, technicians, hell, even janitors we can talk to. And what about parallel research efforts? Certainly other labs would have been involved in the project, even if indirectly?"

McCreary shook his head. "Trust me, Mr. Califano, this was a program of a very different stripe. And as far as we know, there was only one other place in the world where this type of research was ever conducted."

"Yeah?" said Califano. "And where was that?"

McCreary glanced momentarily at Ana Thorne before answering. "Głuszyca, Poland," he said. "During the German occupation. The Nazis apparently had their own version of a Winter Solstice program near the end of World War Two, although not much is known about it."

The quick glance had given Califano two valuable pieces of information. First, he deduced that Thorne was probably the CIA analyst assigned to study the Nazi version of Winter Solstice, or whatever had become of it. Second, there was more to this story than McCreary was telling. *And it hadn't just started this morning.*

"What about the lab itself?" asked Califano. "What happened to all the materials and the lab equipment, and the lab notebooks? That would certainly give us a clue about what was going on there."

"Actually, *I* can answer that question," said Admiral Armstrong. "Thurmond National Laboratory was sealed shut and officially decommissioned in November 1959, using full radiological controls and an electrified exclusion zone of three miles around the entrance. The decommissioning report, which was later destroyed by executive order in 1981 under President Reagan, indicated that Thurmond experienced some sort of extreme incineration event resulting in vitrification of the surrounding rock and complete destruction of the laboratory and all of its contents. There were six fatalities . . . and no survivors."

"Oh yeah?" said Califano with raised eyebrows. "Then where'd *this* guy come from?" He jabbed his thumb toward the window overlooking examination room 2.

There was silence until Armstrong finally spoke up. "Bill, he does have a point. Have you sent an inspection team down into the lab yet?"

"Not yet," said McCreary. "We wanted to gather as much information as we could before attempting to go in." He stared down at the grotesque body of the man in examination room 2. "Honestly, we're just not sure what to expect down there."

"Well," said Armstrong. "It doesn't look like we'll be getting any more useful information from *him*. So what's our next move?"

McCreary closed his eyes for several seconds before responding. "Admiral, may I use Mr. Califano as a dedicated asset on this investigation?"

"Yes. He's all yours."

"Good. Then here's how we should proceed. Ana, please provide Mr. Califano with a transcript of everything the patient has said since he's been here. Don't leave anything out. I want every utterance, no matter how incoherent or nonsensical. Also, give him a copy of the statement that the woman at the diner gave to the police. Mr. Califano, I want you to crunch that information—"

"Whoa, let me stop you right there, Doc," said Califano. "I know what you're getting at. You want me to crunch all this info to see if there are any relevancy hits or unexpected trails. And I'm happy to do that. But don't give me transcripts. I need raw data. I'll take all the video feed that you have of Santa Claus here. And I know you have it, too." He pointed to the two cameras mounted on either side of the examination room, both trained on the patient. "In fact, I see from the red lights that you're recording him right now. And I want to talk to that woman at the diner *myself*, and to the EMTs and the police officers who responded to her 911 call. In fact, now that I think of it, I want to talk to the 911 operator, and I want a copy of the 911 tape. Also, I'll need all the clothes this guy was wearing when he wandered into that diner. Was there anything in his pockets?"

McCreary looked stunned. "Uh, yes. A wallet and a set of keys. We can give you pictures of everyth—"

"I don't want pictures. I'm telling you, Doc, I need *raw data*. Give me his clothes, and the wallet, and the keys, and anything else you have of his. Once I have all the data, *then* I can crunch it."

McCreary gave Admiral Armstrong a concerned look: raised eyebrows, tight lips, deep worry lines around his eyes and mouth.

Armstrong nodded his head ever so slightly.

"Well," said Dr. McCreary curtly. "Admiral Armstrong did say you were thorough." He took a deep breath and released it. "Very well. Ana, set up a work space for Mr. Califano in building one where he can go through the patient's personal effects. There's a vacant office down the hall from mine that we can probably use as a workroom. And please see to it that he's provided with all the raw video footage of the patient."

"*All* of it?" asked Thorne.

McCreary pursed his lips before answering. "Yes, all of it."

From this, Califano deduced that he'd likely be seeing some unsavory interrogation techniques. "What about the lady at the diner?" he asked.

McCreary checked his watch. "I'll arrange for a flight first thing in the morning. In the meantime, we'll provide you with everything you need here tonight." He paused a moment and met Califano's eyes. "I trust you'll be able to get us some answers by morning?"

Califano shrugged. He wasn't making any promises.

McCreary looked annoyed. "Ana will be your CIA escort while you're here. She needs to be with you at *all times*. No exceptions. Understood?"

Califano glanced at Ana and was unable to keep his eyes from momentarily walking up and down her body. "No problem at all." This came out a bit slimier than he'd intended.

Thorne's expression never changed.

"Oh, and I'll need access to the DOE server tonight," Califano added.

"Ana can arrange that for you," said McCreary, motioning toward Thorne. "Now, before I leave, is there anything *else* you need tonight, Mr. Califano?"

"Yeah, just one more thing." Califano held McCreary's gaze for a moment. "I need you to tell me the *whole* story about Winter Solstice."

Admiral Armstrong interjected. "Michael—"

"It's okay," said McCreary calmly. He took a step closer to Califano and appeared to be sizing him up. At six foot three, McCreary was a full two inches taller than Califano, and his considerable heft gave him a hulking presence, albeit in an oafish sort of way.

Califano stood his ground. "I mean, you've got a program called Disruptive Technology Analysis and Intervention. You're obviously mobilizing a lot of resources to get to the bottom of this Winter Solstice program. But, at the same time, you're telling me you have no idea what it's about." He shrugged. "Sorry, Doc. I'm not buying it."

McCreary removed his glasses with an exaggerated flourish. "Mr. Califano," he said calmly. "You are treading in a very sensitive area here. The number of people who know *anything* about this program is six. Four of them are standing in this room right now. The other two are the director of the CIA and the president of the United States. So if there are certain facts that I have *chosen* not to divulge to you, well . . . there's a reason for that. I'm sure you remember the concept of 'need to know' from your SCI training. I assure you, at this point, you have everything you *need* to know about Winter Solstice. Is that clear?"

Several profanities were streaming through Califano's

mind, "Fuck you" being chief among them. But none of them escaped his lips. He was in full control of his emotions now. *Relax*, he told himself. *Let it go.* He glanced at Admiral Armstrong and then back at McCreary. "I understand," he said in a restrained voice. "Perfectly."

6

MALACHI WASTED no time. It was getting darker and colder by the minute, and he knew he was close to something important. He quickly made his way to the railroad tracks and, facing east, aligned himself with the front wall of the Thurmond coal depot. The rain was still picking up, pelting his face and causing cold trickles to run down the back of his neck.

He began walking east between the two rusty rails, counting each step softly to himself as he went. After several steps, he stopped. *Something wasn't right.* The horizontal railroad ties were spaced about twenty inches apart, significantly shorter than the distance of his stride. Once again, he used logic as his guide. If ninety-two was intended to convey a particular distance—a map to some particular location along the tracks—then the most logical unit of measure would not be a man's inconsistent stride but, rather, the uniform spacing of the horizontal railroad ties along the track.

He quickly retreated and began his count again, this time counting each wooden slat as it passed beneath his feet. He reached ninety-two in less than two minutes and stopped abruptly. He looked down at the wooden tie he was standing on and observed a single red paint mark near the center of the tie—the same shade of red he'd seen on the wall.

This was it.

Crouching low and washing the beam of his carbide lantern along the ground, he scrutinized every inch of the weathered railroad tie, but found nothing of particular interest. Other than the red dab of paint about three inches from the transverse center of the beam, this railroad tie looked like all the others.

He stepped off the tracks into the woods and returned a few minutes later with a large, sturdy stick. Using it like a crude shovel, he attempted to gouge through the gravel on either side of the railroad tie where the red dot was. After several minutes, however, he abandoned this effort as futile. Beneath the top layer of coarse gravel was another layer of finely crushed gravel that was packed so tightly it resembled asphalt. He realized he would not be able to excavate farther beneath this tie without metal tools. Which he did not have. Although his pocketknife came to mind, he immediately dismissed the notion of using it as a gouging or digging tool. *Digging is not the answer.*

As darkness encroached, Malachi stood and puzzled over this situation for several minutes. Someone had gone to the trouble of leading him here, most likely his contacts, whoever they were. And those people would have known he'd be arriving without metal tools. Therefore, requiring him to dig would not be logical.

He looked again at the red dot on the railroad tie, which he illuminated for a long time in the beam of his carbide lamp. *What am I missing?* The dot was a few inches off center, a bit closer to the north rail than the south. *Was that significant?* To find out, he trained his lamp northward, using the railroad tie as a directional guide. The light bounced around for a few seconds in the woods before something suddenly caught his eye.

A splash of red.

Using the beam of his lantern to guide his way, Malachi crept into the pine forest that separated the railroad tracks from the New River and slowly made his way to the large granite boulder that he'd spied from the tracks. Up close and shining his light directly upon it, he could now clearly see a bright smudge of red paint on its southern face, the same hue as the other markings. *This had to be it.*

Working quickly, Malachi swept his light all around the circumference of the boulder. At first, he saw nothing of particular interest. On his second pass, however, he spotted a smaller boulder wedged up against the main boulder in a peculiar manner. It looked . . . movable. Using both hands and all the strength in his back and arms, he managed to slowly tilt the smaller boulder away and push it over. What remained in its place was a relatively soft, dry patch of soil about two feet in diameter. He kicked at it several times with the heel of his shoe until he suddenly heard a hollow thump.

What's this?

Like a terrier after its prey, Malachi immediately dropped to his hands and knees and began frantically scooping away the loose topsoil until he could get his fingers around the top edges of the hollow object. He could tell right away it was a small metal box of some sort. But it was stuck tightly in the soil. Clearly, it had been there for some time, perhaps years. He kept digging, using his bare fingers to rake away the compact soil all around the edges of the box. As the dirt became denser, his long fingernails began to bend back painfully and break. Eventually, he was forced to cease digging and trim his fingernails again using his small pocketknife. When he was finished, he resumed digging with increased vigor. The box was getting looser. Looser . . .

With a loud grunt, Malachi extracted the mysterious metal box from its burial place. He placed it on the ground next to the overturned boulder that had once concealed it, and he plopped down beside it on both knees, exhausted, wet, and filthy. After wiping away most of the dirt from the top and sides of the box, he carefully inspected its exterior in the beam of his lantern. As far as he could tell, there were no markings on the box at all. It appeared to be a generic, heavy-duty security container, olive drab, with a latch that was obviously meant to hold a lock, although there was none there.

Slowly, he unlatched the lid of the box and tipped it open, illuminating the contents with his lantern. The interior was lined with gray foam, and had a single, rectangular recess in the center into which a cylindrical object had been snuggly fitted. Malachi studied the object for a few seconds before gently prying it loose from its foam housing. It weighed about ten ounces and was wrapped entirely in heavy, opaque plastic wrapping. Slowly, he turned the object over several times in his fingers, observing no markings of any kind on the outside packaging.

Using his knife, Malachi carefully cut away the opaque wrapping, revealing a marine-grade, waterproof canister, like those used to keep personal belongings dry while boating. The canister was constructed of heavy-duty plastic, with a screw-off lid and no apparent markings on the outside. He shook the canister slightly and could hear something soft bouncing around inside. Slowly, he unscrewed and removed the lid and dumped the contents of the canister into his grimy hand.

The sole object was a tri-folded sheet of cream-colored stationery, which Malachi immediately unfolded and read. The following sentences were written in neat, cursive script:

1. Everything has changed.
2. Elijah is a traitor. Don't trust him.
3. Go to the third church and ask for Qaset:

4. They are tracking your watch.

The last sentence sent a sudden jolt through Malachi's body. He took off his watch and inspected it suspiciously in the light of his lantern. It looked entirely normal to him and seemed to be functioning properly, other than showing the wrong time. He held it close to his ear and heard only the soft ticking of an ordinary wristwatch. But then he began to hear something else. Something unusual, far in the distance. A thumping, rhythmic sound that seemed to be getting closer.

A helicopter.

Malachi stood up and heaved his watch into the woods as far as he could. The chopper noise was getting louder by the second. *Shit. They were coming for him. And he had no idea why.* Terrified, he quickly shoved the note into his coat pocket and snatched the security container off the ground, frantically pulling out its foam insert and inspecting every square inch of the interior for any additional clues. There were none. Frustrated, he tossed the container into the woods with a grunt and looked around frantically for a suitable plan.

The rotor noise was still intensifying. A moment later, Malachi spotted a white light in the darkening sky, moving steadily from right to left and growing larger. Then he saw the outline of the approaching helicopter—sleek and black against the moonless sky, and even closer than he'd thought.

A primal instinct jumped instantly into his brain.

Run!

7

"WE'RE LOST, ain't we?" said Bethany Tremont to her longtime boyfriend Billy. "I can't believe I let you talk me into this." They were driving eastbound on Route 25 in Billy's midnight-blue Chevy Impala. The car's headlights pierced deep into the rainy darkness, illuminating both sides of the otherwise empty road.

"Shut the fuck up," Billy responded, as he often did in response to her complaints. Then he reconsidered. "Shit. Sorry, baby. I'm just frustrated here. Did we miss a turn or something?"

Bethany flicked on the passenger-side light and reread the directions to their friends' party cabin for the fourth time. "East on Route 25 for sixteen miles, right on Beury Mountain Road, eight miles straight, then left into the campsite."

"Dang. This ain't right. We shoulda turned at that last big fork. Can't you find it on your iPhone?"

"I wish." Bethany held up her iPhone. "No signal."

"Shit."

"Just turn around," Bethany said. "We're in the middle of . . . *Holy shit! Look out!*"

Billy slammed on the brakes and held his breath as the Impala skidded and shuddered toward a motionless, silhouetted figure in the middle of the road. "What the fuck!" Billy exclaimed as the Impala's antilock brakes finally completed their job of bringing the sedan to a stop about five feet from the motionless man. In the headlights, he was a tall, dark figure with a leather coat and long, crazy hair. And now he was coming toward them.

"Is that a cop?" asked Billy nervously.

"He don't look like no cop."

"What the f—"

"Billy, let's get out of here! Back up! Back up!"

But the man was already at Billy's window. Bethany hit the automatic door locks just as the man attempted to open the driver's-side door, pulling the latch violently several times.

"Billy, drive!" Bethany screamed. "Drive!"

Billy put the car in drive. But at the same moment, the driver's-side window smashed into a spiderweb of shards as a steel carbine lantern came flying through it.

"What the f—! Get off me!" screamed Billy as a man's arm came through the hole in the window and grabbed hold of his shirt, yanking him hard toward the door. The Impala lurched forward and slowly turned left, bumping down a gravel embankment and thwacking through a thick patch of briars before returning to the road.

Bethany screamed louder than she'd ever screamed in her life.

The stranger's entire upper torso was now through the

broken window. Billy grunted and cursed as he struggled with the man. Within seconds, the stranger had Billy in a stranglehold.

"Stop!" Bethany shrieked. "You're killing him!"

Billy's head was cranked awkwardly to one side, locked firmly beneath the man's arm as he walked alongside the slowing car. Billy was making suffocating noises and frantically trying to undo his seat belt to free himself from the deadly choke hold. Seconds later, he succeeded.

The car stopped abruptly as Billy hit the brakes. In an instant, the driver's-side door was open and Billy was out of the car, thrown viciously to the ground. The next moment, the stranger was in the driver's seat. He shut the door and looked at Bethany for a second. He was dripping wet and breathing heavily. The car slowly began accelerating forward.

"Please," Bethany whimpered. "Oh, Jesus Christ, please don't hurt me."

The car was still driving forward slowly. Through teary eyes, Bethany looked at the man's face, which was covered with matted, muddy facial hair. His eyes were expressionless, his long, gray hair wet and tangled. "Please," she blubbered. "Please don't . . ." She allowed her eyes to drift downward to his hands, which were filthy, and then to his fingernails, which were like . . . *claws*. "Oh my *God*!" she shrieked in terror. Just then, she felt the warm flow of urine in her seat.

The man slammed on the brakes. "Get out," he said.

Bethany was petrified and could not move.

"Get out!" the man ordered again.

This time, she obeyed. Ten seconds later, she was out of the car, sobbing, on hands and knees in the middle of the rainswept road as the Impala sped off into the darkness.

Billy caught up with her a few seconds later, bloody, bruised, and breathless. "Shit. Baby, you okay? Gimme your phone. I'll call 911."

Bethany could barely get the words out of her mouth between sobs: "No . . . signal."

8

H E HAD been known as Elijah many years ago. It was just a code name, but one that he'd put a great deal of thought into at the time. *Elijah, to whom the mantle of God's power was given.*

Benjamin Fulcher reclined in the plush leather chair of his home office and took in the view of the pastoral Dutch countryside outside the window. Rolling fields and pastures extended far into the distance, dotted with sheep and cows and the occasional wind turbine with massive triblades rotating slowly in the breeze. The sky above was an unusual collage of high white wisps and darker, faster storm clouds near the ground. *Ah, late autumn. What a splendid season.*

The seventy-eight-year-old British expatriate took a long sip of tea from a china cup and thought about his biblical namesake, Elijah, a prophet who had received from God a mantle of awesome power and knowledge. Elijah wielded that power righteously for the good of all mankind and then passed the mantle to his worthy successor, Elisha, before being whisked away to heaven in a whirlwind. Fulcher rubbed his chin and pondered how interesting it was that the very first thing Elisha did with his newly acquired power was part the mighty Jordan River. *Just as Joshua had done five hundred years earlier.*

Yes, Fulcher concluded. A conspicuous display of strength and power meant to instill fear among Elisha's enemies and inspire wonder and amazement in his followers. An earthly demonstration of the mysterious powers of the universe.

A brilliant strategy.

Fulcher closed his eyes for a moment and tried to visualize exactly what it must have been like when Joseph and Elisha parted the Jordan River. *Was there a flash? How long did the process take? Was there extensive flooding upstream?* These thoughts were suddenly interrupted by the intrusive ringing of a telephone. With effort, the man hoisted himself from his chair and, with the aid of his walking cane, made his way slowly across the room to the ringing phone. *Curse this broken body.*

Finally, he lifted the receiver to his ear. "Hello?" he said in a British accent, slightly out of breath.

"It's Krupnov," said a man with a deep Russian accent.

"Yes?"

"There's been a signal from Thurmond. We think it's Malachi."

Fulcher closed his eyes for a moment, and a smile of relief slowly crept across his face. *At long last, Malachi has returned. And the timing could not be better.*

"But there's a problem," said Krupnov.

"Oh?"

"The tracking device . . . he apparently removed it. My men haven't been able to find him."

The smile quickly vanished from Fulcher's face. "Vlad, I'm sure I don't need to remind you of how important it is to find Malachi. He's critical to our plan."

"Of *course* I know that!" snapped Krupnov. "My men are looking for him as we speak. And if they don't find him soon, I'll go there myself to finish the job."

"I'm sure you will." Fulcher paused and considered what Krupnov probably meant by "finish the job" himself. *It would not be pretty.* Krupnov's organization was known for getting things done, but not necessarily peacefully, or humanely for that matter. On the other hand, they had unique resources at their disposal that were absolutely necessary for this plan to work. *Si guarda al fine*, Fulcher mused. *One must consider the final result.* "The timing is interesting, don't you think?" he asked after a long pause.

"You mean because of London?"

"Yes, Vlad. Carl Jung would have called this a splendid example of synchronicity."

"I don't know who the hell Carl Jung is. It's just a coincidence, nothing more."

Fulcher laughed quietly to himself. "Don't you know what a coincidence is, Vlad?"

Krupnov was silent.

"A coincidence is merely God's way of remaining anonymous."

Krupnov sighed heavily. "Look, I don't have time for philosophy right now. I'll keep you posted on Malachi. Meanwhile, all the arrangements have been made for the London material to be brought to Severodvinsk. I trust you'll be accompanying it?"

"Yes," said Fulcher. "I'll be there."

"Good," said Krupnov. He ended the call without another word.

Fulcher hung up the phone and walked painstakingly back to his chair with the aid of his cane. He sat down and took another sip of his tea, which he was pleased to find was still reasonably warm.

Before long, his thoughts were back with Joshua and Elisha and the parting of the Jordan River . . . and the awesome power of the Joshua Stone.

9

Hᴏᴡ's ɪᴛ going?" asked Ana Thorne.

Califano swiveled in his chair and watched with interest as Ana walked into the workroom. She'd been in and out of the workroom all night, helping him set up the secure connection to the DOE server, bringing in the patient's personal effects, and helping parse through more than fifteen hours of video from the examination room. But this was different. Now she was wearing a pair of tight yoga pants and a gray CIA sweatshirt. Califano couldn't help but stare. "Hitting the gym?" he asked.

"Just wanted to get out of my suit. This was all I had. They brought up a pair of sweats for you if you want them. There's a bathroom down the hall where you can change."

"Maybe later."

Ana stepped forward and pointed at the computer screen. "Any results yet?"

Califano leaned back and stretched his cramped muscles. "Well, one thing's for sure. This guy does appear to be Franz Holzberg."

"Yeah, like I told you, we ran a bone-structure analysis based on photographs of him in the late fifties. It's either him or it's the best surgical transformation I've ever seen."

Califano nodded in agreement. "What's odd, though, is that all his personal effects are from the same era. Look at this. His shirt and trousers were made in Germany, part of a Walter Rauscher suit that was hand-tailored sometime in the mid-1950s. His shoes are Johnsonian wing tips, made between 1952 and 1960. His hat is from Hutatelier Fuhrmann in Berlin, which went out of business in 1972. He has a receipt in his wallet from the Woolworth's in Beckley dated September 14, 1959. And check this out." Califano fanned five bills across the desk. "He has twenty-two dollars cash in his wallet: a ten, two fives, and two ones. And every single one of these bills is dated prior to 1959. Hell, even his underwear is vintage." He paused to ponder these facts for a moment. "Wherever this guy's been for the past fifty years, he hasn't gotten out much."

"Yeah," said Ana quietly. "What about the things he said in the examination room? Any hits on those?"

"Some." Califano tapped a few keys on the keyboard and pulled up a customized spreadsheet on the screen. "I've broken them into three groups. In one group, there are personal names. I counted three: Mildred, Millie, and what sounded like Opie. The first two were easy. His wife's name was Mildred. She died in 1956. I found a collection of Holzberg's personal correspondence in an online database at Princeton, and in some of his letters, he calls his wife Millie. So no mystery there. But I have no idea about Opie. Still working on that one."

"What's the next category?"

"Next, we have several expressions about time. Or, more specifically, about the timing or sequence of events. In several places, you could hear him muttering, '*Es ging alles so schnell.*'"

"Which means . . . ?"

"'Everything happened at once.' He also said, '*Nicht genug Zeit,*' or 'Not enough time,' on several occasions."

"Interesting."

"Another word he used was '*Synchronizität,*' which means synchronicity. You familiar with that concept?"

Ana shrugged. "It's like synchronization, right? Everything happening in a precise sequence?"

"Not quite. Synchronicity is a philosophical theory that basically says two seemingly unrelated events may, in fact, be linked in some invisible way."

"Okay . . ."

"It's just a fancy way of saying that things that look like coincidences sometimes aren't. There might be some link between them that you can't see. Or maybe *nobody* can see. Kind of like it's part of a pattern, but you can't see the whole pattern at once, just bits and pieces of it."

Ana pursed her lips and bobbed her head slowly from side to side, apparently not yet convinced that "synchronicity" was anything meaningful.

"Anyway," said Califano, pointing back to his spreadsheet. "The third category is where I put all the miscellaneous things he said that were either indecipherable or nonsensical. Of these, there are really only three phrases that seem worth pursuing. First, he mentioned something called '*Bogentechnik.*'"

"Which means what?"

"Best that I can tell, it's a bending technique, or a bowing technique."

"Okay."

"Another interesting phrase was something he said in English several times. 'Murder of science.'"

"Oh yeah. I remember him saying that, too."

"It seems like such a unique phrase, but I'm not getting any clean relational hits on it."

Ana shrugged. "Sounds like he thinks science is under attack."

"I suppose. But it's kind of a weird way of saying it. And it doesn't seem to fit with the context of anything else he said. Just sticks out like a sore thumb, which is why my program is having such a hard time with it."

"Are you getting *any* hits on it?"

"Nothing meaningful. Clarence Darrow apparently used similar language during the Scopes 'Monkey Trial', arguing that fundamentalists were trying to grab science by the throat and throttle it to death. But I've seen no evidence that Holzberg himself was passionate about that issue. At least, he never mentioned it in any of his writings. There was also some guy in the nineteenth century who used the phrase 'murder of science' in an essay about the influence of money on science. But, again, there's no particular correlation there."

"Could just be nonsense," said Ana. "I mean, the guy *is* showing signs of dementia."

"Yeah, maybe." Califano mulled over that possibility for a moment and then pointed back to the spreadsheet. "Anyway, the last thing he said tonight was, '*Es gibt zehn mehr.*'"

"What does that mean?"

"Something like 'There are ten more.'"

Ana looked confused. "Ten more of *what*?"

Califano shrugged. "No idea."

Ana yawned and checked her watch. "All right. Well, we've got a flight in four hours, so I'm going to get some sleep. There's a cot and linens out in the hall for you. Just let the guard know when you want them brought in."

"Okay. But, *hey*, wait a second." Califano said this just as Ana was turning to leave.

"Hmm?"

"Dr. McCreary said you were supposed to stay with me *at all times.* So I thought, you know—"

"Stop right there," said Ana, cutting him off. She paused for few seconds before continuing. "Mike, did you know the CIA has an entire training course on flirting? Literally, the psychology of flirting."

"Uh, no." Califano's voice was suddenly quieter now, lacking its previous ring of self-assurance. He fidgeted perceptively in his chair.

Ana sashayed over to where Califano was seated and leaned down provocatively until her hair was dangling in his face. "Sensuality," she said softly. "Sexuality. Seduction. These are all tools that can be exploited by a skilled agent to gather information from a target. These techniques work especially well when deployed by women, and men are particularly vulnerable to them. No offense. It's just science."

"None taken. I guess."

Ana reached out and gently stroked the collar of Califano's jacket. "That's why the CIA provides special training in this area to all of its covert officers, both men and women. We learn how to use these techniques *and* how to avoid getting ensnared by them."

"But I wasn't . . . I mean, I didn't mean to—"

"Shhh. You didn't need to, Mike." Ana pushed herself away from the chair and brushed her hair back. "That's what I was trying to tell you before. You telegraph your emotions like a neon sign. I knew you were about to say something suggestive, probably something corny sprinkled with a tiny hint of sexual innuendo. Our psychologists call that technique 'escalation.'"

"No, I—"

"Come on, Mike." Ana straightened her back and crossed her arms. "I've been with the agency for twelve years now. And one thing I've learned is that it's best just to nip these things in the bud. Get them out in the open. So, just to be clear, just to make sure there is no confusion about this going forward, I take my job very, *very* seriously. And I *don't* mix business with pleasure. Okay?"

Califano sat in stunned silence. Thorne had, in fact, just nailed him to the wall. He *had* been just about to say something suggestive to her. It was going to be some lame joke about having a slumber party in the workroom. The joke had not even crossed the threshold of vocalization before Ana sensed it was coming and "nipped it in the bud." *Damn, did he really telegraph his emotions that much? Or was Ana Thorne just a goddamn mind reader?* Whatever the case, the contours of their working relationship were now clearly defined. *Just as well*, he thought.

"We good?" Ana asked with a crooked smile.

"Yeah, sure. Thanks for the clarification." Califano maintained a neutral expression, as if nothing she'd said had bothered him in the slightest. But, in truth, Ana had just drilled straight into his ego. *And it hurt*. "All business, no pleasure. Got it."

Ana uncrossed her arms and seemed to soften just a bit, perhaps sensing that she'd been a little too tough. "Look, it's nothing personal. I've just learned—"

"No, I got it. Like you said, it's best just to be clear about these things. Avoid misunderstandings. That's my policy, too."

"Right. Okay. Then I'll see you in the morning."

Ana had not quite reached the door when Califano

called out from behind her. "Hey, can I ask you a question?"

Ana turned around apprehensively. "As long as it's not a *personal* question, then yes."

Califano stood and approached her. "Well, I'm actually not sure if it's personal or if it's something related to your work. But in the interest of *nipping things in the bud*, as you say, I'd like to just get this out in the open." He stopped when they were face-to-face.

Ana already knew what the question was. She could see it in his eyes, which were focused on the right side of her head, where her mangled ear and scarred neck were barely visible beneath her hair. "It happened when I was seven," she said flatly. *Best to get it out of the way*, she figured. At least, that's what twenty-five years of experience with these scars had taught her.

"Was it a fire?" Califano asked, his voice softening with the appropriate degree of compassion.

"Car accident." Which was partly true, insofar as she'd been *in* a car when a bomb exploded nearby. Ana now braced herself for the inevitable follow-up questions, of which there were always many.

To her surprise, though, Califano said nothing further except, "I'm sorry."

"Don't be," Ana mumbled. Califano was already making his way back to his computer. Now it was Ana's turn to satiate her curiosity. "Hey, I've got a question for you."

Califano turned. "Nothing *personal*, I hope."

"Well, I would put this more in the category of work related, since I like to know as much as possible about the people I work with."

Califano already knew what was coming, but he said nothing. *Let her ask*, he told himself.

"It probably won't come as a surprise that I did a background check on you after Admiral Armstrong insisted that you be involved with this project." Ana shrugged. "Standard protocol."

"Uh-huh. And stalking me at work? That was standard protocol, too?"

"No, that was more to satisfy my own curiosity. You see, when I checked your record, I noticed a gap of about three years between when you finished graduate school and when you started at DOE. I'm curious as to what you were doing during those three years."

Califano shrugged. "Research."

"Research. Really?"

Califano flinched. "Look, if you already know, then why don't you just tell me. Or are you waiting for me to *telegraph* it to you?"

"Mike, I know you're a convicted felon."

Califano's heart skipped a beat. He *hated* those words. *Convicted. Felon.*

Ana was inching closer now. "I don't know what you did, because your record is scrubbed cleaner than any I've ever seen. I mean, seriously, I've never seen a more conspicuous blank in a person's record. State and local police—nothing. FBI—nothing. Military—nothing. BOP—nothing."

As Califano knew all too well, "BOP" stood for Federal Bureau of Prisons.

Ana continued, still inching forward. "But I know for a *fact* that you spent time in federal prison. Ashland, Kentucky, was it?"

"Wait a sec—"

Ana cut him off. "Nope. My turn. Now, I can see that you've got the trust of Admiral Armstrong. So I can only assume you've got your life together and that you've atoned for whatever sins you committed in the past. And that's great. Good for you. But here at the CIA, we're kind of sensitive about people who've actually spent time in *federal prison.* I'm sure you can understand why. So here's my simple question for you. What were you in for?"

Califano was on the verge of saying something incredibly stupid, but he managed to stop himself. *Let it go. Let it go.* That was the refrain running through his mind. But for some reason, he couldn't. Not like this. He longed to give his side of the story, to explain what had really happened, to make her . . . *what, respect him?* He doubted that was going to happen, even if he told her everything. Besides, Admiral Armstrong had made it clear that he was never to tell *anyone* about his past. And that included CIA officers. Even pretty ones with green eyes and wicked psychological skills.

Califano took a deep breath and waited for the emotional storm surge in his body to subside. When it finally did, he locked eyes with Ana and said calmly, "I know where you got those scars."

Ana seemed physically startled by this comment. She cocked her head back, and, for the first time since Califano met her, she stumbled over her words. "You don't know sh— I mean, of course you do; I just *told* you how I got them."

"No. I know *where* you got them. As in geographically."

Ana was quiet for several seconds as she processed this comment. "You think this is funny?" she said finally. "Some sort of game?"

"No, not at all. In fact, guess what? I'm just as serious about my job as you are about yours. So while you were out changing into your yoga outfit, I did my own little background check . . . *on you.*"

"Impossible," Ana muttered.

"Hardly. To begin with, your real name isn't Thorne, although Ana is your real first name. Short for Anastazija, if I'm not mistaken."

Ana was icily quiet.

"You have an undergraduate degree in political science

from Georgetown. Graduated with honors. The only Bs you got were in physics, calculus, and art history. You grew up in Danbury, Connecticut, and went to boarding school at Choate. Mom and Dad are both doctors, which explains the pricey private school. You speak fluent Croatian, which confused me at first until I learned that you were adopted at age eight. You were recruited by the CIA while you were still at Georgetown, and you've been here ever since. You've been an analyst, a field agent, an assistant section head at the embassy in Athens. And your newest gig, assistant director of DTAI." Califano was on a roll, but he suddenly paused and cocked his head to one side. "Must not leave a lot of time for a personal life, huh? You live alone, and you've never been married." Califano gestured with an open palm. "Should I go on?"

"No," replied Ana with a bitter smile. "You should go fuck yourself."

Califano didn't miss a beat. "So, wait. It was okay for you to spy on me at work, but because I did a little extra-curricular research on you, now I'm way over the line. Is that it?"

Ana shook her head. "You know what? This conversation is over. And if I find out that you violated the CIA's security protocol with your little hacking expedition, you're going to be seeing a lot *more* of Ashland, Kentucky, is that clear? And not even Admiral Armstrong will be able to save you."

Just then, there was a knock on the door, and the security guard from outside eased the door open and poked his head through. "Everything all right in here? I heard some commotion."

"It's fine, Joey," Ana said in an exasperated tone. "We're just finishing up here."

The guard closed the door, and Ana turned back to face

Califano. "Look," she said, doing her best to de-escalate the situation. "Let's just keep this professional, okay? You stay out of my personal life, I'll stay out of yours."

Califano was silent for a few seconds before forcing a smile. "Deal."

Ana was just turning to leave when Califano decided to add one last comment. "*Lijepe snove,*" he said in remarkably good Croatian. *Sweet dreams.* He even got the intonation almost exactly right.

Ana's posture stiffened slightly, but she did not otherwise move, or blink, or say anything for several seconds. Finally, she turned and left without saying another word.

Califano watched her leave and immediately wanted to punch himself in the face. *Crap, that was stupid.* Ana Thorne was precisely the type of woman who would drive him crazy eventually, if he let her. She was like a *puzzle*. Something to solve. But he doubted he would ever be able to solve *that* puzzle. More likely, he'd wind up in a straitjacket. He dragged both hands over his face and eventually turned his attention back to the computer screen, hoping for little more than a distraction.

He got one.

Something on the screen immediately caught his eye. The relevancy engine had turned up a new result. He clicked on it and was surprised by what appeared on the screen. After checking it twice, he picked up the phone and dialed a ten-digit outside number.

"Hello?" said a groggy male voice on the third ring.

"Hey, it's Mike Califano. You said to call you at any hour if I found something important."

"Yeah."

"I think you're gonna want to see this."

10

TAWNYA JOHNSON checked the Budweiser clock on the wall of the Stop & Shop convenience store. It read 3:05 A.M. God, she hated this time of night—the midpoint of the graveyard shift. The dead hour. No one to talk to. Nothing to do but stare out the window at the traffic whizzing by on Highway 68. *Where are all these people going, anyway?* she wondered.

Most nights, the Stop & Shop stayed reasonably busy until about 1:30 A.M., when the last of the long-haul truckers and traveling salesmen bedded down for the night at the Huntsman Motel next door. For the next hour after that, a few stragglers still came in for cigarettes, snacks, and beer. But then the "dead hour" began, which lasted until the early birds started showing up around 4:30 A.M. for their morning coffee. It was the solitude of this two-hour stretch that Tawnya truly hated.

A pair of bright headlights suddenly flashed through

the store window, and Tawnya watched with curiosity as a
dark blue Chevy Impala pulled slowly into the parking lot. A
few seconds later, a long-haired man in a black leather coat
got out and made his way to the front door of the store. He
seemed tentative, glancing behind him several times before
entering the store. *Shit*, Tawnya thought when she finally
got a good look at him. She'd seen all types in this store, but
this guy was something else. If not for his late-model car,
she would have guessed he was homeless.

"How ya doin'," she called out as he entered.

The man mumbled something unintelligible and
headed back into the aisles. Tawnya watched him carefully
in the convex security mirror in the far corner of the store
as he moved slowly from aisle to aisle, picking up various
items and cradling them in one arm. He spent nearly five
minutes at the magazine rack in the back, where he seemed
mesmerized by the magazine covers and newspapers.
Finally, he brought his armful of items to the counter and
dropped them in front of Tawnya.

Tawnya tried not to look at the man's face at all. She was
used to dealing with toothless locals, stoned kids, grizzled
truckers, and even actual homeless people, but this guy was
different. His face and hands were . . . *filthy*. His long gray
hair and beard were unruly and clumped together with
mud in places. *And those nails . . . my God*. As quickly as she
could, Tawnya rang up his purchases: fingernail clippers;
scissors; shaving cream; disposable razors; a toothbrush;
toothpaste; two ham-and-cheese sandwiches; a bottle of
water; *Time*, *U.S. News & World Report*, and *USA Today*. "Is
that all?" she asked.

"Do you have cigarettes?" asked the man in an educated
Northeastern accent.

Tawnya was taken aback by his spoken words, which
did not match his appearance at all. He sounded . . . smart.

Which would explain all the newsmagazines, she figured. "Yeah, they're back here. What kind you want?"

"Chesterfields."

"Chesterfields?" Tawnya searched in vain for a few seconds. "Uh, we ain't got those."

"Camels, then," said the man.

Tawnya rang up the cigarettes and reported the total: "Fifty-eight thirty-five."

"Excuse me?"

"Fifty-eight dollars and thirty-five cents," Tawnya repeated slowly.

The man seemed confused by that total but quickly retrieved two fifty-dollar bills from his pocket and handed them to her. Tawnya decided to skip the step of holding them up to the light, as all Stop & Shop employees were trained to do for bills over ten dollars. She wanted this guy *gone* and didn't care if she had to take a couple of bogus bills to do it. She quickly made change and placed it on the counter in front of the man, opting not to put it in his hand as she would normally do. *I ain't touching those fingernails*, she thought.

The man scooped up the change and grabbed the two plastic shopping bags that Tawnya had filled with his purchases. "Thanks," he said.

Tawnya watched as the man exited the store and got back into his blue sedan. He sat there for several minutes in the bright light of the storefront, flipping through the newsmagazines with tremendous interest. *Strange old guy*, Tawnya thought, desperately wishing he would leave. Finally, to her great relief, the blue sedan pulled slowly out of the parking lot and turned left onto the access road leading to the highway. Tawnya noticed that the driver's-side window was broken, although she didn't think much of it. She saw all sorts of beat-up cars around here, and a broken window wasn't necessarily out of the ordinary. Besides, she was just glad the guy was gone. A quiet night in the store didn't seem so bad after all, she decided.

What Tawnya did not notice was that the man had merely pulled into the motel parking lot next door.

Malachi closed and locked the door to room 132 of the Huntsman Motel and headed straight to the bathroom. He flipped on the light and gazed in amazement at his reflection in the bathroom mirror. He shook his head slowly in disbelief as he touched his gray hair and beard and gently traced the fine wrinkles around his eyes. Although he could see his reflection clearly, he simply could not fathom that the man staring back at him . . . was *him*.

Fingernails first, he decided. He glanced down and noticed that they'd finally stopped growing at their previously inexplicable rate. Whatever process had been taking place in his body for the past twenty-four hours seemed to be finally coming to an end. He unwrapped the clippers he'd bought and quickly went about grooming his fingernails and toenails to a respectable length. Then, unwrapping the scissors he'd purchased, he went to work on his hair. First, he clipped his beard and mustache short and shaved the remaining whiskers with a disposable razor. Then he did the best he could with his wild mane of gray hair, cutting it close to the scalp until it passably resembled a buzz cut. This process took the better part of an hour.

Finally, with the grooming process complete, he washed his face and hands thoroughly with soap and water and dried off with a clean towel. With his face now clean shaven and his hair reasonably groomed, he gazed once more upon his reflection in the mirror. He certainly looked different. His skin was pallid and wrinkled, his cheeks sunken, his eyes dull and tired. Yet, with his facial hair gone and his hair cropped short, he could finally see *himself* in the middle-aged face staring back at him. Same eyes. Same nose. Same mouth. *But so many wrinkles . . .*

Malachi removed his shirt and flexed his muscles in the mirror. The skin on his chest and arms was a bit baggy, but his muscle tone underneath was essentially the same as he remembered. And this was the strangest thing of all—he didn't *feel* like he looked. The man in the mirror looked old and weathered, but, inside, Malachi felt strong and energized. He moved his body all around the bathroom, watching his reflection in the mirror to prove this to himself. He marched in place for several seconds, lifting each knee high above his waist. Then he twisted his torso all around with his hands on his hips. Finally, he did twenty jumping jacks in rapid succession. His movements during all of these exercises were confident and strong, which was precisely how he felt.

All of this was beyond Malachi's comprehension. Indeed, there were so many things he did not understand about his situation that he'd already begun flirting with a terrifying self-diagnosis: schizophrenia.

All the while, new memories continued trickling into his mind, arriving in sporadic bursts with no logical connection or context. Often, these memories consisted of just a single word or phrase, or a brief recollection of some isolated event. At the moment, he was recalling a beautiful woman with black hair and a long white dress. Then the memory vanished, replaced with a darker memory of some undefined fear . . . and betrayal. He seized upon that last thought—trying once again to conjure up the memory of the gunshots. But, as before, his memory of that event consisted of only disconnected impressions. Surprise. Anger. Blood. And his escape into the darkness.

An idea suddenly popped into his mind. Scanning the

motel room, he quickly spotted a pen and a small pad of paper near the phone on the nightstand. *He needed to start writing these things down.* Logic would eventually help him piece it all together.

He began by jotting down the single word that had just flashed into his mind at that very moment: "Jasher."

11

CIA HEADQUARTERS, LANGLEY, VIRGINIA

"HAVE YOU gotten any sleep?" asked Dr. Bill McCreary as he entered the small workroom.

"Not really," replied Califano. He was still seated in front of the computer monitor where he'd been all night, fingers tapping furiously at the keyboard. It was 4:12 A.M.

"That's what I figured." McCreary approached and placed a mug of fresh coffee on the desk in front of Califano. "Here, I thought you might need this." The mug was emblazoned with the official CIA seal: the head of a bald eagle above an argent shield inscribed with a sixteen-point compass rose. The compass rose represented the agency's endless quest for information; the shield represented defense. *Information as defense.*

Califano took a sip—black and unsweetened, just the way he liked it. "Thanks."

"So, whatcha got?"

Califano resumed typing as he talked. "As you know,

my program crawls the entire worldwide digisphere looking for relational hits. Everything from credit card trans-
actions, travel reservations, online searches, news stories,
blogs, e-mails, police reports, SEC filings, you name it. The
more data you feed it, the better it gets at finding statistically significant relationships between what I call 'independent informational entities' or IIEs."

"Right," said McCreary. He sipped from his own mug as
he watched Califano expertly navigating screen after screen
of complex statistical data. *The master at work.*

Califano continued. "I've been feeding it raw data all
night, but it wasn't until a couple of hours ago that it started
kicking back good hits." He performed a final, exaggerated
keystroke and sat back as the screen suddenly changed to
a colorful graph of squiggly lines and corresponding color-
coded labels. The lines changed shape every few seconds as
the program continuously updated the underlying statistical information. The result looked like a wriggling tangle of
multicolored spaghetti.

McCreary understood it, though. He leaned forward,
acutely interested in what he was seeing.

"Each of these lines," said Califano, "represents a time-
based statistical quantification of the relationship between
two IIEs. It could be the relationship between a person and
a particular place, for instance. Or between a particular
place and a specific date. Or it could be the relationship
between two people. Or anything else under the sun. You
get the picture, right?"

McCreary nodded.

"Now obviously there are an infinite number of IIEs in
the world and an infinite number of relationships among
them. But we're only interested in those relationships that
have a strong statistical correlation to the data that we've
fed the system, right?"

"Sure. Our program works the same way," said McCreary.

Of course it does. "Now, what you're seeing here," Califano said, pointing to the screen, "are several dozen IIE relationships that have a statistically significant correlation to the data set I've provided, which includes everything from Dr. Holzberg's hat size and preferred brand of underwear to the geographic coordinates of Thurmond and Fire Creek, and everything in between."

"So, what are these relationships?" asked McCreary, anxious to get to the point.

"I'll get to that in a second. A more interesting question is *when* are these relationships?" Califano tapped a few keys, and the graph on the screen suddenly changed scale. "Check this out. I did a retroactive analysis to see what these same relationships looked like for the past six months. See that?" He pointed with his index finger to a slow ramp up and then a sudden spike that occurred in the middle of the graph, about three months before, followed by another spike near the end of the graph. "That second spike was yesterday morning. Just about the time our friend Holzberg wandered into the diner in Fire Creek."

"What the—" McCreary straightened his posture, and an expression of concern suddenly flashed across his face. "But those could be *our* activities, right?"

"Nope. I already filtered those out. These relationships are all independent of our activities." Califano tapped a few more keys on the keyboard and brought up another screen on the monitor. "Now, to answer your previous question, here are the independent relationships whose relevancy scores suddenly hit the roof yesterday morning. This screen shows the first five in order of relevance."

McCreary leaned forward and began reading the list to himself. "What the hell?" he whispered.

No.	IIE1	IIE2
1	Vladamir Krupnov	Krupnov Energy, ZAO
2	Vladamir Krupnov	Severodvinsk, Russia
3	Vladamir Krupnov	Skolkovo Innovation Center
4	Vladamir Krupnov	Arkhangelsk, Russia
5	Arkhangelsk, Russia	Stephen Haroldson

McCreary appeared stunned. "You sure about this?"

"I'm positive. The relevancy scores for these relationships tower far above the noise and are actually on par with the relevancy scores of our own activities. In other words, either these guys in Russia know everything we know . . . or some weird shit is happening over there, too."

"Jesus," said McCreary, shaking his head. "Who are these people?"

Califano rolled his chair to the other side of the room and grabbed a stack of about twenty pages off the ink-jet printer. "Here, I prepared a report for you."

McCreary took the stack of papers and gave Califano a look that showed he was impressed.

"Vladamir Krupnov is a Russian businessman with ties to the Russian government and the Russian mob."

"Kind of the same thing these days, isn't it?" said McCreary.

"Uh-huh. He made a ton of money a few years ago brokering natural gas rights in Siberia to European venture funds. Of course, you can't do something like that in Russia unless you have close ties to the Russian government, which he does. He was the director of the Skolkovo Innovation Center for several years, which the Russian government has been trying to develop for years into a Russian Silicon Valley."

"And Krupnov Energy is his company?"

"Yep. It appears to be a start-up company, although

there's not much info about it. No website, no press releases, or anything like that. I did find a registration with the Russian Federal Tax Service about a year ago for Krupnov's 'ZAO' status—the Russian equivalent of an LLC."

"Any indication of what type of energy they're involved in?"

"From the looks of things, nuclear. But that's just a guess."

"And what about Stephen Haroldson?"

"Yeah, that's an odd one. As far as I can tell, he works for the British Civil Service, some sort of assistant manager in the Department of Work and Pension. Lives with his wife in a small row house in northwest London. He's booked travel to Arkhangelsk, which is what landed him on this list. But I'm not sure what his relationship is with Krupnov, if any. I'll keep looking, though."

McCreary dragged his hand over his face. "Christ," he mumbled. "The Russians. I'm gonna have to get the director involved." After that, he was quiet for a very long time.

Califano finally broke the silence. "Hey, Doc, something else just popped up."

"Hmm?"

"Take a look." Califano rolled his chair out of the way to make room for McCreary.

McCreary stepped forward and quickly read the document on the screen. It appeared to be an excerpt from a police log, documenting a radio broadcast sent by a West Virginia state trooper last night. Two of Califano's relevancy terms were highlighted in bold type.

Broadcast Time: 2134
Responding Unit(s): 312
Event: Carjacking (Code 215)

Occurred: 40 minutes ago
Location: State Road 15, approx. 2 miles east of
                Beury Mtn. Rd.
Direction: Suspect fled east on State Road 15
Suspect(s): Caucasian male, 55–65 years old,
                long gray hair, full beard (gray), long
                fingernails, black leather coat
Weapon: Heavy object
Property Stolen: 2010 Chevy Impala 4dr sedan,
                dark blue. Tag no.: WV/YHD–522
Ambulance requested
EOT

"What do you think?" asked Califano.

McCreary shrugged. "What, just because he had long hair and fingernails?"

"No, man. Look at the location. Route 15 and *Beury Mountain Road*. That's less than ten miles from the Thurmond lab."

McCreary stared at the screen for several seconds, rubbing his temples. It was almost as if he didn't *want* to see the connection.

Califano interrupted his concentration. "Hey, you can think what you want. But it looks to me like we've got another crazy Santa Claus out there with long fingernails . . . and a car."

"Shit," McCreary muttered. "Where's Ana?"

"I'm right here," said Ana Thorne, entering the room at that moment. She was still in her yoga pants and sweatshirt. Her hair was in disarray from sleeping on a cot. "What's going on?" she asked, rubbing her eyes.

"Michael can fill you in. There are recent events in Russia that look very concerning. And we may have another boomerang from Thurmond out there. He's mobile . . . and potentially violent. We need to bring him in right away. Understand?"

"Uh, sure," said Thorne stoically. "But what events in Russia? I haven't seen—"

McCreary cut her off. "Michael will fill you in." He turned to Califano. "Michael, call Admiral Armstrong and ask him to meet us before our flight this morning. We've got a lot of work to do."

"Will do," said Califano. He was still puzzling over the odd word McCreary had used to describe the carjacker: a "boomerang."

"Meanwhile," said McCreary glumly, "I've got to go brief the director about all of this. And I'm sure he won't be pleased." He opened the door to leave but stopped short. "Oh, and, Michael . . ."

"Hmm?"

"Good job with this." McCreary held up the twenty-page report. "Please give copies to Ana and Admiral Armstrong." He turned and left the room, closing the door behind him.

Ana was still standing in the middle of the room with messy hair and sleepy eyes. She gawked incredulously at Califano. "I lie down for *three hours* . . ."

Califano shrugged. "What can I say? Things move fast around here."

12

G ENTLEMEN, WELCOME," said Vladamir Krupnov to his two guests, who had just arrived at the Talagi Airport by way of Helsinki. "Welcome to Arkhangelsk, the city of angels."

Krupnov, fifty-one, was tall and trim. He had a weathered, almost leathery face, clean shaven and accentuated by graying hair, which was groomed in a military-style buzz cut. He wore a long black overcoat over a thick turtleneck sweater and black pants. "I hope your flight was not too uncomfortable," he said. He removed one leather glove and extended his hand to the older of the two men, Benjamin Fulcher—the British expatriate who had once been known as Elijah among a certain elite group.

"It was fine," said Fulcher, accepting Krupnov's handshake. He repositioned his walking cane and gestured toward the man next to him. "May I introduce Stephen Haroldson."

"Yes, yes, of course," said Krupnov, enthusiastically shaking Haroldson's hand. "A pleasure to finally meet you."

"Likewise," said Haroldson meekly. He was a diminutive man in his midfifties, nearly bald, with a weak chin and all the self-confidence of a mouse.

"Have you got your bags?" asked Krupnov.

Both men nodded.

"Very good, then. Please come with me. Our driver is waiting." As they walked through the bunkerlike terminal, Krupnov narrated a short history of the airport. "It was once a military airbase," he explained. "What we called PVO, or Soviet Air Defense Forces. When I was in the Soviet navy, I passed through this airport several times on my way to antisubmarine exercises in the White Sea. And trust me, it was no more charming then than it is now."

Outside, a shiny black Mercedes sedan was waiting for them in the snow-covered driveway in front of the terminal. It was approaching dusk and snowing lightly. The driver quickly got out of the sedan to help with the bags. He was a tree trunk of a man, with fleshy features and a massive neck, and a blue blazer that looked two sizes too small for him. After loading the bags into the trunk, he opened the rear door for the two guests, and they climbed in and seated themselves in the backseat. Then he did the same for Krupnov with the front-passenger's door. A minute later, they were under way.

"Gentlemen," said Krupnov as the sedan slowly rolled away from the airport, "we will be in Severodvinsk in about forty minutes. On the way, you will have a lovely view of the Dvina River from the Severodvinsk bridge. After that, please sit back and relax until we pass through the security checkpoint in Severodvinsk and arrive at our destination. I have arranged for a private dinner, where we can discuss business."

"Is all of this really necessary?" asked Haroldson nervously. "I mean, I have what you want. Can't we just—"

"Mr. Haroldson," said Krupnov firmly. "I appreciate your enthusiasm, and I understand your desire to get things done quickly. But—" He paused for a moment, his tone softening just a bit. "I must insist that we postpone any discussion of this until dinner."

Haroldson nodded and seemed to understand. This was Russia, after all. Even in the age of "democracy," you never knew who might be listening.

"In the meantime," said Krupnov, "please enjoy the view."

Several minutes passed in silence before Haroldson spoke again. "Um, would it be possible to stop at the hotel before dinner? I'd like to clean up."

"Actually, there has been a slight change of plans concerning the hotel," said Krupnov. "I have arranged much nicer accommodations for you than the Volna Hotel, where I originally had you booked. When you see it, I think you'll agree it was a good decision."

Haroldson looked uncomfortable with this new plan but said nothing else for the remainder of the trip.

Forty minutes later, the Mercedes cleared security and entered the Sevmash shipyard in Severodvinsk and slowly made its way through the gritty, industrial landscape of massive warehouses, office buildings, machine shops, and crisscrossing railroad tracks. Finally, they reached the waterfront area of the shipyard on the Dvina River. The driver parked in a reserved space in front of Pier 16 and quickly got out and opened the doors for the passengers.

Krupnov emerged eagerly from the sedan. "Gentlemen," he said with a flourish, "this is your hotel for tonight." He pointed to a sleek yacht moored at the very end of Pier 16.

The two-hundred-foot vessel was splendidly lighted inside and out, giving it a warm, festive appearance in the otherwise bleak environment of the frigid, snow-covered shipyard. "This yacht belongs to my dear friend Makarova, who runs the commercial division of the shipyard. He designed it himself, and I understand he has already received orders to build several more. The name of this vessel is *Belyi Prizrak*, which in Russian means 'White Ghost.' As you can see, the design is very modern."

Indeed, the vessel had an unusual, futuristic appearance, with highly stylized curved lines, an inverted bow, and a large flat afterdeck that was obviously designed to accommodate a helicopter. The hull and superstructure were entirely white, punctuated by long, sleek, tinted windows that appeared nearly black in contrast.

"Come," said Krupnov. "Misha will bring your bags."

The three men made their way down the snowy pier and were greeted at the end by two crewmen in thick orange parkas, who helped them aboard the *Belyi Prizrak*. Twenty minutes later, the vessel was under way in the Dvina River, heading south toward the White Sea.

Dinner was served in the lavish dining room by a uniformed waitstaff. They started with an appetizer of crepes and red caviar, followed by *ukha*, a fish broth soup, followed by small plates of smoked mackerel; raw *salo*, or fatty bacon; and pickled tomatoes. Finally, a main course of minced-meat *pelmeni*, leeks, and boiled potatoes was served to each of the three men.

As the *Belyi Prizrak* cruised slowly along the industrial waterfront, sporadic welding activity could be seen onshore through the dining room's long windows.

"Looks busy," said Fulcher, nodding toward the shoreline.

"Yes," Krupnov replied. He had just finished refilling everyone's wineglass with an expensive French Bordeaux. "In the Soviet era, this was known as Shipyard 402, the largest shipyard in the world and a very famous one in Russia. It was here that Russia's first nuclear-powered submarine, K-3, was built. Many other nuclear submarines were also built here, including the *Akula*, the largest submarine ever built, even to this day."

"So are they working on submarines in those dry docks?" asked Haroldson, pointing to two adjacent, brightly lit dry docks that appeared to be the center of tremendous activity.

"No. In those dry docks, they are building two Lomonosov-class floating power stations, the first of their kind in the world. On the left is the *Abraham Alikhanov*. On the right is the *Georgy Flyorov*. We are funding these through the Skolkovo Innovation Center. . . . " Krupnov's voice suddenly trailed off as he noticed that Haroldson had barely touched his *pelmeni*. "Is the food not to your liking, Mr. Haroldson?"

"What? Oh no, it's fine. It's just, well . . . I guess I'm not that hungry." He took a small sip of wine and looked down at his food again, poking it around with his fork.

Now Krupnov focused all his attention on Haroldson. "Tell me, what do you plan to do with the money? I imagine a million euros will be a big change for you and your wife."

Haroldson shifted uncomfortably in his seat. "Uh . . . we'd like to travel."

"I see," said Krupnov with a smile. "And you've already received our advance, have you not?"

"Oh, yes," said Haroldson meekly. "Fifty thousand euros. Quite helpful to pay off expenses."

"I'm happy to hear that," said Krupnov. "As you know, the remainder will be wired—"

Just then a waiter knocked and entered the dining room. He and a second waiter quickly cleared the dinner plates and set out dessert, a *baba romovaya* cake with rum sauce and fresh berries. They poured cognac for everyone and then quickly left the room.

"Try the cake," said Krupnov to Haroldson. "It's delicious."

Haroldson took a small bite and nodded his head unenthusiastically.

Krupnov leaned back in his chair and savored a slow sip of his cognac, studying Haroldson's face over the rim of his glass. "So," he said after a pause, "tell me more about your father. How exactly did he come into possession of this material?"

Haroldson cleared his throat and gestured toward the elderly British expatriate next to him. "Oh, I . . . I assumed Mr. Fulcher had already told you all about it."

"Well, yes. He told me your father found it in Tunisia, during the war. But I'd like to hear more details. From *you*." Krupnov took another sip of his cognac. "If you don't mind, that is."

"No, I don't mind. But I . . . I can only tell you what my father told me, just before he died in the hospital this past July."

"Go on," said Krupnov.

"Right. So it took place when he was in the army, during the North African campaign in 1943."

As the men sipped their drinks, Haroldson proceeded to recount the remarkable tale that his father, William Haroldson, had told him just hours before he died at the age of eighty-seven.

13

PRIVATE WILLIAM Haroldson checked his watch and felt nauseous: *4:40 A.M.—five minutes to zero.* He tightened the chin strap of his pith helmet, leaned back against the inside of the Bedford, and let the heavy vibration of the idling engine spread throughout his body. He and fifteen other members of the British Eleventh Hussars Regiment sat knee to knee inside the canopied cargo bay of the sweltering truck, part of a mile-long column of tanks, armored cars, and personnel transports of the Seventh Armored Division, idling in the darkness thirty miles southwest of Tunis.

The muffled shouts of sergeants outside the vehicle suddenly grew louder. There was a loud slap on the truck door, and a deep voice from outside bellowed, "Go, go, go!" With a horrific gnashing of gears, the Bedford lurched forward toward the German line.

As the truck bounced along the desert road, a lance

corporal sitting across from William motioned for him to do something with his rifle. William didn't understand. "What?" he asked above the roar of the engine.

Annoyed, the more experienced soldier grabbed the rifle from between William's legs, yanked the bolt mechanism backward, and pressed it forward with a metallic *ka-chink*. Then he reached into his own ammunition pouch and retrieved a single .303-caliber round. He quickly ejected the ten-round charger from William's rifle, added the additional bullet, and pressed the charger back into place. He handed the rifle back to William, barrel up. "Ten in the charger, one in the chamber," he shouted in a thick Manchester accent.

William nodded.

"The Bosche are waiting for us down there, mate," said the lance corporal. "You'd better be ready."

William nodded again.

"This is it, boys," yelled William's squad leader as the rickety Bedford bumped and pitched its way down from the high ground at Medjez-el-Bab to the desert floor below. "Heads low."

William slinked down as low as he could, until his helmet was clanking hard against the metal wall of the truck bed. A solitary thought was reverberating in his mind: *I don't want to die.*

The first enemy blast came just minutes later—a thundering *ka-pow* that lifted the truck's rear wheels off the ground and shredded its canvas canopy. The powerful concussion left William gasping for air, his ears ringing painfully. The truck slammed down with a gut-wrenching impact, and all sixteen men inside flew around like toy soldiers, banging heads, limbs, and rifles. Miraculously, the truck restarted and began accelerating again. William scampered back to his seat, clutching his rifle. He could hear the *rat-tat-tat* of the gunner in the cab firing his heavy Bren—a tripod-mounted machine gun. *The Germans were close.*

Another explosion. The troop carrier lurched violently to the left as sand and rocks sprayed into the cargo compartment through the torn canopy. The Bren gunner was still firing rounds in a mechanical staccato, *rat-tat-tat-tat*, as the transport slid to an abrupt halt.

"Out!" screamed the squad leader. William followed his comrades as they scrambled with their weapons out of the back of the truck and onto the sandy road. The sun was just breaking the horizon, illuminating the eastern sky in a brilliant orange.

Suddenly, there was automatic gunfire from behind, and a young man next to William—an eighteen-year-old private just like him—grunted loudly and fell to the sand with several bullet holes in his back.

"Behind the truck!" screamed the squad leader before he, too, was cut down by a storm of German bullets.

Frantic, William ducked low and followed his squad mates off the road and behind the Bedford. Bullets were slamming hard into the other side of the truck as William flattened to the ground. From his new vantage point beneath the truck, he could see the source of the bullets. A German Panzer tank was approaching fast from the south, its small front portal flickering with muzzle flashes. At the top of the Bedford, the Bren gunner was still firing a steady stream of British bullets, but to no avail. The Nazi tank was invulnerable.

William watched in horror as the massive Panzer stopped short, pivoted, and trained its long barrel directly on the Bedford. Somebody shouted, "Run!" But before William could even lift himself off the ground, a tremendous explosion blasted sand and heat into his face, temporarily blinding him. Instinctively, he buried his face in his arm.

When he looked up, he was surprised to see the German tank in flames, the apparent victim of a smaller British Crusader tank, now visible through the smoke of the wreckage.

The lance corporal from Manchester was first to his feet. "Back in the truck," he shouted to the other men. "Now!" As the men clambered back into the truck, more German Panzers were exploding in the crossfire between two columns of British tanks, which were closing together like pincers.

They'd broken the German line.

By the time William's regiment reached the outskirts of Tunis late in the afternoon, Rommel had already surrendered to the Allies.

William's regiment entered the eastern sector of the city, where the process of disarming and interning tens of thousands of dispirited German and Italian troops was already in full swing. William's squad was assigned to "the medina"—the old quarter of Tunis—a byzantine patchwork of cobblestone streets, open-air souks, and ancient buildings. Their orders were to clear every building to ensure that no enemy holdouts were lurking inside.

"Come on, mate," said the lance corporal from Manchester, slapping William on the back as he walked past. William had stopped momentarily to take in the impressive view along the Rue de la Kasbah, a palm-lined promenade that cut through the heart of the medina. He had read about Tunis as part of his Roman history lessons, his favorite subject in school. Here, in 255 B.C., the Carthaginians had defeated the mighty Roman army in the Battle of Tunis, using thousands of cavalry and Nubian elephants under the command of Xanthippus, a Greek mercenary. Beneath the swaying palm trees of the Rue de la Kasbah,

William imagined Xanthippus parading his elephant army triumphantly through the streets of Carthage.

"Let's go," shouted Manchester, motioning with his arm. William caught up with him, and the pair continued walking along the Rue de la Kasbah toward the towering edifice at the end of the street.

"Would you look at that?" said Manchester as they approached the massive building.

"It's a mosque," William said. "You can tell from the minaret." He pointed to the ornately decorated square tower that rose high above the rest of the building. The exterior walls of the sprawling mosque were colonnaded in a Romanesque style, enclosing more than an acre of space within.

"Strangest mosque I've ever seen," said the lance corporal.

William studied the crude city map that his platoon commander had given him. "Says here it's the Great Mosque of Al-Zaytuna. Actually, I've heard of it before."

"You don't say."

"I remember reading about a famous mosque in Tunis that served as a major university in the Middle Ages. I think this is it."

Manchester eyed him curiously. "A history buff, are you?"

William nodded. "My father teaches history at Clifton College."

Manchester smirked, apparently amused by that fact. Then he slung his rifle over his shoulder and started off toward the mosque. "Come on, then."

The two soldiers reached the Al-Zaytuna mosque and entered the long portico that extended the entire length of the west side of the building. The arched portico was supported by dozens of ornate Roman columns, which the builders of the mosque had salvaged twelve hundred years earlier from the ruins of Carthage, just across Lake Tunis to the east.

They approached the first heavy wooden door and exchanged glances. Slowly, Manchester pushed the door open with a squeak, and the pair entered the mosque with rifles at the ready. After passing through a narrow archway, they entered a vast courtyard, covering nearly three-quarters of an acre, with a large fountain in the middle. In the fading twilight, William could just barely make out the red-and-white geometric pattern of the tile pavers covering the ground.

"Over there," said Manchester quietly. He nodded toward an open door in the northeast corner of the courtyard, which led into a portion of the building near the minaret.

William peered in that direction and saw the faint glow of candlelight emanating from the doorway. Someone was inside, in violation of the citywide curfew. Before William could say anything, Manchester was already on the move. William caught up with him a few steps later, and the two made their way across the courtyard and took up positions on either side of the open doorway. There, they readied their rifles. William gripped his with two sweaty hands.

"Hear that?" Manchester whispered.

Through the open doorway, William could hear a sharp, metal-on-metal sound repeating in rapid succession. *Chink. Chink. Chink.* It stopped for a moment, then resumed. *Chink. Chink. Chink. Chink.*

Manchester stepped quietly through the open doorway. William took a deep breath and followed, his stomach churning, in knots. He didn't like this one bit.

They now stood at one end of a long hallway with narrow windows on the exterior side facing the darkening sky.

At the other end of the hallway, a horseshoe-shaped arch-way framed a set of descending stairs. The flickering can-dlelight and the metallic noise were coming from down the stairs. Manchester pressed his finger to his lips and silently mouthed, "Shhh." Then he started cautiously down the hall-way toward the stairs with William following close behind.

The noise continued in periodic spurts. *Chink. Chink. Chink.*

They passed through the horseshoe-shaped archway and stopped at the top of the stairs. Manchester motioned for William to stay put, then pointed to his eyes and the hallway behind them, signaling to *keep a lookout behind us*.

William nodded and watched as the lance corpo-ral descended the steps to a landing about six feet below, turned, and disappeared around the corner. It was at that moment that William realized something awful.

The metallic noise had stopped.

That thought had no sooner crossed William's mind when chaos suddenly erupted below. He heard Manchester shout, "What the f—!" followed immediately by scrapes, thumps, and grunts, and then a strange gurgling noise. These noises echoed loudly throughout the stone stairwell.

William hesitated for just a moment. Then he bounded down the stairs, rounded the corner at the landing, and stopped dead in his tracks when he saw the gruesome spectacle below him. Manchester was lying faceup at the bottom of the stairs, his throat slit wide open from ear to ear, his body writhing as blood gushed from his neck in all directions.

William recoiled in horror, his heart nearly bursting through his chest. At the edge of his vision, he saw some-thing moving away in the room beyond. Someone, or *some-thing*, had just ducked out of sight.

Panicked, William clambered down the steps and

dropped to one knee beside his comrade's body. "Oh, God," he whispered, not knowing what to do. The lance corporal's spasms continued for several seconds, then faded and finally stopped. He was dead.

Terrified, William scanned the room for any movement. *Nothing.* Everything was still now.

The room, which appeared to be a meditation or prayer hall of some sort, was a large rectangular space with two rows of six marble columns supporting the ceiling in a network of symmetrical arches. A massive brass candelabra hung low in the center of the room, bathing the columned space in dancing yellow light. The floor was an intricate mosaic of red, black, and white stones arranged in a traditional Arabic pattern of intertwining geometric shapes.

William's training had not prepared him for this. *He had to get help.* He stood to leave, but something in the room suddenly caught his eye. On the far side of the room, in an alcove partially obscured by one of the marble columns, an old wooden ladder was propped up against the wall. William leveled his rifle and took one cautious step into the room to get a better view. He could now see a chisel and hammer on the floor near the ladder, surrounded by a white circle of debris. His eyes followed the ladder to the wall, where someone had chiseled out a small hole just above the keystone of the arched alcove. *Strange.*

Suddenly, there was motion nearby.

William turned to see a uniformed Nazi officer charging out of the shadows a few yards away, shrieking and wielding a bloody dagger above his head.

William backpedaled but immediately found himself pinned against the stone wall adjacent to the stairwell. He struggled to get his rifle into firing position as the Nazi attacker bore down on him like a crazed animal. In a panic, William squeezed the trigger of his rifle without aiming. A deafening shot exploded out of the barrel and ricocheted off a nearby column.

He'd missed.

The Nazi officer paused for a second, curled his lips into a mocking smile, then moved in for the kill.

William fumbled the bolt lever of his rifle upward and cycled it rapidly back and forth as the Nazi officer lunged savagely at him with his dagger. *Squeeze the trigger!* The dagger flashed past William's eyes at the exact moment he fired his weapon, again without aiming.

The report of the rifle echoed throughout the columned space. But this time, there was no ricochet.

The Nazi officer stumbled backward as the .303-caliber bullet tore into his stomach, the sharp tip of his swastika-emblazoned dagger just barely missing William's chest. To William's amazement, the man regained his footing a few feet away and slowly stood upright. A widening circle of blood was already soaking through his olive drab tunic. Wincing in pain, the man muttered something in German and began advancing unsteadily toward William, the dagger held feebly in one hand.

William frantically chambered another round and stared in disbelief as the bloodied German officer stumbled toward him. *What was wrong with him?* With no other option, William fired another bullet into the man's torso at close range. The officer's eyes bulged as he absorbed the impact of the second shot and retreated backward several steps. He wavered on shaky legs for a moment, then crumpled to the floor.

William stood for several seconds with his back against the wall, trembling and hyperventilating. His ears were ringing loudly, but from somewhere outside, he could hear distant voices yelling in English. His platoon mates had apparently heard the gunshots and were on their way.

William gawked at the dead Nazi officer on the floor. The man was still gripping the dagger in one hand. A pool of blood was spreading out around his body, onto the mosaic floor. William glanced up at the chiseled hole in the wall and wondered what this was all about. Haltingly, he approached and used his foot to roll the man over onto his back. The dead man's face was thin and clean shaven, his wire-rimmed glasses broken and askew. He looked intelligent, as if he could have been a college professor somewhere. *What was he doing in this mosque? Surely he must have known that Rommel had surrendered to the Allies.*

William spotted a prominent lump in the front pocket of the man's bloody tunic, and he cautiously crouched down and retrieved an object from inside. *It felt strange between his fingers.* As he held it up to the candlelight, he saw that it was a jagged black stone, about two inches in diameter, with an irregular shape and a bit of mortar debris still clinging to its edges. He placed the object in the palm of his other hand and gasped at the resulting phenomenon. *Impossible!*

Just then there were heavy footsteps in the hallway upstairs.

"British army!" someone yelled from above. "Announce yourself."

William's heart skipped a beat. He quickly rose to his feet and shoved the mysterious object into his pocket. "P-P-Private William Haroldson," he yelled back. "Eleventh Hussars, second platoon, first squad."

There was a pause. "Is the area secure, Private?" shouted the voice.

William looked around at the two dead bodies on the floor. "Yes," he answered. "But we need a corpsman."

14

WHAT DID your father do with the stone after that?" asked Vladamir Krupnov.

Stephen Haroldson had just completed the story of his father's experience during the British liberation of Tunis. "He kept it until the end of the war. Then he turned it over to the authorities when he got home. The amazing thing is, he never got any kind of reward or credit for discovering that stone and turning it over. No special recognition. Not even a medal." Haroldson let out a sardonic laugh. "Instead, they told him to forget he'd ever seen it. That it was top secret and that there'd be *repercussions* if he ever told anyone about it . . . even his family." Haroldson's voice cracked on the last word. He cleared his throat and continued. "But what my father never told anyone, until just hours before he died, was that he'd actually broken off a small piece of that stone for himself. As a souvenir."

"Your father was a smart man," said Krupnov.

"He kept it hidden all those years in a small tobacco tin in the attic, in a box with all his army uniforms and his medals, and other souvenirs from the war. He never told anyone about it because he was afraid he'd get in trouble." Haroldson sighed, apparently still sensitive about the recent loss of his father. "Anyway, after he passed, I found the piece of stone in the attic, right where he said it would be. And as soon as I saw it, I knew . . . my God, that must be worth a lot of money. I contacted Mr. Fulcher and he got back to me right away. And, well . . . here I am."

"Yes, here you are," said Krupnov with a crooked smile. He let those words sink in, as if weighing their significance. Then he raised his glass high above the table. "Gentlemen, a toast."

The other two men followed suit a moment later.

"To Mr. Haroldson," said Krupnov.

"Cheers," said Fulcher, as they all clinked their glasses together.

"And to your father," Krupnov added reverently.

"Thank you," said Haroldson.

Krupnov drained his glass and carefully refilled it with more cognac. "Notice the rocking?" he said as he poured. "We're in open water now." He rose from his seat and looked out both windows. "Yes, we're in the Dvina Bay, north of Severodvinsk. See there?" He pointed out the starboard window to the lighted shoreline in the distance. "Sevmesh is about four kilometers that way. And in this direction . . ." He pointed into the darkness out the port window. " . . . is the White Sea, which extends north about two hundred kilometers to the Arctic Circle and the Kola Peninsula. The sea to the north is already frozen over by now."

The other two men nodded and admired the view of the sparkling Severodvinsk shoreline.

Finally, Krupnov resumed his seat, set down his glass, and leaned forward on one elbow. "Now, Mr. Haroldson. If you'll hand me the material, we can complete our transaction, and you and your wife can get on with your lives and all of your exciting travels."

Haroldson swallowed hard. "What about the rest—" He cleared his throat. "The rest of the money?"

Krupnov laughed. "You're not much of a businessman, are you, Mr. Haroldson?"

"Sorry?"

"You see, you've put yourself in a very vulnerable position here with no bargaining power at all. A better strategy would have been to demand that the full amount be placed into escrow before you boarded your flight from Helsinki."

Haroldson looked stunned. "But I . . . I thought . . ." His skin was getting paler by the second. He looked back and forth between the two men at the table.

Krupnov laughed again and slapped the table loudly, causing Haroldson to flinch. "Relax, Mr. Haroldson. I'm a man of my word. I have every intention of wiring the remainder of the money into your account. I can do so in thirty seconds using my phone. But first, I need to see that material with my own eyes."

Haroldson breathed an audible sigh of relief and slowly retrieved a small glass vial from his pocket, placing it on the table in front of Krupnov.

Krupnov picked up the vial with great care and held it up to the light. "Magnificent," he whispered, staring in wonder at the tiny object inside. It was a shard of black stone, about the size of a small watch battery. And it was *floating* inside the vial, suspended inexplicably in midair. "It's quite small," said Krupnov, casting a sideways glance at Haroldson. "You're sure this is the *entire* fragment that your father told you about?"

"Oh, yes. I'm sure."

Krupnov appeared mesmerized as he twisted the vial back and forth between his thumb and finger, watching the object inside bouncing lazily off the sides. Finally, he put the vial down and stared at Haroldson curiously, as if sizing him up. The silence stretched into several seconds and became quite uncomfortable.

"So . . . what about the wire transfer?" asked Haroldson, breaking the silence. He glanced at Fulcher beside him and then back to Krupnov. "You . . . you said you were a man of your word."

"So I am." Krupnov retrieved his cell phone from his breast pocket and pressed a single button. He held it to his ear for a few seconds, then spoke into it in Russian, his voice calm and quiet: *"Da. Zaydi."* He hung up the phone and smiled at Haroldson. "It'll just be a minute."

Thirty seconds later, there was a knock on the door and Misha, the husky sedan driver, entered the dining room. *"Vyzivali?"* he said to Krupnov.

"Gospodin Haroldson khotel by iskupat'sya," said Krupnov.

The sedan driver nodded and immediately walked over to Haroldson and grasped him firmly by the arm, helping him to his feet.

"Wh—what're you doing?" said Haroldson in a confused tone, rising to his feet. "Where are we going?"

"Go with Misha. He'll take care of everything."

"But . . . I don't understand." Haroldson's voice was quickly giving way to panic. Misha prodded him toward the door, less politely now. "Wait!" exclaimed Haroldson, trying in vain to resist. "Please!"

Seconds later, Haroldson and Misha were out of the room.

Krupnov and Fulcher remained seated at the dining room table. They looked at each other in silence for a long while, as the sound of Haroldson's struggling and pleading in the hallway gradually grew more distant. Half a minute later, he could still be heard shouting from the forward stairwell thirty feet away: "I don't want the money! You can keep it. Please, just let me go! I have a wife!"

"A shame," said Fulcher, shaking his head.

Krupnov nodded. He rose to his feet and walked over to the dining room door and gently closed it, shutting out the sound of Haroldson's voice altogether. Then he returned to his seat. "So, do you think this is enough material?" he asked, picking up the glass vial.

"Enough to demonstrate the concept, yes."

Krupnov frowned. "I'm not interested in 'demonstrating the concept.' I'm interested in *making money*." He held up the glass vial containing the floating chip of stone. "So, is this enough to make our reactors work or not?"

Fulcher sighed. "No. We'll need more seed material than that. Which is why it is so critical that we find Malachi. With the material from the Thurmond lab, we should have enough for at least one self-sustaining reactor. Maybe two. And once we find the *rest* of the Joshua Stone . . ."

"Yes, about that," said Krupnov. He reached into his pocket and retrieved a folded sheet of paper, which he quickly unfolded and spread out onto the table. The sheet was a photocopy of a tattered and stained notebook page with the following annotated drawing:

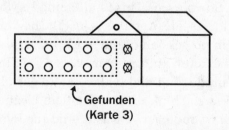

Gefunden
(Karte 3)

"Do you believe Malachi will be able to explain this?" Krupnov asked, somewhat doubtfully.

"Aside from Franz Holzberg himself, Malachi is our best bet."

"You'd better be right," Krupnov intoned sharply. "The *posrednikov* have invested a great deal of money in this project. You originally asked for five million euros, I got you five million. Then you asked for another ten million, and I got it for you. You asked for a reactor, we now have *two* reactors nearly completed. But not enough seed material to make either of them work. And, along the way, I have made certain assurances to the *posrednikov*, not to mention the Russian government. Do you understand what I mean?"

Fulcher nodded.

"I'm not sure you do. This is not England. The *posrednikov* expect results. If we fail . . ."

"Vlad," said the older man calmly. "We won't fail. Are you seriously doubting me now? After what I've just delivered to you?" He pointed to the glass vial on the table. "I was right about that chip, wasn't I?"

Krupnov nodded.

"And I was right about Malachi, too. My timing was just a little off. All we need to do is find him. *Quickly.*"

"*Da*," said Krupnov. "I am leaving for the United States tomorrow morning to supervise that operation myself."

"Good. So you see? This is all going to work out just fine. It *has* to. It's fate. And this is just the beginning. Soon, we will be in possession of the most powerful technology the world has ever known. Our reactors will revolution-ize energy production and make oil and gas obsolete in a matter of years. Think of it: unlimited, clean, renewable energy with no radioactive waste. And the byproduct . . . a material with properties the world has never seen, with limitless applications for military, aerospace, transportation, and more."

"Yes. It will instantly become the world's most valuable commodity," said Krupnov.

"And we alone will possess the critical seed material needed to make it."

"I do like the sound of that," said Krupnov with a smile. He raised his glass and took a sip.

"By the way," said Fulcher after a pause. "What did you tell Misha?"

"Hmm? Oh, I just told him that Mr. Haroldson would like to take a swim tonight."

"Ah."

Seconds later, the flailing body of Stephen Haroldson suddenly flew past the dining room's port window on its way into the frigid waters of the White Sea.

"Well, that eliminates one loose end," said Krupnov.

"What about his wife?"

Krupnov took another sip of his cognac, savoring its smooth, intoxicating flavor. "She's been dead since this morning."

15

DULLES, VIRGINIA

I DON'T trust him," said Ana Thorne to Admiral Armstrong and Dr. McCreary. The three of them were standing on the tarmac in front of Landmark Aviation, one of four fixed-base operators (FBOs) at Dulles International Airport that provided private jet services for corporate clients and wealthy individuals. Thirty yards away, a gleaming white Cessna Citation CJ3 was preparing for takeoff, its twin turbofan engines whirring to life. The object of Thorne's concern, Michael Califano, gazed inquisitively from his window aboard the private jet as the trio conversed about him on the tarmac.

All FBO flights originating from Dulles were required to file publicly accessible flight plans, and this one was no exception. If anyone had bothered to check the Cessna's registration, they would have learned it was registered to the Constellation Aviation Group of Wilmington, Delaware, a full-service aviation company with a highly discreet clientele. The business dealings of Constellation's clients ran the gamut from casino operations to private equity management to commercial real estate. But they all had one thing in common: they were all fake. Or more specifically, they were all front companies for the CIA. Constellation Aviation Group was, in fact, the CIA's private airline, operating around the world twenty-four hours a day, seven days a week.

"First of all," said Ana, nodding subtly toward the plane, "where did he learn to speak Croatian like that? He sounded practically fluent. And I can tell you, unless you grow up a native speaker, you don't pick up that level of proficiency without some serious language training. Where'd he get it? And more important, how did he know *I* spoke it? He would've had to crack into my agency files to get that information, which is illegal."

McCreary cleared his throat and looked at Armstrong with raised eyebrows. "You want to explain?"

Armstrong nodded and took Ana gently by the arm. "Let's go where it's a little quieter."

"I'll tell the pilot to wait," said McCreary, heading toward the jet. "But don't be long. Our flight plan has us taking off by six thirty, which is in twelve minutes. If we're not in the takeoff queue by then, we'll have to file a whole new flight plan."

Armstrong led Ana Thorne toward an empty aircraft hangar nearby. Once they'd reached the relative quiet of the hangar, he turned and spoke. "Michael's a special case. He grew up in Atlantic City, and his father was involved in some bad things. A lot of bad things, actually. When Michael was young, his father spent time in jail for forgery and check fraud. When he got out, he started dealing in counterfeit watches and jewelry, which led to counterfeit prescription drugs and eventually narcotics. On top of all that, he had a terrible gambling habit. When Michael was about twelve, his father got in over his head with a Bratva organization from New York. He'd run up a couple hundred thousand dollars in gambling debts that he couldn't pay off."

"The mob?"

"Uh-huh. So one night, while Michael was at a friend's house, three men broke into his parents' home. They forced his mother and father and fifteen-year-old sister into the basement. They bound and gagged his father and then—" Armstrong cleared his throat. "They raped Michael's mother and sister . . . and cut their throats when they were done."

"Oh, God."

"Then they beat his father to death with a baseball bat."

"Jesus."

"Next morning when Michael got home, he found all three of them in the basement."

Ana winced at the horrible mental image and shook her head.

"Can you imagine finding your entire family like that?"

Ana said nothing. *Actually, she could imagine such a thing.*

"Michael ended up in foster care. Not great in Atlantic City, especially for kids that age. He bounced around from home to home and had a real tough time for a while. But here's the thing: Michael's a prodigy, always has been. He was a phenomenal student, especially in math and science, and his teachers loved him. Despite everything, they kept him on the right path and made sure he applied to college. They even helped him get a scholarship. He ended up at Carnegie Mellon, where he majored in computer science and electrical engineering. Graduated top of his class. Got a scholarship to pursue a master's at MIT . . . an NSA scholarship, actually. And that's where his problems began."

"How so?"

"What happened to his family . . . he carried that around like a ticking time bomb. After all those years, neither the local police nor the FBI had ever solved the crime. Imagine knowing that the animals who did that to your family were still out there, wandering around. I'm sure it ate away at him little by little, until one day something snapped. Or I should say, he *discovered* something that made him snap."

"Which was what?"

Armstrong checked his watch. "We really need to get you on that plane."

"Please tell me," she said.

Armstrong sighed and glanced behind him at the plane. "Michael had developed a specialty in college, which he continued at MIT. He'd become an expert on data mining, which was an emerging field at the time. In fact, by the time he finished his first year at MIT, he'd already created one of the most sophisticated data-mining engines in the world. Single-handedly. As a twenty-two-year-old graduate student."

"Impressive."

"Oh, you have no idea." Armstrong checked his watch again. "Look, we'll have to finish this later. Let's go."

Ana started to protest but saw that Admiral Armstrong wasn't waiting for her. He had already turned around and was heading back toward the plane. She caught up with him a few steps later. "But why does he speak Croatian?" she asked, walking a step behind him.

"Probably learned it on his own," said Armstrong over his shoulder. "From a book."

"Oh, I seriously doubt that," said Ana.

Armstrong stopped short and spun around, nearly causing Ana to crash into him. "Don't," he said.

"Don't what?"

"Don't doubt him. His mind doesn't work like other people's. He's . . . *different*." He released her gaze and turned back toward the plane.

Ana followed close behind. "Okay, just tell me one more thing. What was he in prison for?"

They'd reached the plane. The ladder was down, the engines were spinning, and McCreary was emphatically motioning through his window for Ana to get on board. Armstrong turned slowly and gazed at her. It wasn't a look of anger, exactly. It was more like a warning. "That's classified," he said.

Ana knew she'd crossed a line. In this field, confidential information was always compartmentalized. You knew only what you *needed* to know and nothing more. And it was clear to her that she'd just stepped into the wrong compartment. "Sorry," she mumbled. "It's just—"

Armstrong cut her off. "Ana, you need to go."

Ana nodded reluctantly and made her way up the Cessna's ladder. When she reached the last step, she turned and glanced back at Armstrong.

Armstrong gave her a slight nod and a smile that seemed to say: *You're forgiven, now go.*

The flight to West Virginia took just over thirty minutes. They landed at the Raleigh County Memorial Airport, where three black Ford Explorers were waiting for them on the tarmac. "Courtesy of our DEA friends," said McCreary as they exited the airplane. "Keys are in the vehicles. Michael, you head to Fire Creek and see what you can find. Remember, you're FBI today. Be sure to show your credentials and explain clearly why you're there."

Califano nodded. Today he was Special Agent Michael Califano of the Federal Bureau of Investigation, and he had the badge and ID to prove it. The CIA's disguise people had even provided him with an off-the-rack blue suit, a pair of well-worn leather Oxfords, and a khaki raincoat. This was considered "FBI appropriate."

"You're here to investigate the escape of a mental patient from St. Elizabeth's," said McCreary, repeating the cover story he'd gone over twice on the plane. "Nothing more, nothing less."

"I still think we could do better than that," said Califano. "I mean, seriously, the old 'escaped mental patient' story? Do people still buy that?"

McCreary frowned. "Michael, we're not writing a novel here. It's a cover story that works, okay? It accounts for Holzberg's strange appearance and anything crazy he might have said to people before we took him into custody. Stick to it, okay? No improvising. If you leave people wondering why you're here, they start speculating. I don't want people speculating."

"I got it," said Califano.

Ana kept her eyes fixed on Califano and shook her head slightly. She still didn't trust him, although now she had a bit more empathy for him.

"Ana," said McCreary. "You work with the county sheriff's office and find out everything they have on that carjacking last night. Tell them it's related to the St. Elizabeth's incident, but don't elaborate."

Ana nodded.

"Okay. You've both got your earpieces in, right?"

Thorne and Califano nodded in unison. Each had a tiny earpiece lodged deep in one ear, completely invisible, and a small wireless microphone hidden in their clothing.

"Remember, Michael, when you tap the unit in your breast pocket, everything you say will be picked up and transmitted to both of us. It's voice activated, so it keeps transmitting as long as you're talking. It times out after about one second of silence. Try to keep the line clear unless it's important, okay?"

"Uh-huh."

"I'll head to Thurmond and see what I can find there. Let's meet back here at four thirty."

With that, they separated and headed to their respective SUVs.

Ana paused before getting into her vehicle, and Califano did the same. Their eyes met momentarily over the hoods of their SUVs.

"Anything unusual happens out there," Ana said, "make sure you call us." She was about to say something else but stopped short. "Just . . . don't take any chances, okay? You're not trained for this."

"Got it," said Califano. He waited to see if Ana had anything more to say to him.

She didn't.

A minute later, the three black SUVs exited the municipal airport and headed off in three different directions.

16

IT WAS just after 9:00 A.M. when Mike Califano walked through the front door of the Fire Creek Diner. He observed three old codgers seated in a booth near the front and an elderly woman in an apron behind the counter. He approached the woman. "You Thelma Scott?"

The woman nodded. "That's me, honey."

Califano retrieved the leather ID holder that the CIA people had provided him with and flipped it open to show his FBI credentials. "I'm Special Agent Califano." He felt awkward flashing his badge like that. *It always seemed so natural on TV.* "FBI," he added.

Thelma glanced at Califano's fake FBI badge but showed no particular interest in it.

"Do you mind if I ask you some questions about what happened yesterday?" asked Califano.

Thelma shrugged. "No, I don't mind."

Califano snapped his ID holder shut and motioned with

his head to a vacant booth in the far corner of the diner. "Can we talk over there?"

"Sure."

Thelma and Califano made their way to the empty booth and sat down across from each other. Once they were situated, Califano said, "Okay, please tell me everything you remember about the incident."

Thelma recounted the prior day's events as best she could, pointing several times to the spot on the diner floor where the man had curled up and nearly bled to death. She mentioned the man's strange appearance, his hat, his foreign accent, and the fact that he claimed to have come from the Thurmond National Lab. She also remembered that he'd asked her to call someone.

"Yeah? Who'd he ask you to call?"

"Oh, gosh. It was *Doctor* somebody. Dr. Brown? Dr. Burns? Bernstein . . . hmmm . . . Dr. *Somebody*. Burr . . . Burt . . ." Her voice trailed off.

"That's okay if you can't rem—"

"Reynolds!" she exclaimed. "I was thinking Burt Reynolds. It was Dr. Reynolds. At Princeton. And he gave an old-fashioned number. Like Princeton one two three four, or something like that. That's the way we used to do long distance when I was young. But not anymore . . ."

"Thank you, that's very helpful. Now, did he mention any other names?"

"None that I can think of."

"How about Opie? Did he mention anyone by that name?"

"Opie? No, not that I remember."

"Can you remember anything else he said? Maybe particular phrases that he used?"

Thelma shrugged. "No. Just what I've already told you."

Califano decided not to ask her about the phrase "murder of science." *Might freak her out,* he figured. He could hear McCreary's voice in his head: *I don't want people speculating.* "Okay, Ms. Scott. Is there anything else you can recall about the incident that might be important? Anything at all?"

Thelma fidgeted with her hands and hesitated for a moment, apparently unsure about whether to proceed. "Well, there's one thing." Her voice dropped a notch as she spoke.

"Hmm?"

Thelma looked around the restaurant and then lowered her voice to nearly a whisper. "I think I know who that man was."

"You do?" Califano leaned in closer. "Who was he?"

"Well, I don't know his name per se, but I think he was one of those scientists who used to work up in Thurmond in the fifties. I recognized his voice 'cause he had a German accent. He come in here on Sundays for breakfast when I was still helping my mother on weekends. Said Mom's pancakes reminded him of home." She smiled. "I think what he really liked was my *mother.* Anyway, that's who I think he was."

Califano had nearly forgotten about the cover story he was supposed to be using. But he figured now would be as good a time as any to bring it up. "Actually, ma'am, I think you might be mistaken about that."

"Oh?"

"Yeah. The man who came in here yesterday is an escaped patient from St. Elizabeth's Psychiatric Hospital in Washington, D.C. He's not German. He's not a scientist. And he didn't have anything to do with the Thurmond National Laboratory."

Thelma looked hurt by the suggestion that she was misremembering things. "I'm . . . I'm just telling you what I remember," she said. "You asked if there was anything else I recalled, and I'm telling you what I recalled. If you say I'm wrong, then . . . well . . . so be it. But I know what I saw."

Califano decided to leave it at that. There wasn't much else to say. *Stupid cover story anyway.* "I understand, ma'am. Now, is there anything else you think might be important?"

Thelma looked around again, and her voice dropped even lower. "Well, yeah. Now that you mention it." She paused for a moment. "But first let me ask *you* something."

"Okay . . ."

"Do you know what used to go on up there in Thurmond?"

Califano shrugged and said no. Which was the truth.

"Well, let me tell you something. I was about fifteen or sixteen when they first started doing all that stuff up there. And I remember lots of strange things happening. Most of all, our clocks would get all messed up. And watches, too. You wouldn't notice it at first, but then someone would come to visit from another town, and you'd find out that every clock in Fire Creek was thirty or forty minutes behind. Always behind. Never fast. You'd reset them, but then it would happen again a week later."

"How long did that go on?"

"Better part of a year, as I remember it. Eventually, a couple of the men in town complained about it, on account of it making them late for work at the mines. After that, a man from the government come down here and explained it was all because of solar flare activity or something like that. Not anything to do with the lab."

Califano was nodding along.

"Well, we never really believed that for a second. We knew they were doing something strange up there. But it did get better for a while. After that, clocks just ran a *little* slower, a few minutes each day. Which they still do today, by the way."

"What, even now?"

"Uh-huh. Every clock in town. We're all just used to it, I guess. So we don't really think much about it. But every morning, I have to bump my clock ahead three minutes, just to keep it on time. Same with everyone else. We don't really worry about it none. Doesn't seem to affect anything important."

"Yeah, but it's . . . *strange*," said Califano.

Thelma's eyes widened. "You think *that's* strange? Well, let me tell you what happened to the folks up in Thurmond."

Califano leaned in close. "You mean the people in the lab?"

"No, honey. In the *town*. There was still some folks living up there in Thurmond even after they built that lab. Probably fifty or sixty folks in several families. 'Mountain folk,' I guess you'd call them. Kept to themselves mostly. Never bothered no one. They're long gone now, though. That place has been a ghost town for, lord, fifty years or more."

"So what happened to them? The families in Thurmond?"

"Must have been late summer or early fall of 1959. I was already married and pregnant with my first child. One night, there was some big commotion up on the mountain, in Thurmond. You could hear it all the way down here. Some type of explosion, a big, loud boom, or more of a popping or whooshing sound. Anyway, there were helicopters and searchlights all over the place, and it went on all night long. Next morning, we expected to hear some big news about it. We figured it was a mine explosion or something. But . . . there was *nothing* about it at all. Nothing in the newspaper. No radio reports. Nothing on TV. Nothing. Well, that didn't sit right with folks here. Thurmond's just ten miles up the ridge, and a lot of people in Fire Creek knew people up there. So, some of the men went up to investigate, including my father."

"They drove up there?"

"Well, they tried to, but all the roads was blocked off by the army. So three of them decided to hike off into the woods to see what happened . . ." Thelma paused, apparently trying to recall the exact details of the incident. "They left on a Sunday morning, probably about nine, and didn't come back all day. Sun went down, and they *still* weren't back. Lord, I remember my mother was a wreck that night. She called the police, and they said no one was supposed to be going up there on account of the whole area being . . . what's the word? *Quarter-eened?*"

"Quarantined?"

"Uh-huh, that's it. So no one was being allowed in or out of Thurmond 'cause of the quarantine."

"So what happened to your father and the other men?"

"Well, we thought they must have been put into quarantine with the rest of them. In fact, we were convinced it was radiation or something like that. Everyone was worried sick. But then, out of the blue, they come walking back out of the woods on *Friday*. Five days later. Said they were stopped by military police before they ever reached Thurmond and told to turn around, which they did. So we said: 'Okay, but where you been for the past five days?' And they was totally confused because, according to them, they'd only been gone a few hours."

Califano's brain was working overtime, fitting all this new information into his memory bank and comparing it with what he already knew about Thurmond. "Whoa, whoa. Hold on. They thought they had been gone only a few hours, but it was really *five days*?"

"Uh-huh."

"So . . . did you ever find out what happened?"

"Not exactly," said Thelma. "The quarantine lasted about a month. Nobody went in or out of Thurmond during that entire time. When it was over, the government evacuated everyone from Thurmond and relocated them to temporary housing . . . I think somewhere near Charleston. I never personally saw any of those people again. But I heard from other folks that they was never really the same. They had all types of medical issues. Memory loss and night terrors and such. Government paid for their food and housing and health care, I guess for the rest of their lives. And, like I said, I never saw any of them again."

"What about your father? Did he ever figure out where the five days had gone?"

Thelma shrugged. "It's just like our clocks. The time just *vanished* somehow."

Califano sat quietly for several seconds as his mind processed this bizarre information. Finally, he thanked Thelma for her time and told her she could go. A few minutes later, he put on his overcoat and began making his way to the exit. He smiled and nodded politely at Thelma as he passed by. Then he stopped just short of the door. "Uh, Ms. Scott."

"Yes?"

"You mentioned there's a way to *walk* to Thurmond from here?"

"Well, there *used* to be. There's an old railroad line that goes straight over to Thurmond from here. It doesn't go around Beury's Ridge like the road does. It goes straight over the top. When the coal company was still operating, that's how they got the coke from the furnaces to the coal depot in Thurmond. It's all overgrown now, but back then— yeah, you could walk along the tracks. Probably about ten miles, I'd say. *Hey, Frank!*"

One of the old men in the booth suddenly looked up from his buckwheat pancakes. "Huh?"

"How long's that old branch line to Thurmond? Ten miles, would you say?"

"Yeah, I reckon. Maybe a bit less. Why?"

"This fella wanted to know." Thelma turned back to Califano. "You can still see part of the tracks out there." She pointed toward the back of the restaurant. "Walk straight back into the woods until you reach the old coke ovens. Can't miss 'em. Branch line runs right in front of the ovens."

Califano thanked her and exited the restaurant. Outside, he made an immediate right turn on the sidewalk and then another right turn at the first corner. Then he made a beeline for the woods. He tapped the button for his transmitter as he walked. "Hey, guys, I'm all done in the diner," he said.

A second later, he heard McCreary's voice crackling in his ear: "Anything interesting?"

"Got a name," Califano replied as he walked. "Dr. Reynolds at Princeton. Apparently Holzberg wanted to contact him. I'll feed that into my database when I get a chance and let you know what I find."

"Very good," said McCreary.

"Also," said Califano, "sounds like they were doing some strange stuff in Thurmond. Apparently something that messed up all the clocks around here . . . to this day."

"Oh yeah?" said McCreary. "The locals told you that?"

"Mm-hmm. Thelma Scott says they evacuated and relocated the entire town of Thurmond back in '59 after some sort of explosion." Califano suddenly stopped at the tree line and searched for a path through the woods. He spotted one off to the left and started making his way toward it. As he walked, he pressed the transmit button again. "How about you guys? Anything interesting?"

Ana Thorne's voice came on the line. "Nothing here. Still waiting for the sheriff." She sounded annoyed.

McCreary's voice came on a few seconds after that. "I'm suiting up right now. I'll let you guys know what I find."

Califano immediately stopped walking. *Suiting up?*

He'd worked at DOE long enough to know what that meant. He tapped the transmit button. "Hey, Doc, I thought we needed more information before we could go down into the lab."

There was a long pause before McCreary finally responded. "Keep the line clear, Michael."

The coke ovens in Fire Creek were apparently a popular attraction among the "ghost tour" crowd, as evidenced by the well-worn footpath that led there. Califano followed that path several hundred yards into the woods until it gave way to a large clearing. He stopped at the edge of the clearing and took in the unusual sight that was now spread before him. The morning sun was filtering softly through the trees, illuminating thick pools of swirling fog that still hugged the ground in splotches. The coke ovens themselves were about thirty yards away, at the far edge of the clearing. And Thelma Scott had certainly been right. *You couldn't miss them.*

The coke ovens were part of an enormous brick structure, about twelve feet high and more than two hundred feet long, that stretched deep into the woods. Each of the beehivelike ovens was built directly into the face of this brick structure, creating a long row of semicircular openings, each about six feet in diameter, with a two-foot column between them. This gave the masonry structure a Romanesque appearance, like a crumbling, vine-covered aqueduct that had somehow been transplanted from Tuscany into the West Virginia wilderness.

Califano made his way to the first of the semicircular ovens and poked his head inside. In the dark shadows, he could see that it was shaped like an igloo, with curved brick walls that converged at the top, leaving a small, circular opening, which he guessed was a chimney. Turning away from the ovens, he scanned the forest floor until he spotted the remnants of the train tracks that Thelma Scott had mentioned. The rusty rails were barely visible beneath a tangle of vegetation and forest debris. With some effort, he made his way to the tracks until he was standing directly between the rails. He peered eastward into the forest, in the direction of Thurmond, and observed that the tracks quickly disappeared into the vegetation.

Califano checked his watch; it was just shy of 10:30 A.M. He stood there for a long time, thinking about what Ana had told him earlier this morning: *don't take any chances.* She was right, of course. In fact, he already felt like he was in over his head.

But that had never stopped him before.

With a deep breath, Califano began walking eastward along the tracks, and he was soon deep in the woods.

17

BILL MCCREARY could barely see out of the face mask they'd put over his eyes, nose, and mouth. In frustration, he ripped it off his beefy face for the third time. "It keeps fogging up," he complained.

The radiological control technician at the guard station was apologetic, but firm. "I'm sorry, sir. But you've got to wear that mask at all times beyond this point. No exceptions. Try breathing through your nose. That should cut down on the fogging."

"Jesus," McCreary muttered under his breath. "In all the years you've been here, have you *ever* detected radiation levels above background?"

"No, sir. Not down here. But we don't usually go up to the entrance where you're going. That's a highly restricted area with special radiological controls. In fact, I'm surprised you even got clearance to go up there. I mean . . . everything checks out, so you *are* clear to go. It's just . . .

well, you have to have the proper protective gear if you want to go up there. So if you'll please bear with me . . ."

McCreary waved away the man's assistance. "I'll do it." He slipped the face mask over his broad face once again and tightened the four rubber straps.

"Ready?" asked the technician.

McCreary nodded that he was. He was suited from head to toe in yellow coveralls, cotton gloves, rubber booties over his shoes, a cotton hood, and now the face mask. With his large frame and oversize physique, he looked like a bright yellow Sasquatch.

The technician quickly donned his own face mask, and the two men climbed into an olive drab Polaris Ranger—a two-seat all-terrain vehicle with the Department of Energy seal on the hood. Once they were both buckled in tightly, the technician gunned the ATV, and they began their three-mile ascent to the entrance of the abandoned Thurmond National Laboratory.

The trip took about twenty-five minutes and was bone-rattlingly bumpy at points. *This road doesn't get much use*, McCreary figured. They stopped twice to clear fallen tree limbs and once more to open the final security gate, a heavily padlocked section of barbed-wire fence about one hundred yards from the lab entrance. A large red-and-white sign on the gate read:

**WARNING: HIGH RADIATION AREA
AUTHORIZED PERSONNEL ONLY
USE OF DEADLY FORCE AUTHORIZED**

The technician opened the metal gate and returned to the ATV. "Okay, sir," he shouted through his mask. "Beyond this point is a twenty-minute exposure area. You stay longer than that and you'll exceed your maximum quarterly radiation dosage, which is a violation of federal law. I'll wait right here for you. There's a fifteen-minute alarm on your dosimeter. When that goes off, you've got five minutes to come back. If you're not back here at the end of that, my orders require that I sound the RADCON alarm." He locked eyes with McCreary through their visors. "Please don't make me do that, sir."

McCreary nodded.

"Do you know how to operate your radiation monitor?"

McCreary nodded that he did.

The technician held up the portable radiation detector that was attached to McCreary's coveralls with a lanyard. It was a yellow handheld unit with several buttons and a small digital screen. "It's set to detect gamma and beta radiation," he said. "You'll get audio clicks and a digital readout in milliroentgens per hour. You can change the scale by pushing this button and toggle to counts per minute by pressing this one." He pointed to the two corresponding buttons. "You've got a two-way radio in this pocket." He patted his left breast pocket. "And a flashlight in this pocket." He patted the other pocket. "Any questions?"

McCreary shook his head.

"Okay, then. Good luck, sir."

With that, McCreary lumbered in his radiation suit through the security gate and made his way toward the only structure in sight: a rectangular, bunkerlike building constructed entirely of exposed concrete, with a flat concrete roof, no windows, and a single gray metal door. Attached to one side of the building was a square, windowless tower—also constructed of exposed concrete—that looked to be about thirty feet high. McCreary had a pretty good idea what that was. The radiation monitor began clicking a few times per second as he got closer to the building. He glanced down at the digital display, which indicated less than 0.1 milliroentgen per hour. Nothing to worry about.

He stopped a few feet from the entrance and read the sign that was hanging crookedly beside the door. In faded letters, it read: THURMOND NATIONAL LABORATORY. AUTHORIZED PERSONNEL ONLY. He approached the heavy steel door and tugged gently on its handle. To his surprise, the door began to open. It squeaked loudly at first as the rusty hinges got their first workout in decades. Then the door suddenly fell off the hinges and crashed to the cement sidewalk with a resounding *clank!*

McCreary jumped back to avoid the heavy door. When the commotion subsided, he entered the building cautiously and switched on his flashlight. The radiation monitor was clicking more rapidly now. He glanced down through his foggy visor and saw that it was spiking at about 1.5 milliroentgens per hour. Approximately one hundred times background, but still nothing to worry about.

The building was entirely bare inside except for an L-shaped metal security desk that was bolted to the floor and a large, metal, boothlike structure behind the desk, which was centered within a framework of heavy steel beams that rose high into the enclosed, three-story tower above.

McCreary shined the beam of his flashlight all around the interior of the building, especially the desk area. *Nothing.* No logbooks, no name tags, no security manuals, no remnants of any human activity whatsoever. *As expected.* This place had been well sanitized many years ago.

McCreary now trained his flashlight on the tall metal structure behind the desk. It looked like an oversize phone booth—about seven feet tall with a five-by-five-foot base and a gray metal door in the front. The scaffolding above the structure was draped with steel cables, and there were several large spools attached to what appeared to be hydraulic motors. McCreary recognized this equipment as the lifting mechanism for a mine elevator.

He approached the elevator and noted that his radiation detector was now clicking much more rapidly. As he neared the elevator door, the detector began clicking so rapidly that he had to change the scale by two orders of magnitude. Even then, the clicks were so close together that they sounded like a single, steady tone. He checked the digital readout with his flashlight: 250 milliroentgens per hour. An elevated exposure rate, to be sure. *Although not a twenty-minute zone*, he thought. At this exposure rate, it would take six hours before he exceeded his quarterly limit.

With a gloved hand, McCreary attempted to open the gray steel door that provided entrance to the elevator. It was a bifold design, similar to a bus door, with a sturdy steel handle near the hinge and a narrow rectangular window on each side. He pulled gently on the handle. *Nothing.* He pulled harder, and the door still did not budge. Finally, with all his strength, he yanked hard on the door handle. The door creaked slightly at the hinge but refused to open. It was definitely stuck.

Pressing his Plexiglas visor against one of the two windows in the elevator door, McCreary attempted to see inside, shining his flashlight through the other window to illuminate the space. But, with his foggy visor and the glare of the flashlight on the glass, it was difficult to see much of anything. All he could make out was a tangle of cables and something lumpy on the floor. Frustrated, he gave the door handle another hard tug, but, once again, it did not budge.

McCreary checked the timer on his radiation monitor. Six minutes left. *Crap.* Using his flashlight, he quickly scanned the tower section of the building for something that might be useful, although he had no idea what that might be. After nearly half a minute of searching, he finally spotted something. He made his way quickly to the rear wall of the tower and pried an old fire extinguisher out of its rusty bracket. It popped out with relative ease.

Working quickly, McCreary brought the fire extinguisher to the elevator door, felt its weight in his hands for a moment, then prepared to smash it into one of the glass windows. Just before he did, however, his dosimeter alarmed loudly, adding a shrill overtone to the steady clicking of his radiation detector. Seconds later, he heard the technician's voice crackling over the radio. "Five minutes, sir."

McCreary hesitated just a moment, then proceeded with his plan. He smashed the bottom of the fire extinguisher into the narrow glass window of the elevator door . . . and was amazed when it did not break. *Shatterproof glass.* Redoubling his effort, he again slammed the extinguisher into the glass window. This time, the glass fractured in several places but stayed stubbornly in place. Undeterred, McCreary repeated this process several more times until, finally, his effort was rewarded with a hollow puncturing sound. He'd broken a hole in the glass. With two additional blows, he managed to enlarge the hole enough to get his arm through.

McCreary quickly put the extinguisher down and glanced at the timer on his dosimeter: *three minutes left.* Wasting no time, he thrust his flashlight through the broken glass and pressed his visor into the opening. With the interior of the elevator shaft now well illuminated, he could finally see inside.

It took several seconds to figure out what he was looking at. Then he realized what it was.

It was a giant blob of concrete.

Just then, the radio crackled to life. "Sir, you've got to get out now. Or I have to sound the RADCON alarm."

Perplexed, McCreary took one last look at the large blob of concrete in the elevator shaft. In one corner, he noticed a cubelike metal box with a yellow-and-magenta trefoil symbol on it. He immediately recognized this as a controlled radiation source. *But why would there be a controlled radiation source up here?*

The radio crackled loudly: "Sir, you need to leave *right now!*"

McCreary quickly retreated from the building and waved to the technician beyond the fence as he exited through the doorway. Two minutes later, he was through the gate.

"Did you find what you were looking for?" asked the technician as he closed and padlocked the gate behind them.

"Actually, no," said McCreary, shaking his head and breathing heavily. "Is there any *other* way to get down into the lab?"

The technician looked confused. "No, sir. The lab is sealed shut. You can't get down there at all. I figured you knew that."

McCreary's earpiece suddenly activated and Ana Thorne's voice came on the line. "Hey, I just got an update on Holzberg's burial site in Germany."

McCreary tapped the transmit button beneath his protective clothing. "Go ahead," he said, still breathing heavily.

"Empty. As we suspected."

McCreary was not surprised by this news, but the confirmation that Holzberg's grave was empty still left him baffled. He tapped the transmit button again. "I just checked the entrance to the lab." He paused to catch his breath. "The elevator shaft is sealed with concrete. *Solid concrete.* And the radiation is not coming from below. It's coming from a controlled source on the surface."

"That's . . . surprising," said Ana. She paused for a moment. "So there must be some other way in and out."

"Agreed," said McCreary. "But where?"

Five miles away, Mike Califano listened to this conversation with considerable interest. It proved two things he'd suspected since late last night. First, both McCreary and Thorne apparently believed that Dr. Holzberg had emerged forty-eight hours ago *from the lab*—a lab that was decommissioned and sealed shut in 1959. Which meant they believed, as he now did, that Holzberg had somehow been transported through time. *Like a boomerang.* Califano hadn't wanted to be the first to bring up this theory because it sounded . . . well, crazy. *But now that it was out in the open . . .*

The second thing this conversation confirmed was something Califano already knew: there was a second entrance to the lab. In fact, at this very moment, he was looking directly at it. Califano tapped the transmit button on his radio. "Hey, guys. I think I know where that second entrance is."

There was silence for several seconds before McCreary's voice came on the line. "Where's that, Michael?"

"On the other side of Beury's Ridge. Near an abandoned branch line that connected Fire Creek to the Thurmond depot. The entrance is actually to an older mine called Foster Number Two. I noticed it last night on an old U.S. Bureau of Mines map from 1919 that turned up in my search. Back then, all these mines were operated by the New River Coal Company, and it looks like some of them got interconnected at some point."

"Where are you, Michael?" asked McCreary with rising concern in his voice.

"I'm, uh . . . standing at the entrance to Foster Number Two."

On the other side of Beury Mountain, McCreary motioned frantically for the radiological control technician to stop the ATV. The technician complied and brought the vehicle to a skidding halt on the gravel road. They were about a mile from the guard station.

"Michael, listen to me," said McCreary sternly. "Do *not* go in there, understand?"

There was silence on the line.

"Michael?"

Silence.

"Listen to me. The radiation levels could be sky high down there. Not to mention toxic gases, the lack of oxygen, cave-ins . . . *snakes*. Michael, are you listening to me?"

Silence.

"*Shit,*" McCreary hissed, transmitting that sentiment over the radio. He motioned for the driver to continue.

A short time later, Ana Thorne came on the line. "Bill, you still there?"

McCreary shouted above the noise of the ATV, which was bumping violently along the gravel road. "Yeah, I'm heading back to the guard station. You heard anything from Michael yet?"

"No, but something else has come up. They just found that stolen car. The one from last night."

"Where?"

There was a short pause. "Frostburg, Maryland. At a motel right off Highway 68. The local police have it under surveillance right now."

"Tell them not to move in until we say so."

"Already did that."

"How soon can you get there?"

Another pause. "About three hours, driving."

"No good." McCreary thought for a moment, weighing his options. Then he pressed the transmit button and said, "Tell the state police we need their chopper. If they give you any flak, have Admiral Armstrong make a call . . . to the governor if necessary. I'll meet you at police headquarters in thirty minutes."

"Got it."

"And tell the Frostburg police that if they see this guy, they are to follow him closely *but don't engage him.*"

"Understood."

McCreary waited for the voice-activated feature to time out. Then he turned to the ATV driver and shouted: "Can't this damn thing go any faster?"

18

CALIFANO KNEW he shouldn't go into the mine. Among other concerns, his only source of light was a small aluminum LED flashlight attached to his key chain. Hardly the type of equipment one needed to explore an abandoned coal mine.

He stared into the blackness of the mine entrance for several minutes, earnestly debating whether to go in. The entrance was a rectangular hole, about five feet high and eight feet wide, which had been cut directly into the moss-covered stone face of the mountain. The remnants of a wooden frame and two wooden handrails could still be seen, although the majority of the wooden structure lay in a jumble of half-rotted six-by-six timbers that partially blocked the entrance.

Califano had heard all of McCreary's warnings about the potential dangers inside the mine. In fact, Califano had almost talked himself out of going in, mainly because of the snakes. But that was before something interesting caught his eye.

To the left of the entrance, near the tangle of fallen timbers, Califano spotted a single cigarette butt on the ground. He approached, picked it up, and inspected it closely in the morning sunlight. The tiny gold letters around the circumference of the filter spelled CHESTERFIELD. *Do they even make those anymore?* He pinched the cigarette lightly between his thumb and finger and noted that it was a bit soggy, though still round and firm. Which meant it hadn't been exposed to the elements for very long. Indeed, the butt still contained tobacco and a bit of light gray ash at the end. From that, he deduced that it had been smoked very recently, probably within the past few days.

He put the butt in his coat pocket and inched closer to the mine entrance. A single question was now running through his mind: If Dr. Holzberg had escaped from the lab through this abandoned mine shaft, did that prove the mine was safe? *Not necessarily,* he concluded. Holzberg could have had breathing equipment, although Califano somehow doubted it. The more significant problem was that there were multiple passages through the mine, and just because Holzberg had apparently found one safe passage, that did not mean they were *all* safe.

"Screw it," said Califano under his breath. The only way he was going to find out the truth about the Thurmond lab was to investigate it himself. He energized his tiny LED flashlight and carefully made his way through the tangle of wooden beams. He paused for a few seconds on the other side, then ducked into the mine entrance.

It was cold and damp inside, as he'd expected. Califano halted about six feet inside the entrance, where a few rays of sunlight still managed to filter in from outside. He inspected the walls and ceiling in the broken sunlight and noted that they were made of solid rock, roughly hewn by explosives more than a century ago, but still in excellent shape. He was surprised to find that he could actually stand up inside the mine shaft. In fact, in most places, there was nearly a foot of clearance above his head. Satisfied with the mine's structural integrity, he turned and began making his way down the gently descending ingress shaft of Foster Number 2.

In less than a minute, the entrance behind him was completely out of sight, and the last remaining rays of sunlight were gone. He was now engulfed in the cold and absolute darkness of the subterranean tunnel, which smelled strongly of dank water and sulfur. As his senses gradually acclimated to this new environment, a nagging concern began percolating through his mind: *I'm screwed if I get lost.*

For nearly twenty minutes, Califano navigated the ingress shaft by the glow of his LED flashlight, which provided a surprisingly good level of visibility. As he walked, he pictured in his mind the 1919 Bureau of Mines survey of Foster Number 2. Although he'd only scanned the survey for a few seconds last night, his photographic memory allowed him to "look" at it again, pulling up many of the details in his mind. He recalled that the mine ran generally southeast, with a long, straight ingress shaft that split into more than a dozen parallel shafts about a mile into the mountain. Of those, the southernmost shaft was the most logical place for there to be an unmapped connector to the Thurmond mine.

Eventually, Califano reached a three-way intersection. His memory told him to turn right, which he did. Then, fifty yards later, he reached another intersection—a T. *Left or right?* He struggled for several seconds to visualize this particular intersection on the Bureau of Mines survey, but he couldn't. The survey was not ingrained firmly enough in his mind to access this level of detail. Without a clear map, he knew he would need a consistent plan to avoid getting lost. He decided that, at each T intersection, he would always turn right, which should send him northwest. If he didn't reach a left turn before coming to the end of the shaft, he would reverse direction until he reached a right turn. This method should eventually get him to the southernmost mine shaft. *At least he hoped it would.*

For the next forty minutes, this method worked reasonably well, although it required him to backtrack many times. He noticed along the way that the mine always seemed to go slightly downhill in the southeast direction and slightly uphill in the northwest direction. He assumed this was because the coal seam itself slanted in this fashion. Whatever the reason, this observation proved enormously helpful in navigating the crisscrossing patchwork of shafts.

After nearly an hour, he had finally reached the thirteenth and southernmost shaft. He stood at the T intersection for a moment and was just about to turn right, in accordance with his plan, when something unexpected happened.

He saw a flicker of light.

It occurred very quickly, about fifty yards away—just a brief flash of white light, as if someone had flicked the beam of a flashlight quickly across the wall.

And there it was again.

Califano froze and immediately clicked off his own light. Seconds later, he saw another flicker of light, as if someone was walking with a flashlight down a long tunnel that intersected with the one he was standing in. He tucked his flashlight into his pocket and slowly pulled out his Glock 9 millimeter from its holster and released the safety.

The white light was growing brighter now, the beam playing back and forth across the rough stone face of the tunnel wall. Califano could now hear footsteps and muffled

voices down the passageway. Someone was coming. Judging from the voices, there were at least two of them. *And
they were close.*

Califano quickly took stock of his situation, and it
wasn't good. If he entered the thirteenth shaft and turned
left, he'd be illuminated as soon as the approaching strangers reached the same shaft and rounded their corner to the
right. If he tried to make it past the T intersection before
they arrived, to put himself on the other side of their right
turn, he'd risk being seen momentarily in the beam of their
approaching light, which now resembled a theater spotlight
on the far wall.

That left only one choice: *retreat.*

Califano quickly turned and ran in the opposite direction from which he'd just come, retracing his steps to the
twelfth shaft, approximately fifty yards away. He ran in total
darkness with one hand outstretched because he knew eventually he'd . . .

Bam! And there it was. He hit the wall hard with his
left hand, elbow, and shoulder and winced in silent pain. A
few loose stones fell to the ground around him, and he held
his breath as the gentle clacking sounds echoed throughout the shaft. When the noise subsided, he turned quickly
and listened for the approaching voices. They still seemed
to be conversing in the same muffled tones as before. *They
hadn't heard him.* Just then, he saw reflected light bouncing
toward the cross-connecting shaft he'd just traversed.

He had to move. *But which way?* On instinct, he darted
left, heading southeast and slightly downhill along the
twelfth shaft. He knew this would lead to a dead end, but
that was exactly what he wanted. If the approaching strangers knew the mine layout, they would presumably be turning northwest—away from him. With luck, they wouldn't
see him at the far end of the shaft.

Califano reached the dead end of shaft twelve, then turned and squatted low, waiting for the strangers to arrive. For several tense minutes, he watched as the bouncing white light grew brighter and brighter at the other end of the shaft. During this time, he gradually became aware of a throbbing pain in his temples—a headache that he'd failed to notice before. He found himself longing for an aspirin. Or, better yet, a whole handful. It annoyed him that something as trivial as a headache was interfering with his concentration at this crucial moment.

The voices were growing louder now. Califano could almost make out some of their words, although it was hard to concentrate with his head throbbing so badly. *Jesus*, he thought, shaking his head. Again, he pushed the discomfort aside. He had to focus.

He thought he heard one of the voices say: *"Skolko?"*

"Shest minut," said a second voice in what sounded like Russian.

As Califano tried to process this information, his head continued pounding like a bass drum. *Who are these men, and what are they doing down here? And why are they speaking Russian?*

"Bystryee," said the first man in Russian.

By now, Califano's headache had given way to full-blown dizziness. *Something is seriously wrong with me*, he realized. It was at that exact moment that he remembered where he was: in the southeast corner of the mine, *at the lowest spot*. Suddenly, two terrifying words jumped to the forefront of his mind, cutting through the throbbing pain.

Black damp.

Califano had no sooner formed that thought than two large figures suddenly emerged at the T intersection, their shapes fuzzy behind the blinding lights of their miners' hats. In the glare, Califano thought he saw them wearing full-body jumpsuits . . . and gas masks.

Suddenly, he could no longer focus on anything. *My God, my head!* He winced in pain. And then, a second later, he lost his balance and slumped backward against the rock wall with a grunt.

"*Vy slyshali eto?*" said one of the men through an amp-lfier in his gas mask. Both men stopped and trained their blinding lights toward the dead end of the shaft, where Cal-ifano's body was now lying flat on the ground. One of them pushed a clip into his automatic weapon. The unmistakable metallic click echoed ominously throughout the space.

For several seconds the men's lights washed all over the rough stone wall at the far end of shaft twelve. Cali-fano's limp body, however, was positioned perfectly within the narrow shadow at the base of the wall created by the shaft's natural downward slope. His prone position made him invisible to the searchlights.

After a long while, the second man said, "*Poidem. Tam ne mnogo vreni.*" And the lights began moving away.

Califano barely heard these final words as he drifted toward unconsciousness. He felt the blood draining from his brain. *This is it. The end.* As everything slowly went dark around him, an image of his mother and sister appeared in his mind. They were smiling and carefree, the way he always liked to remember them. *Like angels.* His father, of course, wasn't in the picture at all. Which was also how he liked to remember things.

A moment later, his entire world went black.

19

FROSTBURG, MARYLAND

THE STATE police helicopter set down gracefully in a grass field near Route 40, about half a mile north of Interstate 68. Ana Thorne was the first to emerge from the shiny blue-and-gold chopper. Across the field, she immediately spotted a police officer standing by a parked cruiser on the side of the road, emphatically waving her over. "Looks like our ride's here," she yelled to Bill McCreary, who had just finished easing his hefty frame out of the chopper.

"Good," said McCreary. "Let's go." He broke into a slow jog across the field.

Ana smiled at the sight of McCreary jogging. She hesitated a moment before quickly catching up with him, her long athletic strides putting his lopsided, lumbering gait to shame. They reached the police cruiser half a minute later.

The police officer was tall and lanky, dressed in the khaki-and-brown uniform of the Allegany County Sheriff's Office. He appeared anxious. "You guys from the FBI?" he asked.

"Yeah," said McCreary, breathing heavily and wheezing. "Hop in. I'll take you over."

Ten minutes later, they arrived in the parking lot of the Huntsman Motel and pulled up next to a brown SUV with a gold sheriff's star on the door. The SUV was parked in a remote corner of the lot, away from the view of most of the rooms. Several police officers in khaki-and-brown uniforms were clustered around the sheriff's SUV, and they watched with tremendous interest as McCreary and Thorne emerged from the cruiser. They seemed *especially* interested in Ana Thorne.

"About damn time," said a heavyset man in a tight uniform and a wide-brimmed hat. He broke out of the group and introduced himself as Walter Fitch, the Allegany County sheriff.

McCreary cut right to the chase. "What room's he in?"

"Room 132," replied Fitch.

"What do you know about him?" McCreary asked.

Fitch looked annoyed by McCreary's rapid-fire questions. "Can I, uh . . . see some identification?"

McCreary and Thorne both flashed their fake FBI badges and waited for the sheriff to inspect them.

"Right," said Fitch after a while. "So, we got a tip from the store clerk next door, who saw the APB flash across her computer screen this morning. Said a man came into her store about three A.M. Same description as the carjacking suspect. Long gray hair and beard, long fingernails, midsixties. According to her, he looked like a homeless guy. Filthy and kind of . . . disoriented. He bought a bunch of personal hygiene items like fingernail clippers, razors, and so forth. And he bought some food, cigarettes, and several newsmagazines."

"Did he say anything unusual to her?" asked Ana.

"No, she didn't mention him *saying* anything unusual. In fact, she said he sounded kind of smart. Bought his stuff, said thank you, and left. She did say, though, that he seemed really interested in the magazines and newspapers in the back. 'Mesmerized,' I think was the word she used."

Thorne and McCreary glanced at each other.

"How'd he pay?" Ana asked.

"Cash. Two fifty-dollar bills. We checked them out. They're genuine."

"We'll need to get those from you," said Ana. "What about the car?"

"Right over there." The sheriff pointed to a blue Chevy Impala with West Virginia plates that was parked, front in, about forty yards away. "Tags match. Broken driver's-side window. Owner's registration was in the glove compartment. It's definitely the same car."

"Wait. You went through it already?" said McCreary, unable to disguise his surprise.

Exasperation flashed across Fitch's face. "Yeah, we went through it, okay? We've been here since *nine thirty* this morning. Worked this scene for nearly an hour before we even knew you guys were involved. In fact, we were just about to bust down this guy's door when I got the call from HQ to back off. Been waiting here ever since."

McCreary nodded calmly, but he was not happy. *Jesus,* he thought. *The car's right in front of the guy's room. You think he might have noticed you rifling through it?* He kept these thoughts to himself. "What did you find in the car?" he asked.

"Found an old carbide lamp in the passenger's seat, which is probably what he used to smash the window. Title and registration in the glove compartment. In the console, we found a bag of marijuana. About six ounces. Could've been the owner's, but we're not sure. A pack of rolling papers, a lighter, some CDs, cell phone charger . . . and a bunch of other miscellaneous stuff."

"Is all that stuff still in the car?" Ana asked.

"All except the marijuana." The sheriff paused, noticing their inquisitive looks. "We tagged and bagged it already and sent it to the evidence locker. Standard procedure for drugs and cash." He paused again, observing their continued expressions of confusion. "Look, that stuff tends to disappear real quick if you don't lock it up, okay?"

Ana nodded that she understood. "So what time did the suspect check in here?"

Fitch rubbed his face and exhaled loudly. "I talked to the night manager this morning. Best he could remember, the guy checked in around three fifteen A.M. Same description as before. Long gray hair, beard, fingernails."

"What name did he give?"

"He didn't."

"But . . . I thought hotels were required by law to check ID."

"Come on," said Fitch, laughing sarcastically. "Look at this place. The night manager figured the guy was homeless, so he made him pay up front in cash. Didn't bother to ask for an ID."

"How'd he pay?" Ana asked.

"Same way. Two fifties. Guy said he had a whole wad of them."

Ana suddenly thought about the money they'd found in Dr. Holzberg's wallet. "Can I see those bills?"

Fitch shook his head. "Like I said, young lady, cash and drugs get sent to evidence right away. So if you want to see those bills now, you'll have to go downtown."

"*Or*," Ana retorted. "You can bring them *here*." She held the sheriff's gaze for several seconds, leaving no doubt that she expected him to do just that, and that she did not appreciate being called "young lady."

Fitch bobbed his head back and forth, then scowled and cursed under his breath. "Hey, Davidson!" he barked to one of his deputies. "Go to evidence and bring back those fifties we got from the store, and the hotel register."

"Will do," said the deputy.

"Anything else?" said Fitch.

"Yeah," Ana replied. "Has anyone seen the suspect since he checked in here last night?"

"Nope, we've had the room under surveillance since about nine thirty this morning. No one's come in or out since then. I'm guessing he's sleeping like Rip Van Winkle in there."

"I doubt it," McCreary mumbled.

"Got a room key?" asked Ana.

"Uh-huh."

"Then let's go."

Ten minutes later, they were all in position. Ana Thorne stood beside the door to room 132 with her pistol drawn. One of the sheriff's deputies stood on the other side of the door. Thorne drew a deep breath and nodded for him to proceed.

Keeping his body as far to the side as possible, the deputy slowly inserted the key into the lock. He glanced at Ana one last time, and she nodded for him to continue. Then, in one quick motion, the deputy turned the key clockwise and popped the door open a quarter inch.

At the same moment, Ana stepped forward and gave the door a hard kick. "FBI!" she shouted as she charged in, training her weapon at chest level all around the room.

Empty.

"Bathroom!" Ana shouted, nodding toward the open bathroom door.

The deputy rushed into the bathroom with his weapon leveled. A second later, he yelled, "Clear!"

Ana activated her earpiece. "No one here," she said.

McCreary's voice came on the line. "I'm not surprised."

"Hey, check this out," the deputy called from the bathroom.

Ana entered the dingy bathroom and saw what he was pointing to. The window above the shower stall was wide open. She tapped the transmit button again. "Bill, he went out through a back window. No telling how long ago."

"Probably when he saw a bunch of cops digging through his car," McCreary replied. He sighed and added, "Okay, I'll have a team comb the area behind the motel and put out an APB for the immediate vicinity."

Ana looked down at the bathroom floor, which was covered with mounds of gray hair. She pushed the transmit button again. "Oh, and you can drop the Santa Claus description," she said. "He'll look different now. Short hair and probably clean shaven." She waited for the transmitter to time out, then turned to the deputy and pointed to the mess on the floor. "Bag all of this," she said. "It'll be useful for DNA."

Five minutes later, it seemed the whole police squad was in the room, including Sheriff Fitch. Ana spotted McCreary standing outside, near the doorway, and she made her way over to him.

"Have them box everything up," he instructed her quietly. "We can take the boxes with us tonight."

Ana nodded and was just about to say something when a young police corporal interrupted. "Excuse me, ma'am.

Sheriff asked me to give these to you." He handed her two plastic evidence bags, each containing two fifty-dollar bills.

Ana waited for the cop to leave, then closely inspected one of the bills through the clear plastic bag.

"Checking the date?" asked McCreary quietly.

"Uh-huh. This one says 'Series 1970.'" She quickly checked the other bag. "Series 1971.'" She looked at McCreary, confused. "They postdate 1959 by more than ten years. What do you make of that?"

McCreary shrugged. "Maybe he stole them."

Ana looked unconvinced. "Where would he have stolen a wad of forty-year-old bills?"

McCreary shrugged. "Good point."

"Hey, guys," said another police officer. "Sheriff wants you inside. Thinks he might have found something."

Thorne and McCreary quickly pushed their way through the crowd of policemen inside the motel room. "You got something, Sheriff?" asked McCreary as they approached.

Sheriff Fitch was hunched over the nightstand with his back to them. "Yeah. Got a notepad here that appears to have some residual writing impressions. You could submit it for ESDA analysis, but I don't think that'll be necessary." He straightened, turned around, and held out a small piece of paper between his thumb and forefinger. "Just look at it at an angle to the light."

Ana took the paper carefully by one corner and inspected it closely in the glow of the nightstand lamp. It was a page from a small notepad with several letters prominently indented from someone having written with a ballpoint pen on the preceding page. It took several seconds before the light hit the page just right and a legible word suddenly appeared. "Jasher," she whispered.

"Mean anything to you?" asked the sheriff.

Thorne and McCreary both looked at each other and shook their heads.

Five minutes later, when they were away from the crowd, Ana leaned close to McCreary and whispered emphatically, "We need to have Michael plug this into his program right away."

"Speaking of Michael," said McCreary. "Where the hell is he?"

PART TWO

And he bade them, teach the children of Judah the use of the bow: behold, it is written in the book of Jasher.

HOLY BIBLE, 2 Samuel 1:18

20

A BSOLUTE DARKNESS has a way of playing tricks on your mind. *Am I awake?* Mike Califano wondered. *Am I even alive?* In fact, he was lying in total blackness against a cold, damp wall, nine hundred feet underground. He had lost all orientation as to time and place. Tactile sensation was gone. His sense of sight and sound, even smell, were gone. His only sensation now was a strangely comforting warmth that was spreading from his core to his extremities and head. And, with it, an irresistible desire to sleep.

Yet something deep inside him was fighting . . . resisting . . . *warning* him not to give in to the warmth. He struggled to amplify that voice. *What was it telling him to do?* The answer arrived slowly, like a long-forgotten tune. *Wake up! Now!*

Suddenly, Califano could feel sharp rocks poking painfully against his back, and gravel pressing hard against the right side of his face. Mustering all his remaining energy, he managed to lift his head a few inches off the ground. The feeling of gravel against his face subsided. *Crawl!* Califano obeyed the voice inside his head. Like a bear arising from hibernation, he rose to all fours and began plodding awkwardly on hands and knees away from the wall, struggling mightily to do so. Somewhere in his mind, it began to register that he was crawling uphill. *Yes*, urged the voice. *Uphill is good.*

Inch by agonizing inch, Califano slowly emerged from the invisible cauldron of "black damp" at the end of shaft twelve, a deadly pool of odorless methane and other heavy gases that had almost become his grave. He was gasping desperately for air now, his body instinctively sensing the presence of oxygen. His mind was slowly beginning to clear.

Minutes later he was on his feet again, stumbling groggily in the darkness toward the northwest end of the shaft. *Uphill.* Toward safety. His motor skills were gradually improving. His breathing was becoming more regular. His memory was starting to return. . . .

Califano stopped in his tracks, suddenly remembering where he was. And why. *The lab. The men in miners' hats. And . . .*

Where's my gun?

Shaking off the lingering effects of hypoxia, Califano quickly retrieved his aluminum flashlight from his pocket and clicked it on. With the help of the light, he went back and recovered his gun from the other end of the mine shaft, being careful this time to hold his breath.

Having now recovered his weapon and most of his strength, Califano once again resumed his trek toward the Thurmond lab.

He reached the entrance to the connecting corridor in shaft thirteen and stopped there briefly, half expecting to hear voices coming down the corridor. Hearing nothing, he ventured cautiously into the corridor, flashlight in one hand, pistol in the other, and walked for several minutes until he reached a dead end. *This made no sense at all. Where had those men come from?* Califano quickly scanned the stone walls with his flashlight and soon had his answer. At a height of about six feet was a neatly formed rectangular opening, approximately three feet across. *A cross-ventilation shaft.*

Califano pulled himself up to the lip of the opening and, with great effort, managed to snake his body headfirst into the shaft. Using his flashlight, he peered down the opening and saw that it extended straight for a very long distance and eventually disappeared into darkness. He began carefully making his way along the shaft, propelling himself with his elbows and knees until he reached the other end. He paused there for a moment, bewildered by what he saw as he swept his tiny LED flashlight all around.

Spread below him was a large rectangular room with unpainted cement walls and a high, arched ceiling. The room was crowded with control panels and scientific equipment. *So much for the lab having been destroyed.*

After observing no human activity for more than a minute, Califano eased his body out of the ventilation duct and carefully dropped to the floor. He slowly approached the nearest workstation and inspected it in the beam of his flashlight. It was a large gray console with a flat U-shaped desk portion, a sloped skirt portion, and a tall vertical section beyond that. The skirt portion contained numerous knobs, push buttons, and toggle switches, which presumably would have been within reach of an operator seated at the desk. The vertical portion behind it was studded with dials and gauges of various shapes and sizes. *Definitely late 1950s*, Califano thought. He quickly skimmed some of the labels below the gauges: VOLT. 1, VOLT. 2, AMP. 1, AMP. 2, INLET

PRESS., INLET TEMP., OUTLET PRESS., OUTLET TEMP. *Not particularly informative*.

He noticed two large analog clocks, situated side by side in the middle of the vertical section, which were labeled ATOMICHRON 1 and ATOMICHRON 2. *Why did that name sound familiar?* Then he remembered that he'd read about the Atomichron a few years earlier. It was the world's first commercial atomic clock, based on a cesium standard, and built in the late 1950s by the National Company. *But why would they need two of them?* He looked again at the two clocks mounted on the instrument panel and noticed that they were frozen at different times.

Venturing farther into the room, he next came upon a tall gray cabinet on wheels, containing several racks of gauges and buttons. A metal plaque on the front of the cabinet read AUTOMICHRON NC-2001. *Jesus, that thing should be in a museum*, he thought.

Continuing toward the center of the room, Califano eventually arrived at a large pool of water, about thirty feet across, with a sturdy steel railing circumscribing its entirety. In the middle of the pool was a square structure with no top, which appeared to be a chamber or vault of some sort, about four feet square. It was partially submerged in the pool and was suspended by cables from a steel catwalk that stretched from one side of the pool to the other, about six feet above the surface of the water. Califano observed a tangle of cables and wires, as well as a narrow metal ladder extending from the catwalk down into the partially submerged chamber.

Without question, this was the heart of the lab, the focus of whatever was going on here.

Califano spotted a nearby staircase that led to the elevated catwalk and quickly made his way to it. As he skirted the edge of the pool, he thought about similar pools he'd seen at other DOE laboratories, which were typically associated with "swimming pool"–type nuclear reactors. A pool this size indicated the need for a large heat sink—a way to absorb and dissipate a tremendous amount of energy. But he doubted this was a nuclear reactor.

He reached the stairs and ascended quickly to the top. He paused there for a moment before venturing out onto the catwalk, testing it first with one foot and a portion of his weight. Once satisfied that the structure was sturdy, he eased himself out onto it and inched forward until he was standing directly above the vaultlike structure in the middle of the pool. He shined his light down into it. *Definitely not a nuclear reactor.*

The dry chamber below him was entirely empty except for a tall instrument cabinet in the middle, which appeared identical to the one he'd seen earlier. *The other Automichron.*

At the same moment, something at the far edge of the pool caught his eye. Something . . . floating in the water. *What is that?* He took two more steps along the catwalk and then peered down into the water with his flashlight. He immediately found himself gazing upon the bloated face of a dead man floating belly up in the pool, eyes wide open in terror, staring lifelessly toward the ceiling. The water around him was tinted red with blood. *What the hell?*

Just then, he heard a delicate beep somewhere behind him. He unholstered his Glock and quickly swiveled in the direction of the noise, which had come from the opposite side of the room from where he'd entered. As he quickly scanned the far end of the room with his flashlight, he noticed more workstations, cabinets, wires and cables, a gray metal desk, and . . . *what was that?*

Califano squinted to make out the lumpy object that was lying on the ground near one of the workstations. It took a moment before he realized what it was. A bloody body.

"What the—"

He continued scanning the scene and soon spotted another lifeless body, then another, and another. Four in total, not counting the one in the pool, all bloody and definitely dead.

"Jesus," he whispered, preparing to go investigate.

Just then, he heard another beep. At the same moment, he saw a tiny flicker of red light across the room, just a few feet from the dead bodies. He trained his light on that spot and saw what appeared to be a metal suitcase on the ground, lid open, wires extending in all directions. He followed one pair of the wires with the flashlight until they terminated at a bundle of cylindrical objects about fifteen yards from the suitcase. His heart skipped a beat.

Dynamite.

Another beep. Califano quickly traced another pair of wires with his flashlight and saw that they, too, led to a bundle of dynamite on the other side of the room. Judging from the number of other wires coming out of the suitcase, he concluded there must be at least a dozen such explosive charges throughout the space. Enough to incinerate the entire room. And him with it.

Beep.

Califano didn't waste another second. He scampered back along the catwalk to the stairs, taking them two at a time to the bottom. He made a hard right and darted at full speed toward the other end of the room.

Beep.

Ten seconds later, he reached the end of the room where he'd originally entered. He looked up and saw the ventilation shaft above his head. He leaped up and curled his fingers around a narrow ridge at the bottom lip of the ductwork. It was difficult to get a grip, and his fingers began sliding off.

Beep.

Califano readjusted his grip and with all his remaining strength managed to slowly pull his body up. Several seconds later, his head and torso were in the duct.

Beep.

Come on! He wiggled his body into the rectangular shaft and scrambled on knees and elbows down the steel tunnel, desperately trying to clear the shaft before the explosives detonated. *Ten feet . . . five feet . . . one foot.* Suddenly, there was a deafening *boom* in the lab behind him, followed by a rapid sequence of several more explosions, each as powerful as the last. Califano felt a massive disruption of air and searing heat as his body launched violently out of the shaft and into the air like a human cannonball.

That was the last thing he remembered.

21

VLADAMIR KRUPNOV sat alone in the back of a black Mercedes sedan with today's edition of *Kommersantt*—a Russian business newspaper—folded across his lap. "Misha, how much longer to the airport?" he asked his driver.

"Another twenty or twenty-five minutes," Misha replied.

"Goddamn Moscow traffic," Krupnov mumbled. He opened his newspaper and was just beginning a fresh article when his cell phone suddenly buzzed in the pocket of his blazer.

"*Da?*" he answered.

"Vlad, it's Sashko," said a man in Ukrainian. Alexandre "Sashko" Melnik was Krupnov's most trusted lieutenant and was currently in charge of all of Krupnov Energy's operations in the United States. "We just picked up two more signals from Thurmond," he continued.

"The Soviet team?" asked Krupnov, switching seamlessly from his native Russian to Ukrainian.

"Yes. It appears so. We're going out to find them now. I just wanted to let you know before you got on your flight."

"Excellent. They may have valuable information for us, maybe the material itself. Make sure you bring them in alive. And, Sashko?"

"Yes?"

"Do *not* fuck this one up, understand?"

"*Tak*. I understand."

"You bring them in immediately no matter what you have to do. Is that clear?"

"Yes. The men are assembling now, and we'll have a chopper in the air within twenty minutes."

"Make it ten. I will not tolerate another mistake like you made with Malachi. Understood?"

"Yes, sir."

"And speaking of Malachi, any sign of him?"

The man on the other end of the line hesitated a moment. "No," he replied quietly. "We're still looking for him."

Krupnov cursed under his breath and terminated the call. *Why is this so difficult?* He leaned forward and tapped Misha on the shoulder. "Step on it. I don't want to miss my flight."

22

RESTON, VIRGINIA

A SHRILL NOISE pierced the silence of Ana Thorne's darkened one-bedroom apartment. She awoke immediately, her adrenal glands quickly jumping into action. A moment later, the same shrill sound repeated itself. *The phone.* She picked it up before it could ring a third time.

"Thorne," she said in a raspy voice that belied the fact that she'd gotten only two hours of sleep. It was 4:35 A.M., and she knew perfectly well who was calling. Middle-of-the-night calls used to rattle her, but not anymore. Not since the fateful call that had arrived in this apartment two and a half years ago, informing her that her fiancé had been killed in Afghanistan during a covert CIA operation. No, these days, if someone called in the middle of the night, she could be damn certain it was work. *Who else would it be?*

"Ana, it's Bill. Can you come in?"

"What is it? Is it Mike? Have you heard from him?"

"No," said McCreary glumly. "It's something else."

"On my way." Ana hung up and was out the door in less than five minutes. If her CIA training at Camp Peary had taught her anything, it was how to dress and egress quickly. But before turning off the lights and closing the door to her apartment, she paused and quickly surveyed the living room. She'd lived in this apartment for more than three years. Yet, in all that time, she'd never managed to hang a single picture on the wall. *What's the point?* The place was clean and sparsely furnished, like a hotel room. Which essentially it was. There didn't seem to be any point in trying to personalize it.

Not anymore.

Thorne arrived at CIA headquarters just after 5:00 A.M. and proceeded directly to Bill McCreary's office on the third floor of building 1. The placard on the door read: DTAI TEMPORARY OFFICE. *Wishful thinking,* she thought with a crooked smile. Ana knew that McCreary was still hoping for a bigger space, having arrived at the CIA from DARPA several months ago. But she also knew he wasn't going to get it, at least not anytime soon. There was a certain pecking order to this place, and DTAI was currently at the bottom. She took a deep breath and knocked three times on the door.

"Come in," McCreary yelled.

Ana entered and immediately noticed the hulking presence of Steve Goodwin, McCreary's administrative assistant. *Goon, administrative assistant, whatever.* He was six feet three and made of solid muscle. "What, he's read into this program now, too?" she asked.

"As of last night, yes," said McCreary. "With Califano . . . uh, *missing*, we'll need some extra analytical help. Steve has some experience with data mining, so I figured he could take over where Califano left off. Granted, our program's not as powerful as his, but it'll have to do. For now, anyway. Until he comes back."

"*Is* he coming back?"

McCreary shook his head and exhaled. "Honestly, I don't know."

"Why can't we just send someone down there to look for him? Hell, I'll go."

McCreary frowned. "You know we can't risk that."

Ana nodded reluctantly because she knew he was right. "How's Admiral Armstrong taking it?"

"Not well."

"Yeah. I figured as much." Ana was sympathetic but, of course, didn't show it. She'd noticed the close relationship that Admiral Armstrong and Mike Califano seemed to have. Almost like father and son, or mentor and mentee. She didn't *understand* it, but she had no doubt it was genuine. Which was why she felt bad for Armstrong. It was tough losing someone you cared about. On the other hand, this was the agency, and sometimes people died. *Or sometimes they just disappeared—like her fiancé—and you didn't even have the satisfaction of knowing what had happened to them.* Either way, you had to move on and finish the mission. *The mission always came first.*

"So, what's up?" Ana asked, looking back and forth between McCreary and Goodwin.

"Holzberg's dead," said McCreary.

"What?" Ana had hoped they might be able to extract more information from him after his wound healed—something better than the gibberish they'd gotten from him so far. "When?" she asked.

"About two hours ago. I've ordered an autopsy to confirm the cause of death, but I'm guessing it was old age. Med staff said his organs just started shutting down one

after the other. Same sort of progeria effect we saw earlier with his hair and fingernails. As if he's aging from the
inside out."

"Well, I'm sure the gunshot wound didn't help, either."

"Probably not."

"Did he say anything else while we were gone yesterday?
Anything useful?"

"You can review the tapes yourself," said McCreary.
"But I don't think he did. He was pretty far gone and never
really recovered after Friday night."

"Too bad. He might have been our last hope. How about
our mystery man in Frostburg? Any luck finding him?"

"Not yet. I've got the FBI on it, and we're monitoring
their live feeds." McCreary nodded toward Steve Goodwin,
who was now wearing a pair of headphones and was seated
at a computer workstation on the far side of the room.

"So, what now?" Ana asked.

"We're still working on the stuff we picked up yesterday. The police lifted several dozen prints from the motel
room in Frostburg. No surprise, the place was filthy, so we
got lots of prints. Unfortunately, we aren't sure whose they
are or how long they've been there. I had the FBI run all of
them through IAFIS last night."

"Anything?"

"Two matches, but I don't think either is our guy. One
was a truck driver named Leonard Goff, whose prints were
on file from his service in the marines back in the nine-
ties. FBI tracked him down at his home in Chattanooga last
night. He's not our guy. Just a forty-three-year-old trucker
with a wife and three kids, and no criminal record."

"How about the other guy?"

"*Gal*," McCreary corrected. "Angelina Jones. The county
cops were very familiar with her. She apparently spends a
lot of time at the Huntsman Motel. Said they wouldn't be

surprised if her prints were in every room of that place. Again, not the person we're looking for."

"Okay, so what about the fifties? Anything on those?"

"Got Treasury working on those. First of all, they're genuine. Two 1970 series and two 1971. Ran the serials through the FBI and Treasury databases—no hits. Which means they were never reported stolen from a bank. As for the age of the bills, fifties and hundreds are taken out of circulation about every five years or so. But it's not uncommon to find older ones still in circulation. The folks at Treasury estimated that about five percent of all 1970- and 1971-series fifties are still in circulation today. But the odds of finding *four* of them together . . ."

"Yeah," said Ana, nodding. "I'm betting this guy came from the lab. But somehow he went in at a different time from Holzberg . . ." Her voice trailed off as she pondered that fact.

"Want to hear what we've got on Jasher?"

"Absolutely," said Ana.

McCreary motioned for her to have a seat on the opposite side of his desk.

"You can skip the basics, though. I looked it up online last night."

"Oh, yeah?"

Ana nodded and quickly rattled off what she'd learned from the Internet. "The book of Jasher is one of the so-called 'lost' books of the Bible. Mentioned two or three times in the Old Testament, but a genuine copy has never been found. You've got something else?"

McCreary smiled. "Well, we've got *one* thing I know you'll be interested in." He seated himself at his desk and shuffled through a large stack of papers until he found the particular sheet he was interested in. He adjusted his glasses, skimmed the page for a few seconds, then spoke.

"The most prominent mention of the book of Jasher in the Bible is in Joshua, chapter ten, where it says: *'So the sun stood still, and the moon stopped, till the people had revenge upon their enemies. Is this not written in the book of Jasher? So the sun stood still in the midst of heaven, and did not hasten to go down for about a whole day.'*"

Ana was nodding her head. "Uh-huh. And people have speculated for centuries that God somehow stopped the rotation of the earth for an entire day. I read all about that last night. Ridiculous, of course."

"Okay. But don't jump ahead."

Well, don't waste my time.

"Let's just focus for a minute on what the book of Joshua is all about. Have you read the entire thing?"

"No," Ana conceded with a shrug.

McCreary gave her a bemused look over the top of his glasses, as if to say: *See, you were jumping ahead.* Then he continued. "The book of Joshua is a very important part of the Hebrew Bible and the Old Testament. It tells the story of how the Israelites, having escaped slavery in Egypt and having wandered in the desert for forty years with Moses, finally entered the promised land. The land of Canaan, which they believed was promised to them by God. But when they got there, there were people already living there. Lots of them. Canaanites, Hittites, Amorites, and other tribes. The book of Joshua is really the tale of how the Israelites, under the command of Joshua, defeated all these other tribes, slaughtering many of them, and driving the rest out of Canaan. It's a book about warfare. And conquest."

"Okay . . ."

"So you're wondering why our carjacker from Thurmond is apparently so interested in this stuff?"

"Well, yeah. I mean, what does any of this have to do with what was going on in Thurmond?"

"I'm not entirely sure," McCreary confessed. "But hear me out." He riffled through the stack of papers and extracted another sheet. "Okay, another mention of the book of Jasher in the Bible is in second Samuel." He adjusted his glasses and skimmed the sheet with his finger until he found a particular spot. "After Saul and Jonathan are killed in battle, David is mourning their deaths. The writer of Samuel mentions at this point that David instructed his men to teach the sons of Judah 'the bow.' And then, as if to add credence to this assertion, he says, *'Behold, it is written in the Book of Jasher.'*"

"Isn't there some debate about what 'the bow' is referring to there?"

"Yep. Some translations have it as 'the song' or 'the song of the bow.' Others have it as 'the bow' or 'the use of the bow.' So it was either a song or a weapon. Pretty big difference if you ask me. Anyway, what I find interesting is how the writer of Samuel felt the need to refer to the book of Jasher, an external source, as an authority for this particular point."

"Does anyone know who Jasher was?"

"Actually, it's not who but *what*. Jasher wasn't a person. Most experts who've translated the original Hebrew Bible think that 'Jasher' means 'Upright,' which would mean these two references in Joshua and Samuel were to something called the 'book of the Upright.' Some later Latin translations used *'Liber Justorum,'* which means 'book of the Upright Ones.' Whatever it means, the book of Jasher was apparently an important, authoritative book at the time Joshua and Samuel were written."

"Which was when?"

"Sometime around fourteen hundred B.C."

Ana let out an ironic laugh.

"What's so funny?" McCreary asked.

"I don't know, it's just . . . why are we sitting here talking about stuff that was written, what, three thousand years ago? I mean, Thurmond National Laboratory was built in the 1950s. The particular event we're interested in took place in 1959. The director of the lab was Franz Holzberg, one of the most brilliant scientists of the twentieth century. Do you really think he cared about what some desert scribe wrote down in fourteen hundred B.C.? I mean, seriously . . ."

"I know. I know. I've had the same thoughts running through my head all night. But *someone* in that motel room wrote down the word 'Jasher.'"

"Yeah, but how do we even know it was *our* guy? Could have been someone else. Hell, maybe the happy hooker—what's her name, Angelina—maybe she was interested in biblical mysteries. Who knows?"

"Yep, I considered that, too," said McCreary. "But trust me, there's a connection."

"Well, get to it already!" With just two hours of sleep last night, Ana was in no mood for riddles.

"Okay, I guess I've kept you in suspense long enough." McCreary pulled a half-inch-thick stapled bundle of paper from his stack and slid it across the desk to Ana. "Steve found this in an online academic database."

Ana picked it up and read the title: *The Book of Jasher: Word of God or Work of Fraud?*

"It's a doctoral dissertation," said McCreary. "Written in 1961 by a divinity school student at Princeton. Check out his name."

Ana's eyes darted to the bottom-right-hand corner of the cover page. "Thomas J. Reynolds," she said quietly to herself.

"Recognize it?"

It took a few seconds before it suddenly hit her. "Dr. *Reynolds*. Michael mentioned that name on the radio yes-

terday. He said that Holzberg had wanted to contact someone named Dr. Reynolds . . . *at Princeton*." She was excited
for a moment, but her enthusiasm quickly began to wane.
"But Reynolds is a pretty common name."

"Sure it is. But Jasher, Reynolds, Princeton. How many
coincidences do you need?"

Ana nodded. He was right. "Plus the date," she said.
"Reynolds would have been a Ph.D. candidate in the 1950s,
within the same time frame that Holzberg was at the Institute of Advanced Studies."

"In *Princeton*," added McCreary.

"Right." Ana churned this information in her head for
a few seconds. "So is this guy still alive? Do we know where
he is?"

"Way ahead of you." McCreary pulled a sheet of paper
from his stack. "Thomas J. Reynolds is alive and well. He's
eighty years old and lives in Satellite Beach, Florida, with
his wife, Betty. Here's the address." He handed her the paper,
then looked at his watch. "If you leave now, you can be there
by breakfast."

"What, you've already set it up?"

McCreary nodded. "There's a plane waiting for you at
Landmark Aviation."

Ana stood to leave but hesitated. "What about—"

McCreary cut her off. "Let me worry about Mike. You, go."

23

EVERYTHING WAS happening in slow motion. A man in a gas mask was spraying machine-gun fire in every direction. Bright flashes emanated from the gun's muzzle as the man swept the weapon back and forth, mowing down everyone in its path. There was screaming and scraping and scuffling all around. And blood. *So much blood.* Yet the dreamer himself couldn't move. His feet were fixed to the floor of the laboratory, his eyes focused intently on the shooter. He waited for the man to turn in his direction. *He had to see the man's eyes. He had to know.* The shooter turned slowly, as if suspended in time, until his eyes gradually came into view through his visor.

Malachi awoke with a start, breathing heavily and sweating despite the cold. Obviously, he'd drifted off. *But for how long?* "Damn," he whispered, surprised that it was already light outside. He quickly scanned his surroundings and was relieved to find nothing of immediate concern.

He was still alone in the rustic cabin he'd broken into last night, deep in the Savage River State Forest, about twenty-five miles southwest of Frostburg.

There was no heat or electricity in this cabin, nor furniture for that matter. Malachi had slept in a sitting position on the pine floor, with his back propped against the rough-cut interior wall of the cabin. With great effort, he rose and stretched his stiff and aching limbs. His legs, especially, were painfully sore from yesterday's fourteen-hour trek through the woods, which he'd accomplished using a series of hiking trails that ran along the Savage River, darting off into the woods whenever he heard an approaching hiker.

After yesterday morning, he'd decided he could not risk hitchhiking or stealing another car. Not around here. Not after seeing a team of policemen rifling through the car he'd stolen the night before. His instincts were telling him that he had to keep running. He needed to find his contacts . . . and avoid getting caught in the process.

Malachi peeked through one of the grimy windows of the cabin and saw an endless forest of spruce trees, awash in the dim gray light of an early morning October sky. Then he quickly looked out the other five windows of the cabin and saw the same terrain in every direction. *Now what?*

As he pondered that question, he shook a cigarette loose from his pack and pressed it between his lips. He lit it with a flick of his lighter and drew in a deep, satisfying breath. The warm smoke felt good in his lungs and helped clear his mind. He could tell his memory was improving, although very slowly. For instance, he could now specifically remember entering the Thurmond lab on a moonless spring night. He remembered that he was on an important mission, that he had an objective, that there were specific rules he was to follow. He lingered on that last thought for a moment. *Rules. Something about time. It was important to check his watch*. He tried to hold on to that particular memory, but it quickly evaporated into nothingness.

Frustrated, he reached into his pocket and retrieved the small piece of paper and pen that he'd taken from the Huntsman Motel yesterday morning. Since then, he'd added a few more items to his list—random thoughts that seemed to carry some special significance, and which had popped into his mind during his hike. The paper now had four items scrawled in uneven handwriting:

Jasher
White House
Opal
Ellipse

Malachi added a fifth: "Time." He had no idea what any of this meant, aside from the obvious fact that the White House was the home of the president, opal was a type of stone, and an ellipse was a geometric shape. He certainly had no idea about "Jasher." He slowly shook his head, desperately trying to piece it all together. *This was maddening.*

For a long while, he just stared out the window into the woods, doing his best to push his emotions aside and focus on logic. *Concentrate*, he told himself. *Let logic be your guide*. He drew a deep drag from his cigarette and once again began methodically ticking through the things he could deduce based on the facts he knew.

First and foremost, he knew it was no longer 1972. According to the magazines he'd bought the other night, the year was now 2013. Malachi tilted his head back and blew out a long stream of smoke. *Jesus. How could he have lost four decades of his life?* No doubt, this had something to do with the experiments taking place in Thurmond. *Something about time.*

Malachi felt the same feelings of confusion and bewilderment that he'd experienced last night starting to well up inside him again. *Where had he been all this time? In a coma? Or was he simply crazy?* With effort, he pushed these thoughts aside and forced himself, once again, to focus on logic. *What else did he know?*

He knew that someone had been expecting him in Thurmond. His contacts. A man and a woman. They had left clues for him that only he could solve. And apparently he'd had some type of training or preparation that allowed him to solve those clues. In other words, all of this had been prearranged, and Malachi himself had been a part of it. *But why? What was he supposed to have accomplished?*

His contacts had certainly not left him much to go on. A cryptic note with instructions to go to the "Third Church." *Meaningless drivel.* He had no idea who Elijah was. *And where was this "Third Church" he was supposed to go to?*

Malachi retrieved the sheet of stationery from his pocket and studied the strange arrangement of symbols in the middle of the page, which appeared to consist of two numbers and two letters arranged around an octagon with a cross in the middle:

What did this mean? He noted that the numbers 17 and 16 were in reverse numerical order. *Was this significant? Did this have something to do with going backward? Perhaps time was going backward.*

Putting the numbers aside for a moment, Malachi next considered the letters *K* and *I*. Unlike the numbers, these letters were not consecutive in the alphabet. The letter *J* should have been between them, but it was missing. Or, more precisely, the letter *J* had been replaced with a cross in this puzzle. *But why? Or was "KI" an acronym for something?* Malachi had already mulled over those two letters endlessly, trying in vain to trigger some meaningful memory. *King Isaac? King's Island?* Nothing seemed to fit. Nor did his knowledge of chemistry offer any logical answers. As he knew, *K* was the chemical symbol for potassium, and *I* was the symbol for iodine. Two elements on nearly opposite sides of the periodic table. Potassium, far to the left, had a single valence electron that it wanted to get rid of. Iodine, nearly on the far right of the periodic table, had seven valence electrons and desperately wanted one more to complete its valence shell. Therefore, chemically speaking, these two elements were nearly a perfect match to form an ionic compound. Which they often did. Potassium iodide, or KI, was a common, naturally occurring salt, and an important component of iodized table salt, usually sold in supermarkets. *But what did potassium iodide have to do with anything?*

Malachi took a last puff of his cigarette and dropped it on the floor, grinding it out with his shoe. He glanced at his own notes again, which seemed to be pointing him toward Washington, D.C. *But to do what? Knock on the door of the White House and announce his presence?* Actually, he entertained that idea for quite some time before finally dismissing it. *No*, he decided. There had to be a better plan.

He felt his stomach growl and was reminded once again of how terribly hungry he was. He hadn't eaten in more than thirty hours, and his body was desperately craving food. This was why he did not trust his senses at first when he began to smell something delicious in the air. *When you're starving, everything starts to look and smell like food.* After a couple of minutes, though, he simply could not ignore the unmistakable aroma of . . . *bacon*. It seemed to be seeping through the cracks in the cabin.

Malachi slowly unlatched the front door and eased it open a few inches. As he did, the tantalizing smell of sizzling bacon suddenly wafted inside. *Someone was cooking breakfast nearby.*

He immediately drew his pistol and ventured out the front door and into the woods. He stopped for a moment and took note of the light breeze that was blowing from the southwest. He turned in that direction and began making his way stealthily through the dense forest. The smell of frying bacon grew steadily stronger until, finally, he saw its source—a neighboring cabin in the woods, about seventy yards away. A thin stream of smoke was twirling out of the cabin's river-stone chimney.

Malachi continued creeping toward the back of the neighboring cabin with his pistol drawn, until he was close enough to see through one of the windows. For a while, he saw nothing at all. Then, suddenly, he saw movement. A man in a red flannel shirt and boxer shorts, then an attractive woman in a pink robe. She was cradling a coffee cup, and the man seemed to be carrying something . . . a spatula. Now they were kissing and smiling.

Malachi moved quickly around the side of the cabin toward the front door, ducking low to avoid being seen through the windows. As he rounded the corner to the front, he saw a forest-green Land Rover parked in the dirt driveway that led away from the cabin and disappeared into the woods. *Perfect.* He quickly approached the front door, clicked off the safety of his pistol, and prepared to enter.

Five seconds later, Malachi pounded open the front door with a rapid series of powerful kicks. The door splintered on the third kick and flew wide open, into the cabin.

He burst in with his weapon drawn and shouted, "On the floor!"

The woman in the pink robe dropped her coffee and shrieked in terror. She backed away quickly and shrank to the floor until she was huddled in a tight ball against the wall.

The man in the red flannel shirt, however, proved much more brazen than Malachi had expected. He was a brutish man with a square jaw and a massive chest. He stood his ground in the middle of the cabin with a large cast-iron skillet held in both hands above his head like a baseball bat. He appeared poised to charge at Malachi.

Malachi leveled his pistol directly at the man's chest. "It'll be the last thing you do," he warned.

The man stood motionless, seething and breathing heavily for several seconds. Then, slowly, he returned the skillet to the hearth with a loud *clank*.

"On the floor," Malachi ordered, motioning with his pistol for the man to join the woman in the pink robe, who was now whimpering uncontrollably near the back wall.

The man in flannel reluctantly obeyed. "What do you want?" he asked gruffly as he sat down next to the woman.

"Car keys," said Malachi.

"Shit," the man huffed. "Are you serious?"

"Where are they?" Malachi demanded.

The man shook his head and let out an incredulous laugh. "In my jeans pocket. Over there." He pointed toward a pile of clothes next to a rustic pine bed on the far side of the cabin.

Malachi slowly backed away from the couple, keeping his weapon trained on them at all times.

"You're making a big fucking mistake, buddy," said the man in flannel.

The woman next to him piped up, her voice squeaky

with fear. "Dave, please . . . just . . . just shut up. Please . . ."

"Good advice," said Malachi, still inching his way toward the pile of clothes on the floor. When he got there, he bent down and retrieved a set of keys from the front pocket of a pair of faded jeans on the floor. He glanced down and saw that the leather key chain was embossed with the words RANGE ROVER.

"Take it," said the woman in a shaky voice. "Please . . . just go."

Malachi felt genuinely sorry for this woman, who was obviously terrified. He was about to say "Sorry" when her male companion decided to add one last macho comment.

"You're going to regret this, asshole."

Malachi had had enough of this guy's mouth. He took three quick steps toward him and trained his pistol directly between his eyes. He turned to the woman in the pink robe and said, "Your boyfriend's not very smart."

The woman broke down in sobs. "Oh God, please don't do this. Please . . . don't." She closed her eyes tightly, apparently waiting for Malachi to pull the trigger.

As for the man in flannel, he had suddenly lost his voice. He was now staring silently at the gun, mouth agape, eyes wide open. His face seemed to be getting paler by the second.

Malachi maintained his firing stance for several seconds, then he began backing away slowly. When he reached the front door, he turned and quickly made his way to the vehicle.

Twenty seconds later, the Range Rover roared to life and tore away from the cabin at high speed.

A single question now occupied Malachi's mind. *How do I get to Washington, D.C., from here?*

24

A NA THORNE rang the doorbell of 131 Montecito Drive in Satellite Beach and stepped back, awaiting a response. The house, located in an upscale golf community, was part of a tasteful, Mediterranean-style duplex with cream-colored stucco exterior walls and a brown tiled roof. The doormat on the front stoop read:

> *As for me and my house,*
> *we will serve the Lord.*
> *—Joshua 24:15.*

As she waited, Ana reminded herself of her fake identity for this meeting. Today she was "Ana Griffin," a freelance writer from Baltimore.

After a few seconds, the door swung open slowly, and an elderly man in khaki slacks and a bright yellow golf shirt appeared. He was a tall, birdlike man with sagging jowls, black-rimmed glasses, and patches of white hair on either side of an otherwise bald head. "Hello," he said in a voice that sounded much younger than he looked. "Are you Ana?"

"Yes," said Ana. "I'm Ana Griffin. Thanks for meeting with me on such short notice."

"Oh, it was no trouble," said the man, extending his hand. "I'm Tom Reynolds. Come on in."

Ana followed the man inside to a tastefully furnished living room, where they both sat down on a chocolate-brown leather couch. "This is a lovely home," she said.

"Thanks. We like it down here. Moved down about ten years ago from Boston after I retired from the ministry. My wife, Betty, does all the decorating, so I really can't take credit for anything."

"Is she here?"

"Uh, no. Today's one of her golf days, so she's out with her friends." Reynolds pointed to a framed photograph on the table behind the couch, showing four smiling, gray-haired women in golf attire holding a trophy. "She never misses golf."

"Which one's your wife?"

"Betty's on the left in the blue sweater. Believe it or not, she never golfed a day in her life until we moved down here. Now she can't get enough of it. She's darn good, too. Better than me, anyway."

"She's lovely."

"Yep. I'm a lucky man."

After several more minutes of small talk, Ana finally got to the point. "As I explained on the phone," she said, "I'm working on a book about Franz Holzberg. I understand you were friends with him at Princeton, is that right?"

"Friends?" Reynolds pondered that word for a moment. "I'd say we were more like acquaintances. He was at the Institute of Advanced Studies. I was in the Department of

Religion at Princeton, working on my doctorate. But yes, some of our interests, shall we say . . . *intersected*."

"How so?" Ana removed a notepad and pen from her purse and prepared to take notes.

Reynolds cleared his throat. "Well . . . if you're writing a book about him, I assume you're familiar with how Franz Holzberg came to the United States in the first place?"

In fact, Ana knew all about Dr. Holzberg's entry into the United States in 1948, but much of what she knew was highly classified. So she had to be careful not to reveal anything that would have been beyond the knowledge of a diligent scholar using publicly available sources. "You mean Project Paperclip?" she said, referring to the once-secret OSS program in which hundreds of German scientists, mathematicians, and engineers were funneled into the United States in the aftermath of World War II. The existence of Project Paperclip had been well known for decades, although many of its details remained highly secret.

"Yes, exactly," said Reynolds. "Franz Holzberg was recruited fairly late in that program, sometime around 1948 or '49. Since his background was in physics, they parked him at the Institute of Advanced Studies at Princeton, where he overlapped for several years with Einstein and Oppenheimer and others of that ilk. It was quite a concentration of brainpower in those days. A lot of interesting things going on."

"So you were explaining how the two of you had similar interests . . ."

"Yes. I met Franz in the fall of 1955. As I said, I was pursuing my doctorate in religious studies. And it turned out that Franz had an interest in the Bible, too, particularly the Gospels of the Old Testament. But his interests were not in what I would call the *religious* aspects of the Bible."

"Oh?"

"No, Franz was more interested in certain aspects in

the Bible that he thought related, somehow, to his own field of study—theoretical physics."

"Like what?"

"Well, I remember he was very keen on the book of Joshua and some of the events described in that Gospel."

"You talked to him specifically about these things?"

"Oh, yes. Over a period of about two and a half years, I would say from late 1956 to early 1959. We were in the same circle of friends at that time. He was older than I was, but I was friends with some of his younger colleagues, and we would all get together for dinner or coffee and just, you know . . . *talk* about things. It was a very exciting time. And by the way, Franz was not the only scientist from the institute who was interested in religion in those days."

"Who else was?"

"Well, for instance, Albert Einstein often sat in on lectures at the Princeton Theological Seminary and sometimes provided critiques. He even gave a few lectures there himself. But that was before my time. Benjamin Fulcher, another well-known physicist who was there at that time, was quite interested in religious studies. My point is, there was a great synergism in those days between the scientists at the institute, especially the physicists, and students of religion like me."

"Why do you think that was?"

"I don't know, exactly. Perhaps it was a sense of optimism in those early days, when so many amazing discoveries were being made, that science would eventually reveal *every* mystery of the universe. At which point, science and religion would simply merge into one cohesive, universally accepted understanding of the cosmos, and we would all implicitly understand who we are and why we're here. At least, that was one view."

"You mentioned that Dr. Holzberg was particularly

interested in the book of Joshua. Can you tell me more about that?"

Reynolds smiled. "I can tell you a *lot* about that. How much time do you have?"

Ana shrugged. "All day."

Reynolds looked genuinely excited by this prospect, and Ana sensed that he probably missed this sort of intellectual discussion. "Wait right here," he said. He disappeared through a doorway and returned a minute later carrying a large black book that Ana recognized as the Holy Bible. He sat down with the book in his lap and thumbed quickly through several pages. "Joshua, Joshua," he mumbled. "Ah, here we go." He paused for a few seconds before continuing. "By the way," he asked, "do you belong to any particular religious denomination?"

Ana had to think about that one for a second. She hadn't bothered to assign the fictional "Ana Griffin" any specific religion. So, as a fallback, she just used her own. "I was raised as a Presbyterian," she replied. "But I don't really attend church anymore."

"Fair enough," said Reynolds. "But I'm sure you're familiar with the story of Exodus. How Moses led the Israelites out of Egypt and how they wandered in the desert for forty years."

"Generally, yes."

"And at the end of those forty years, after all the elders except Moses had died off, the decision was made to invade Canaan to conquer the promised land for Israel, as God had commanded."

"Uh-huh."

"At the age of a hundred and twenty, Moses died in sight of the promised land, never having set foot there. So Joshua was appointed as the new leader of the Israelites, and he quickly went about preparing to lead his people into battle.

His first challenge was how to get them across the Jordan River."

Ana was nodding along politely. But she really wished the conversation would hurry up and steer back toward Dr. Holzberg, or at least something more . . . *relevant*. But she knew she had to be patient.

"Crossing the Jordan would be no easy task," Reynolds continued. "Here, let me show you a map." He flipped to the back of his Bible, which contained a series of annotated maps of the Holy Land. Then he placed the Bible on the coffee table, opened to a two-page map of the Middle East, circa 1400 BCE. "The first thing you need to realize," he said, "is that the Jordan was a much more powerful river in those days than it is now. Nowadays, it is heavily diverted for irrigation and drinking water, and there are various flood-control levees in place. But back then, it was just a raw and natural river. Very powerful. As you can see, it runs from the Sea of Galilee in the north, up here"—he tapped the appropriate spot on the map—"to the Dead Sea in the south, down here." He pointed to the Dead Sea on the map. "Along the way, it picks up runoff from the mountains and hillsides that extend all along the Jordan Valley on both sides." He indicated these features on the map, tracing both sides of the Jordan River with his bony finger.

"Mmm-hmm." Ana craned her neck to see the map.

"Now, Joshua was leading an army of *forty thousand* men, plus horses and cattle and supply carts and so forth. So getting that entire fighting force across the river was not going to be an easy task. To make matters worse, it was springtime, which meant the Jordan was flooding. In other words, it would have been flowing even faster and wider than normal."

"So how *did* he get across?" After all this buildup, Ana genuinely wanted to know.

"Well, let me read you the actual account from the book of Joshua." He leaned over the coffee table and flipped through the Bible until he found the right spot. "Okay, I'm reading now from Joshua chapter three, verses fourteen to seventeen:

> *'And it came to pass, when the people removed from their tents, to pass over Jordan, and the priests bearing the ark of the covenant before the people; and as they that bore the ark were come unto Jordan, and the feet of the priests that bore the ark were dipped in the brim of the water, (for Jordan overfloweth all his banks all the time of harvest,) that the waters which came down from above stood and rose up upon an heap very far from the city Adam, that is beside Zaretan: and those that came down toward the sea of the plain, even the salt sea, failed, and were cut off: and the people passed over right against Jericho. And the priests that bore the ark of the covenant of the Lord stood firm on dry ground in the midst of Jordan, and all the Israelites passed over on dry ground, until all the people were passed clean over Jordan.'"*

"Sorry," said Ana, shaking her head. "I sort of lost you there. *What* exactly happened?"

Reynolds flashed a smile. "It's okay. The King James lingo is sometimes hard to follow if you're not used to it. In a nutshell, Joshua instructed the priests to carry the Ark of the Covenant to the edge of the Jordan River. And as soon as the priests' feet touched the water, a miracle occurred. The river began swelling up to the north of their location—rising up in a 'heap,' as the Bible says—and it ran dry to the south, all the way to the 'salt sea,' which is the Dead Sea. This allowed the Israelite army to cross over the dry riverbed to the south and make their way to the city of Jericho, which was their first military target."

"I see," said Ana, bobbing her head up and down. "Very interesting." In fact, though, she didn't find any of this biblical stuff interesting. What she *really* wanted to know was how it related, if at all, to Dr. Holzberg and the strange events that were taking place in and around Thurmond. *Time to steer this conversation.* "And was this something that Dr. Holzberg was particularly interested in?" she asked.

"Oh, yes. He was very interested in the river-crossing story."

"How so?"

"Well, he . . . he had a theory about how this miracle occurred. From a *physics* perspective, that is."

Okay, now we're getting somewhere. "And what was that?"

Reynolds laughed and shook his head. "You're going to think I'm crazy."

"No, I won't. I promise."

"Okay, but I'm only telling you what Franz conveyed to me back then. In fact, at times, he was quite emphatic about it."

"I understand," said Ana, nodding for him to continue.

Reynolds sat back on the couch and appeared to be collecting his thoughts for a few seconds. "Okay," he began. "Franz believed this event—the stopping of the Jordan River—was the result of what he called 'time dilation.'"

Ana immediately stopped writing in her notepad. *Time dilation.* "Did he elaborate?"

Reynolds cleared his throat. "He did, although I'm not sure I remember all the details. He and his students had all sorts of complex calculations. They would fill entire blackboards with this stuff. And I certainly don't remember any of those details. But, in general, I remember what he said."

"Go on."

"As Franz explained it to me, time is relative. So it can appear to slow down in one area relative to another. He would often give the example of a three-dimensional sphere centered on a particular point or object. That point or object would have to have enormous gravity or some other unusual physical property. I was never really clear on that principle. Anyway, time inside this sphere would run more slowly relative to time outside the sphere. So if you had such a sphere extending across a river that, say, flows from north to south like the Jordan, then, as the water enters the sphere from the north, it travels more slowly than the water immediately behind it. So the river begins to back up. Eventually, it floods to the north. On the other side, the water that has just left the sphere flowing south will travel faster than the water immediately behind it, which is still within the sphere. As a result, the river will eventually run dry to the south, or nearly dry. And that's as good as I can explain it."

Ana's brain was suddenly spinning. "And what . . . what is it about this material that it would cause such a time dilation?"

Reynolds shrugged and gave a sheepish smile. "Beats me. Like I said, Franz and his students had all sorts of calculations and theories, but all of that stuff went over my head."

"Who were these students you keep mentioning?"

"Well, they weren't technically 'students.' The institute doesn't really work that way. In fact, it's not officially part of the Princeton academic structure at all. But there was a group of younger people who sort of idolized Franz and did his bidding, if you will. I guess you could call them acolytes, to borrow a word from my field. And I would say there were basically three of them in those days. One of them was Gary Freer, who was also a friend of mine from church. Then there was, uh . . . let me see . . . Irwin Michelson, another theoretical physicist. And then there was Opal."

"Opal? Who was that?"

Reynolds looked a bit surprised by the question. "Opal? She was a, uh . . . a very pretty young woman. Part of Franz's circle of friends." He shrugged, indicating that there was nothing left to say about her.

"Remember her last name?"

Reynolds thought for a moment and shook his head. "I don't."

Ana was writing all of this down as fast as she could. When she had finished, she decided to change the subject. "What can you tell me about the book of Jasher?"

Reynolds's eyebrows suddenly arched up. "The book of Jasher?" He rubbed his chin thoughtfully for a moment, then stood up from the couch and gestured for Ana to follow him. "Come, let me show you something."

25

VLADAMIR KRUPNOV peered out the cockpit window of the Schweizer helicopter and admired the splendid view of the Hillcrest estate below him. The Hillcrest mansion, guesthouse, barn, and pool were situated on twenty-three acres of rolling, manicured lawns and gardens. The maple and ash trees dotting the grounds were ablaze in bright autumn colors. Although Krupnov had been here several times before, this was the first time he'd arrived at the compound by helicopter. Today was an important day, though, and there was no time to waste.

The chopper gently touched down in an open area of grass behind the barn, and a man in a gray tracksuit and sunglasses quickly jogged over and greeted Krupnov as he hopped from the passenger side of the cockpit. Once they were clear of the spinning rotor, Krupnov turned and gave the pilot a quick wave, and the small chopper revved up and lifted off the ground.

"Where are they?" Krupnov barked in Ukrainian to his trusted lieutenant, Sashko, as the chopper rose into the sky behind them and banked away.

"In the guesthouse," said Sashko. He pointed to the white building adjacent to the mansion. "We brought them in late last night. It took a while to find them in the dark because they were very confused."

"Did they have the material?"

Sashko shook his head slowly, clearly disappointed.

Krupnov cursed in Russian and frowned. "Let's go."

As the two men made their way to the compound's guesthouse, Krupnov reflected on what a perfect location this was for their activities. A ten-million-dollar estate in the heart of Virginia horse country. Here, no one batted an eyelash when a helicopter landed on the lawn or a fleet of limousines arrived at the front gate. With the maintenance and upkeep of a place like this, no one thought twice about unmarked vans and trucks coming and going at all hours of the day and night. Moreover, the entire estate was fenced, and there was an armed security guard at the entrance twenty-four hours a day. And all of this was considered perfectly normal around here. To the residents of Middleburg, Hillcrest was just another mansion owned by some shadowy European or Middle Eastern billionaire who hardly ever visited but who apparently let his friends use the place year-round. *Yes, Hillcrest was perfect.*

Krupnov and Sashko strutted quickly past the barn and the pool until they arrived at the guesthouse, a tastefully converted stable with white clapboard siding and a red tin roof. Krupnov opened the front door and headed straight upstairs to the master bedroom. As he entered the room, he immediately observed two heavily bearded men tied to wooden chairs. "*Ne khuya sebe,*" he whispered as he approached. *Fuck me.* The two restrained men had long white hair and beards, as if they were in their seventies or eighties. Yet their bodies looked relatively healthy, even muscular, beneath their ragged and filthy clothes.

Krupnov glanced around at the other two men in the room. Like Sashko, they were Ukrainians, unshaven, cocky, and dressed in nearly identical tracksuits. One had an Uzi machine gun slung across his shoulder. The other held a pistol. These men were officially considered "security specialists" for Krupnov Energy, although most of them were former members of the Ukrainian mafia.

One of the restrained men groaned and rolled his head lazily to one side.

Krupnov stepped forward and bent down until he was looking directly into the man's hazy eyes. "What's your name?" he said in heavily accented English.

The man did not reply.

"They don't remember nothing," said the man with the machine gun. "Not even their names."

Krupnov carefully studied the bearded man's dull eyes and pale skin. Then he glanced down at the man's hands. "*Shcho za khren!*" he said with surprise. "What's happened to his fingernails?"

"They keep growing," said Sashko with a shrug. "They weren't that long when we picked them up last night. But now . . . well, you can see. Their hair is the same way. It's been growing all night. Weird, huh?"

Krupnov did not respond. He recalled Fulcher mentioning that something like this might happen. *Physiological artifacts*, he'd called it. Krupnov looked over at the other bearded man, who looked to be in even worse shape than the first. The second man's head was down, chin on his chest, eyes closed. Apparently, he was unconscious.

"Have they been this way the whole time?" asked Krupnov.

"No," replied Sashko. "They were confused last night when we found them. And very agitated. They fought with us for a long time, which is why we eventually had to subdue them and tie them up like this. They were like . . . wild animals. We had to sedate them just so they wouldn't hurt themselves."

"Sedate them with what?"

Sashko pointed to a small glass vial and two syringes on the nightstand by the bed. "Propofol."

Shit. Krupnov needed these men to communicate. He turned back to the semiconscious man and stared directly into his eyes. "Can you hear me?" he said in English.

The man stared back blankly and said nothing.

Krupnov repeated the same question in Russian: *"Ty menya slyshish?"*

The man groaned unintelligibly.

This gave Krupnov a spark of hope. He stood up straight and hesitated a moment before suddenly slapping the man brutally across the face, hoping to wake him up.

The bearded man grunted loudly and seemed to be coming to.

Krupnov slapped him again and then bent down toward him. "You are Yuri Chaika," he said in Russian. "Yes?"

The bearded man shook his head slightly and mumbled, *"Ya ne pomnyu." I don't remember.*

"You're a KGB agent," said Krupnov emphatically. "You were on a mission for the Soviet Union. Surely you remember this?"

Once again, the bearded man shook his head lazily from side to side. *"Ya ne pomnyu." I don't remember.*

Anger flashed across Krupnov's face. He cursed and slowly backed away.

"It was the same last night," said Sashko. "They remember nothing. It's as if their memories have been erased."

"You searched their clothes? Their pockets? Did they have *anything*?"

Sashko shook his head. "Nothing."

Damn it. Krupnov considered his options and finally instructed Sashko to set up a videoconference.

Sashko left the room and returned several minutes later with a laptop computer. He set it up on a small table at the foot of the bed and worked the keyboard and touch pad for a few minutes until the videoconference was ready. "He's on," Sashko said quietly.

Krupnov leaned over the table and saw the face of Benjamin Fulcher on the screen. "How are things going there?" Krupnov asked in English.

"We're busy preparing for our demonstration," said Fulcher. "And I have a lot to do before I leave for Italy tomorrow morning. I hope you're contacting me with some good news."

"I'm afraid not," said Krupnov glumly. "We have the two men in custody. The ones who emerged from the mine last night. But they don't have the material."

The elderly man on the screen frowned. "Do they know where it is? Can they tell us *anything* helpful?"

Krupnov shook his head. "They remember *nothing*. Here, take a look." Krupnov turned the computer so that Fulcher could have a view of the two bearded men. After several seconds, he turned the screen back around. "They're like zombies."

On the screen, Fulcher bridged his fingers and bent his forehead down until it was touching his fingertips. "My God, I had no idea the physiological effects would be so severe."

"So, what do we do now?" Krupnov asked in a sharp tone. "You assured me that everything would work out fine, remember? I think you called it *fate*."

"And it will," said Fulcher calmly. "The material is obviously with Malachi. We simply need to find him."

"*Da*," said Krupnov. "We will find him. You can count on it." He cast a quick glance at Sashko.

"Good," said Fulcher on the screen. "Then we have nothing to worry about. Now, if you'll excuse me, there are many things left to do for our demonstration that I must attend to. Let me know when you find Malachi." A moment later, the screen went dark.

Krupnov closed his eyes and cursed under his breath.

"Vlad?" said Sashko. "What should we do with these guys?" He motioned toward the two bearded men.

Krupnov considered the question for several seconds before answering with a shrug, "I don't have room in my organization for zombies. Get rid of them." He quickly turned and left the room.

As Krupnov approached the stairs at the end of the hallway, he hesitated for a moment, wondering whether he'd made the right call. Perhaps those two washed-up Soviet agents might be useful at some point down the road. He was still turning that possibility over in his mind when he suddenly heard a muffled *pop!* from the bedroom, followed two seconds later by another *pop!*

Too late now.

26

Holy cow," exclaimed Ana Thorne as she entered the large office on the second floor of Tom Reynolds's home.

"Yeah, my wife doesn't like it much," said Reynolds with a grin. "But a man has to have a hobby."

Ana looked around and marveled at the sheer amount of clutter in the room. Nearly every square inch of horizontal and vertical space was occupied by something, save for the ceiling and a clear patch on the carpeted floor. She took a few steps into the room and approached the wall on the left. It was covered, from floor to ceiling, with old maps, handwritten notes, and several reprints of classical artwork. She noticed some crude "biblical" maps, like the one Reynolds had shown her earlier, depicting various features of the Holy Land. Other maps, however, were modern topographical survey maps—quite colorful and detailed. She approached one of these and read the legend: HYDROLOGICAL SURVEY OF THE JORDAN RIVER BASIN.

"I've found it helps to understand the geology of the area," said Reynolds, still standing in the doorway.

"What are all these?" Ana pointed to the intricate network of colored thumbtacks and yarn that stretched across the entire wall, connecting numerous points on the maps and even some of the paintings and etchings. Many of the lengths of yarn were labeled with tiny tabs of paper that had letters or numbers written on them.

"Oh, just a system I use to keep track of connections. If I were better with computers, I probably wouldn't need to do it this way. But, well . . . this is how I've always done it."

"Impressive," said Ana with a nod. *In a "mad scientist" sort of way.* She continued scanning the wall until she reached a colorful print of a Renaissance-style painting that was pinned to the wall with four thumbtacks.

"*The Crossing of the Jordan* by Raphael," said Reynolds. "The original is in the Vatican. I've seen it in person. It's beautiful."

Ana inspected the Raphael painting closely. It depicted four men dressed in plain robes, like friars, carrying a large house-shaped box on their shoulders, presumably the Ark of the Covenant. A bearded man with flowing white hair—presumably God—was holding back the flow of the Jordan River with his hands and right shoulder. Joshua was in the forefront, dressed like a Roman legionnaire in a silver breastplate and white pleated kilt with gold trim. His helmet was adorned with a brilliant plume of white feathers. He was leading an army of thousands of men on foot and horseback across the dry riverbed as God himself held back the raging waters.

"Not accurate, of course," said Reynolds. "Joshua would not have been dressed like a Roman military officer. He certainly wouldn't have had body armor or a bronze helmet, or nice sandals, for that matter. The Israelites had just spent forty years in the desert. Joshua himself was born into slavery in Egypt and lived nearly his entire life in the wilderness among hundreds of thousands of people who had no permanent home. In reality, Joshua and his army would have looked more like bedouins—basically, vagabonds. Which is what made their conquest of Canaan all the more amazing."

Ana turned her attention back to the wall.

"Take the next picture, for instance," said Reynolds. He pointed to a smaller, black-and-white etching next to the Raphael print. "It's called *The Fall of the Walls of Jericho*, by John Martin."

Ana inspected the dark print, which depicted a dramatic scene of mayhem and destruction. An army of soldiers watched from the foothills of Jericho as the massive walls of the fortified city came tumbling down amidst a swirling dark sky and bolts of lightning.

"Jericho was a powerful city at that time," said Reynolds. "Yet Joshua chose it as his first military target. That would be like the Hondurans deciding to conquer America and choosing Washington, D.C., as their first target."

"How did they get the walls to come down like that?"

"Actually," said Reynolds. "They used the ark."

"Again?"

"Yes. God instructed Joshua to have his men carry the Ark of the Covenant around the walls of Jericho once a day for six days, blowing rams' horns as they did. On the seventh day, the men circled the city seven times with the ark. And then, with one last blast of the rams' horns and with all of Joshua's men shouting at the tops of their lungs, the walls of Jericho came crumbling down."

Nonsense, thought Ana. But she kept this sentiment to herself, nodding politely with a straight face. "So does Jericho still exist?"

"Oh, yes," Reynolds replied. "It's located in the Palestinian territories, on the West Bank." He stepped forward and indicated the location of modern Jericho on one of the maps on the wall. "In fact, Jericho is one of the oldest continuously inhabited cities in the world. Archaeologists have found evidence of civilization there since at least 9000 B.C. And, more important, there's clear evidence of a massively destructive event in Jericho around 1400 B.C., about the time of Joshua's conquest. There's even evidence that the city's walls were destroyed during that event."

"Really?"

Reynolds nodded enthusiastically. "The most famous excavation of Jericho, and probably the most thorough to date, was Kathleen Kenyon's work in the late 1950s. She concluded that the Bronze Age city of Jericho, including its surrounding walls, was destroyed in a single cataclysmic event in approximately 1500 B.C., which is about a century earlier than the biblical account in Joshua. But more recent studies and carbon dating have shown that her estimate was slightly off. The actual date was closer to 1400 B.C., which would coincide nearly exactly with the Old Testament account. Of course, people still differ on this, but the evidence is very strong."

"Interesting," said Ana. "And what about *this* picture?" She pointed to a large, majestic depiction of an epic event, complete with swirling clouds and dramatic scenery.

"Ah, that's an interesting one," said Reynolds. "Another work by John Martin from the early nineteenth century. It's called *Joshua Commands the Sun to Stand Still over Gibeon*. And it depicts the story that is told in Joshua, chapter ten, of the Israelites' defeat of five Amorite kings and their armies at Gibeon."

Ana traced a strand of bright pink yarn from the painting to a modern political map of Israel and Palestine. "Is this Gibeon?"

"Yes. Near the present-day village of Al-Jeeb in the Palestinian territories. It's situated on a high hill on the outskirts of Jerusalem. A very strategic location in ancient times."

Ana remembered the "sun standing still" story from her research last night and recalled that it involved the book of Jasher. "So what happened there?" she asked.

"Well . . . Joshua's crushing defeat of Jericho had sent shock waves throughout the territory of Canaan. At that time, each city in Canaan was essentially its own kingdom or city-state. Some of these city-states decided to make peace with the Israelites rather than risk being destroyed like Jericho. Gibeon was one of those cities that preferred peace to war. With Gibeon under their control, the Israelites now had a strategic stronghold in this hilly area here." Reynolds pointed to the area around Gibeon on one of the biblical maps. "And that really worried the surrounding city-states, especially Jerusalem, which was less than ten miles away. So five kings from these surrounding city-states decided to join forces and attack Gibeon, in order to drive out the Israelites, but also to send a message to the other cities in Canaan that they should not make peace with the Israelites."

"And how did that turn out for them?"

Reynolds let out a dry laugh. "Not good. When Joshua heard what was happening, he quickly marshaled his forces and led an all-night march to Gibeon, where he launched a surprise attack on the Amorite army. He crushed them at Gibeon and soon had them on the run . . . all the way along the road from Beth Horon to Azekah, which is way down here." Reynolds pointed to Azekah on the biblical map.

"So what about the sun-standing-still part?"

"Well, Joshua wasn't satisfied with just repelling the Amorites from Gibeon. He wanted to utterly destroy them . . . to eliminate their ability to regroup and fight again, and probably also to send his own message to the other cities in Canaan. But the day was coming to an end, and he needed more time to finish the job. So, according to the Bible, he commanded the sun to stand still in the sky, which it did. For about a whole day. You might say that Joshua bought himself more time, *literally*, to complete his mission."

"And is this where the book of Jasher comes in?"

"Yes," said Reynolds, nodding. "This is one of two places in the Old Testament where the book of Jasher is specifically mentioned." He pulled a small Bible from one of the crowded bookshelves in the room and quickly flipped to the correct page. "In the King James version, it says: '*And the sun stood still, and the moon stayed, until the people avenged themselves upon their enemies. Is not this written in the book of Jasher?*'"

"And what, exactly, *is* the 'book of Jasher'?"

Reynolds laughed. "You're opening up a whole can of worms there." He swept his hand all around the cluttered room. "As you can see, I've spent many years trying to answer that question."

"*And . . . ?*"

"And . . . the only thing I can tell you for sure is that it isn't *this*." He pulled a thin booklet from the shelf and held it up. Then he pulled another booklet from the same shelf and held it up in his other hand. "And it's probably not this, either."

"Those are the two books you analyzed in your Ph.D. dissertation?"

Reynolds looked surprised. "You dug up that old thing?"

Ana shrugged. "Just wanted to be prepared for today. I have to admit, though, I couldn't really follow all of it."

Reynolds smiled. "That's okay, neither could the thesis committee at Princeton." He paused, apparently collecting his thoughts. "How about I just give you the short version?"

"That would be great."

"Okay, let's start with the easy one first." He handed
Ana one of the two booklets, a pamphlet-size volume with a
thick paper cover that was yellowed with age and well worn
around the edges.

Ana read the title:

The Book of Jasher
with Testimonies and Notes
Translated into English from the Hebrew by Flaccus
*   Albinus Alcuinus,*
who went on a Pilgrimage into the Holy Land, and
*   Persia,*
where he discovered this volume, in the city of Gazna.

The publication date was MDCCCXXIX.

"A well-documented fraud," said Reynolds after he'd
given her a moment to review the cover. "It was first published in 1751, and then again in 1829, which is the version
you're holding now. It contains so many anachronisms and
contextual flaws that no serious student of Hebrew or the
Bible believes it's a translation of an ancient Hebrew document, let alone the book of Jasher."

"Hmm." Ana took one last look at the forgery and
handed it back to Reynolds. He then gave her the other
booklet, which was very similar in size and appearance,
and also showed signs of age. Ana read the title:

The Book of Jasher,
referenced to in
Joshua and Second Samuel

At the bottom of the front cover was the imprint of M.
M. Noah & A. S. Gould and a publication date of 1840.

"This one's a much closer call," said Reynolds. "It was published in Hebrew in Venice in 1625. The 1625 version indicates that an earlier version was published in Naples in 1552, but nobody has ever found that version. The version you're holding is the first English translation, which was published by Mordechai Noah in New York in 1840."

"What does it say?" asked Ana, already skimming through the pages.

"Well, for the most part, it tracks the stories of the Old Testament, from Adam and Eve to Noah and the Great Flood to Exodus and Israel's conquest of the promised land. Some of the wording is different, and in many places it's much more condensed. But, in general, it tracks the Hebrew Bible pretty well."

"Wait. So it doesn't contain anything new or different? How about the story of the sun standing still—what does it say about that?"

Reynolds shrugged and took the book back from her. "That story is recounted in chapter eighty-eight." He flipped to a page near the end of the book. "Just like the Bible, it describes Joshua's army chasing the Amorites along the road to Azekah, smiting them along the way. And then it says: *The day was declining toward evening, and Joshua said in the sight of all the people, Sun, stand thou still upon Gibeon, and thou moon in the valley of Ajalon, until the nation shall have revenged itself upon its enemies. And the Lord harkened to the voice of Joshua, and the sun stood still in the midst of the heavens, and it stood still six and thirty moments, and the moon also stood still and hastened not to go down a whole day.'"

"That's it?"

"Were you expecting something else?"

"I . . . I don't know," said Ana. In fact, she *had* been expecting something else. If not a revelation, then at least a clue as to why a researcher from the Thurmond National

Laboratory would be so intensely interested in the book of Jasher. *This doesn't add up.* "What does 'six and thirty moments' mean?" she asked.

Reynolds shrugged. "I don't know. And apparently neither did the person who translated the original Hebrew back in 1840. He placed an asterisk by the word 'moments' and explained that the original Hebrew version used the word 'times.' In other words, the original text referred to the sun standing still for 'six and thirty times.' But the translator said he'd never seen that term before and didn't know what it meant. So he used the word 'moments' instead."

Ana was quiet for a long time as she digested all of this information. "So, do you think this version is genuine?"

Reynolds blew out a long breath and shook his head. "I've been going back and forth about that my whole career. These days, most experts seem to be split right down the middle. About half think it's a genuine transcription of an original Hebrew document dating from at least the eighth century B.C. The other half think it originated sometime during the Middle Ages, nothing more than a copy or paraphrasing of the Hebrew Bible. And there's evidence to support both sides."

"What do *you* think?"

"I . . . *don't* think it's authentic," he said after a long pause. "But not because of the minor flaws in Hebrew grammar or the discrepancies between this book and other cross-referenced texts. No, my feeling is actually based on something Franz Holzberg told me way back when I was a grad student."

Okay, here we go. "And what was that?"

Reynolds seemed hesitant to say. He cocked his head slightly to the side and asked, "What kind of book are you writing, exactly?"

"It's a comprehensive biography of Franz Holzberg.

From his early childhood in Limburg, Germany, through his work at Humboldt University in Berlin, to his time at the Institute of Advanced Studies, his relationship with Einstein and Oppenheimer and others, and his views on everything from politics to religion. Why? Is there something that you're concerned about being in the book?"

Reynolds closed his eyes for a few seconds, apparently contemplating this question. Finally, he replied, "No. I guess not."

Ana waited patiently as Reynolds continued collecting his thoughts. "Okay. I've never told anyone this before. Not even my wife. This is something Franz told me in strict confidence, and he asked me to keep it secret. Which I have. All these years." He paused for a moment, apparently still debating whether to continue. "But I . . . I suppose it's time."

Ana nodded for him to continue.

Reynolds retrieved his small Bible and thumbed quickly to a particular page. "Joshua chapter 4 explains what happened after the Israelites successfully crossed over the dry bed of the Jordan River. At that point, Joshua summoned twelve of his men—one from each of the twelve tribes of Israel—and instructed them to *pass over before the ark of the Lord your God into the midst of Jordan, and take ye up every man of you a stone upon his shoulder, according unto the number of the tribes of the children of Israel.*" Reynolds looked up from the book.

"What did they do with the twelve stones?" Ana asked.

"That's explained in verse twenty: *And those twelve stones, which they took out of Jordan, did Joshua pitch in Gilgal.*" Reynolds stepped forward and pointed to the map of modern Israel and Palestine. "Gilgal would have been right about here, just east of Jericho, which is where the Israelite army had set up camp as they prepared to attack Jericho. This is where the Bible says they constructed a memorial using the twelve stones that had been collected during the crossing of the Jordan River."

"Does the book of Jasher say something different?"

"Well, that's just it," said Reynolds. "The 1625 version doesn't say *anything* about this event. It skips that part of the story completely. Which I always thought was odd because, in most places, the translation tracks the book of Joshua very closely. Yet, when it comes to these important stones being taken from the Jordan River and erected at Gilgal, it's completely silent."

"But you said the book of Jasher is condensed in places, compared to the Bible. So maybe that part just got left out."

"Sure, that's possible," said Reynolds. "But that's where Franz's comments come in. You see, Franz was very interested in the story of these twelve stones. He called them 'seeds.'"

"Seeds?"

"Uh-huh. Or sometimes he would say 'seed material.' According to him, that's what was actually in the Ark of the Covenant. And he described a way that this seed material could be piled up together to create a self-sustaining reaction of some sort. Like they did at the University of Chicago back in the early days of nuclear research."

Ana nodded. She remembered reading about the world's first self-sustained nuclear reactor, which had been built in 1942 in a very unusual, and risky, location: directly beneath the bleachers of an unused sports field at the University of Chicago. They achieved sustained nuclear fission by piling blocks of uranium and graphite into a large mound until it eventually reached "critical mass," the point at which fission becomes self-sustaining. This crude reactor was dubbed "CP1," an acronym for "Chicago Pile 1."

"Anyway," Reynolds continued. "Franz and I were talking one day—just a private conversation between the two of us—and he told me that he believed these twelve stones were used during the Battle of Gibeon . . . to create the long day." He nodded toward the John Martin painting of Joshua commanding the sun to stand still.

"Wait. How were they used to make the sun stand still?"

Reynolds shrugged. "Again, Franz was able to explain it using complex physics and mathematical equations. As best I can recall, it was the same phenomenon that was used to slow down the flow of the Jordan River, but on a larger scale. 'Time dilation,' he called it. He said that with enough of this material, you could create a large sphere where time ran more slowly. If you were inside the sphere looking out, it would seem like the sun was standing still because the rays of light would actually slow down when they hit the sphere, just like the flow of the river."

This was making Ana's head hurt. "Okay," she said, rubbing her temples. "So, how does this relate to the book of Jasher? You said something Dr. Holzberg told you made you believe that the Venice version was not authentic."

"Right," said Reynolds, nodding. "When I asked Franz how he knew all this stuff, he told me in strict confidence that he'd once seen a *German* translation of the book of Jasher, which went into great detail about the seed material. According to him, this German version was not a paraphrasing of the Hebrew Bible, like the ones we have here. Instead, it was a book that basically explained how to use these special stones in warfare. A military tactics manual of sorts. And, according to Franz, this German translation also described precisely where the stones were located."

"Which was where?"

"That he didn't say."

Of course not. Ana shook her head slowly. "And all of

this was according to some German translation of the book of Jasher that he said he'd seen?"

Reynolds nodded.

Ana felt as if her head was going to explode. She needed to sit down and sort through all this information and figure out what—if anything—was actually meaningful. "Did Dr. Holzberg say where he got access to this German book of Jasher?"

Reynolds gave her a curious look before answering. "Well . . . I presume from the people he was working for during the war. *The Nazis.*"

Something suddenly clicked in Ana's mind. She knew that Dr. Holzberg had been forced by the Nazis to work on scientific research projects during the war. But now something about *where* he'd worked suddenly made sense.

"Oh, and there's one more thing," Reynolds added.

"Hmm?"

"Remember I said there was a second mention of the book of Jasher in the Old Testament?"

"Uh-huh. It's in the book of Samuel, right?"

"Right. In the second book of Samuel." He quickly flipped through his Bible until he reached chapter one, verse eighteen. "Here, David is mourning the deaths of Saul and Jonathan. And the Bible says, *'He bade them teach the children of Judah the use of the bow: behold, it is written in the book of Jasher.'*"

"Okay . . ."

"Well, it turns out there is a tremendous dispute about what the word 'bow' means in this passage. The Hebrew word is Qaset, which can mean 'bow' like a weapon or 'bow' like bending. The context of this particular phrase is very odd, though. And that has led scholars to interpret it very differently over the years. Some have interpreted it to mean

the 'song of the bow,' since David is performing a lamentation, which would traditionally include poetry or songs.
Others have interpreted it to mean the 'use of the bow,' as in
the use of a bow and arrow."

"So which is it?"

"Well, in fact, the actual Hebrew text doesn't say 'song
of' or 'use of.' It literally says 'teach the children of Judah *the
bow*, which is written in the book of Jasher.'"

"Okay . . ."

"According to Franz Holzberg, 'the bow' was actually
the name of a technique—a military tactic, if you will—
that was described in the book of Jasher. So, in this passage
in second Samuel, what David is actually instructing the
Israelites to do is teach each subsequent generation the bow
technique, as described in the book of Jasher."

"And what technique would that be?"

Reynolds cleared his throat and removed his glasses.
"According to Franz, the bow was a technique for bending . . . *time*."

27

ROME, ITALY

THE HOUSE LIGHTS slowly dimmed in the Enrico Fermi Lecture Hall at the Sapienza University of Rome, and the audience broke into thunderous applause. The event's keynote speaker approached the lectern slowly, with the help of a cane. When he finally reached the lectern, he smiled and nodded appreciatively at the audience, waiting patiently for the applause to die down. Finally, the lecture hall fell silent, and a single bright spotlight now illuminated the man behind the podium, Dr. Benjamin Fulcher.

Fulcher was one of the most famous physicists in the world. He was best known for his theoretical work on quantum entanglement, for which he was awarded the Nobel Prize in Physics in 1975. He had completed most of that groundbreaking research while in residence at the Institute of Advanced Studies in Princeton from 1957 to 1973. After that, he held a tenured chair at Cambridge University for several years until leaving England altogether in the early 1980s to become the general director of the European Organization for Nuclear Research (CERN), a post he'd held until just about six months ago, when he abruptly left for unknown reasons.

"Friends and colleagues," said Dr. Fulcher in a crisp British accent and a voice that was nuanced and mellowed with age. "Thank you for giving me this great honor of addressing such a distinguished gathering of scholars and scientists. I am proud to call to order the forty-seventh annual meeting of the International Society of Theoretical Physicists and Chemists."

At that, the audience erupted in applause, which continued for nearly half a minute, until Fulcher finally signaled for it to subside.

"It is wonderful to be part of this important international symposium, where we will once again explore the outer reaches of physics, expand the boundaries of mankind's knowledge and understanding of the physical universe . . . and *dream*." He paused for effect after putting heavy emphasis on the word "dream." "Yes, my friends. *Dream*. For that is what we theoretical physicists and chemists do, is it not? We seek to understand the mysteries of the universe by first dreaming of how things *might* work . . . if only light had mass, or particles traveled in waves, or time and space were relative, or what have you. The dream, you see, is the spark that leads to the theory that leads to the model that, if you're lucky, leads to the truth. And while some of you may call this process theorizing or hypothesizing, I prefer to call it what it is . . . *dreaming*."

The audience was suddenly abuzz with quiet whispers. Fulcher waited patiently for this activity to run its course. And this was precisely why he had been chosen as this year's keynote speaker. Aside from being a Nobel laureate and the former director general of CERN, Benjamin Fulcher was also a consummate showman. Always a bit offbeat, always provocative, always entertaining, Fulcher had a reputation for elevating physics to the level of religion. He spoke like a televangelist and, for an hour or so, could make even the most introverted physicist feel like a god. And they loved him for it.

"Today, I would like to talk about gravity. A simple concept, I know. Especially for such an impressive gathering of scientific minds like yours." He shrugged impishly. "Just gravity. That humble, predictable phenomenon that mankind has known about since the first caveman dropped a rock on his foot. That elementary concept that our forefather Sir Isaac Newton pondered more than three centuries ago." Fulcher paused and shielded his eyes from the glare of the spotlight so he could observe the reaction of his audience. As he expected, they were hanging on his every word.

"Of course, we all know that gravity is anything but simple. Indeed, with the thousands of years of collective knowledge in this room, and with lifetimes of work by giants such as Newton, Einstein, and Holzberg, we *still* cannot answer the most fundamental question about gravity. Namely, what *is* it?"

As Fulcher expected, the crowed suddenly buzzed at this provocative statement. Many in the audience apparently believed that they *did* know the answer to that question. But Fulcher knew otherwise.

"Of course, we can measure gravity," he said, quieting the crowd down. "Yes, Newton deduced long ago that two objects in space will attract each other with a force proportional to their masses and inversely proportional to the distance between them. That was the *law*, so to speak . . . until Einstein taught us that it wasn't. Einstein taught us that matter, energy, space, and time are all interrelated. That matter warps the fabric of space-time, like a bowling ball resting on a soft mattress, which then causes other objects around it to move in curved paths instead of straight lines. This, as you know, is a central tenant of Einstein's theory of general relatively: that gravity is the result of a disruption in the continuum of space-time."

Fulcher noted that his audience was no longer murmuring and whispering. *He had them*.

"But of course general relativity has its faults, doesn't it?" Fulcher again blocked the spotlight with his hand and saw that many heads in the audience were nodding in agreement. "For one thing, it doesn't jibe well with quantum mechanics. Things that happen on a very small scale, such as inside an atom, don't seem to obey general relativity. And general relativity also doesn't cooperate very well with the standard model of the cosmos, which predicts that only *five percent* of the universe is actually made up of the type of matter contemplated by Einstein—that is, atoms and molecules and subatomic particles. The rest of the universe is apparently made of something else, some mysterious dark matter that finds no place in Newtonian physics, or, for that matter, in Einstein's model. So, for the past thirty years, we have struggled to harmonize Einstein's theory of general relativity with quantum mechanics and with what we can readily observe with our telescopes and modern instrumentation. The result has been . . . well, a stunning failure."

There were some rumblings in the audience following that provocative comment.

"Yes, we have string theory," Fulcher continued, raising his voice over the crowd noise. "Which models our universe as a four-dimensional membrane in an eleven-dimensional manifold."

More rumblings.

"We have Horava gravity, shifting gravity, supergravity, M-theory, and many, many variations on string theory. And yes, some of these theories do a good job of harmonizing general relativity and quantum theory, and I'm not here to discuss which of these theories does a better job than the others. After all, I wouldn't want to start a riot."

There was a smattering of laughter in the audience.

"My point is," continued Fulcher, "none of these theories explains *why* gravity occurs. And none is fully satisfactory as a comprehensive theory of gravity." He paused to let the audience absorb this point. "Ladies and gentlemen, gravity is still a mystery to us. The year is 2013. Man has walked on the moon. Our spacecraft have touched Mars and Jupiter and Venus. In the past decade alone, we've managed to wire nearly the entire human race into a cohesive neural network called the Internet. *Yet we still do not know what causes gravity.*" He paused for a moment and added with a grin, "I know you smart people don't like to hear that . . . but it's true."

There was some laughter in the audience. Others in the audience, however, were shifting in their seats, gesticulating emphatically as they exchanged quiet commentary with their neighbors. Fulcher watched this activity with a wry smile. He'd hit a nerve, and he knew it.

"Now," said Fulcher, once again taking control of the room. "Allow me to offer my own personal perspective on what gravity is." He paused and cleared his throat. "First, I think it's safe to say that gravity is a force. And, since it remains a mystery to this day, I think it's fair to call it a *mysterious* force."

A few chuckles could be heard in the audience.

"A mysterious force that pervades the universe, that imbues every particle in the cosmos with a common purpose. A common code of conduct, if you will. So that every physical thing in the universe, even things that suddenly spring into existence from another form—like gases and minerals in the stars or life here on earth—is automatically and indelibly tasked with the same common instruction: to *attract*. Well, I don't know about you . . . but that sounds to me like something an intelligent creator would do."

Suddenly, the audience erupted in a variety of ways, ranging from reverent whispers to open laughter to even a few angry and mocking comments shouted toward the stage. Benjamin Fulcher was well known in the physics community as a rare but vocal minority: *a deist*.

Fulcher raised his voice above the commotion. "To solve gravity . . . that is, to truly put it under the control of man, would be to stare directly into the face of God. And, ladies and gentlemen . . . *we are nearly there*." He paused for several seconds, and the crowd eventually quieted down. "Now, we are all familiar with entanglement theory. The idea that two particles that are born in the same quantum event are somehow *entangled* with each other such that, even if you separate them by a great distance, they can somehow share information instantaneously. As we've learned through decades of experimentation, particularly the recent work at CERN, this information appears to travel faster than the speed of light. For instance, if you measure the spin of one of these paired particles, the other paired particle will instantly change its spin in response . . . even if they are separated by many miles." Fulcher blocked the spotlight and saw many people in the room nodding along.

"Now, this has been proven over and over again in a variety of experiments. Yet it was something that utterly confounded Einstein. As you know, he called this phenomenon 'spooky action at a distance.' 'Spooky' because it didn't seem to obey his cardinal rule of relativity, which is that *nothing*—not even information itself—can travel faster than the speed of light. So, if we are to abide by this speed limit, then we must assume that quantum entanglement, like gravity, involves some sort of warping of space-time. In other words, the information that is being transmitted between these entangled particles only *appears* to be traveling faster than the speed of light. In reality, there is a time dilation—perhaps an imperceptibly thin tunnel between these two particles—where time runs faster than it does on the outside."

The audience was now very still and quiet.

"Now, you are probably wondering why I even brought up this issue of quantum entanglement when I'm supposed to be talking about gravity. Well, it's because I want you to imagine, if you will, that the Big Bang—the birth of our universe—was a single quantum event that caused every particle and packet of energy released in that event to become entangled. And I want you to imagine that this entanglement effect persisted indefinitely, even after the energy and matter from the Big Bang changed form and began creating gases and minerals, suns and moons, comets and planets, and everything we see around us." He swept his arm dramatically around the room. "Now I want you to imagine that gravity is simply a physical manifestation of this quantum entanglement. That is, every particle in the universe is attracted to every other particle because they were all born in the same quantum event and possess the same lingering effects of entanglement. *Now . . .*"

Fulcher had been on a roll, but suddenly he stopped talking. He let the silence grow as he looked back and forth across the audience, setting up his next sentence for maximum impact.

"Now," Fulcher continued, a bit more quietly. "I want you to imagine that there is a material that does *not* obey gravity. In other words, it floats in air." Fulcher used his hands to simulate the effect of an object floating above the podium.

There was some murmuring in the crowd.

"Well, if such a material *did* exist, and you forced it to become entangled with a secondary material, say nickel or iron . . . well, imagine the type of time dilation that would occur. And imagine how much energy would be released as each atom of the secondary material made the transition from the gravity state to the nongravity state." He stopped for a moment and scanned the audience from left to right. "Wouldn't that be something?"

Fulcher paused again, noting that the audience was oddly quiet. He shaded his eyes and searched their faces. For the most part, he saw only confusion and bewilderment.

They're not ready for this, he thought. *But they will be . . . soon.*

"Just some food for thought," Fulcher said, shrugging his shoulders. "Something for you to *dream* about." He finished his presentation by calling out and thanking some individual members of the society and providing an overview of the plenary sessions and subcommittee meetings that were to follow in the next two days. Then, in conclusion, he thanked the audience and bid them all good night. He stepped away from the podium to a modest round of applause.

As Fulcher made his way backstage, he was immediately met by Eduardo Bruni, president of the Italian chapter of the ISTPC, which was hosting this event.

"How'd I do?" Fulcher asked.

"Oh, that was quite . . . interesting," said Bruni.

Fulcher was just about to say something when his cell phone rang in the breast pocket of his blazer. "Excuse me," he said, hobbling away to a quiet corner. Once he was alone, he answered the phone. "Hello?"

"Doctor, it's me," said Vladamir Krupnov. "I've received

word from the team in Severodvinsk that the demonstration is ready to proceed."

"Excellent," said Fulcher.

"But unfortunately I need to stay here in the United States. There is still some . . . unfinished business."

Fulcher understood. *Malachi was still on the run.* "Don't worry, I can handle the demonstration," he said. "As long as someone can get me into the shipyard."

"Misha will escort you," said Krupnov. "And I'll arrange to be linked in by video." He paused for a moment. "You are confident this demonstration will work?"

"Absolutely."

"Then we will be one step closer to our goal."

"Indeed," said Fulcher. "All that is needed now is the material from Thurmond and Malachi's help with the map. Vlad, he is the key to our plan. We *must* find him."

"Don't worry," said Krupnov. "I know exactly where he's going, and we'll be waiting for him there. It's just a matter of time."

"Let's hope it's soon."

28

MIKE CALIFANO felt as if he'd been hit on the side of his head with a tire iron. The explosion in the lab had tossed him like a rag doll into a solid wall of jagged shale. He must have blacked out. As he gradually came to, he found himself lying prostrate on the ground, trying to figure out for the better part of a minute *who* he was, *where* he was, and what he was doing there. As he slowly worked through these questions, he gradually became aware of a strange dot of light in the distance. *What is that?* At length, he realized it was his flashlight, on the ground a few yards away.

With a great throbbing pain in his head, Califano rose slowly to his feet. He took stock of his physical condition. Other than the right side of his head, which hurt like hell, everything else seemed intact and reasonably functional. Nothing missing. Nothing broken. *But everything sore.* With considerable pain, he made his way over to where his flashlight lay and retrieved it from the ground. As he did, he noticed blood on his hand. He reached up and gently touched the right side of his forehead, which was wet. Then he looked down at his hand in the beam of the flashlight. Fresh blood . . . and lots of it.

Shit.

Ignoring the pain in his head and his aching muscles, Califano gradually made his way down the connecting shaft to the old Foster Number 2 mine, heading back the way he'd come in. This time, he did not need to perform the trial-and-error method to find his way out. He'd memorized the entire layout during his journey into the mine.

As the minutes ticked by, Califano's muscles gradually loosened up, and he was soon able to pick up the pace to something close to normal walking speed. *Ninth shaft. Turn right and then left. Eighth shaft. Turn left.* He was making good progress at this, and even starting to feel a little better, when he suddenly started thinking about the two men with gas masks and guns he'd seen on the way in. *Who were they? Were they responsible for the dead bodies in the lab? And the explosion?* Suddenly, he stopped walking.

Where are they now?

Instinctively, Califano placed his hand on his weapon, reassuring himself that it was still in its holster. He stood motionless for some time, listening carefully to the ambient noise in the mine. *Those men could still be down here,* he realized. *Lying in wait.* For nearly a minute, he listened intensely but heard only the rhythmic echoes of dripping water and his own heavy breathing. He was alone.

He continued on, much more cautiously now. *Fourth shaft. Turn left, then right. Third shaft. Left again, then right.* Eventually, he reached the long ingress shaft where he'd originally entered and walked straight along this shaft for about ten minutes. He could feel the incline gradually getting steeper. *He was getting close.* Finally, he saw light at the end of the tunnel. Except instead of daylight . . . it was *moonlight*.

Califano slowly approached the mine's entrance and puzzled over this fact. *Why was it nighttime?* He still had no answer to this question as he emerged cautiously from the mine entrance and enjoyed his first breath of crisp autumn air. The clean air felt good in his lungs and helped alleviate some of the throbbing pain in his head. *But something wasn't right.*

Without moving, Califano looked up and saw a crescent moon high overhead in a starry sky. *Strange.* Before him in the moonlight was the thick tangle of old wooden timbers that he'd originally crawled through to get into this mine. Beyond that, he could see only the dark outline of the mountain forest and little else. He remained in this position for some time, straining to detect any evidence of danger. But, once again, the only sounds he heard were those of nature.

He checked his watch: 1:45 P.M., which was exactly what he expected. He'd entered the mine around 11:00 A.M., and he couldn't have been down there longer than a couple of hours. *Right?* He pondered this question for a few seconds. *Was it possible he'd passed out for the entire afternoon?* He shook his head and eventually gave up trying to figure this out. Something was definitely awry.

Califano tapped the switch for his radio, and he heard it crackle slightly in his ear. "Ana?" he said quietly. "Bill?"

No response.

He let the radio time out and tried again. "Hey, guys, it's Mike. You there?"

Silence.

Califano looked around one last time and then slowly began climbing his way through the thicket of old wooden beams. With his sore muscles and painful head injury, this proved much more difficult than it had been the first time, and much more time consuming. When he finally emerged from beneath the last wooden beam that separated the mine entrance from the surrounding forest, he scanned the dark tree line before him and immediately realized something was wrong.

He heard a noise and reached for his gun. But it was too late.

"Don't move!" shouted a deep voice from somewhere in the woods. "Keep your hands where we can see them."

We?

Suddenly, the entire area was awash in blinding white light as two pole-mounted spotlights in the woods suddenly switched on with the loud click of an electromechanical breaker.

Califano was momentarily blinded. After all the time he'd spent in the dark mine, the bright light was like a knife to his brain, making his head hurt much worse than it had before. He squinted and shielded his eyes as best he could with his hands. Through the blinding light, he could just barely make out three or four figures. They appeared to be wearing military fatigues of some sort. And they were carrying machine guns. Califano squinted harder and could now tell they were aiming their machines guns . . . *at him.*

Someone was now approaching from behind the spotlights. Califano could hear the crunching of feet on the dry leaves, and he watched in disbelief as the person's face gradually came out of the blinding light and into focus. It was a large man in camouflage fatigues and combat boots. No insignia. No name tag. And he looked serious.

"Who the fuck are you?" Califano demanded.

The man said nothing and proceeded to frisk Califano thoroughly, shoulders to feet, front and back. Within seconds, he had removed Califano's Glock from its holster, dropped the clip out, and ejected the chambered round. Obviously, this man knew what he was doing.

"Mr. Califano," said the man in a deadly serious tone. "Please come with me."

29

ANA THORNE cursed and pushed redial on her secure satellite phone. The CIA was still working out the bugs in its dedicated worldwide phone network, which had been put in place after the embarrassing "outing" in Lebanon of several of its agents, whose commercial cell phones had been hacked. Of course, the fact that Thorne was now traveling at 480 knots at an altitude of 20,000 feet didn't help, either. She pressed the phone to her ear and waited for Bill McCreary to pick up again.

"Yeah?" said McCreary after the first ring.

"Bill, it's me again. The call dropped off. What were you saying about the names I gave you?" An hour earlier, she'd asked McCreary to research the people Reynolds had identified as Dr. Holzberg's "acolytes" at Princeton in the late 1950s.

"As I was saying," said McCreary, "Gary Freer worked for Bell Labs for thirty years and then Xerox. Retired in 1998. Died of colon cancer in 2005. He's survived by his wife and two daughters, and seven grandchildren. I couldn't find anything out of the ordinary about him. Irwin Michelson disappeared in 1959, just about the same time as Holzberg. Official report was a small plane crash near Portland, Oregon. But I suspect he was involved in Winter Solstice. I bet he was down in the Thurmond lab with Holzberg."

"Makes sense. What about the woman, Opal?"

"Yeah, I wanted to ask you about her. Are you sure you got that name right? I couldn't find anything about an 'Opal' that matches the information you gave me. No record of anyone with that name ever being at Princeton or in any way associated with the Institute of Advanced Studies. Is it possible you got the name wrong?"

"I don't think so," said Ana. "I wrote it down and double-checked the spelling with Reynolds. I'm almost positive that's the name he gave me. Did you come up with *any* women at Princeton in the late 1950s who might have been part of Dr. Holzberg's inner circle?"

"Nope."

"That's odd." Ana's voice trailed off as a new thought suddenly occurred to her. "Opie," she said.

"Hmm?"

"One of the names Dr. Holzberg muttered before he died was Opie, wasn't it?"

"Yeah, I think so."

"Could be a nickname for Opal, right?"

"Could be. But I still didn't come up with any women matching the description you gave me."

"That's weird," said Ana quietly. *Opal the mystery woman.* "Hey, can you check one more name for me?"

"Sure, who?"

"Benjamin Fulcher."

"You mean Nobel Prize–winning, famous physicist Benjamin Fulcher? You want me to check him out?"

"Yeah, I do. Thanks."

Ana hung up the phone and reclined in her seat, pondering the day's events. *Something just didn't add up.*

30

LANGLEY, VIRGINIA

"WELL, LOOK who it is," said Bill McCreary. He spoke these words to Mike Califano, who had just emerged from a black Apache helicopter at the rear of the CIA headquarters building. The two men quickly cleared the rotor zone and made their way to the headquarters building, where they stopped just short of the entrance.

Califano was still badly shaken up. His face and shirt collar were covered with blood, and his hands and clothes were filthy. He had a jagged, two-inch laceration and large scrapes on the right side of his forehead, which were thoroughly caked with blood and dirt. A green thermal blanket was draped around his arms and shoulders.

"What the hell?" said Califano. "You sent a bunch of SEALs to grab me in the woods? I thought they were going to kill me!"

"Sorry, Mike. We couldn't take any chances."

"Bullshit! You could've just called me on the radio if you wanted me to come in."

McCreary held out his open palms. "Mike, you've been missing for *three days*."

Califano's face suddenly twisted into an expression of confusion. "*What?*"

"Yeah. It's Monday night right now. You went down into the mine on *Saturday morning*. We weren't sure if you were ever coming out of there, or what condition you'd be in if you did. I had those guys camped out in front of the entrance just to make sure you got back here safely. And they *had* to disarm you because . . . well, to be honest, we didn't know what kind of physiological or psychological effects there might be. And by the way, those weren't SEALs. Although some of them used to be."

Califano still looked utterly confused. "But I . . . I was only down there for a couple of hours." He extended his left arm. "Look at my watch."

"I know," said McCreary. His tone was calm and soothing, almost patronizing. "I'll explain it all when you get to the workroom. But first we need to get you looked at. Medics should be here any—"

Califano cut him off. "I saw the lab."

"You what?"

"I saw it. I went in. And then someone blew it up. Almost blew me up with it."

Now it was McCreary's turn to look confused. "You mean just now? Just when you were down there?"

"Yeah, man. Just now. I was down there, and I saw a bunch of stuff. There was some sort of swimming pool–type test rig, and Atomichron clocks, and instrument panels. Then all of a sudden I heard a beep and noticed there were explosives all over the fucking place. I ran like hell and barely got out of there before it blew."

"Shit," McCreary whispered. His eyebrows were scrunched together in an expression of confusion.

"Oh, and there were bodies. I counted at least five, including one in the cooling pool. They looked like they'd been shot *recently*. And there were two men leaving the mine just as I was going in. They were wearing gas masks and carrying guns." Califano paused and took a deep breath. "Seriously, Doc, something really strange is going on down there."

McCreary was just about to say something when his phone rang. He answered it quietly, listened for a few seconds, then turned back to Califano. "Med staff's on their way." Moments later, an ambulance pulled up to the circular driveway behind the building, and two paramedics jumped out.

Califano waved them off. "I'm fine," he yelled to them.

"Michael, you have to go with them. They need to look at your head."

"No offense, Doc, but I really don't want any CIA people examining my head, okay?"

"Come on, you know what I mean." McCreary pointed to his bloody right temple. "Your *cut*. It needs stitches."

Califano lowered his voice to nearly a whisper. "Just tell me this. Am I gonna end up strapped to a bed like Holzberg? Drugged up and crazy?" He held McCreary's gaze for a moment. "Well . . . *am I*?"

"No," said McCreary reassuringly. "Of course not. They're going to stitch you up, run some basic tests. Blood work, that sort of thing. And you'll be back with us in a couple of hours. Look, we've got a lot of stuff to cover, so we don't want you out of commission any longer than necessary. All right?"

Califano accepted this assurance and felt a little better. "Yeah, I guess."

"Good. Now go get yourself fixed up. You look like shit."

Califano managed a smile. Then he turned and made his way over to the ambulance.

. . . .

It was nearly 11:00 P.M. when Califano finally returned to the workroom in building 1. Ana Thorne, who had just gotten back from Florida, was still in the process of updating Dr. McCreary and Admiral Armstrong about what she'd learned.

"I'm back," Califano announced, entering the room with Steve Goodwin.

McCreary, Thorne, and Admiral Armstrong all rose to their feet to greet him.

Califano looked much better now than he had a few hours ago. He had showered and was now wearing a set of clean gray sweats, courtesy of the folks in the medical unit. He also had twelve stitches on the right side of his head, neatly dressed with a small, square bandage.

Ana was the first to speak. "Michael," she said in a tone that was somewhere between *Glad to see you* and *I can't believe you're still alive.* She walked over to him and gave him a quick hug.

A hug from Ana Thorne? Califano marveled over this and quickly reciprocated, making the embrace last just a little longer than intended.

"Michael," said Admiral Armstrong, putting his hand on Califano's shoulder. "Looks like you got yourself pretty banged up there."

"Yeah, just a bit."

Armstrong's grip tightened on Califano's shoulder, and his tone suddenly sharpened. "And just what the *hell* were you thinking going down into that mine all alone? Completely unprepared. And without one iota of authority?"

"Yeah," Califano mumbled. "Not my brightest idea, I'll admit."

Armstrong shook his head and let out an exasperated breath. "And yet, amazingly, not your stupidest either. Not by a long shot."

Finally, McCreary spoke. "Michael, we're all glad you're back." He motioned toward an empty chair. "Come have a seat and I'll catch you up with where we are. Then I want to hear all about your adventure in the lab."

They all took seats around a small conference table in the back of the room, except for McCreary, who remained standing. "Michael," he said. "What I'm about to tell you is highly classified."

"Isn't *all* of this stuff?"

"Yes, but this gets into a whole different channel. I wasn't authorized to tell you this before—"

"Whoa, whoa, whoa," said Califano, stiffening in his chair. "You weren't *authorized*?" An incredulous look spread over his face as he digested this comment. "Dude, I almost *died* down there. What, exactly, were you holding back?"

"Calm down, Michael," said Admiral Armstrong. "He's getting to it."

"Look," said McCreary sternly. "You weren't even supposed to go down there, okay? *You* violated protocol, not me. So don't start casting stones."

"Okay, we get it," said Armstrong, trying to keep the peace. "We're all on the same team here."

Califano exhaled and nodded. *Shit. They were right.* He'd crossed way over the line by going down into that mine. And he had no one to blame but himself for his injuries. "Sorry," he mumbled. "Guess I'm still a little worked up."

"It's okay," said McCreary. "You've been through a lot." He paused for several seconds to collect his thoughts. "Okay, let me first explain about the time."

For the next twenty minutes, Dr. McCreary explained in great detail about the "time dilation" technology at the heart of the Winter Solstice program. He explained that time dilation is a phenomenon whereby two different observers in two frames of reference experience time differently. He explained the classic example of the "twins paradox." One identical twin stays on earth while the other travels through space at nearly the speed of light. When the traveling twin returns, he is chronologically much younger than his sibling, because of time dilation. That is, because time ticked by much more slowly for the traveler than it did for his brother back on earth. Finally, he explained that all of this was precisely as predicted by Einstein's theory of relativity.

"And it's been proven?" asked Califano.

"Absolutely," said McCreary. "A very simple example is the clocks on our GPS satellites. They have to be adjusted by about thirty-five microseconds per day to account for the effects of time dilation. There are actually two different opposing effects at play there. Time runs a bit slower on board the satellites due to their high speed relative to the earth's surface, and it runs a bit faster because of the difference in gravity between where the satellites are and where we are. Those two effects offset each other so that, overall, the clocks run a tiny bit slower on board the satellites than they do here on earth. And this has all been proven in countless experiments."

"I knew about the speed thing," said Califano. "But I didn't know that gravity also causes time dilation."

"According to Einstein, it does. What Einstein's theory of general relativity says is that time and space are flexible. They can be stretched. And what stretches them are objects with mass. So if you take a massive planet like earth and you plop it onto the so-called space-time continuum, it will distort that continuum and cause other objects to be attracted to the depression in the continuum, just like water circling a drain. According to Einstein, *that* is the real explanation for gravity. It's a phenomenon we observe because of the disruption of space-time. The farther you get from a massive object, the less distortion of time and space you are subjected to, and, therefore, the less gravity you feel. In simplistic terms, gravity slows time down by distorting it. And as you escape a gravitational field, time speeds up."

"Can you *feel* it slowing down and speeding up?" asked Ana.

"No. Each person in each frame of reference experiences time perfectly normally. So a second always feels like a second and a minute always feels like a minute, no matter where you are. It's only when you *compare* two things in two different frames of reference, like a clock on a GPS satellite versus a clock on the ground, that you notice the effects of time dilation."

"And is that what happened to me?" Califano asked.

"Yes," said McCreary, nodding. "And you were *very* lucky. Apparently, what you experienced were just the lingering aftereffects of a previous time-dilation event. If you'd been exposed to the full thing, we wouldn't be seeing you for a long, long time."

Califano furrowed his brow. "I don't understand. You mean the event that happened way back in 1959?"

McCreary walked over to a nearby whiteboard and uncapped a dry-erase marker. "Here, let me show you what I think happened." He quickly drew a bell curve on the whiteboard and labeled it as follows:

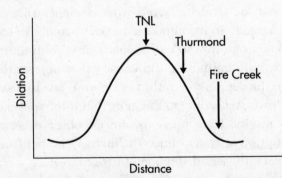

"On October 5, 1959, the researchers at Thurmond National Laboratory inadvertently triggered a massive time-dilation event," said McCreary. "Time inside the lab slowed way down compared to time outside the lab. How much did it slow down? We can't know for sure. For instance, if the actual event lasted only ten seconds in the lab, and we know that fifty-four years have elapsed since 1959, then the ratio would be something like 170 million to 1. If the event lasted an hour, then that ratio is more like 470,000 to 1. But whatever the ratio, time was *crawling* inside the lab, compared to outside, okay?"

Everyone at the table nodded. Indeed, this was the only logical explanation for Dr. Holzberg's sudden appearance in Fire Creek after going missing in the lab fifty-four years earlier.

"Based on what we know about time disruption in Thurmond and Fire Creek, it appears that the effects of this time-dilation event varied inversely with the distance from the lab, as I've shown here." He pointed to the bell curve on the whiteboard. "Thurmond was only a mile from the lab, and it experienced a dramatic disruption of time. So much so that the entire town was quarantined and then evacuated."

"Yeah, the lady at the diner told me about that," said Califano. "She also said the people who were relocated had all sorts of health issues, like loss of memory."

McCreary nodded. "It appears this time-dilation phenomenon can have severe effects on the human body, including some manifestations of rapid aging." He pointed again to his bell curve. "Now, Fire Creek here is about ten miles from the lab, and I understand the time disruption effects were much less severe there."

"Three minutes a day," said Califano. "That's what Thelma Scott said. Every clock in town has been running three minutes slow since 1959."

"Incredible," Ana remarked, shaking her head. "How could that *not* have been reported in the news?"

Califano laughed. "If you saw Fire Creek, you'd know. It's like the town that time forgot. *Literally.*"

Admiral Armstrong interjected. "Bill, why couldn't they have rescued those people down in the lab in 1959?"

"They probably tried," said McCreary. "But rescuing someone from a time-dilation event like this would be very difficult. Think about it. You send the elevator down, but the closer it gets to the lab, the slower time runs. So it could take *years*, in outside time, just to get an elevator down to the lab. And then it would take years to get it back up."

There was silence around the table as everyone tried to wrap their minds around that concept.

"Look, we don't know what rescue efforts were undertaken, if any," said McCreary. "What we *do* know is that by November 1959, the decision was made to seal off the lab entirely, with everyone still trapped inside. My guess is they wanted to prevent anyone or anything from going in . . . or *out*. So they sealed the elevator shaft with concrete and created a fenced-in exclusion zone with a three-mile radius around the lab. They used the specter of radiation to keep people away, which was a pretty effective ploy. In truth, there probably never was any radiation associated with this event. In fact, what I saw up in Thurmond was a controlled gamma source in the elevator shaft that was probably placed there when the lab was decommissioned. This would have given the *appearance* that radiation was streaming from inside the lab. But I think we now have living proof that it isn't." He gestured toward Mike Califano.

Now Califano spoke up. "So how come Dr. Holzberg was trapped down there for, like, fifty years, but I only lost a few days?"

"Ah," said McCreary. He quickly drew another curve on the whiteboard, and labeled it as follows:

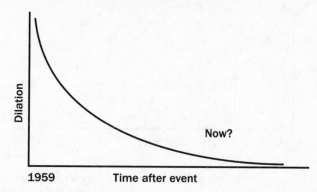

"I'm guessing that the effects of time dilation decay something like this. Back in 1959, when this event first occurred, the time dilation was tremendous. For all we know, it might have taken them *decades* in our time just to get through the first few seconds of the event down there. But, as time moves on, the dilation becomes less and less. Until eventually, it returns to normal. So let's see . . ." McCreary scrawled some numbers on the whiteboard. "You say you experienced an elapsed time of about two and a half hours, or a hundred and fifty minutes. Elapsed time outside the lab was two and a half days, or about three thousand six hundred minutes. That means you experienced a time-dilation ratio of about twenty-four to one. As I said, you're damn lucky it wasn't twenty-four *thousand* to one, or you'd still be down there."

"What about our carjacker?" Ana asked. "He's been spending fifty-dollar bills that weren't even printed until 1970 and '71. Assuming he came from the lab, how do you explain that?"

"Easy," said McCreary. He quickly added some features to his second graph, so it looked like this:

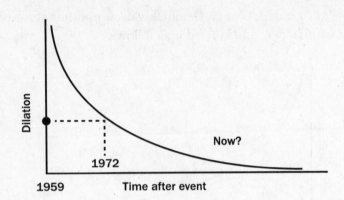

"Let's assume that guy entered the lab in 1972. In that case, he would have been exposed to time-dilation effects that were much less severe than what were experienced by Dr. Holzberg and the original crew. Perhaps the time-dilation ratio would have been cut in half by then, or even by two-thirds."

There were baffled looks all around the table.

"Think about it this way," said McCreary. "Put yourself in the shoes of Dr. Holzberg. It's October 5, 1959, and a strange event has just occurred in the lab. Perhaps this event lasted for just a few seconds. But, unbeknownst to you, during that short span of time, *ten years* have gone by outside the lab. You go out and check the elevator shaft, and you discover, to your horror, that it's been sealed with concrete. You're trapped. A few more seconds tick by and suddenly someone arrives in the lab who says they're from 1972. You wonder: *How can it be 1972 already? It was 1959 just a minute ago.* And then you wonder: *How did this person even get down here with the elevator shaft sealed?* And this guy says: 'I know an escape route. A secret passage.'"

"Actually, it's a cross-ventilation shaft to Foster Number Two," said Califano.

"Fine, a ventilation shaft," said McCreary. He pointed to his graph. "By now, it's already 1995 or 2000 outside the lab. But to *you*, Dr. Holzberg, it still feels like 1959. And to your new acquaintance, the carjacker, it still feels like 1972." McCreary suddenly turned to Califano. "Mike, how long did it take to get out of the lab through that shaft?"

Califano shrugged. "I dunno. Maybe five minutes."

"Okay," said McCreary. "So it takes five more minutes to get through this ventilation shaft and into the adjacent mine. Meanwhile, another ten or twelve years has gone by outside. You finally make it out, and it's 2013. So you, Dr. Holzberg, have lost fifty-four years, and your rescuer, our carjacker, has lost forty-one years. But you both come out of the lab at nearly the same time."

Everyone was quiet for a while until Califano spoke up. "A couple of problems with your time line, Doc."

"Hmm?"

"Well, first of all, who shot Dr. Holzberg in the gut? Was it the carjacker, or was it someone else? Second, who killed all those people in the lab? Like I told you, I saw at least five bodies down there. And I know gunshot wounds when I see them. And third—and this is a big one—who set those explosives that blew up the lab? Remember, I saw two people heading *out* through Foster Number Two when I was coming in. They were wearing gas masks, and they were armed. My guess is, they're the culprits. So where are they on your time line?"

"All good points," said McCreary. "And here's the answer. Those people you saw could have entered the lab at *any* time. They could have entered the lab in 1975, or 1980, or 1985, or really *any* time. But from the perspective of Dr. Holzberg and the others inside the lab, it still would have seemed like those men with guns came in just a short time after the original event. Everything would have happened in the blink of an eye. Perhaps Dr. Holzberg was caught in the crossfire and managed to escape, while the rest of the lab crew was killed. We just don't know."

"Jesus," said Admiral Armstrong. "I don't know about you people, but my head is starting to hurt. Just tell me this, Bill. What do we do now?"

"For starters," McCreary said. "We need to find that Thurmond material ASAP. We can't risk it falling into the wrong hands. As you can see, this is a very powerful technology. The effects of a larger-scale dilation event could be catastrophic. Not to mention that whoever controls this technology will have a tremendous technological edge over the United States. If the Russians are involved, as we suspect they are, then that's even more of a concern."

Ana rose to her feet. "To find this material, we need to find that carjacker. I'm convinced he's the key to all of this."

"And where are we going to find him?" Califano asked.

Ana arched her eyebrows and nodded toward the computer that Califano had been using three days earlier to run his data-mining program. "Isn't that your job?"

31

THE RUSSIAN icebreaker *Burnyi* slowly made its way through the snow-covered ice that blanketed this region of the White Sea eight months out of the year. The ice was relatively thin for late October—only about six inches in most places—due to the unusually mild weather this year in the Arctic. But this was still a challenge for the *Burnyi*, a timeworn, diesel-powered icebreaker out of Severodvinsk. Especially with the heavy barge it was towing.

Seventy miles due south, just at the edge of the winter ice sheet, the sleek, white *Belyi Prizrak* glided gracefully through the frigid blue water of the White Sea. On board, a group of powerful men were assembled in the yacht's plush media room. Seated among four rows of red theater-style chairs were five high-ranking officials of the Russian government, including the first deputy prime minister and three Russian generals in full uniform; two representatives of the Chinese Defense Ministry; and one representative from the Atomic Energy Organization of Iran. In the back row were four older men who simply described themselves as *posrednikov* or "facilitators." These were powerful—and dangerous—men with connections in both high and low places. They were the type of men who put the word "crony" in "crony capitalism," which was what passed for free enterprise these days in Russia. In the front row, seated by himself with his legs crossed and a stoic expression on his face, was Nobel Prize laureate Dr. Benjamin Fulcher.

Vladamir Krupnov, president and cofounder of Krupnov Energy, suddenly appeared on the room's large plasma television screen. "Gentlemen," he said with a dramatic flourish. "Welcome aboard the *Belyi Prizrak*. I apologize that I could not be here in person for this historic event. But if all goes as planned today, you will soon be witnessing the greatest technological accomplishment in Russia since the launch of *Sputnik*. Because of your tremendous support and patience, and your continued financial generosity, we are now in a position to announce that Krupnov Energy will be the first and *only* company in the world with the capability to harness mankind's greatest untapped energy source . . . *gravity*."

The small crowd did not stir at all. The dignitaries and other men assembled in the media room had all heard this promise many times before. What they wanted to see today were *results*.

"This is just a demonstration, of course," continued Krupnov. "But I think you will soon see that your investments in Krupnov Energy have been well placed." Krupnov gestured toward Dr. Fulcher. "So without further ado, may I introduce Dr. Benjamin Fulcher."

Fulcher rose slowly with the help of his cane and turned toward the small audience. "Lights, please," he said. The lights slowly dimmed in the media room and a video began playing on the screen behind him. "It all begins with a small seed," he said. As he spoke, a small glass vial appeared on the screen with a tiny black shard floating lazily inside it. The camera zoomed in slowly until the floating object took up most of the screen.

There was a collective murmur in the room as the seated dignitaries began exchanging emphatic whispers.

"This," continued Fulcher, "is one of the rarest substances on earth . . . perhaps in the entire universe. We are tremendously lucky to have this small bit in our possession. And I assure you, there is more on the way. This tiny seed material is what makes all of this technology possible."

"How does it float like that?" asked the Russian first deputy prime minister.

Fulcher collected his thoughts for a moment before answering. "Let's just say, for the sake of argument, that the force of gravity we experience all around us emanated from a single event known as the Big Bang."

The first deputy prime minister shrugged and nodded his head.

"So all matter is attracted to all other matter because, in the beginning, it existed as just a single pinpoint of incredibly dense matter and energy, and it wants to return to that state. Let's just accept that assumption as true."

The first deputy prime minister nodded again.

"If that *is* true, then the material you see here on the screen somehow escaped the Big Bang. In other words, this material came to us from somewhere else, somewhere that was not involved in the Big Bang. And, as a result, this material is not imbued with the property that we call 'gravity.'"

"But . . . where could this material have come from if not from the Big Bang?" asked the Iranian official.

Fulcher shrugged. "Another universe, perhaps. Or another dimension. Both possibilities are supported by modern string theory. Or, if you like, you could just say it came from God."

There were a few chuckles among the group. Fulcher, however, did not laugh or give any sign that he was joking. *Because he wasn't.*

"The question of where it came from is not terribly important," said Fulcher. "What *is* important is that, under the right conditions, this seed material has the ability to influence other material." Fulcher looked around the room to make sure this notion had sunk in. "This seed material," he explained slowly, "can make ordinary material give up its gravitational force. And *that*, gentlemen, is what allows our reactor to convert gravity . . . into energy."

"Can you explain how the gravity reactor works?" asked one of the Chinese officials.

Fulcher clicked a button, and the screen behind him suddenly transitioned to a slick animation of nuclear fission. "I can explain it best by comparing it to a conventional fission reactor. As you know, a fission reactor converts mass into energy. It does this by breaking an unstable uranium atom into fragments and using the released energy to heat water, which then runs turbines to generate electricity. But where does the energy come from? Well, if you were to weigh all the fragments that are left over after the uranium atom is broken up during fission and compare it to the original, intact atom, you would find there is a very tiny difference in mass. This is called the mass deficit, and this is where the energy actually comes from. The missing mass has been transformed directly into energy according to the formula E equals mc squared." Fulcher paused for a moment and looked all around the small audience. "Of course, this was considered impossible a hundred years ago. Now it powers ships and submarines and entire cities. Next slide, please."

The screen changed to a simplified animation of Fulcher's gravity reactor.

"Our reactor is based on a similar principle. But instead of converting *mass* into energy, it converts *gravity* into energy. As I explained earlier, we start with a special seed material, which has the capability of influencing a secondary material, causing it to release its gravitational force. This results in a 'gravitational deficit,' and energy is simultaneously released according to the formula E equals mc squared, where *m* is the mass of the material that has transitioned to the nongravitational state."

"And what is the secondary material that you use?" asked one of the Russian generals.

"For today's demonstration, we will be using nickel. But virtually any dense mineral will work, such as iron or copper, or zinc, or even alloys such as steel. In time, we will be able to harvest the spent secondary material from the reactor. And I'm sure you gentlemen can imagine the many uses it will have."

"It will float?" asked the first deputy prime minister. "Just like the object we saw earlier?"

Fulcher nodded. "Yes, it will."

"What about radiation?" asked the Iranian scientist.

"There is no release of radiation from our reactor because the atoms are not being broken apart, as they are with fission. Therefore, when we harvest the spent secondary material, it will not be radioactive." Fulcher paused. "There is, however, one important side effect. Which is why we are conducting this demonstration out here in the open ocean."

"You mean time dilation," said the Iranian.

Fulcher nodded. "Yes. It is most problematic during reactor start-up, and it diminishes over time. We believe that, once we have enough material to create a self-sustaining reaction, the time-dilation effect will reach a steady-state condition that can be easily managed. Perhaps it will be a factor of just slightly less than one. In other words, time will run just a bit slower in the vicinity of the reactor, but this should not affect operations or present any sort of health hazard. As a precaution, however, we are designing our first reactors to be placed out at sea. Long transmission lines will carry electrical power to the grid."

Krupnov's face suddenly appeared on the screen again. "Gentlemen, it is not necessary to get bogged down in these details right now. Our technology will provide clean energy from a natural resource that, while it may not be renewable, is certainly abundant." He swept his arms dramatically around the room he was sitting in, which happened to be the library of the Hillcrest mansion in Middleburg, Virginia. "We are talking about converting *gravity* into energy. As a side benefit, we will be harvesting gravity-free material from these reactors. The quantity will be quite small at first, but, as it accumulates, just *imagine* the possibilities. And, unlike with conventional nuclear power, we will no longer have to worry about radiation." He paused and watched the Russian generals and the Chinese officials nodding enthusiastically. "The only price we must pay is the inconvenience of a few isolated 'time pockets.' Easily manageable, as Dr. Fulcher explained. And totally harmless."

Dr. Fulcher checked his watch and interrupted. "Gentlemen, I believe our demonstration is nearly ready. Please sit back and watch the screen. We have remote cameras on board the reactor barge, and thanks to the Russian navy we have two helicopters in the vicinity that will provide aerial shots. Ah, here we are."

As Fulcher spoke, the plasma screen switched to a four-way split screen, showing two live shots of the reactor vessel and two overhead shots of the mobile power station, floating by itself in the frozen White Sea.

"The demonstration will begin in approximately five minutes," said Fulcher. "Gentlemen . . . prepare to witness history."

32

PETTY OFFICER First Class Carlos Mendez poured himself another cup of coffee, the third one for the day. *So much for cutting down*, he thought. It was 4:20 P.M., and he was the only person awake in the small monitoring station that the U.S. Navy maintained on Bjømøya (Bear) Island, a sparsely populated Norwegian island in the Barents Sea. His supervisor, Senior Chief Petty Officer Lionel Brown, was asleep in an adjacent room. In another hour and forty minutes, he'd wake up the chief, and they'd switch places. Until then, he'd need at least one more cup of coffee to stay awake.

The Bear Island facility was one of the few remaining manned SOSUS outposts maintained by the U.S. Navy. For more than four decades, Bear Island had acted as an early warning station in the European Arctic region, notifying the U.S. military whenever Russian submarines came in and out of the White Sea. Mendez presumed this was a much more exciting job during the Cold War, when Soviet submarine activity was a frequent and menacing threat. Today, the Bear Island assignment was really just a twelve-month exercise in boredom and solitude.

But that was about to change.

Mendez twisted a rotary switch to channel 1 and inspected the low-frequency array, or LOFAR, display that appeared on the large screen on his control panel. He studied the grayish display for several seconds and then made a notation in his log indicating "NOI" or nothing of interest. Then he clicked the rotary switch to the next transducer in the four-hundred-mile underwater SOSUS array that stretched from the Svalbard Islands near the Arctic Circle to Tromsø at the northern tip of the Norwegian mainland. This process continued for several minutes.

As the LOFAR display for the fourteenth transducer in the array began cascading down his screen, Mendez immediately realized something was seriously wrong. Instead of a light gray color with a few random splotches of dark gray, the entire screen was filling with dark gray, with large splotches of black. *What the hell?*

Mendez knew this could not possibly be correct. An acoustic contact such as a surface ship or submarine would create thin vertical stripes of black or dark gray on the display, corresponding to discrete "tonals," or sustained frequencies, caused by rotating equipment. But here, the *entire screen* was lighting up with what appeared to be low-frequency acoustic energy. If this display was accurate, that would mean some sort of massive event was occurring in the White Sea that was somehow producing a wide swath of intense, low-frequency energy. Mendez's first thought was that it was an undersea earthquake.

He quickly rolled his chair to the far side of the room, where a seismograph was dutifully recording every terrestrial bump and tremor taking place in the Arctic region. He scanned the graph and shook his head. It was flat. *So much for the earthquake theory.*

Mendez slid back to his console and switched to the next transducer in the SOSUS array, which was located twenty miles south of the previous one he'd checked. The result was the same. As before, the screen began filling in with dark gray and splotches of black. "Jesus," he whispered. *I need to wake up the chief.*

Before he could get to his feet, Mendez heard the distinct beeping of an urgent "FLASH" message. He swiveled at his console and read the incoming message on his computer screen. It was an automated error message from USNO, the U.S. Naval Observatory in Washington, D.C.

Like GPS satellites in space, the underwater SOSUS array had to be frequently synchronized with an ultra-precise time signal generated by an array of forty-four atomic clocks, known collectively as the "master clock." These clocks were located at the U.S. Naval Observatory at Thirty-fourth Street and Massachusetts Avenue in northwest Washington, D.C., also the home of the vice president of the United States. The forty-four atomic clocks were strategically distributed among twenty shock-resistant and environmentally controlled "clock vaults" at the secure facility to ensure continuity in the event of a natural or man-made disaster.

Mendez studied the message, which consisted of a single line of alphanumeric symbols:

NSS4 ER02 10120913.15.220011Z CD –2.913553E6

What the hell? Mendez could not believe what he was seeing. "Yo, Chief!" he yelled in the direction of the bunk room.

Thirty seconds later, a groggy Senior Chief Brown came

stumbling out of the bunk room, rubbing his eyes. "What's going on?"

Mendez pointed at the display screen on his console, which was still dark gray with splotches of black.

"Whoa," said Brown.

As they both watched, the top of the display suddenly began transitioning back to a normal, light gray color. This color quickly cascaded down the screen until the display was back to normal thirty seconds later.

"What the hell was that?" asked Brown.

"I don't know. All the arrays went dark gray like that about two minutes ago. Something big must have happened."

"Earthquake?"

Mendez shook his head. "Seismo's flat. And check *this* out." He pointed to the automated FLASH error message on the screen, which had been generated a minute before by USNO.

Senior Chief Brown leaned down and carefully studied the message. "Holy shit," he said when he reached the part of the message that read "CD –2.913553E6." "That's almost . . . *thirty seconds*," he said.

"Yeah. But is that really possible?" asked Mendez. "I mean, is there any way our clocks suddenly slowed down thirty seconds compared to the master clock?"

"I don't think so," said Brown. "Get the USNO watch officer on the phone right away."

33

"DON'T YOU ever sleep?" asked Ana Thorne as she entered the DTAI workroom at 5:15 A.M.

"It's overrated," deadpanned Califano without looking up from his computer. His fingers were typing furiously on the keyboard.

"Anything interesting?"

Califano finished typing and finally gave in to the urge to check out Ana in her yoga pants. "Yeah, I found a few things."

"Like what?"

Califano swiveled back toward his screen and cracked his knuckles. Ana walked up close behind him and leaned over his shoulder. "First of all," said Califano, "we got the DNA analysis back from that carjacking incident in Maryland."

"The one at the cabin near the Savage River?"

"Uh-huh, about twenty-five miles south of Frostburg. The FBI found cigarette butts in the cabin next door. Doc

McCreary asked them to run an expedited DNA analysis on the saliva residue and compare it to that hair you found on the bathroom floor in Frostburg."

"And . . . ?"

Califano clicked his mouse, and a detailed forensic DNA report immediately appeared on the screen, including a chart of twenty-two genetic markers and comparative scores for two samples labeled SPECIMEN 1 and SPECIMEN 2.

"Uh, help me out here," said Ana.

Califano pointed to the conclusion at the very bottom of the report, which said: "Likelihood of match: 99.99%."

"So that's our guy then. Wait. It *is* a guy's DNA, right?"

Califano nodded and pointed to the AMEL genetic marker in the middle of the chart, indicating "XY" for both specimens. "Yep, it's a guy."

"And we've got an APB out for his vehicle?"

"Uh-huh. A 2012 forest-green Range Rover Sport with Maryland tags YRT 886. We've got every local, state, and federal law enforcement agency in the area looking for it right now. And there's something else, too."

"Hmm?"

"Remember I told you I found a cigarette butt near the mine entrance in Thurmond? Well, I had Steve run it over to the FBI last night, and they did the same DNA analysis on it as they did on the cigarettes from the cabin."

"They matched?"

Califano nodded. "Ninety-nine percent. So whoever this dude is, he definitely came out of that mine."

"I figured as much."

Just then, Admiral Armstrong barged into the room without even a perfunctory knock. He had his cell phone pressed to his ear, and he appeared to be in the middle of an intense conversation. "Yes, sir," he said subserviently. "Yes, sir. We're on it." He paused for a moment and appeared to be getting an earful from the other end. "I understand, Mr. President. Yes, sir."

Admiral Armstrong terminated his call and immediately turned to Thorne and Califano. "We've got problems."

"What's going on?" Califano asked.

Armstrong pointed to Califano's computer. "Get me into NSASI and I'll show you."

Califano quickly manipulated his mouse and tapped on his keyboard until an NSA dialogue box suddenly appeared on the screen. He paused for a moment and then typed in a very long password, all from memory. A moment later, a window appeared on the screen that was prominently marked across the top with the words RESTRICTED NSASI DATA. AUTHORIZED PERSONNEL ONLY.

Ana immediately recognized NSASI as the acronym for National Security Agency Satellite Intelligence. "Um, I don't think I'm cleared for this," she said.

"You are now," said Admiral Armstrong. "Michael, can you put it on the big screen?"

Califano pressed a button on his keyboard and then swiveled around and turned on the projector. Seconds later, the NSASI main page appeared on the screen at the front of the room.

Moments later, Bill McCreary entered the room, out of breath and harried. "I just got your message," he said to Armstrong. "What's going on?"

"I'll show you in a second." Armstrong retrieved a slip of paper from his pocket and handed it to Califano. "Call this up."

Califano quickly navigated through a series of screens, typing in information here and there until, finally, a sharp photographic image appeared. He enlarged it and carefully centered it on the screen. Everyone in the room stared at it for a few seconds, trying to figure out what it was.

"This is satellite imagery from about three hours ago," said Armstrong. "The area we're looking at here is in the White Sea, about ninety miles northwest of Severodvinsk, in northern Russia. Hit Play, please."

Califano clicked a virtual button on the screen, and the satellite imagery suddenly began moving.

"What's that black line in the middle?" asked Ana.

"The white stuff you see here is ice," said Armstrong, indicating with his finger. "Right now, the White Sea is mostly frozen in the north, and that black line you see is an icebreaker pushing its way through the sheet ice. And you see that thing behind it?"

"Yeah," said Ana.

"That's a barge that's being towed out to sea."

"What kind of barge?" asked McCreary.

"The name of the vessel is the *Georgy Flyorov*. It's one of two floating power stations currently being built in Severodvinsk. Unfortunately, we don't know much about them."

"What's it doing out in the middle of the White Sea?" Ana asked.

"You'll see in a minute. Michael, can you speed it up a bit?"

Califano clicked another button on the screen and the video of the icebreaker suddenly sped up. In the time-lapse video, the icebreaker quickly punched a long path through the ice, maneuvered in circles several times to create a large swath of open water, then retreated south along the path it had just cleared, leaving the *Georgy Flyorov* floating all alone in a circle of open water in the White Sea.

"Okay, right here," said Armstrong. "Go back to normal speed."

Califano complied, and the video resumed as before.

Ana shrugged after a pause. "I don't see anything happening."

"Just wait," said Armstrong. His eyes were fixated on the image. "It's coming . . . *now*."

As everyone in the room watched in astonishment, a bright flash suddenly enveloped the barge, causing it to disappear from view.

"What the hell," McCreary whispered.

"Keep watching," said Armstrong. A second later, the bright flash was gone. And so was the *Georgy Flyorov*.

"Did it sink?" asked Ana, her eyebrows scrunched tightly together.

McCreary was shaking his head slowly back and forth. *He knew what was happening.*

"Keep watching," said Armstrong.

About ninety seconds later the barge suddenly reappeared on the screen.

"Holy crap," said Califano.

"I don't get it," said Ana incredulously. "One second it's gone, then it reappears?"

McCreary was still shaking his head. "They've got it," he said quietly. Everyone turned to look at him.

"They've got *what*?" asked Ana.

"Whatever material Dr. Holzberg was using for his experiments in Thurmond. They've got some of it, too."

"But how?"

"I don't know," said McCreary. "But this is bad. Very, very bad. The long-term effects of this could be . . ." His voice trailed off as he resumed shaking his head slowly back and forth.

Meanwhile, Admiral Armstrong leaned over Califano's shoulder and typed in some information on the keyboard. Suddenly another window from the NSASI database appeared on the large screen. "This might give you some idea. This is from the Air Force Second Space Operations Squadron in Colorado. They're the guys who control the GPS constellation and do all the maintenance and adjustments on the satellites. This is a top-secret message that was sent about two hours ago to all military users of the GPS system." The message on the screen was written in military broadcast format:

FROM: Commander, 2SOPS (USAF)
TO: All GPSMIL subscribers
INFO: DHS, NASA, DARPA, NSA
TOP SECRET NOFORN
MSGID/GPSALERT/COM2SOPS//
GENTEXT/CRITICAL GPS EVENT AFFECTING ACCURACY

1. At 1113Z today, all GPS clocks experienced an unexpected error ranging from +1 to +12 microseconds.
2. The cause of the error is unknown and is currently under investigation.
3. The problem was corrected at 1149Z with an interim clock adjustment.
4. Civilian GPS accuracy was not affected. However, military GPS accuracy may have been affected between 1113Z and 1149Z. All subscribers are advised to review GPS-derived data from this period.//

"Does that mean the clocks on the GPS satellites suddenly sped up relative to the earth?" Ana asked.

"That's one possibility," said Armstrong. "The other is that time on earth suddenly *slowed down*."

There was silence in the room for several seconds, which was eventually broken by a knock on the door. The door opened slowly and Steve Goodwin entered tentatively with a piece of paper. "Sorry to bother you. I thought you'd want to have this immediately."

McCreary grabbed the paper from Goodwin and quickly skimmed it. Suddenly, his eyes got wide. "Shit," he whispered, glancing at his watch. "This was five minutes ago." He looked at Califano and Thorne. "You two have to go. *Right now!*"

PART THREE

O sacred, wise, and wisdom-giving plant,
Mother of science, now I feel thy power
Within me clear, not only to discern
Things in their causes, but to trace the ways
Of highest agents, deemed however wise.
Queen of this universe, do not believe
Those rigid threats of death; ye shall not die:
How should ye? By the fruit? It gives you life
To knowledge.

John Milton, *Paradise Lost*, Book IX

34

M ALACHI SLOWED down the stolen Range Rover as he reached the 1600 block of Constitution Avenue in northwest D.C. Something had caught his attention—a giant flaming sword ensconced in a granite monument about twenty yards off the road. He quickly pulled over and parked. It was just past 6:00 A.M. on Sunday morning, and this usually crowded area of the city was uncharacteristically empty. It was too cold and too early for the tourists.

Malachi sat for a long while in the idling vehicle, transfixed by the flaming sword and the large expanse of grass behind it. *Yes, this all seemed so familiar to him now. He'd been here before.*

With her.

With his gaze still fixed on the flaming sword, Malachi alighted from the Range Rover and donned his black leather coat. It was a cold, damp morning with dark clouds gathering low to the ground. He buttoned his coat to the top and flipped up his collar against the wind. As an afterthought, he patted his right pocket and felt the hard outline of his pistol. *He might need this today.* With his other hand, he felt a hard lump in his left coat pocket—the object he'd retrieved from the Thurmond lab. *The purpose of his mission.*

Malachi lit a cigarette and looked around in all directions. Vehicular traffic on Constitution Avenue was extremely light, and the sidewalks on both sides of the wide avenue were entirely empty. Across Constitution Avenue, the Washington Monument rose high into the sky, nearly poking into the swirling storm clouds overhead. Malachi considered the monument for a moment, intrigued by its pagan significance. A white Egyptianesque obelisk keeping constant watch over the nation's capital. Then he turned his attention back to the wide expanse of grass to his right: the Ellipse—formally called President's Park—a large, oval park situated between the south side of the White House and Constitution Avenue. He took a long drag of his cigarette and held the smoke in his lungs. *This felt right. The Ellipse, the White House, the flaming sword.*

Finally, it was all coming together.

Malachi blew out a stream of smoke and tossed his cigarette to the ground. Then, looking all around and seeing no one on the sidewalk or in the park, he quickly made his way to the granite memorial that housed the giant, flaming sword of gold that had caught his attention from the road. Below the sword were three large words, deeply inscribed in granite and highlighted in gold leaf:

To Our Dead

Malachi recognized this as the Second Division Memorial, honoring members of the Second U.S. Infantry Division who died in World War I, World War II, and Korea.

He'd been here before.

Standing alone a few feet from the steps of the memorial, he carefully studied its unusual layout. The main portion of the monument was constructed of thick granite slabs, arranged so as to leave a large rectangular opening resembling a doorway in the middle. Beyond this open doorway were the manicured grounds of the Ellipse and the White House. But the doorway itself was blocked . . . by the giant, flaming sword held aloft by a disembodied hand. The sword and the hand were covered in bright gold leaf, making them stand out brilliantly against the somber granite backdrop of the memorial. It was a stunning visual effect, meant to reflect the Second Division's bravery in repelling the German army during World War I. Yet Malachi knew there was a deeper significance to this flaming sword. It took a few minutes, but it finally came to him in the form of a Bible verse:

So he drove out the man; and he placed at the east of the Garden of Eden cherubims, and a flaming sword which turned every way, to keep the way of the tree of life.

This verse was from the book of Genesis, just after Adam and Eve had been cast out of the Garden of Eden for eating the forbidden fruit from the tree of knowledge. As Malachi now recalled, the flaming sword was put in place by God to protect the Garden of Eden from further trespass by man.

Man had taken enough from the garden.

Malachi now gazed north beyond the flaming sword. He could just barely see the top of the White House in the distance. An American flag on the roof was waving furiously in the stiff morning breeze. *Was that his destination?*

Still uncertain about his final plan, Malachi ventured onward toward the White House. He walked with both hands in his pockets, chin down against the wind, virtually alone on the Ellipse at this early hour. Gradually, he followed the Ellipse road to the right until he found himself on Fifteenth Street, heading north. This street was a bit busier than the Ellipse, though still generally free of pedestrian traffic. As he walked, Malachi thought about the note that had been left for him in Thurmond, which he still had not entirely solved. Go to the "Third Church," it had instructed. And ask for "Qaset."

Malachi mulled over these instructions as he walked steadily up Fifteenth Street. *Was the White House the Third Church? And if so, who was Qaset?*

Malachi still had not solved these questions when he passed by a guard shack at Fifteenth and Pennsylvania Avenue, one of the main access points to the White House grounds. On instinct, he stopped and stared. He was now under the watchful gaze of two armed Secret Service agents inside the guard shack, just a few feet away. Malachi turned and approached the men.

"Can I help you?" asked one of the armed guards, a tall man in a white-and-black uniform.

Malachi became acutely aware of the pistol in his coat pocket. *This will end badly if I make a mistake*, he realized. He was also keenly aware that his appearance probably made him seem very suspicious to these guards. He was a middle-aged man in filthy clothes, with a three-day-old beard and badly trimmed hair. And this was the *White House*—home of the most powerful man in the world. *Be careful*, he told himself.

"Sir?" said the guard with growing concern in his voice.

"Um, yes," Malachi replied. "Could you tell me where I can find Qaset?"

The guard looked confused. "Cassette? Is that what you said?"

"No. Qaset with a *Q*." Malachi spelled the word out: "Q-A-S-E-T."

The two guards looked at each other and shrugged. "Sir, I suggest you try the White House Visitor Center." The tall guard pointed to his right. "It's at Fifteenth and E, and it opens at seven thirty. They should be able to answer all your questions."

Malachi thanked the guard and quickly turned away. He'd pushed his luck far enough with these men. As he started to stroll in the direction of the visitor center, however, something suddenly clicked in his mind. Something the guard had said. He immediately stopped in this tracks, paused, and reversed direction.

He'd been wrong all along. The Third Church was not the White House. But now he knew exactly where it was.

"Where's he going?" asked Mike Califano over the wireless radio. He was standing half a block away, in front of the Willard Hotel, watching every move Malachi made.

"The guards just directed him south," said Ana through her concealed microphone. "Probably to the visitor center." She was standing about fifty yards south on Fifteenth Street, between Pennsylvania and H. "Wait," she said. "He just turned around. Now he's heading north on Fifteenth. Mike, you got him?"

"I see him," said Califano.

Suddenly, Bill McCreary's voice came on the line. He was monitoring the entire operation from his office in Langley. "Stay with him," he warned. "But don't engage just yet. Let's see where he goes."

Malachi walked briskly north on Fifteenth Street, then turned left onto the wide walking street that runs behind the White House. When he reached a point adjacent to the north lawn of the White House, he quickly turned right and entered Lafayette Square Park.

"Got him?" asked Califano over the radio.

"Yep," replied Ana. She was about thirty yards behind Malachi, walking nonchalantly and gazing in all directions like a tourist on an early morning stroll to see the White House. "He's in the park now," she said quietly over the radio. "Heading north."

Malachi picked up his pace as he followed the redbrick walkways through Lafayette Park. He rounded the circular fence surrounding the Jackson memorial and paused for a moment, taking in the sight of General Andrew Jackson in full military regalia striking a majestic pose atop a rearing warhorse during the Battle of New Orleans. *Magnificent*, he thought. He was just about to turn when he noticed a woman at the edge of the park near the White House. *Was that the same woman he'd seen back on Fifteenth Street?* He considered that possibility for a few seconds, carefully studying her clothes and body type. Finally, he dismissed it. The Third Church beckoned.

And he was close.

"Shit, I think he saw me," said Ana in a hushed tone over the radio. "He's out of the park now. Just crossed H Street, and he's heading north on Sixteenth."

"Yeah, I see him," said Califano, who had just arrived at the northeast corner of Lafayette Square. "Fall back so he doesn't spot you again. I'll close in from here." Califano picked up his pace and walked briskly toward the corner of Sixteenth and H. To a casual observer, he looked like a lobbyist or diplomat, perhaps late for a Sunday power breakfast at the Hay-Adams. "Where the hell's he going?" he whispered into his microphone.

"I don't know," said Ana, who was still lingering at the south end of the park.

McCreary's voice cut in again. "Remember, stay close. But don't engage until we see where he's going."

Malachi walked by the pale yellow church on the corner of Sixteenth and H and paused for a moment to admire its simple, Greek Revivalist design. He recognized this as St. John's Episcopal Church, where every U.S. president since James Madison had attended services at least once. At the front of the church, six white columns supported an exquisitely proportioned triangular pediment. The steeple consisted of a three-tiered angular structure culminating in a gold-leafed dome topped by a weather vane. There was no cross atop this "church of presidents."

Malachi turned and continued northward on Sixteenth Street. Past the Hay-Adams hotel with its stately columns and ornate Renaissance architecture. Past the AFL-CIO headquarters—a sleek, modern study in limestone and rectangles. Past the pricey apartments at the corner of Sixteenth and I Streets, a frequent home away from home for diplomats and powerful lobbyists.

Malachi stopped abruptly on the southwest corner of Sixteenth and I Streets and glanced quickly behind him. *Was he being followed?* He scanned the entire block that he'd just traveled, searching especially for the blond woman he'd seen in the park a few minutes earlier. But she was gone. He spotted a man in a tan overcoat who appeared to be making his way hastily toward the Hay-Adams hotel. Two doormen in top hats and tails in front of the hotel were preparing to greet him. *Nothing out of the ordinary*, Malachi decided.

He now turned his gaze across the intersection, and his pulse suddenly quickened.

He had arrived.

In a flurry, he reached into his pocket and extracted the cream-colored sheet of stationery that he'd retrieved from the buried canister in Thurmond. He unfolded it and reviewed the unusal cryptogram that had been baffling him for days:

This was it. He looked across the street at the building that was located precisely between Sixteenth and Seventeenth Streets and K and I Streets. He now recalled that Washington, D.C., has no J Street because, in the eighteenth century, the letters *I* and *J* were considered redundant, or at least confusingly similar. In any event, the building he was now staring at was located almost *precisely* where the octagon was on his sheet of stationery. He looked down again at the cryptogram, marveling at its clever simplicity. Then, once again, he looked up and gazed upon what was arguably the most controversial and enigmatic building in the entire city of Washington, D.C. An octagonal concrete bunker with no apparent windows or doors.

"The Third Church," he said quietly to himself.

35

WASHINGTON, D.C.

MALACHI CAREFULLY studied the iconic building at 910 Sixteenth Street, just two blocks from the White House. The unusual building was constructed entirely of exposed concrete and was shaped like a tall, octagonal prism, with a flat roof and no windows or doors facing the street. From Malachi's vantage point at the corner of Sixteenth and I, the building looked like a bunker from the Cold War era—drab and imposing, almost menacing in its appearance.

And this was not by accident.

The octagonal building at 910 Sixteenth Street was, in fact, a veritable monument to the Brutalist school of architecture, a harsh style that had flourished in this city in the late 1960s before dying a quick, and largely unmourned, death. As an architectural philosophy, Brutalism sprang from a socialist, utopian view of the world. Regimented, domineering, downright totalitarian in form, Brutalism envisioned an urban society of complacent workers and residents, all neatly compartmentalized into low-cost, über-efficient fabrications of unadorned functionality. The concept of Brutalism was to dominate the urban landscape, forcing residents to conform to a new, progressive way of living: modern, functional, supremely efficient, and, above all, intelligently designed.

The result of this style, however, was anything but utopian. The naked concrete exteriors weathered poorly, turning ugly over time. The tall, fortresslike walls attracted graffiti, and their shadowy angles provided sanctuary for junkies, vagabonds, and criminals, eventually transforming many Brutalist-inspired neighborhoods into urban combat zones.

As Malachi knew, the Brutalist prism at 910 Sixteenth Street was not an apartment building or a residential project of any kind. Nor was it an office building, a library, a post office, or any other sort of government building. Instead, this structure had a much different purpose—one that most people found astonishing given the building's stolid appearance.

On one side of the octagonal structure, a large square slab of concrete jutted out perpendicularly about ten feet, as if an entire piece of the building had been pulled out by force and left to dangle precariously above the brick walkway below, supported only by one vertical edge. Affixed to this giant slab of concrete were twenty bronze bells.

Malachi crossed the intersection at Sixteenth and K and continued north on Sixteenth Street until he could read the full message that was written along the east side of the building. The words were formed by large black metal letters, bolted directly to the building's concrete facade. They read:

Third Church of Christ, Scientist

"The Third Church," Malachi whispered. His heart began racing as he realized, without a doubt, that this was his destination. *Here he would fulfill his destiny.*

He also knew that he'd been here before . . . *with her.* Although, judging from the condition of the building, his last visit must have been many, many years ago. He gazed up at the building's windowless facade, which loomed high above Sixteenth Street, and noted that the concrete was badly stained at the top. Long, triangular splotches streaked down like tears along the sides of the building, the result of decades of dirty storm runoff from the building's flat, and poorly conceived, octagonal roof. Malachi could remember distinctly when the concrete walls of this building were sleek and clean, its walkways flat and weed free, its twenty bronze bells gleaming brilliantly in the sun. Now, those same bells were black with grime, and the entire building seemed dingy and neglected. *What happened to this place?*

Malachi continued farther up Sixteenth Street until he was able to turn left into the church's courtyard. Like the rest of this austere building, the courtyard was stark and angular, paved nearly entirely with bricks except for a few soft planting areas along the sides and a single leafless tree in the middle. The landscape was minimalist to the extreme, bordering on harsh.

Malachi passed through the courtyard and slowly approached the wide, rectangular entryway adjoining the courtyard, on the east side of the building. Above the entryway was the building's sole window, with nearly the same rectangular dimensions as the entryway. He glanced all around the courtyard and confirmed that he was still alone. Then, just as he was about to enter the building, he paused and took note of the date that was pressed deeply into the concrete wall near the entryway: 1970. The year of the building's completion.

Malachi repeated this in his mind, 1970. *When everything was new.* He took one last look around the courtyard. Then he quickly entered the building through one of the tinted glass doors and disappeared inside.

"He's inside the building," said Mike Califano, who had been observing Malachi from across Sixteenth Street. His words were broadcast via secure satellite radio to Ana Thorne, who was a few blocks south, and to Bill McCreary at CIA headquarters.

"*What* building?" asked McCreary, who was still struggling to keep track of this operation from his office.

"Nine ten Sixteenth Street, Northwest," said Califano quickly. "It's the Third Church of Christ, Scientist. Can you tell us anything about it?"

"Stand by," said McCreary. Back at CIA headquarters, he and Steve Goodwin began furiously looking up information about the address.

"Mike, where are you?" asked Ana over the radio.

"Just crossing Sixteenth Street, heading into the courtyard behind the building. Where are you?"

"Southwest corner of Seventeenth and I," said Ana. She paused for a moment. "Hey, I think I can get to the courtyard from here. I see an alleyway across the street. I'm heading there now." Ana terminated her transmission and quickly crossed over I Street and made her way to what appeared to be a narrow passage that ran along the west side of the octagonal church.

"You're correct," said McCreary a few seconds later, his voice crackling over the radio. In his office at Langley, he was already looking at a detailed satellite image of the church on his computer screen. "The alleyway goes straight through to the courtyard."

Ana entered the dark alleyway on I Street and was immediately struck by the smell of urine and human filth. "Jesus," she whispered, shaking her head. Apparently, this alley was popular with the homeless. And she could see why. It was nearly covered along its entire length by a concrete overhang with long strands of vegetation hanging down from above. *Perfect shelter.* Because of this odd feature, the gray sky was visible only through a narrow slit between the overhanging planter and the west side of the octagonal building. *Strange design*, Ana thought as she quickly made her way through the tunnel-like passage toward the courtyard on the other side.

As she neared the end of the passageway, she could see more of the sparse courtyard as it gradually came into view. She saw a leafless tree in the center, surrounded by a large expanse of uneven brick pavers. She saw several concrete benches near the planting areas. But one thing she did *not* see was Mike Califano.

"Hey, I'm coming up on the courtyard now," said Ana through her concealed microphone. "Where are you?" Those words had no sooner left her lips than she sensed a commotion in the vegetation above her head. At first, she thought it was a rat or some other urban animal. But it wasn't.

A man dropped through the narrow opening above the alleyway without warning, landing a few feet in front of her with impressive acrobatic skill. He wore a black ski mask pulled over his face and carried a suppressor-enhanced pistol in one hand, which he was now leveling at her chest.

Ana flinched, but her instincts quickly kicked in. Three options immediately coursed through her mind, none of them good. Fleeing would not work because she was stuck in the middle of a narrow passageway facing an armed man. Charging forward wouldn't work, either. The man had a pistol aimed at her chest, and she could tell his finger was resting on the trigger. Her third option wasn't any better. She could try to draw her weapon, but she knew she wouldn't be fast enough. *Nothing left to do but stall.*

"What do you want?" she asked. "You want money? I've got—"

"Shut up," said the man through his ski mask. He stiffened his firing arm, then slowly lifted the barrel until it was level with her forehead. "Hands up."

Ana blew out a long, frustrated breath. Then she slowly raised her hands.

The man whose code name was Malachi passed through the church lobby and took a left at the interior stairwell that circumscribed the building's massive atrium, known as "the sanctuary." He climbed the steps to an intermediate platform and approached the first door on his right and gently tugged on its handle. *Locked.* Undeterred, he proceeded several feet down the hallway and checked the next door. It, too, was locked.

"Can I help you?" called out a woman from behind.

Malachi spun and observed a thin, silver-haired woman in a white dress and a large beaded necklace draped around her neck. She looked to be in her midseventies or perhaps early eighties.

Malachi hesitated. "I'm . . . looking for Qaset."

The woman approached slowly, her eyes widening with each deliberate step. At a distance of several feet, she stopped and squinted at Malachi's face. "Daniel?" she said tentatively.

Daniel. That name eased slowly and comfortably into Malachi's brain, and he found himself nodding in agreement.

The woman slowly closed the remaining distance between them. "My God," she whispered. "You've barely changed." She reached out and gently touched his unshaven face. "Just a few wrinkles." Then she glanced at his hair. "But your hair . . . it's gray."

Malachi smiled slightly and nodded. "Yours, too."

"Oh," said the woman, shaking her head. "I'm so old, I'm surprised you even recognize me." There was a long, awkward pause. "You . . . *do* recognize me, don't you?"

Malachi started to say something but stopped short. He still did not trust his memory.

"Go ahead," said the woman reassuringly. "Say it."

Malachi studied the woman's face for several more seconds, tilting his head from side to side. Then, in an unsure tone, he said, "Opal?"

The woman smiled and nodded. "Yes, Daniel. It's me."

Ana Thorne watched in disbelief as the man in the black ski mask approached and put the barrel of his gun just inches from her forehead. With his free hand, he began patting her down for weapons, starting at her shoulders and working his way down. He hadn't quite made it to her underarm holster when his hand groped crudely across her breasts. For a split second, his eyes darted downward to see what he was grabbing.

And that was all the time she needed. Ana's right knee exploded upward into the man's crotch, landing with a satisfying thud. Simultaneously, she smashed her right forearm into the man's firing arm, knocking it violently out of place.

A noise-suppressed round whizzed past Ana's head and ricocheted off one of the concrete walls of the passageway.

The man keeled forward, wincing in agony. Ana was tempted to deliver a downward thrust kick to the back of his skull, which, given her martial arts training, probably would have killed him. But protocol required otherwise. She had no idea who this man was, and like it or not, deadly force was not authorized in this situation.

Not yet anyway.

Ana quickly pulled her Glock 9 millimeter from its holster beneath her jacket and aimed it at the top of the man's head. As he arose slowly from his bent-over position, she adjusted her aim until her weapon was trained at the center of his chest. *Center of mass*, per her CIA training. "Don't move," she warned.

The man locked eyes with her through his ski mask. A tense moment passed, and his eyes began to narrow slightly. Then, in a flash, he raised his weapon to fire.

Ana beat him to it. She fired twice in rapid succession, placing a noise-suppressed 9-millimeter round in the man's chest and another in his forehead before he hit the ground. The CIA's "double tap" technique, just as she'd been trained. *Now* deadly forced was authorized. She watched as the man collapsed to the ground in a lifeless heap.

Moments later, the dark outline of another man appeared at the north end of the alleyway, blocking out the light. Ana saw the unmistakable shape of a pistol in his hand. She immediately raised her Glock to fire.

"Ana!" said a voice.

Ana's heart skipped a beat. It was Califano.

"Shit!" she exclaimed angrily. "Don't *ever* do that again. I almost shot you."

"You all right?" Califano asked as he jogged toward her and gawked at the dead man on the ground.

"I'm fine, but we've got company. Come on."

The crackly voice of Bill McCreary came on the line. "What the hell's going on?" he asked.

Ana tapped her microphone as she jogged. "I'll explain later." She didn't have time for Q and A right now.

Seconds later, Ana and Califano emerged from the passageway and quickly made their way to the church entrance. "Where the hell were you?" Ana whispered angrily as she holstered her weapon. She nodded for Califano to do the same with his pistol.

Califano looked confused. "What? I was right here. Waiting for you."

Ana looked annoyed. "Never mind. Let's go in."

The two of them entered the church and found themselves standing alone in a small, unlit lobby with a polished terra cotta floor. Ana pressed her index finger to her lips and listened carefully for several seconds. The building was eerily silent.

"Where is everyone?" Califano whispered.

Ana pointed to a sign on the wall, which read:

Third Church of Christ, Scientist
Sanctuary Closed for Repairs
9:30 A.M. Sunday Services Next Door
in the Reading Room

"Ah," Califano whispered.

Ana again pressed a finger to her lips and pointed emphatically with her other hand toward the hallway beyond the lobby.

Califano heard it now, too. The unmistakable sound of high-heeled shoes clicking loudly across a hard floor. Califano reached instinctively for his weapon, but Ana stopped his arm before he could withdraw it. She slowly shook her head no. *Protocol*.

A moment later, a petite, middle-aged woman in a bright

blue dress rounded the corner and came into the lobby. "Oh," she said, looking a bit startled. "I thought I heard someone in here. God's love to both of you."

"And to you," said Ana.

"Are you visiting us for the first time?" asked the woman in a gentle voice. As she spoke, she dropped her car keys into her purse.

"Um, yes," said Ana. "We just moved to the area, and we're looking around for a new church."

An idea suddenly popped into Califano's mind. "Actually, we're newlyweds," he said with a crooked smile. "Just got married last week." He glanced down at his ring finger. "We're, uh . . . still waiting for our rings to get sized."

Ana shot him a sideways glance.

"Oh, how wonderful," said the woman in blue. She gave Ana a big smile. "You must be so happy."

Ana forced a smile. "Thrilled."

"Well, may God bless your marriage with boundless love."

"Amen," said Califano. At the same time, he wrapped his arm tightly around Ana's waist and planted a kiss on her cheek. Ana blushed and forced another smile.

The woman in blue laughed nervously. "Oh, my. Well, I'm sorry our main building is closed due to some storm damage. But we'll be holding services next door at nine thirty. I'm heading over there now to set up if you'd like to join me."

"Thanks," said Ana. She wiped her cheek and gave Califano a none-too-subtle jab in the ribs. "But we'd like to look around here a bit, if that's okay. It looks like such a cool building."

"Uh, sure. I guess that'd be okay. Just be careful wherever you see buckets on the floor. We've got a very leaky roof."

"We will," said Ana. She thanked the woman and then

quickly turned and proceeded toward the wide, angular staircase on the left side of the lobby.

Califano caught up with her halfway up the stairs.

"What the hell was that?" Ana whispered over her shoulder as she climbed the steps two at a time. It was an unusual staircase, angling clockwise at even intervals as it hugged the octagonal contours of the building. The stairwell was dark, with just a bit of indirect natural light filtering down from the skylights above.

"Just playing my part," Califano replied, still two steps behind her. "Trying to be a little creative."

Thorne stopped abruptly on the steps and turned to face him. "*Stop* trying to be 'creative.' It's going to get us both killed. Just follow protocol, got it?"

"Yeah, I got it." Califano mumbled these words with something close to sincerity.

Ana swiveled her head. The sound of low voices could suddenly be heard through a slightly open door at the top of the stairs. She slowly withdrew her weapon and approached the door. Califano followed close behind.

Ana reached the door first and eased it open a few inches, holding her breath as she did. When it was cracked open just wide enough, she slipped through and found herself standing on a wide balcony, gazing down into a cavernous octagonal sanctuary with no windows and very little light. In the semidarkness she could see dozens of long metal pews arranged in horizontal rows facing the pulpit. About half of them were covered with blue tarps, apparently to protect them from the leaking roof above. Other metal pews were arranged in three long balcony sections, including the one on which she now stood. The pulpit below was situated on a raised stage at the front of the sanctuary, which was dominated by sleek, geometric shapes of cement and metal, all in keeping with the Brutalist design of the church. Behind the pulpit, in large metal letters fastened directly to the naked cement wall, was the following quotation:

**If Science is not God,
then truth is but an accident.**

Ana suddenly heard the voices again and her eyes were immediately drawn to a dark corner of the sanctuary near the pulpit. As her eyes adjusted to the darkness, two figures gradually came into view, a man in a black coat and a shorter, elderly woman in a white dress. *Why did that woman look familiar?*

The man and woman were facing each other, speaking in hushed tones. Because of the angular design of the sanctuary, Ana could hear some of what they were saying, although their words were fading in and out in waves.

". . . did you see . . . is he alive. . .?" asked the woman.

"Yes," said the man. ". . . wounded. I helped him . . . then we got separated . . ."

". . . the stone?" asked the woman.

The man's response was garbled.

Ana wanted to hear more, but she knew it was time to move in. They couldn't take any more chances, especially given what had happened outside. She quickly turned to signal Califano through the open door.

But he was gone.

Shit, Ana mouthed. Just then, her earpiece crackled to life and she heard Califano's voice speaking very softly in her ear. "Look up," he said.

36

COME ON, Steve. Find me something." Bill McCreary was hovering nervously over Steve Goodwin's shoulder at the computer terminal in the DTAI workroom at CIA head-quarters.

Goodwin mashed furiously on the computer keyboard with his beefy fingers. "I'm working on it, boss."

"Damn it, work *faster*." McCreary quickly paced away to the other side of the room. "Ana?" he said quietly into his radio transmitter. "Mike?" For the third time in as many minutes, there was no response at all. "Crap," he whispered. *This was quickly becoming a disaster.*

McCreary's cell phone buzzed. "Yeah?" he answered sharply.

"Bill, it's Bob Armstrong. Anything yet?"

"No, Admiral," said McCreary in an exasperated tone. "I've lost all contact with them. To tell you the truth, I'm about ready to call in the big guns."

"I wouldn't do that."

"What, you think I *want* to? Sure, that's just what we need. Some big clusterfuck two blocks from the White House. You think we'll be able to keep a lid on this stuff after that?"

"Then don't do it. Just give them a little more time. You've got to trust your people to get the job done."

McCreary exhaled loudly. "Admiral, I'm going to level with you. I don't trust your guy Califano at all. He's a loose cannon. He doesn't follow protocol. Hell, I don't think he even knows what the word 'protocol' *means*. And honestly . . . he's just weird."

Armstrong laughed dryly. "Bill, you worked at DARPA. Don't tell me you haven't worked with some weird people before."

"Yeah, some of the folks at DARPA are quirky. Maybe you could even call them weird. But Califano . . . he's more like *criminally insane*. I'm telling you, I just don't trust him."

"Well, *I do*," said Armstrong firmly. "I'll stake my career on it."

"You may have to," McCreary muttered.

"Hey, boss?" said Steve Goodwin over his shoulder.

"I gotta go," said McCreary. He abruptly terminated the call with Admiral Armstrong and turned his attention to Goodwin. "Yeah? You got something?"

"Maybe. Take a listen." Goodwin clicked his mouse and turned up the volume on his computer. Suddenly, sporadic voices could be heard crackling over the speakers amid a high level of static.

McCreary stepped closer so he could hear better. The voices were just barely audible over the heavy static.

"*Ty na mista?*" said one man's voice.

"*Tak, vse gotovo,*" said another.

"What the hell language is that?" McCreary asked.

"Not sure," said Goodwin. "Sounds like Russian or maybe Polish. It's hard to tell."

"Where's it coming from?"

"The Secret Service has scanners that continuously monitor all point-to-point radio transmissions near the White House. I'm picking this up from one of their feeds at 467.6875 megahertz. It's probably a commercial walkie-talkie, and my guess is it's being used within about five blocks of the White House."

"That would include the church, right?"

"Uh-huh."

"Send the feed to our language folks. Let's find out what language it is and what they're saying."

"Already did that. I'm just waiting—" Goodwin paused and skimmed a message that had just popped onto his screen. "Here it is. The language is Ukrainian. It's a group of eight to ten men, and they seem to be positioning themselves for some sort of operation. One of them— Hold on. I just got another one." Goodwin was quiet for a moment as he skimmed a new message.

"Come on, what is it?" asked McCreary impatiently.

Goodwin shook his head. "Take a look."

McCreary leaned over Goodwin's shoulder and read the translation that had just been provided by the CIA's Ukrainian language specialist:

SPEAKER 1:   *[Garbled] What about the woman?*

SPEAKER 2:   *Kill her if you need to. We only need [Garbled, phonetic: mal-uh-kī]. He has the [Garbled, phonetic: Thur-mond] material.*

SPEAKER 1:   *Understood. Take him alive?*

SPEAKER 2:   *Yes, alive. We need him to lead us to the [Garbled].*

"Who the hell is Malachi?" McCreary asked.

"That must be our carjacker from Thurmond."

"And what do they think he's going to lead them to?"

Goodwin shrugged. "Don't know, boss."

McCreary shook his head slowly and wiped his brow. *Christ. This was turning into a disaster.* He pressed the transmit button on his microphone. "Ana and Mike, if you can hear me, the church is crawling with foreign operatives. Could be as many as ten of them. And they're looking for someone named Malachi, who we think is our guy from Thurmond. Be careful."

There was still no response.

Shit.

37

WASHINGTON, D.C.

IT WAS too late.

By the time Ana Thorne saw the man in the ski mask swinging onto her balcony from above, she had no time to react. The man hit her square in the stomach with both feet, and she flew backward into an unforgiving cement wall. The powerful blow knocked the wind out of her and left her momentarily disoriented and gasping for breath. Within seconds the man had regained his footing and was now aiming his pistol directly at her forehead. Ana could tell from the look in his eyes that he wasn't interested in talking. *He was going to kill her.*

A gunshot suddenly exploded, and Ana instinctively closed her eyes. Yet she felt no pain. She opened her eyes a moment later and found, to her amazement, that the man had missed. Without hesitation, she raised her own weapon. But as she did, she noticed something odd about the masked gunman. He was lowering his pistol and stumbling toward her. Then, all at once, he collapsed face-first onto the balcony floor with a loud thud.

Ana now understood. The man hadn't missed at all. *He'd been shot in the back*. Frantically, she scanned the sanctuary for the source of the bullet, fearing that another one might be heading her way. She immediately spotted a man in the balcony across from her, barely visible within the deep shadows of the church. *He had a gun*.

A man's voice suddenly buzzed in her ear. "You're welcome," said Mike Califano.

Ana looked again and saw that the man in the opposite balcony was waving to her. *Unbelievable*. She shook her head in amazement. Then, as much as she tried to suppress it, she smiled. "That was a damn good shot," she whispered into her concealed microphone. If Califano responded at all, she never heard it. Because, at that very moment, all hell broke loose in the sanctuary below.

"Move in now!" yelled Vladamir Krupnov into his small walkie-talkie. From his vantage point in the rear upper balcony, he watched as five of his Ukrainian goons burst into the sanctuary from all directions. All of these men were wearing tracksuits and black ski masks, and carrying compact Uzi machine guns.

The man and the woman behind the pulpit were already on the move, having heard the commotion in the balcony a few seconds earlier. "This way," said the elderly woman in white. She and Malachi darted to an adjacent doorway and quickly disappeared.

Krupnov grimaced as he watched the pair disappearing through the doorway. *Malachi must not escape!* He was just about to bark another order into his walkie-talkie when a sound-suppressed gunshot suddenly punctured the air to his right. In the same instant, he saw one of his men in the sanctuary stumble and hit the floor.

Goddamnit! Krupnov seethed. He immediately spotted the source of the gunshot. It was a blond woman in the side balcony to his right. *And she was preparing to fire again.* Before she could, Krupnov hoisted his Uzi and unleashed a firestorm of bullets in her direction. "*Chertovsky suka!*" he screamed. *Fucking bitch!* The woman in the balcony immediately went down and disappeared from view.

"You all right?" whispered Mike Califano into his microphone after the machine-gun fire had subsided. He was crouching low behind the wall of his own balcony.

No response.

Shit. Still ducking low, Califano scrambled to the balcony doorway and burst out into the landing outside. With his pistol raised, he quickly scanned the darkened stairs in both directions. It appeared to be clear. "Ana, you okay?" he repeated into his microphone, louder this time. Seconds ticked by with no response.

Finally, the voice of Ana Thorne crackled in his ear. "I'm fine," she said in a strained voice.

"You hit?"

"No. Just got the wind knocked out of me."

Califano breathed a sigh of relief. *Thank God.* He tapped his transmit button again. "They went through a door at the front of the sanctuary. Right side if you're facing the pulpit."

"Got it," said Ana. "Bill, can you help us out with the layout of this place?"

Bill McCreary's voice came on the line a second later. "Oh, so you *can* hear me," he said in an exasperated tone.

"Yeah, Bill. We can hear you," whispered Ana. "It's been a little busy here, okay? How about that layout?"

. . . .

Back at CIA headquarters, McCreary was still pulling up the original architectural drawings of the iconic church on his computer screen. "Give me a second."

"We don't *have* a second," Ana whispered emphatically.

As luck would have it, the Third Church of Christ, Scientist, at Sixteenth and K, had been the subject of a lengthy and contentious legal battle concerning its status as a historic landmark. The owners of the church and the congregation itself wanted the structure torn down and replaced with something more "churchlike." The District of Columbia, however, insisted that the building was historical and wanted it preserved as an exemplar of the short-lived Brutalist movement in the city. To the surprise of nobody, the district won. As a result of this legal skirmish, the building's exterior and interior designs were now well documented and permanently preserved.

Strange that the government would want to preserve such an eyesore, McCreary thought as he finally got the right architectural drawing on his screen. "Okay," he said over the secure radio network. "The door to the right of the pulpit, as you're facing it, leads to a small vestibule, about eight by twelve feet. On the other side of that, through a doorway, is a midlevel landing with two sets of stairs. One set leads down to a hallway that connects to the front lobby on the east side of the building, where you guys probably came in. The other set leads up to the back of the sanctuary."

"How many exits are there?" asked Califano.

"Uh . . . three. The main entrance is on the east side. There's a delivery entrance on the I Street side, and a fire exit on the west side, which goes into that alley where Ana was earlier."

Where I almost got killed, Ana thought.

"Those dudes are gonna have all those exits covered," said Califano.

"Yeah," said Ana. "But I think that old lady knows another way out."

"What makes you so sure?" asked Califano.

"Woman's intuition." As Ana spoke, she slipped carefully through the door of her balcony and quickly scanned the stairs in both directions. There were stairs going up to her right, which angled clockwise and disappeared. And there were stairs going down to her left, angling counterclockwise toward the lobby. "Jesus," she whispered into her microphone. "This place reminds me of one of those crazy Escher drawings."

"I know," said Califano. "Stairs everywhere."

"Okay, here's the plan," whispered Ana. "Mike, you head upstairs toward the back of the sanctuary. Be careful, though. The shooter may still be up there. I'll head downstairs to the lobby. I think I know where they're heading."

"On my way," said Califano.

"Be careful, guys," McCreary said nervously.

"Where are we going?" whispered Malachi.

"This way," urged the elderly woman in white who called herself Opal. She was moving surprisingly fast for a woman her age. With Malachi in tow, she headed straight upstairs, banked right into a hallway, then walked quickly toward the main lobby. As she neared the lobby, she spotted a man in a black ski mask about thirty feet away, patrolling the front door with a machine gun. Apparently, he had not seen them yet. She took two more careful steps in that direction, then quickly darted left into a darkened doorway. Malachi followed her through the doorway and disappeared.

. . . .

Mike Califano climbed the angular stairs toward the back of the church. With each forty-five-degree turn of the stairwell, the shadows and indirect lighting shifted dramatically, creating a bewildering "fun house" effect. As he ascended these steps, a troubling thought began easing into his brain. *Why am I heading up?*

Califano stopped in his tracks. *To hell with woman's intuition.* He had his *own* intuition, namely that nobody trying to escape a building ever runs *up.* Without a second thought, he reversed direction and began descending the stairs. *Fuck protocol.*

"Keep going," said the elderly woman in white. "It's a long way down." Malachi nodded and continued descending the narrow cement stairs in the dank stairwell, which was dimly lit with incandescent bulbs at each landing. Opal followed close behind him.

"What is this place?" Malachi asked over his shoulder.

"It's a parking garage."

Malachi paused at the landing for level 2. "Keep going?"

"Yes," said Opal. "Down one more."

Fifteen seconds later, they exited into a vacant parking deck, forty feet below the octagonal church. The space was sparsely lit by overhead fluorescent bulbs, several of which were flickering badly. The cavernous parking deck was entirely empty and eerily quiet, like a tomb.

"Shhh," said Opal. "Did you hear that?"

Malachi nodded. He could hear faint footsteps in the stairwell behind them. He quickly pulled his pistol from his coat pocket.

Opal eyed the weapon disapprovingly and shook her head. "Violence is not the answer, Daniel."

Malachi stared blankly, unsure of how to respond.

"If it comes to that, your weapon will be useless anyway. Put it away."

Malachi reluctantly complied.

"This way," said Opal, motioning emphatically toward a metal door nearby, which was prominently marked with the yellow-and-black symbol for a fallout shelter—three yellow triangles embedded in a black circle. She quickly made her way to the door and punched an access code into a small keypad on the wall next to it. The metal door immediately clicked open and the two of them slipped through and entered a dark stairwell. "Leave the door open so we can see," she said. Then she carefully led Malachi down one more flight of stairs, around a corner, and into a wide, nearly pitch-black space.

Malachi strained to see into the darkness. The flickering fluorescent lighting that bled through the open doorway provided just enough illumination that he could tell there were concrete walls and a concrete floor. He could also make out the shapes of desks and consoles and other structures clustered together in groups, extending far into the darkness. "What is this place?" he whispered.

Opal paused. "*This* is the reason the government won't let the congregation build a new church on this site. Until about twelve years ago, this was the official nuclear fallout shelter for the White House. There's a passageway on the other side that connects directly to the basement of the west wing. Or at least there used to be. It's sealed shut now."

"But . . . how do *you* have access?"

The woman laughed softly. "Honey, I *designed* this place."

· · · ·

"Hey, boss?" said Steve Goodwin, who was seated at his computer in the DTAI workroom at the CIA.

"Yeah?" said McCreary.

"Did you say there were *three* exits in that building?"

"Uh-huh."

"Well, I just got another translation from our language people. Looks like those Ukrainians are covering *four* exits."

"Huh?" McCreary's heart skipped a beat as he looked up from his computer terminal. "Where's the fourth exit?"

Goodwin carefully studied the translation on the screen. "Uh . . . it's the service entrance at the back of the Hay-Adams hotel at Sixteenth and H."

"What the—" McCreary immediately swiveled in his chair and began typing furiously on his keyboard. Two minutes later, his screen was full of top-secret information about the fallout shelter beneath the Third Church of Christ, Scientist, and the secret passageway that ran deep beneath Sixteenth Street, connecting the White House to the Brutalist octagonal church, with an intermediate escape point behind the Hay-Adams hotel. "I can't believe I missed this," he said, shaking his head. He quickly pressed transmit on his microphone. "Ana? Mike?"

No response.

"If you guys can hear me, there's a tunnel beneath the church that runs along Sixteenth Street toward the White House. There's an access point behind the Hay-Adams. And somehow these Ukrainian guys know all about it."

38

A NA THORNE could no longer hear anything in her earpiece. She was twenty feet beneath the Third Church of
Christ, Scientist, on the first level of the building's underground parking garage. With her Glock at the ready, she
quickly canvassed the space. Two cars were parked along
the east wall, near the stairwell. She presumed one of them
belonged to the church lady in the blue dress, whom she'd
noticed dropping her car keys into her purse earlier this
morning. Other than that, the garage was entirely empty.
And quiet.

On the north wall, about twenty yards away, Ana spotted an overhead sectional door, about twice the size of a
residential garage door. She assumed this was the connection to the building next door, which she knew would
be the only way for vehicles to get in and out of here. She
studied the door carefully. *Did they escape through there?*
Overhead doors like that typically opened and closed very

slowly. Plus, they were designed to stay open for fifteen or twenty seconds after a vehicle passed through. She shook her head and quickly dismissed the idea. The timing just didn't work. If the woman and man had gone through that door, it would still be open.

They must have gone somewhere else.

Frustrated, Ana retreated to the stairwell and began climbing back toward the main level of the church. A second later, she stopped. Shuffling feet and voices could now be heard overhead. *Someone was coming down . . . and fast.* Ana quickly backtracked to the parking platform and ducked behind one of the two parked cars. The voices were growing louder.

"*Kudy vony pijshly?*" she heard a man's voice say.

"*Tudy,*" said another.

Moments later, Ana saw two goons with ski masks and machine guns rounding the corner of the stairwell. They were moving fast and breathing hard. They rounded the corner at the first level and continued descending toward the lower levels of the garage without even pausing.

Ana cocked her head in confusion. *What do they know that I don't?* When the men were safely out of view, she quickly looked around and spotted the vehicle ramp that descended to the next level. *That would be the long way down*, she realized. But at least she wouldn't risk being heard in the stairwell, which was like an echo chamber.

She immediately began sprinting toward the ramp.

"Where the hell is it?" said Mike Califano into his microphone as he made his way south along Sixteenth Street toward the Hay-Adams hotel. Two blocks behind him, a dead Ukrainian thug with a bullet in his head marked the spot where Califano had escaped from the octagonal church a few minutes earlier, through the fire door in the alleyway.

"It's in the back," said McCreary over the radio. "Between the hotel and the chamber of commerce building. Look for an alley that runs along the north side of the hotel."

"Okay, I see it," said Califano. He quickly crossed over Sixteenth Street and made his way down the narrow alley until he reached a patch of asphalt behind the Hay-Adams hotel. The area was lined with Dumpsters and linen carts and was entirely enclosed by walls except for the alley entrance, which was just wide enough for small delivery trucks to come in and out.

"What exactly am I looking for?" Califano whispered as he scanned the area.

"Probably a metal cover of some sort on the ground," McCreary replied over the radio. "It might look like a cellar door or a hatch."

"Hold on." Califano terminated the transmission and stood still for a moment, trying to discern the direction of a metallic noise he'd just heard. It sounded like it had come from behind one of the Dumpsters. That's when he noticed that one Dumpster was angled sharply away from the wall, unlike the others. He unholstered his noise-suppressed pistol and stepped cautiously toward the askew Dumpster until his shoulder was pressed tightly against it. He could hear a metallic grinding noise on the other side, and periodic grunts. *What the hell is that?*

Califano inched along the side the Dumpster until he was at the corner. Then, in one swift motion, he turned and leveled his weapon at a man who was hunched over a metal access hatch on the ground, apparently trying to pry it open with a crowbar. "Freeze!" he ordered.

The man with the crowbar was clearly startled. He stood with the crowbar in one hand and a stupefied expression on his face. He was a large man, with a massive jaw and a crooked nose. He was dressed in blue pants, a dungaree shirt, and a blue jacket with the Hay-Adams logo embroidered on one side.

"What are you doing here?" Califano demanded.

The big man spoke with a slight Slavic accent. "I was told to get hatch open. I . . . I work for hotel."

Califano wasn't convinced. But he certainly wasn't going to shoot a man who might be telling the truth. He was still considering his options when a crackling noise suddenly emanated from the man's shirt pocket. It was a walkie-talkie.

"*Nomeru try, chy htos vyjshov?*" said a man's voice over the walkie-talkie.

Califano immediately trained his pistol at the man's head. "Drop the crowbar."

In an instant, the Ukrainian man swung the crowbar at Califano's head like a baseball bat. Califano fired his weapon and ducked as the crowbar whizzed an inch over his head. The bullet ricocheted off a brick wall behind the Dumpster. When Califano looked up, the man was nearly on top of him, swinging the crowbar straight down toward his face.

Califano dove to his left but could not escape the crowbar as it landed hard on his right shoulder, sending an excruciating burst of pain all through his body and causing him to lose his grip on his pistol. The Glock went skittering across the asphalt.

Califano scampered away on hands and feet, unable to regain his full balance. He turned and fell backward as the Ukrainian barreled toward him with the heavy crowbar raised high over his head. "*Zgin vybludok!*" the brute shouted through gritted teeth.

Califano had no idea what that meant, but it didn't sound good. A second later, the man brought the crowbar crashing down toward Califano's head. Califano rolled away and the crowbar clanked violently against the asphalt near his ear.

Califano gained his feet and had just enough time to turn and see the Ukrainian charging toward him again at full speed, grunting like an animal. Instinctively, Califano lowered his stance and tackled the man around the waist, exploding upward at just the right moment to send the Ukrainian somersaulting over his head. As the man flew through the air behind him, Califano searched frantically for his weapon, which he spotted near the Dumpster. He lunged for it and quickly scooped it off the ground.

With his gun now gripped in his hand, Califano spun to see a crowbar swinging viciously toward his face. He arched back and allowed the crowbar to fan harmlessly past his nose. In the next instant, he raised his firing arm and pulled the trigger. A suppressed shot split the air, and the big man instantly lurched backward with a wound in his chest. Califano fired another round, and the man stumbled backward again into the Dumpster, dropping the crowbar to the ground with a clank.

Califano moved in for a final shot. But he saw it wouldn't be necessary. The man's eyes were bulging out, and blood was dribbling from his mouth. A second later, his knees buckled and he began sliding slowly down the side of the Dumpster until he crumpled lifelessly to the ground.

"What's going on?" asked Bill McCreary over the radio.

Califano tapped his transmitter. "Company," he said, still trying to catch his breath. He paused for a moment, making sure the coast was clear. Then he picked up the crowbar and quickly made his way behind the Dumpster.

Time to find out what's beneath this hatch.

· · · ·

"I . . . I don't understand," said Malachi. He was follow-ing close behind the woman in the white dress, Opal, as she carefully made her way through the darkened fallout shelter beneath Sixteenth Street. The darkness was nearly absolute, save for a scintilla of flickering light still bleeding through from the stairwell behind them.

"I know you're confused," said Opal over her shoul-der. "You must have lost some part of your memory. We knew that would be a risk, and I'm *so* sorry about that." She stopped at a closed steel door. "Do you have a light?"

"Uh, I've got this." Malachi reached into his breast pocket and retrieved his lighter. He flicked it in one motion, and the metal door before them suddenly lit up in danc-ing hues of yellow and orange. The letters HA-1 were promi-nently stenciled in the middle of the door.

"The Hay-Adams," said the woman quietly. She opened the door and quickly passed through.

Malachi followed the woman through the security door and used his lighter to navigate their way through a short tunnel that terminated at a small, square room. *A dead end.* Four cement walls towered high above them, with pin-pricks of natural light filtering down through some sort of cover at the top. This gave Malachi the impression that they were standing at the bottom of a covered well. "What is this place?" he asked.

The woman pointed to a set of sturdy steel rungs that formed a ladder extending upward, embedded in one of the walls. "It's an escape shaft," she said.

Seconds later, they heard footsteps and shuffling noises in the fallout shelter behind them. And they saw the wash of flashlights flitting back and forth across the opening to the shaft. "Hurry," said the woman, motioning for Malachi to scale the ladder.

Malachi had no sooner stepped onto the first rung than

the metal hatch above them began rattling violently, as if someone was trying to pry it open.

"We're trapped," the woman whispered.

"What do we do?"

The woman closed her eyes for a moment, apparently deep in thought. Meanwhile, the footsteps behind them were getting louder, and the flashlight beams were growing brighter. Above them, the rattling noise was growing even more intense. "Give me the stone," she said.

Malachi retrieved the lump from his pocket and gripped it firmly in one hand. "I still don't understand. What is this for?"

The woman looked surprised. "Haven't you noticed its unusual properties?"

"I have, but . . . I still don't know what it does."

The woman took the stone gently from Malachi's grasp and held it out in front of her with both hands. "Let me show you." She slowly drew the stone close to her chest and touched it to a black oval pendant dangling from a chain around her neck.

Immediately, something strange began to happen. Malachi could *feel* it. An aura of light began emanating from the woman's chest. "No," he said, slowly backing away.

"Daniel, stay close!" the woman yelled. "This is our only chance!"

No, Malachi thought. *This feels wrong.* He watched in bewilderment as the swirling light enveloped the woman completely and began spreading toward him. He continued backing away into the tunnel. Then, as the light began encroaching into the tunnel, he turned and bolted headlong into the darkness.

Straight toward his pursuers.

39

MIKE CALIFANO could clearly hear voices beneath the steel hatch, which was located in the small service courtyard behind the Hay-Adams hotel. At first, they were muffled and indiscernible. But then he heard a woman scream, "Daniel, stay close! This is our only chance!" Seconds later, a bright flash of white light shot up through the cracks and holes around the edges of the hatch, dissipating a moment later. This was accompanied by a soft whooshing sound.

Califano shielded his eyes. *What the hell was that?* Moments later, he returned to his work with the crowbar. With one final heave, he managed to pop the steel hatch free from its internal locking mechanism. Then, with effort, he tilted the hatch open on its hinges and pushed it over, wincing a bit at the pain in his shoulder. As the hatch fell aside, Califano peered down into the square shaft that now lay uncovered behind the Dumpster. The gray morning light penetrated several feet into the shaft, but the bottom was still heavily obscured by shadows.

Should I climb down?

Califano was still contemplating this idea when he suddenly heard a commotion below. Multiple voices could be heard shouting in Ukrainian. A man yelled out in English: "Don't shoot!" After that, there was relative silence for several seconds until the dead man's walkie-talkie on the other side of the Dumpster suddenly came to life. *"My zahopyly Malachi!"* reported a nearly breathless man in Ukrainian.

They'd captured Malachi.

The next moment, Califano saw moving beams of light illuminating the bottom of the shaft below him. He stared down and was surprised to see that it was empty. *Where did the woman go?* he wondered.

The radio in the dead man's shirt suddenly crackled again. *"Nomeru try, chy htos vyjshov?"*

Califano didn't know exactly what that meant, but he had a hunch. *"Nomeru try"* meant "number three," which was apparently the designation of the gunman who now lay dead against the Dumpster, with two bullet holes in his chest. Number three's teammates apparently wanted to know if anyone had come up this way.

"Nomeru try?" said the man's voice again over the radio.

Califano scurried around the Dumpster and quickly retrieved the radio from the dead man's shirt. He pressed the transmit button and paused for a moment as he tried to recall a particular page from a Ukrainian phrase book he'd once perused in college. A moment later, an exact image of that page flashed into his mind. *"Nemaye,"* he answered in passable Ukrainian. Which meant: *No.*

Califano returned to the shaft and peered down into it. He observed that the flashlight beams were now getting dimmer. The men were retreating back toward the church. Califano's next thought was: *Where's Ana?*

Vladamir Krupnov stood alone, seething in the alleyway behind the Third Church of Christ, Scientist. Two of his men lay dead on the brick walkway nearby.

Imbeciles. How could they have let this happen? Two more of his men had gone down inside the church, shot by that blond bitch. *She will pay for that.*

Just then, Sashko Melnik—his trusted lieutenant—entered the alley through the fire exit. He was breathing hard and sweating. "Vlad, the men are on their way to the egress point."

"And Malachi?"

"They've got him subdued. We'll be ready to go momentarily."

Krupnov did not move at first. He was still staring at the bodies on the ground, stroking the thick stubble on his chin. *A heavy price to pay. But at least they'd achieved their objective.*

"But, Vlad . . ."

From the tone of his lieutenant's voice, Krupnov could tell bad news was coming.

Sashko cast his eyes downward and shook his head. "He doesn't have the stone."

Anger immediately flashed across Krupnov's face as he struggled mightily to maintain his composure. "Impossible," he growled. "What about the old woman?"

Sashko shook his head remorsefully. "We couldn't find her."

"How could you not find her? She's a fucking *old woman!*"

Sashko was silent. He had no answer.

Krupnov was about to say something else when he suddenly heard sirens a few blocks away. They were getting louder by the second. *Damn it.* "We have to go."

Ana Thorne was just approaching the still-open security door to the fallout shelter when she suddenly saw flashlight beams bouncing toward her from the other side. *Oh, no. They're coming back.* She immediately sprinted away from the door and headed for cover at the far end of the parking deck. She had just turned a corner when three men in black ski masks came barreling through the doorway behind her.

Ana halted and carefully peeked back around the corner. At a distance of about thirty feet, she observed two goons frog-marching the man in the black leather coat through the security door. *Malachi.* The third goon was scanning the entire space with his machine gun at the ready. Ana immediately pulled back just as the third man looked in her direction. *Did he see me?*

A tense moment passed. Then she heard the men scuffling quickly toward the stairwell. *Which meant there was still a chance.* Ana immediately took off up the ramp toward the upper parking platforms, sprinting at full speed. If she hurried, she could still beat them to the top and surprise them. *At least it was worth a shot.*

A minute later, Ana arrived breathlessly on the first parking level and made a beeline for the two parked cars near the stairwell. She knew she would have only seconds to pull this off because the men would be coming up the stairwell at any moment. As she neared the stairwell, however, she realized that something was amiss. She stopped between the parked cars and strained between heavy breaths to hear any sounds at all coming from the stairwell. There were none. It was completely silent.

Where the hell did they go?

Ana quickly considered her options. She could climb the stairs back to the church, which, when last she checked, was crawling with goons with machine guns. *Or . . .* She looked across the parking platform at the large overhead door that provided vehicle access to the adjacent building. *Plan B.*

The car to Ana's left was a late-model Toyota Prius, just the type of car she imagined the church lady in the blue dress would probably drive. She gently lifted the door handle and was not entirely surprised when the door popped open. *Church lady is a trusting soul.* Within seconds, she spotted the exact item she needed: an electronic pass that provided access to the adjacent parking garage.

Krupnov and his henchman Sashko stood anxiously beside a white Ecoline van at the egress point, ready to go. Approaching sirens could still be heard nearby, although they seemed a bit more muted now. Inside the van, a cacophony of thumping, scraping, and grunting could be heard as four of Krupnov's goons worked hard to bind Malachi's hands and feet with duct tape, tape his mouth shut, and pull an opaque hood over his head.

"Where's number three?" Krupnov demanded.

Sashko shook his head. "He hasn't responded to his radio for several minutes. I don't know what happened to him."

Krupnov shook his head. *Unbelievable.* He may have lost *five* men today. And he still didn't have the Thurmond material. He suddenly pictured the grim faces of the *posrednikov*, the "facilitators" back in Russia. They were going to kill him if he failed to recover this material. *Literally kill him.* And not in a painless way.

"I should kill all of you," Krupnov hissed. "Right here and now. Where the *fuck* is number three?"

"Maybe he found the stone," said Sashko encouragingly. "Maybe that's what's taking him so long."

Krupnov said nothing for several seconds as the sirens continued to grow louder. Finally, he spat angrily on the ground and turned to Sashko. "Let's go."

Sashko nodded and climbed into the driver's seat. Krupnov was just making his way toward the passenger's side when something very unexpected happened behind him.

His luck was about to change.

Ana pressed the church lady's key pass against the electronic reader, and the overhead garage door began lifting slowly off the ground. She waited impatiently for the door to rise high enough that she could squeeze beneath it. Finally, when there was just enough room, she ducked low and scampered through.

"Don't move!" said a man's voice in a thick Russian accent.

Ana slowly rose to her feet and instantly realized her mistake. There were six of them in all, four thugs with black ski masks and two without. They were standing in front of a long white van with machine guns aimed directly at her. And there was nowhere to run. *They had her.* She could hear grunting and muffled screams emanating from the van, which she presumed was the man they called Malachi.

One of the two unmasked men slowly stepped forward until his face was very close to hers. Without saying a word, he gripped her face tightly with one hand and squeezed it until it hurt. He pulled her face toward his, forcing her to look directly into his icy blue eyes. Their lips were nearly touching. "You've caused me a great deal of trouble today," he said in a thick Russian accent.

"Who are you?" Ana asked through puckered lips.

"Someone you should not have fucked with," said Vladamir Krupnov. He released her face with a cruel shove, causing her to stumble backward a few steps. Then, without warning, he smashed the butt of his gun viciously into the side of her head.

It was the last thing she remembered before everything went black.

40

BEHIND THE HAY-ADAMS HOTEL, WASHINGTON, D.C.

MIKE CALIFANO pressed the transmit button for his microphone. "Ana, you there?" It was the third time he'd tried to raise her on the radio. Once again, there was no response at all. *Not good*.

The voice of Bill McCreary suddenly came on the line. "Michael, is that you?"

"Yeah, it's me."

"What's wrong with your voice?" McCreary asked. "It sounds weird."

"It sounds fine to me," said Califano. "Has anyone heard from Ana?"

"No," replied McCreary grimly. "Nothing from her in a while."

"I hear police sirens everywhere," said Califano. "Are they finding anything?"

There was a long pause before McCreary finally came back on the line. "Yes, Steve's monitoring all the police radio runs. They're apparently responding to gunshots fired at the

Third Church of Christ, Scientist. They've found two bodies in the alley behind the church . . . and they just found another one in the sanctuary. All of them white males."

"I suppose that's good news," Califano mumbled. As hard as he tried, he could not shake the disturbing image of Ana Thorne lying dead or dying in an underground bunker somewhere. And this was dredging up all sorts of raw emotions and memories that he desperately wished he could suppress right now.

"Michael?" said Bill McCreary.

But Califano was now lost in nightmarish thoughts about his murdered mother and sister.

"Michael?"

"Huh? Yeah?"

"What about the woman you saw? Do you know where she went?"

This snapped Califano out of his trance. *The woman in the white dress.* He stepped quickly to the edge of the shaft behind the Dumpster and peered down again into the darkness. *The white flash. He'd seen that phenomenon before. In the satellite video this morning.* "Hold on," he said.

For the next thirty seconds, Califano searched all around the service courtyard until he returned with a flat brick that he'd found in a small pile of replacement pavers. He brought it to the edge of the shaft, held it high over the center of the opening, then let it drop. He watched with anticipation as the brick fell through the shaft and disappeared into the darkness. At the exact moment when he expected to hear it land at the bottom with a loud clank . . . he heard nothing.

He quickly tapped the button for his microphone. "Bill, I think I know where she is. And I think she has the stone."

. . . .

Back at CIA headquarters, Bill McCreary was intensely interested in Califano's comment about the woman and the stone, and he was still puzzled by the odd tone of Califano's voice, which seemed to have mysteriously dropped several octaves. But all of this was suddenly interrupted by a strange commotion coming over the radio. Someone had just activated their transmitter but wasn't talking. Instead, thumping and scraping noises could be heard, along with sporadic, muffled voices in the background. *And something else.* McCreary strained to make it out. Eventually, he realized it was the sound of a revving engine and shifting gears. These noises went on for several seconds and then abruptly stopped as the transmitter apparently timed out.

"Mike, did you hear that?" McCreary asked over the radio.

"Sort of," said Califano a couple of seconds later. His voice came over the speakers in the DTAI workroom in a deep, unnatural baritone. "Was that Ana?"

Before McCreary could answer, Steve Goodwin shouted an urgent report from across the room. "Police just received a report of a suspicious white van that left the garage next door to the church about three minutes ago. Last seen heading north on Sixteenth."

McCreary immediately relayed that information to Califano.

"I'm on it," Califano said. He quickly began running in the direction of the black Chevy Tahoe that he and Ana had parked on Fifteenth Street earlier that morning. As he ran, he tapped the button for his transmitter. "Hey, Bill," he said between breaths.

"Yeah?"

"You may want to have someone cover the access points to that fallout shelter. Especially behind the hotel. I think we have a little time situation going on down there."

"Got it," said McCreary. "And by the way, your voice seems back to normal."

Ana Thorne was thinking about trains. The rhythmic bumping and jostling as the wheels rolled over uneven tracks. The noise of engines and horns and passengers shouting out the windows to friends and loved ones. She loved trains. They reminded her of holidays with her family as a little girl. The train ride from their home in Zagreb to Pula on the Mediterranean coast was always the most exciting. Watching the countryside whiz by as she anticipated the first magical feeling of sand between her toes and the cool blue waves of the Mediterranean Sea. Of course, that was before the war . . . before the explosion that killed her family and left her ear and neck badly scarred . . . before she was forced to start a new life with a new family in the United States.

Suddenly, very different noises were intruding into her thoughts. The constant shifting and downshifting of an automobile engine. Sporadic thumping and squealing brakes. And the ugly voices of angry men. These were not the joyous shouts of happy passengers on holiday. She opened her eyes, and the world was still black. It took her a moment to realize why. She had an opaque hood over her head.

Ana tried to move her arms and legs but couldn't. Her wrists were secured tightly behind her back and her legs were bound together at the ankles. She tried screaming, but her mouth was apparently taped shut. She was lying on her side on the hard metal floor of a cargo van, feeling every bump and pothole in the road as the van sped north out of the city. Her head throbbed terribly because of the brutal blow by the man with the Russian accent.

Ana did her best to keep track of what was going on

around her. She knew she could still collect valuable intelligence in this situation. In fact, she'd been specifically trained to do just that.

A man nearby was speaking English with a heavy Slavic accent. "Tell me what this is," he demanded.

"I'm telling you, I don't know," said a second man in American English. Ana deduced that this was probably the carjacker from Thurmond. *Malachi.*

Suddenly, there was the sound of a vicious slap, and the American man grunted in agony.

"You are Malachi, are you not?" asked the first man.

"Yes. I already told you that."

"Then answer my question. *Tell me what this is!*"

There were several seconds of silence followed by another brutal slap and the sounds of a man grunting in extreme pain.

"Give me that," said a third man. Ana recognized his voice as that of the Russian who had struck her with his gun. She deduced that he must be the leader of this group of thugs. She heard the sound of rustling paper being transferred from one hand to another. *So the thing they are asking about is on a sheet of paper.*

"These men are going to kill you if you don't answer their questions," said the Russian. "Do you understand that? Good. Now, I can help you avoid that fate, but only if you cooperate with me."

Good cop, bad cop, Ana thought. A classic interrogation technique, and one of the most effective.

"I understand you don't recognize this exact drawing," said the Russian. "But have you ever seen anything *like* this before?"

"I don't know," said the American man after a pause. "Maybe."

"When?"

"A long time ago . . . with her."

"Who? The woman you met at the church today?"

"Yeah."

"What's her name?"

"Opal."

"And what did she tell you about the twelve stones shown in this sketch?"

"I . . . I don't remember anything about twelve stones. I swear."

The Russian sighed. "I can't help you if you won't help me."

There was some jostling as the men apparently repositioned themselves in the back of the van. Then, suddenly, there was another brutal slap, and the American man cried out in agony.

Moments later, Ana felt her own head being lifted up and her body being rudely dragged across the floor of the van. Someone grabbed her beneath her arms and propped her up into a sitting position against the side of the van. She could feel the bite of sticky duct tape around her wrists and over her mouth. Then, suddenly, she felt the warmth of another person's face next to her own. She heard heavy breathing and could feel hot breath on her ear. She could see just a bit of flesh color through her hood.

"You're next," whispered the Russian man into her ear. His voice was sinister, and tinged with a kind of sadistic pleasure that made her skin crawl.

41

THE BLACK CHEVY TAHOE barreled down Sixteenth Street like a freight train with Mike Califano at the wheel. In the past ten minutes, it had been photographed no fewer than three times by red-light cameras as Califano blew through intersection after intersection with little more than a tap on the brakes. He didn't care. He had to catch that white van.

"I don't see it," he barked into his microphone as he scanned every cross street he passed. "Any idea where it went?"

The voice of Steve Goodwin came on the line a moment later. "Mike. This is Steve. I'm taking over for Dr. McCreary because he had to step out."

"All right, big guy. Tell me where that white van went."

"I'm looking at raw feeds from all the DHS cameras in the district. Just give me another minute."

"Dude, I'm doing seventy. In a minute, I'll be in Maryland."

"Okay, I got it," said Goodwin after a few seconds. "A white van matching the description just passed Connecticut westbound on M. You're going the wrong way."

Shit. Califano immediately slammed on the brakes and maneuvered the bulky Tahoe through a squealing U-turn in the intersection of Sixteenth and T Streets. Two minutes later, he swerved sharply onto M Street, heading west. "All right, I'm on M Street now." He was doing his best to swerve through traffic, which was much heavier on M Street than it had been on Sixteenth. He finally reached the intersection of M and Connecticut Avenue and stopped abruptly at a red light. He scanned the intersection in all directions but saw no white vans. "Should I keep going straight?"

"Stand by," said Goodwin calmly. "I've got all the DHS cameras west of Connecticut, and I've seen nothing in Foggy Bottom. Nothing on Constitution. Nothing on E Street. Nothing on any of the bri— Wait, here we go." Goodwin paused for a moment. "Okay, I just saw a white van heading westbound on K, going down into the tunnel beneath Washington Circle. Looks like it's heading toward the Whitehurst Freeway."

Califano thought about the Whitehurst Freeway for a moment. As he recalled, it was a limited-access road throughout its entire stretch through Georgetown—no on-ramps or off-ramps. "Steve," he said quickly. "Call the metro police and have them block off Whitehurst where it intersects with Canal Road. We can trap them there."

"Will do," said Goodwin.

Califano cut the wheel left and screeched onto Twenty-first Street southbound. Two blocks later, he hit the brakes and banked a hard right onto K Street. He accelerated and the Tahoe lurched down into the tunnel that stretched about a hundred and fifty yards beneath Washington Circle. Seeing that the tunnel was clear ahead, Califano gunned the accelerator, and the Tahoe's powerful engine responded with a roar. At nearly sixty miles per hour, however, Califano suddenly saw brake lights ahead, just beyond the tunnel exit. *Oh shit. Red light.*

Califano swerved into the eastbound lane just as the Tahoe emerged from the Washington Circle tunnel with its wheels slightly off the ground and whizzed by a line of stopped cars at Twenty-sixth and K. That's when he saw the oncoming delivery truck heading straight toward him in the eastbound lane, blasting its horn. *Crap!* He instinctively cut the wheel to the right, missing the truck by inches and narrowly avoiding the last of the stopped cars on his right. Two seconds later, the Tahoe careened up an on-ramp and onto the elevated Whitehurst Freeway. Califano slowed the vehicle and let out a relieved breath. *Damn, that was close.* He activated his microphone. "Steve, I'm on the Whitehurst now."

"Roadblock should be in place," said Goodwin. "They just got there."

The elevated Whitehurst Freeway cut straight through the tony waterfront section of Georgetown, running parallel to the Potomac River about a hundred feet from the water's edge. This drove Georgetowners crazy because it blocked their view of the river. In fact, they had petitioned for decades to get the Whitehurst torn down. But that was never going to happen. Not as long as it provided an easy commuting route for certain politicians and the well-heeled denizens who lived just upriver in Palisades and in the close-in suburbs of Virginia and Maryland.

Califano brought the Tahoe to an abrupt halt behind two lanes of stopped vehicles. *The roadblock.* He jumped out and began sprinting toward Canal Road along the concrete barrier on the left-hand side of the freeway. He unholstered his pistol as he ran, drawing incredulous looks from a few drivers inside their stopped vehicles. As the pavement began sloping down toward Canal Road, Califano could now see the blue flashing lights of the roadblock ahead.

And there it was.

Three vehicles back from the roadblock on the left-hand side of the freeway was a Ford E-350 van—white, just like the description of the van that had been spotted near the church. *That had to be it.* Califano slowed his pace and approached the van carefully. As he did, he saw two armed D.C. policemen approaching from the other side. "Mike Califano," he shouted to them. "CIA."

The cops nodded but didn't look terribly impressed. One of them signaled for Califano to stay back. He complied. *Let's just see how this goes,* he figured. With his pistol still drawn, he watched from about thirty feet away as one of the cops carefully opened the driver's-side door with his gun drawn. He appeared to be giving the driver an order. A moment later, the driver got out of the van.

Right away, Califano could tell something was wrong. The driver was short and Hispanic looking, and he was wearing cargo shorts and a white T-shirt. *None of the thugs back at the church looked anything like that.* He continued watching with concern as the cop frisked the man and placed him in handcuffs against the van. *No, no, no. This was all wrong.*

Califano quickly changed positions so he could see the other side of the van. The cop on the other side had another man in handcuffs. He, too, was Hispanic and dressed in shorts, a T-shirt, and a painter's cap.

Califano shook his head and began approaching the vehicle, ignoring what the police officer had told him to do.

"Stay back, sir," said the cop on the passenger side.

Califano kept walking. "I'm with the CIA. I'm the one who ordered this roadblock."

The cop eyed Califano suspiciously and trained his pistol on him. "Stay back."

Califano ignored the cop and continued walking straight toward the van until he reached the cargo door on the passenger side. He hesitated just a moment before pulling hard on the handle and sliding the door wide open.

Empty.

The only contents of the van were a few paint cans, some paint-spattered tarps, and a small stepladder.

Shit! Wrong van.

"Who are you?" whispered the Russian man into Ana Thorne's ear.

She was sitting with her back against the side of a moving vehicle, with her hands and feet bound, mouth taped shut, and the opaque hood still over her head. She could tell the vehicle was out of the city now, traveling fast on a relatively smooth highway with light traffic. She tried to speak but could only manage to vibrate her voice box. "Mmmmph. Mmm. Mmmmph."

Suddenly there was light as the man pulled off her hood. Ana winced and quickly looked all around, taking stock of her situation. The Russian man was beside her, to the right. Another goon in a tracksuit was sitting across from her, leering at her with some sort of stupid grin. The driver and three other men were in front. And the man they called Malachi was on the floor in the middle of the cargo section, with his feet and hands bound tightly with duct tape. His face was bruised and swollen, and a mixture of blood and saliva was drooling out of his mouth, forming a frothy pool of red on the van floor. For a moment, he caught her gaze and held it. He looked confused . . . and terrified.

The Russian man grabbed one edge of the tape covering Ana's mouth and ripped it off in one cruel motion.

"Ow!" Ana shouted as the adhesive tape pulled painfully away from her skin.

"Ready to talk now?" asked Vladamir Krupnov as he squatted down in front of her.

Ana stared back impassively.

"What's your name?"

"Ana Thorne," she said flatly, in accordance with CIA protocol.

"Who do you work for?"

"U.S. Department of State," she replied without hesitation. This, too, was in accordance with standard CIA protocol. Her default employer was *always* the State Department. In fact, if anyone had ever bothered to check, they would have found a complete employment file on her at the State Department, including W-2s, performance evaluations, and even an EEOC complaint against a previous supervisor who'd harassed her. All fake, of course.

Krupnov was quiet for a while, apparently weighing her answer. "State Department, hmm?"

Ana shrugged. "That's where I work."

Krupnov snorted and curled his lips into a crooked smile. With the back of his hand, he gently stroked her cheek and allowed his hand to drift slowly down her neck, stopping at the scarred region just below her ear. "What's this?" He clucked his tongue several times. "What a shame." His hand continued drifting downward along the curves of her body until it reached her inner thigh, where it rested for several seconds. He leaned in close and whispered into her ear, "Young lady, if you don't start telling me the truth, this is going to get very, *very* messy."

Ana swallowed hard but said nothing.

Krupnov's face remained close to Ana's ear for several seconds. She could hear him inhaling deeply, apparently savoring the aroma of her hair. Then he suddenly pushed back and retrieved a folded piece of paper from his pocket. He unfolded it and held it up for her to see. It appeared to be a photocopy of a tattered notebook page containing a crude sketch of some sort of building with twelve circles in a rectangular box, ten of which were grouped together with dashed lines. There was some German writing scrawled beneath the sketch.

Ana stared at the drawing and did her best to conceal her surprise. *She'd seen something almost identical at Tom Reynolds's house.*

"Do you recognize this?" asked Krupnov. He studied her eyes closely as he awaited her response.

"No," she lied.

Krupnov did not react at first. Finally, after a long pause, he exhaled loudly and turned to the thug behind him, who still had the same stupid grin on his face. *"Vascha Cherga,"* he said with a shrug.

Your turn.

Mike Califano returned to his vehicle and tapped the button for his microphone. "Steve," he said emphatically. "Get these guys to clear this roadblock *now*. They won't listen to me for some reason."

"On it," said Goodwin.

As Califano waited impatiently for the roadblock to clear, he pulled his cell phone from his pocket and speed-dialed Admiral Armstrong. He pressed the phone to his ear but heard no ringing for several seconds. Then he held the phone up and saw that he had no service. *What the hell?* He tapped his microphone again. "Hey, Steve. Can you patch me through to Admiral Armstrong? My phone's not working."

"Stand by," said Goodwin. A few seconds later, he came back on the line. "By the way, that roadblock should be clearing now."

Good. At least one of us has some pull around here.

As the traffic began to inch forward, Admiral Armstrong came on the line. "Armstrong," he said curtly.

"Admiral. It's Mike Califano. I was wondering if you could have your satellite boys help us find a white van that left the city about fifteen minutes ago. I know there'll be a ton of them on the road, but maybe they can help narrow it down somehow." He paused and exhaled. "I think they have Ana."

"I wish I could help, Mike. But we're having a crisis of our own here. Have you been listening to the news?"

"Uh, no. I've been kind of busy."

"Satellites are all out of sync. GPS, civilian, and all of ours, too. Some sort of problem with the master clock."

Of course, Califano thought. "The master clock's at the Naval Observatory. That's about two miles from the Hay-Adams."

"So?"

"I saw a bright flash there about twenty minutes ago. Just like the one we saw in the White Sea."

"Twenty minutes ago, you say? Yep, makes sense. *Damn.* If it screwed up the master clock even half a second, that would wreak havoc with our satellites. Is someone looking into it?"

By now, the traffic on the Whitehurst Freeway was moving swiftly. "Dr. McCreary's on it," said Califano.

"Oh, that makes me feel a lot better," Armstrong muttered. "Look, I gotta go. Good luck."

Califano shook his head as he accelerated the Tahoe forward. Seconds later, he passed the police car at the bottom of the off-ramp and turned left onto Canal Road. *Time to regroup.* He eased the Tahoe up to cruising speed and glanced momentarily at the gravel towpath of the C&O Canal whizzing by on his left, where mules once pulled canal boats into the city two centuries before. He turned on the Tahoe's radio and quickly found a news station. A man with a deep voice was in the middle of a rambling broadcast:

> *. . . appears to be a worldwide outage. Anyone who has GPS in their car or on their mobile phone or tablet computer will probably notice that they're not able to acquire any satellite signals. Many cellular phone networks also appear to be down. And again, this appears to be a worldwide problem. We're getting reports now that airports are suspending flights until further notice. FAA regulations require a functioning GPS, so, until the system comes back, all commercial flights are temporarily grounded. Once again, we are reporting a major, worldwide disruption in the global positioning system and other critical satellites. We will continue to keep you updated after this short commercial message . . .*

Califano turned down the volume and shook his head. *Jesus.* It was amazing what a little slippage in time could do. No wonder Dr. McCreary was so adamant about preventing this technology from falling into the wrong hands.

His thoughts quickly shifted back to the white van . . . and Ana Thorne. They were taking her somewhere. *But where? Likely somewhere close by, or at least within driving distance.* He wished he had his data-mining program available to him right now. At least that would save him a trip back to CIA headquarters—valuable time that he could not afford to lose right now.

He tapped the transmit button. "Hey, Steve? Have you ever used my data-mining program?"

"No," said Goodwin. "Only Dr. McCreary's."

"Looks like today's your lucky day."

42

BILL MCCREARY was staring down at the bloody corpse of a man who was slumped awkwardly against a trash bin with two bullet holes in his chest. *Califano's work, no doubt.* Looking up, he once again scanned the service courtyard behind the Hay-Adams hotel for the vertical shaft that was supposed to be here, the one that provided access to the fallout shelter beneath the Third Church of Christ, Scientist. *Where is it?* He'd already circled the courtyard once with no success, and he was just about to do so again when he suddenly realized what he'd been overlooking the whole time.

The Dumpster.

With care, he stepped over the dead man's legs and made his way around the corner of the Dumpster.

And there it was.

He was now standing at the edge of a square hole, about four feet across with a heavy steel access panel that was flipped over on its hinges. He observed a steel ladder secured to one side of the shaft, which extended downward and disappeared into the darkness below. He energized his powerful flashlight and pointed it straight down into the shaft, illuminating the bottom some forty feet below. It looked to be empty, but the cement bottom was shimmering, much like an asphalt road on a hot day. He considered this fact for a moment, then he reached into his pocket and pulled out a quarter. With his flashlight still illuminating the shaft, he held the coin above the opening for a moment and released it, watching as it fell straight down, spinning and glinting in the beam of the flashlight.

Until it suddenly vanished near the bottom.

"Whoa." He continued watching the shaft for several seconds, utterly amazed, half expecting the quarter to suddenly reappear and hit the bottom. But it never did.

"Hello?" he shouted down into the shaft. His voice reverberated in the narrow vertical space and then quickly dissipated, with just the faintest echo still audible somewhere deep below.

Aside from the echo, there was no reply.

He checked his digital watch, which read 7:42 A.M. He wondered whether that was still the correct time. After all, he'd heard the reports on the way into the district about the GPS satellites falling out of sync. *And now he knew why.* He suspected the entire city of Washington, D.C., had just experienced a very mild time dilation. Perhaps on the order of a few seconds, maybe less for most areas. And most people never even knew about it. Except for the GPS issue, of course.

McCreary also now understood why Califano's voice had sounded so funny on the radio. Standing at this very spot, Califano would have been at the peak of the bell curve, experiencing a much higher time-dilation factor than the folks back at Langley, who were probably experiencing little or none at all. That had apparently created something akin to a Doppler effect, making Califano's voice sound deeper than normal.

"Steve, can you hear me?" McCreary said into his microphone.

Steve Goodwin answered a few seconds later. "Yeah, boss."

"How do I sound?"

"Like Barry White."

McCreary nodded knowingly and then peered down into the shaft. *Of course, the highest time-dilation factor would be down there.*

McCreary considered his options for a few minutes, repeatedly checking the shaft with his flashlight to see if anything had changed. It hadn't.

Finally, blowing out a long, nervous breath, he eased his large, oafish frame onto the first rung of the ladder. *Time to find out where my quarter went.*

43

D O YOU *want* to die?" asked Vladamir Krupnov in a measured tone that bordered on politeness.

The man strapped to the chair in front of him, Malachi, shook his head. His face was badly bruised and bloody. His left eye was swollen completely shut and was about the same size and color as a plum. His other eye didn't look much better, although at least it was still open a slit. The man's cheeks were puffy and raw from repeated beatings, and his lips were grotesquely swollen and bleeding.

"Then I suggest you start making yourself useful to me," said Krupnov in the same measured tone. He paused to gauge Malachi's reaction. "Do you understand?"

Malachi nodded slowly.

"Good," said Krupnov. "It's very important that you understand that." He stepped away and returned a few seconds later pulling a wooden chair slowly across the pine floor of the guesthouse's master bedroom. He sat down

directly in front of Malachi and stared into his one functioning eye. "You see, the moment I feel you are no longer
useful to me . . . the moment I think you are wasting my
time . . . *that* is the moment you will die. Is that clear?"

Malachi nodded his head lackadaisically. He appeared
to be on the verge of unconsciousness.

"And after everything you've been through, that would be
a shame. Don't you agree?"

Malachi did not respond.

"So let's go through this again," said Krupnov. "And
please try to be more helpful this time."

Malachi closed his one good eye and nodded.

"Okay. You entered the Thurmond lab in the spring of
1972, hmm?"

Malachi nodded feebly.

"Early March?"

Malachi nodded again.

"And, at that time, you were working for MOSS."

"A volunteer," said Malachi through swollen lips.

Krupnov smiled. "Right. A *volunteer* for MOSS."

Malachi nodded his head in agreement.

"And you had two simple tasks. Recover the material
from the lab . . ."

Malachi nodded.

"And obtain the map from Dr. Holzberg showing the
location of the remaining stones."

Malachi closed his right eye and slowly shook his head
from side to side. A quiet groan of frustration arose from his
throat. "I don't remember a map," he said with great effort.

Krupnov sighed and then rose to his feet with a tremendous show of disappointment. He raised his right hand
and was poised to strike Malachi brutally across the face
when a voice behind him suddenly called out, "Let me talk
to him."

Krupnov dropped his hand and turned toward the laptop computer behind him, which was displaying a live video shot of Dr. Benjamin Fulcher. "Bring me closer," Fulcher said.

Krupnov slid the laptop computer to the edge of the table. Then he and Sashko lifted Malachi's chair and maneuvered it until it was directly facing the laptop computer.

"Daniel, do you recognize me?" asked Fulcher via the secure video link.

Malachi tilted his head, trying to get a better view of the screen through the remaining field of vision in his right eye. After several seconds, he slowly nodded his head up and down. "Elijah," he mumbled.

"Yes, of course you remember me," said Fulcher. "We were a team. *MOSS*. The Mother of Science Society." Fulcher said these words slowly, almost reverently. Then his tone suddenly changed. "Silly organization," he said with a dismissive shake of his head. "Save humanity from itself," he said mockingly. "Prevent man from doing what he is *destined* to do . . . which is to consume the apple of knowledge to the core. Chew it up. Digest it. So that we ourselves can become like God. It's not a tragedy to be prevented. It's *fate*."

Malachi remained motionless. If he had any expression on his face at all, it was impossible to see beneath his injuries.

"You were a fool, Daniel."

"I fulfilled my destiny," mumbled Malachi through painfully swollen lips.

"You fulfilled nothing," Fulcher sneered. "You were blinded by your devotion to Opal and misguided by a childish philosophy."

"I was called by God."

"Ha! God doesn't call men to service. God is a *mechanism*. A contraption of ingenious design that we are destined to solve . . . and master. *Deus ex machina*. Are we slaves to the machine, Daniel? No. It serves *us*."

"*Deus summus est ens aeternum, infinitum*," said Malachi in labored measure.

"Do not quote Newton to *me!*" Fulcher said, seething. "He wrote that portion of the Scholium under duress, and everybody knows it. Newton didn't believe in a living God any more than he believed in heaven and hell. He understood the truth. That the clockwork universe *is* God. And man is the clock winder. Why is that so hard for you to accept? Hmm? God gave us a machine, and we are meant to run it."

Malachi remained silent.

"What a shame you wasted your youth on this claptrap. Look at you now. Gray hair and wrinkles and nothing to show for it. Although, I must say, I'm surprised by this interesting aging effect. Gray hair and wrinkles . . . yet your body looks youthful. Perhaps time dilation causes *cellular* aging, inside out, but with no atrophy. Interesting . . ." His voice trailed off as he appeared to contemplate this phenomenon for several seconds. "Well, to tell you the truth, I didn't know what kind of physiological artifacts there might be. I suppose it was unethical to experiment on you like that." He paused for a moment and smirked. "But you were such an eager volunteer. Who was I to stand in your way?"

"So you knew," said Malachi slowly.

"What, that you'd be gone for a very long time? Oh yes, I knew that. Of course, I didn't think it would take *this* long. But, fortunately, I'm a patient man." He cocked his head to one side. "But what of your lovely Opal? You must have been quite surprised to see her wrinkly old face."

Malachi's face grew slightly more contorted than it already was.

"Tell me, Daniel, is your devotion to her just as strong? Are you still willing to sacrifice everything for her?"

Malachi closed his one good eye and said nothing.

"Time is running short," said Fulcher. "So I'm only going to ask you this once. But before you answer, you should understand something. I am going to solve this puzzle with or without your help. Einstein may have been confounded by it, and my dear friend Franz Holzberg may have failed miserably with it. But *I will not*. Time and gravity are the final dimensions to be conquered, and I am on the cusp of controlling both. Finally, man's destiny will be achieved. We will be our own God."

"You're crazy," mumbled Malachi.

"Crazy? Or heretical? There's a difference, you know. I'm quite proud to be among heretics like Galileo, Copernicus, and Newton. But I digress. Right now, the only thing *you* need to worry about is whether you still love Opal."

Malachi lifted his head. "What are you talking about?"

Fulcher's face twisted into a patronizing smile. "Daniel. We know exactly where she is. And as soon as her little time bubble decays—and that shouldn't take too long—we'll have her *and* the Thurmond material in our possession. So, like I said, I'm only going to ask you this one time. If you want to spare your dear Opal a great deal of pain and suffering, I suggest you tell us what we want to know. *Right now.*"

Malachi was already shaking his head back and forth. "I'm telling you—"

"Shut up," said Fulcher. He held a sheet of paper up to the camera. It was the same drawing of the houselike structure and twelve circles with German notation beneath them that they'd shown him in the van. "Daniel, I want to know where these remaining stones are located." He pointed to the dashed box that enclosed ten of the small circles. "I know they're all together. And Franz Holzberg knew exactly where. Now tell me how to find them."

Malachi closed his eyes and was silent for a very long time. Finally, he dropped his head and muttered, "I *don't know*."

Fulcher pursed his lips tightly and abruptly stood up. A second later, he bent down so that his face filled the entire computer screen. "You're a goddamned fool," he said with a scowl. He paused and shook his head. "Vlad, he's all yours."

Ana Thorne was lying facedown on a soft bed, her hands secured tightly behind her back with several layers of duct tape. Her ankles, too, were taped tightly together. At the moment, she was thinking about the last time she'd been tied up like this, which was twelve years ago.

It was during her CIA training at Camp Peary, when she'd received a full day's instruction on how to escape from various types of restraints, everything from ropes to handcuffs to nylon zip ties. During that training, she'd learned that some restraints were easier to escape from than others. And one of the easiest of all . . . was duct tape.

She turned her head and sized up the unshaven goon who had been guarding her in this small bedroom for the past hour. He wore gray warm-up pants and a grimy wifebeater undershirt with a gold chain dangling around his neck. At the moment, he was leaning back in his chair near the door with what appeared to be a Beretta 9-millimeter pistol in his lap. For the past hour, he'd been rocking back and forth in that chair, chewing gum like a cow and leering at her with the same stupid expression that he'd worn in the van.

Ana knew exactly what he was thinking. *And it was time*

to give him what he wanted. With some effort, she rolled herself over onto her back and sat up on the edge of the bed so that she was facing the man. Her jacket was open, exposing her white, form-fitting tank top. "Hey," she said, tipping her head back slightly.

The man did not respond at first, although he was obviously enjoying the view.

"Hey," she said again, her voice soft and beckoning.

"What do you want?" said the man with a thick Ukrainian accent. He seemed very apprehensive about what was happening.

Maybe he's not as dumb as he looks, Ana thought, considering this possibility for a moment. *No, he probably is.* She arched her back and let out a sensuous groan. "Ahh, I just need someone to scratch my back. God, that would feel *sooo* good right now."

The man stared back at her and continued chewing his gum.

"Can't you just scratch it a little?" asked Ana in full flirtation mode. "That's all I need. Just a little scratch." She squirmed her torso all around. "Come on, don't be mean."

The man watched impassively as Ana moved her body around with catlike grace.

Ana could tell he was ready to cave. "No?" she asked softly, sounding a bit dejected. "Not even a little scratch?" She pouted. *And that was all it took.*

"*Dobre,*" said the goon, rolling his eyes. He stood and tucked his pistol into the back of his waistband, then slowly approached the bed. He drew near and pressed his crotch and stomach up against her as he reached over and scratched her back with one hand. "Like this?" he asked. With his other hand, he reached around and cupped one of her breasts and began squeezing it.

In an instant, Ana brought her unbound hands around

and grabbed the man's pistol from the back of his pants. Amazingly, he didn't even seem to notice at first. He was still scratching her back and fondling her breast. Then Ana jabbed the barrel of the Beretta hard into the man's stomach.

Now he noticed. *"Vy poviya!"* he shouted as he brought his massive hand up to strike her across the face.

But Ana wasn't about to let that happen. She pulled the Beretta's trigger, and a 9-millimeter round instantly exploded into the man's stomach. He winced and looked down in disbelief at the growing circle of red on his grimy white undershirt. "You . . . *bitch*," he sputtered. He grabbed the wound tightly with both hands and gawked as blood leaked in great volumes between his fingers. He stumbled backward into a nightstand, knocking it over and sending its lamp and telephone crashing to the floor. Two seconds later, he hit the floor and grunted in pain as he slowly drew his knees to his chest and assumed the fetal position.

Meanwhile, Ana quickly unraveled the duct tape around her ankles. She was nearly done when she heard the heavy footsteps of someone fast approaching in the hallway outside the door.

With her feet finally free, she hopped off the bed and rushed to the opposite side of the room, where two wooden doors were located side by side. She turned the handle of the first and swung it open wide. *A closet.* She quickly moved to the next door and checked its handle. *Locked.*

Just then, the door from the hallway began to open. Ana barely had time to train her newly acquired Beretta toward the door before it flew wide open and a thug in a tracksuit came barging into the room brandishing a compact Uzi machine gun. He took one look at his fallen comrade on the floor, then immediately began firing his weapon in Ana's direction. In the same instant, she pulled the Beretta's trigger three times in rapid succession. The deafening sound of gunshots filled the small room. Ana flinched as the door beside her exploded into splinters and the window behind her instantaneously shattered. Drywall, plaster, and bits of broken glass flew in every direction.

Ana was sure she'd been hit. She looked up and saw the man with the machine gun tumbling backward with two bullet wounds in his chest. *Center of mass.* Then she checked her own body and was amazed to find that she hadn't been hit at all.

A miracle.

Suddenly, more footsteps and voices could be heard from somewhere inside the house. *She had to get out of there.* She glanced at the shattered window behind her and was surprised to see a red metal roof directly beneath it—apparently a covering for some sort of porch or walkway attached to the house. She approached and quickly knocked out the remaining shards of glass from the frame and removed the screen. Then, with one last glance behind her, she crawled through the window and hopped down onto the red metal roof below.

The metal roof was sloped . . . *and slippery.* She found herself sliding quickly toward the edge, and there was no stopping it. Two seconds later, she tumbled awkwardly over the edge and into the bushes eight feet below, where she landed in a painful tangle of branches and holly leaves. She slowly worked her way free of this mess and flopped ungracefully onto the mulched planting bed beside the guesthouse.

She rose to her feet and took stock of her situation. Other than scrapes and cuts, she was fine. For the moment, it was eerily quiet. She gazed out over the manicured grounds of the Hillcrest estate and could see a mansion and swimming pool about fifty yards away, and a barn beyond that. *But where was everyone?*

Her answer came a moment later in the form of automatic gunfire. The mulch in front of her suddenly exploded as a torrent of bullets whizzed close by her head and into the ground. Several rounds pinged loudly off the metal roof above her and ricocheted into the distance. Someone was apparently firing from the bedroom window above her but did not have a clear shot. When the gunfire subsided a few seconds later, she ran.

She sprinted at full speed until she reached the open lawn between the guesthouse and the pool. *Which way?* She paused momentarily and stole a quick glance behind her. To her horror, she saw three goons rushing out of the guesthouse, shouting wildly and pointing toward her. She saw one of them leveling his weapon, preparing to fire.

Ana immediately turned right and sprinted away as a stream of bullets whizzed through the space where she'd been standing a second before. She passed the pool area behind the main mansion and continued at full speed toward the open fields beyond the barn. *Not good*, she realized. *Out in the open, exposed.* Out of the corner of her eye, she spotted two more men with guns exiting the back of the mansion and making their way through the pool area.

Great. Five men on her trail, and she was heading straight for an open field. *Target practice.*

Twenty seconds later, Ana passed the barn and continued racing toward the open field beyond it. It was a terrible plan. But, unfortunately, it was the only one she had. The closest of her pursuers was now about thirty yards away and gaining steadily. She could hear shouts in Ukrainian and sporadic bursts of automatic gunfire behind her. But she dared not look back, not even for a second. *Keep running!*

Suddenly, a new sound was permeating the air. It was a rhythmic, thumping noise that seemed to have arisen from out of nowhere, and it grew quickly until it was deafening overhead. *And then she saw it.* A black helicopter suddenly swooped low over her head and banked sharply into the air, coming to a low-altitude hover about thirty yards away, facing directly toward her. *Oh shit.* She was forced to stop running because of the intense rotor wash.

Without warning, muzzle flashes suddenly erupted from the chopper's twin 20-millimeter cannons. Ana instinctively hit the ground. As she did, she noticed the grass behind her being violently torn up in two straight lines extending back toward the houses. A split second later, two of the five goons behind her lurched backward in a splatter of blood and fell to the ground. The other three goons were now sprinting away in different directions.

The pitch of the chopper's engines began changing. Ana looked up and saw that the MH-60L Blackhawk had now turned sideways and was descending. She shook her head in disbelief and immediately got to her feet. As the chopper touched down about twenty yards away, she began making her way toward it with great effort, leaning forward against the heavy rotor wash. As she approached, the side door of the Blackhawk opened.

And there was the smiling face of Mike Califano.

Unbelievable.

Califano was crouching low in the doorway with four CIA special ops guys behind him. Two of them jumped out immediately and helped Ana into the chopper. Once she was safely aboard, the other two special ops guys jumped out onto the lawn. She watched as the four of them regrouped momentarily and quickly fanned out and headed toward the mansion and guesthouse.

The pitch of the Blackhawk's powerful engines suddenly increased and the chopper began rising into the air.

"You all right?" Califano shouted over the noise.

Ana looked at him and nodded. "Don't let this go to your head," she said between breaths. "But you've got impeccable timing."

Califano shrugged. "Just had to be a little creative."

Ana smiled and reached out her hand, letting it come to rest on his shoulder. "Yeah. Thanks for that."

Four hundred yards away, a black BMW 750i was quietly leaving the Hillcrest estate at the same moment the Blackhawk helicopter was lifting off the ground.

"Not too fast," warned Vladamir Krupnov from the backseat. "We don't want to attract attention."

"I understand," said Sashko Melnik.

The BMW cruised north on Route 626 for several minutes and was soon indistinguishable from the other luxury vehicles heading off to various Sunday activities in the picturesque Virginia countryside.

44

HELL OF a day," said Mike Califano as he eased himself into one of the chairs around the small conference table in the DTAI workroom. Ana Thorne and Steve Goodwin were there, too, seated at the table.

"That's an understatement," muttered Ana.

"Anyone heard from Doc McCreary?" asked Califano.

Goodwin and Thorne both shook their heads.

"That can't be good," Califano mumbled.

"Should we wait for Admiral Armstrong?" asked Goodwin. "He said he'd be—"

"I'm here," announced Armstrong as he entered the workroom. "Finally got all the birds on the same clock. Crisis averted. Lives saved. Jesus, what a mess."

"So everyone's got their navigation systems back?" asked Ana.

"Yeah, and their cell phones and satellite TVs, too," Armstrong replied. "More important, NSA has all its spy satellites back. I'm telling you, I don't *ever* want to go through that again. President's still trying to decide whether he needs to address the nation about this tonight. In the meantime, will one of you geniuses *please* explain what the hell happened?"

The three "geniuses" at the table looked at each other, trying to figure out who should go first. Finally, Califano spoke. "I guess I'll start." For the next fifteen minutes, he explained to Admiral Armstrong everything that had happened that day, including the events at the Third Church of Christ, Scientist; the Russian and Ukrainian thugs; the man in the black leather coat and the old woman in white; the underground bomb shelter; and the bright flash behind the Hay-Adams hotel. He also explained how Steve Goodwin was able to use Califano's data-mining program to figure out that the Hillcrest estate in Middleburg was the center of all this activity.

"Good job, Steve," said Ana.

"Thanks. But Mike talked me through it."

Finally, Califano concluded with an account of the Blackhawk landing at the Hillcrest estate and Ana Thorne's escape.

"So these Russian assholes—Krupnov Energy—did they actually recover the material they were looking for? I mean, do we have to worry about more of these time events coming from Russia?"

"Yes and no," said Ana.

"Not what I was hoping to hear," Armstrong grumbled.

Ana straightened in her chair. "From what I could tell, Admiral, they did *not* recover any of the material from Thurmond. Of course, they obviously have *some* material, which we saw the effects of in the White Sea. But it sounded to me like they're still looking for more."

Armstrong was confused. "Wait. Other than the Thurmond material, where else do they expect to find more of this stuff?"

"Ah," said Ana. She turned to Califano. "Mike, can you put something on the screen for me? It's probably on the Internet."

"Sure." Califano rolled his chair over to his computer workstation. At the same time, Goodwin turned on the projector and lowered the screen at the front of the room.

"Okay, where to?" asked Califano, as the Google Web site slowly came into focus on the screen.

"Find me an image of the Madaba map."

"Madaba? Like M-A-D-A-B-A?"

"Uh-huh."

Seconds later, an image of an incredibly detailed mosaic map appeared on the screen.

"Whoa," said Goodwin. "What's that?"

"This is the oldest known map of the Holy Land," Ana explained. "It's located on the floor of an old Byzantine church in Madaba, Jordan, which dates from at least the sixth century A.D. I saw a copy of this same map on the wall of Dr. Reynolds's home office in Florida. And there was one feature in particular he was very interested in."

"Which was what?" asked Califano.

Ana stood and pointed to a spot on the lower-right-hand side of the map. "Can you focus in right about . . . here?"

Califano manipulated the image and eventually succeeded in zooming in on that particular spot. On the screen was a mosaic version of a houselike structure and twelve circles, similar to what Ana had been shown in the van:

"The men in the van asked me about a sketch that looked a lot like this," she said. "Except it'd been photocopied from some old notebook, and it had notations on it in German. I recognized it right away because Tom Reynolds explained this exact feature of the Madaba map to me at his house."

"And what do those words say?" asked Admiral Armstrong, pointing to the words above the house structure.

"In Greek, it says *Galgala-tokai Dodekalithon*, which means the town of Galgala with twelve stones."

"And are those the twelve stones there?" asked Califano, pointing to the white circles.

"Uh-huh. The book of Joshua talks a lot about those twelve stones, and Dr. Holzberg was apparently very interested in them, too."

"Of course," whispered Califano to himself.

"What's that?" asked Ana.

"Remember what Dr. Holzberg said? 'There are ten more.' Ten more *stones*. It totally makes sense now. He was worried about someone finding the other ten stones."

Ana nodded. "I think you're right. And there's more. The sketch they asked me about in the van was annotated like this." She stepped forward and drew an imaginary X over two of the white circles in the lower-right-hand corner. "These two stones had X's through them."

"Meaning what?" Armstrong asked.

"I don't know. Could mean they've been found and retrieved. Who knows?" She next drew an imaginary box around the remaining ten stones. "These ten stones were boxed together like this and labeled as *'Gefunden, Karte three.'*"

"Found, see map three," said Califano, translating from the German.

"Thanks, I was just about to say that. Anyway, those guys in the van were really interested in these ten stones. I think *this* is what they're still trying to get their hands on. In addition to the Thurmond material, of course."

"Hmm," said Armstrong, stroking his chin. "And what exactly do these twelve stones do?"

"Good question," said Ana. For the next twenty minutes, she repeated everything she'd learned from Tom Reynolds, including the accounts from the book of Joshua, the differing claims about the book of Jasher, and the three-thousand-year-old dispute regarding the word "Qaset" in the second book of Samuel. "What's interesting," she said in conclusion, "is that Dr. Holzberg apparently believed 'Qaset' referred to a technique for bending *time*."

"*Bogentechnik*," said Califano.

"Huh?" Armstrong looked momentarily confused.

"*Bogentechnik*. That's the word Dr. Holzberg used to describe it. It means 'bending technique' in German."

Armstrong was rubbing his eyes and his temples with both hands. "Okay, this is all very interesting. But where is the Thurmond material *right now*? Isn't that what we should be most concerned with?"

"Absolutely," said Califano. "To the best of my knowledge, that material is still with the woman in the white dress who we saw at the church."

"Her name is Opal," said Ana. "I overheard them calling her that."

"And this *Opal* woman is the one you overheard down in the bomb shelter, the one you think caused the time incident that screwed up all of our satellites?"

Califano nodded. "As best as I could tell."

"And you say Bill McCreary went to check it out?"

"Uh-huh."

"And that was, what, about seven hours ago?"

Califano checked his watch. "A little more, actually."

"And no one's heard from him since?" said Armstrong.

"Well, speaking from experience," said Califano, "we may not be seeing him for a while."

Armstrong rolled his eyes and groaned. "Great. I'm sure the president will be thrilled to hear that. And what about this other person? The one they had in the back of the van with you, Ana?"

"They called him Malachi," said Ana. "But I'm still not sure who he was or how he fits into everything."

"Any chance we could just *ask* him?"

Ana shook her head slowly. "Unfortunately, no. He didn't make it. Spec ops found him shot in the head."

"Great," said Armstrong. "So all our answers lie with this woman Opal. And we don't know where she is or when she's coming back. Did I get that right? Is that what I'm supposed to tell the president?"

All three of the "geniuses" around the table nodded their heads slowly.

Armstrong was just about to say something else when there was a knock on the door and it slowly swung open. On the other side of the door was Bill McCreary. He stepped into the workroom and then turned and ushered in another person who was standing behind him.

It was the elderly woman in white from the church.

"Everyone," said McCreary. "I'd like you to meet Opal Chauvenet."

45

"WE ARE both dead," said Vladamir Krupnov with barely suppressed panic in his voice. "Do you understand that?"

Dr. Benjamin Fulcher held the phone to his ear and pulled back the drapes of his hotel room overlooking the Baixa district of Lisbon. "Calm down, Vlad. Where are you right now?"

"I'm not going to tell you that over the phone. They might be listening."

"Who?"

"You know goddamn well who. The *posrednikov*."

"You're being paranoid."

"Perhaps. But that's because I know them. *You don't.* Trust me, Doctor. If we fail at this, you will not see the light of the next day. It won't matter where you are or what you're doing. They will find you . . . and kill you. The *posrednikov* don't tolerate people who waste their money."

"I'm not afraid," said Fulcher.

"Well, you should be."

"We will not fail."

"Your confidence is admirable, Doctor. But honestly, it's wearing on my nerves. You didn't just see your entire team wiped out in one day." Krupnov cursed under his breath in Russian. "That blond *d'yoval*. I should have blown her brains out when I had the chance."

"Listen, Vlad. I'm sorry about your men. We knew this was a risky business when we started. But even if the Thurmond material is out of our reach, there are still at least ten more seed stones up for grabs. That's more than enough to carry out our plan."

"What are you talking about?" said Krupnov sharply. "You heard Malachi. He didn't know *anything* about those stones. And even if he did, he's dead now. The woman, Opal, she's probably with the Americans by now. So we are no closer to those ten stones than we were before. Probably further away."

"Vlad—"

"No, Doctor. We promised them that we were close to bringing this plan to completion. The *posrednikov* will hold us to that promise. If you don't understand that, then you are a fool. I don't care if you do have a Nobel Prize."

"Vlad, we will keep our promise."

"How?"

"Have you ever heard the expression that there's more than one way to skin a cat?"

"No. We don't skin cats in Russia."

"It just means there's more than one way to accomplish a goal. You may be right about Malachi and the woman. But I have discovered something quite remarkable about this tiny stone. Something I'd overlooked before."

"You mean the material we got from Haroldson? The

small chip that his father took from the stone he found in Tunis?"

"Yes. I retrieved it after we finished the demonstration in the White Sea, and I have it with me now. There's something about it that I believe will solve all of our problems."

"And what's that?"

"I'll explain later. Just be ready to travel. I'll give you instructions shortly."

Fulcher terminated the call and immediately turned his attention back to the small apparatus that he'd set up on the desk of the hotel room three hours ago. It consisted of a glass ball about the size of a basketball, which had a small opening in the top that was covered with tape. The glass ball was striped with black longitude and latitude lines so that it looked like a globe without the geographical features. It was sitting atop a makeshift gimbal structure that Fulcher had carefully aligned three hours before to point due north, after taking into full consideration the local magnetic declination of the Lisbon area.

Fulcher bent down and carefully inspected the tiny black chip that was floating inside the glass ball. It hadn't moved for the past half hour, which meant it had finally achieved a steady state. "Excellent," he whispered. He took precise note of the position of the chip as it pressed gently against the side of the glass ball.

Like attracts like.

He jotted the information down on a scrap piece of paper and then hobbled over to a Mercator map of the world that was spread out across the hotel room's dining table. Using a ruler, a protractor, and a black pen, Fulcher carefully placed a dot on his location in Lisbon and then plotted a line in the exact direction indicated by the tiny floating chip in the glass ball. It was the third line that he'd drawn on the map in the past twenty-four hours. The first had originated in Severodvinsk, Russia, and extended south. The second had originated in Almaty, Kazakhstan, and extended southwest. And now this line, which began in Lisbon and extended southeast. They all intersected at nearly the same point, forming a tiny triangle known to navigators around the world as a "fix."

Fulcher stood up with some effort and tapped his finger on the small triangle of intersecting lines. "Remarkable," he whispered. "After all this time."

He quickly retrieved his cell phone and dialed Krupnov.

"*Da?*" Krupnov answered.

"Vlad, I know where those ten stones are located. Be in Istanbul tomorrow afternoon. I'll arrange a private flight from there."

"Are you sure?"

A smile crept across Fulcher's face. "Sure as clockwork. Just make sure you're there."

46

CIA HEADQUARTERS, LANGLEY, VIRGINIA

WHO ARE YOU?" asked Ana Thorne of the elderly woman in the white dress, whom McCreary had introduced a minute earlier as Opal Chauvenet. The woman was seated in a chair with her legs crossed, hands in her lap, looking very matronly. McCreary was seated beside her, and Ana was slowly pacing around the room as she awaited an answer.

"My full name is Ophelia Josephine Chauvenet," said the woman. "But everyone has called me Opal since the day I was born." She spoke in a slightly wavering voice with a mild upstate New York accent.

Ana wasn't sure what to ask next. *Explain everything!* was what she wanted to say. But she settled for something smaller in scope. "What were you doing in the church this morning?"

The woman let out a sigh. "It's a long story. Should I start at the beginning?"

Ana, Califano, and Armstrong all answered in unison, *"Yes!"*

The woman laughed quietly and nodded her head. "Okay." She paused for a moment to collect her thoughts, and then she began. "In June of 1947, when I was nineteen years old, I was asked by Bill Donovan to help him with an operation they were conducting to get certain scientists and engineers out of Germany and into the United States."

"Wait. Bill Donovan? As in *Wild* Bill Donovan, the founder of OSS?" Ana was referring to the Office of Strategic Services, the immediate predecessor of the CIA.

"Yes," said Opal. "He was a friend of my father's. They grew up together in Buffalo and served in the same unit during the First World War."

"And you're referring to Project Paperclip?" Ana asked.

Opal nodded. "I was in college at that time, studying civil engineering. Bill felt I would bring a certain *'woman's touch,'* as he called it, to the operation. At that time, we were competing with the Russians for the top German talent, so there was a certain degree of *enticing* that had to be done to encourage the best scientists and engineers to come with us instead of them."

Ana nodded that she understood. *Sex appeal. The oldest trick in the book.*

"I was assigned to Franz Holzberg, a physicist who had worked during the war on secret Nazi projects in the Wenceslas mine complex in Poland."

Ana suddenly stopped pacing. "It was Die Glocke, wasn't it? That's what he was working on."

Opal nodded. "Yes. That was our belief at the time. It's why Bill Donovan was so interested in bringing him to the United States."

"Wait," said Califano, who was seated at his computer, across the room. "Die Glocke? You mean the antigravity stuff that the Nazis were supposedly working on at the end of the war?"

"Yes," said Opal.

All around the room, there were slow nods of recognition. *It made sense.*

"And why were *you* assigned to Franz Holzberg?"

Opal flashed a lovely smile and subtly rolled one of her shoulders forward.

With that, Ana had her answer. Even in her eighties, Opal still had a certain indelible beauty. *And at nineteen, she would have been a stunner in high heels.*

"We knew Franz had a certain *reputation*, shall we say. He was thirty-six years old, married, with no children, and quite handsome for a physicist. And like a lot of men in those days, he liked the company of younger women."

On the other side of the room, Califano was nodding along. He recalled the comment from Thelma Scott at the diner in Fire Creek about how Dr. Holzberg would often stop by the diner on Sundays. Allegedly because he liked the "pancakes."

"So you were sent over to cozy up to him?" asked Ana. "Give him a little extra reason to come to the U.S.?"

Opal smiled. "You got it."

"I guess it worked," said Admiral Armstrong. "I mean, he did come to the U.S."

"Actually, it worked a little *too* well." Opal looked down with a wistful smile. "I fell madly in love with him. When he took up residence at Princeton in 1948, I dropped out of school and moved there myself." She paused for a moment, as if trying to conjure up some long-lost emotion. Then she shrugged her shoulders. "We were having an affair."

Which is why we couldn't find any record of you at Princeton, Ana realized. "You were part of his small circle of friends, weren't you? His group of acolytes."

"Yes, I was. It was a very exciting time. Franz was working on things that just . . . blew people's minds. Albert Einstein was involved, too, which was amazing. And then, of course, there was the material itself."

Ana pulled up a chair and sat down close to Opal. "Yes, tell us about the material."

"Well, let's see . . . Franz brought the first stone with him from Germany. He said it was the only thing he managed to save from his lab in Wenceslas when Poland was liberated by the Allies."

"What do you mean the *first* stone?" Ana asked. "How many were there?"

Bill McCreary suddenly spoke up. "Ana, she's referring to two black stones. One about the size of a golf ball; the other about this big." He held up his thumb and finger about an inch apart. "We've got both of them downstairs in our vault right now. The first one, which Holzberg brought with him from Germany, was the smaller of the two stones."

"Remember," Opal warned. "Don't let them touch."

McCreary nodded. "Don't worry. We won't."

Ana was momentarily at a loss for words as she looked back and forth between Opal and McCreary. "Uh . . . how about a little more information here?" she pleaded.

McCreary spoke again. "The time-dilation incident behind the Hay-Adams. It was caused when Opal touched the two stones together. It was a very small dilation, as these things go. It faded just after I got there. The reason we couldn't see her at the bottom of the escape shaft is that time dilation refracts light, just like water does. But unlike water, which creates a smooth interface between two media with different light transmission speeds, time dilation creates a steady gradient of transmission speeds, which causes objects to be completely obscured from view."

"It's one of the Qaset techniques," said Opal.

Ana's head was about to explode as she tried to process all this information at once.

Opal apparently sensed her frustration. "You see, when Franz came to the U.S. in 1948, he had a small black stone with him that had these very unusual properties. Most notably, it floated in air. He said the Nazis had recovered it from a church or mosque somewhere in Turkey. And his initial research at the Institute of Advanced Studies was focused entirely on that small stone. It was just he and Einstein working on it at first. Then, about three years later, the institute came into possession of a much larger stone with the same unusual properties."

"The second stone," McCreary added. "It was provided by British Intelligence. Recovered during the British invasion of Tunis in 1943. In 1951, the Brits sent a young physicist named Benjamin Fulcher to Princeton with the Tunis stone in order to collaborate with Einstein and Holzberg in trying to figure out its properties. It was a binational project and highly classified, as you can imagine. Einstein died in 1955, and after that, Fulcher and Holzberg continued the research without him."

"But Franz never trusted Ben," Opal added. "Something about him was very off-putting. I felt it, too. He had a real lust for glory that neither Franz nor Albert shared."

"And how do you know about the Qaset techniques," Ana asked.

"From Franz." She paused when she saw the surprised looks around the room. "Franz told me *everything* back then. We were very, very close. He told me all about the book of Jasher and the Joshua Stone, and the many other things he'd learned working for the Nazis. He hated the Nazis and was itching to divulge their secrets."

"Did he tell you about the lab in Thurmond, West Virginia?" asked Admiral Armstrong.

"Not at first. But eventually . . . yes." Opal paused before continuing. "It was early spring in 1959 when he first announced that he'd be gone for at least six months, off to some secret lab. I cried my eyes out for days, until he eventually broke down and told me where he was going and what he'd be working on. He said he'd try to arrange a way for me to visit, but he never did. The last time I saw Franz was on May 4, 1959. When he left, he gave me a beautiful black-stone necklace." Instinctively, she reached for the necklace, but it was gone. "It was to remember him by, but also for safekeeping."

"What do you mean, for safekeeping?" Ana asked.

"It was the small stone that he'd brought from Germany. The 'first stone.' He'd made it into a necklace for me. I think he was afraid Ben Fulcher might get hold of it."

Ana looked amazed. "So he made the floating black stone into a *necklace*?"

"Yes," said Opal with a sweet smile. "It was perfect. It was framed in silver and looked just like a chunk of uncut onyx. Sort of the au naturel style that was just coming into vogue at that time. And no one ever guessed its special significance."

Unbelievable, Ana thought. She decided it was time to switch gears. "What can you tell us about Malachi?"

Opal's eyes suddenly grew large. "Is he okay? Where is he?"

There were glances all around the table, and Ana eventually shook her head slowly. "I'm . . . sorry." She sensed this was coming as bad news for Opal.

Opal lowered her head and brought both hands to her eyes. "Oh, it's my fault," she muttered beneath her hands.

"What is?" asked Ana gently.

"I got him into this mess. I should have put my foot down and said *no*."

Ana gave Opal a few seconds to work through her emotions before asking, "Can you tell us about it?"

Opal finally lifted her head and regained her composure. "It was all Ben Fulcher's idea."

"What was?"

"To go down into the lab to rescue Franz and the stone."

"When was this?" asked Ana.

Opal searched her recollection. "It was . . . 1971. October or November, when Ben first broached the idea."

"And how, exactly, did this come about?"

Opal took a deep breath and looked all around the room. "First, I need to explain to you about MOSS. The Mother of Science Society."

Across the croom, Califano slapped his forehead. "*Mother* of science," he said. "Not '*murder*' of science." He snapped his fingers, angry at himself for the mistake.

Opal continued. "A few of us in Franz's circle formed a group that we called the Mother of Science Society."

"And the point of this society was what, exactly?" asked Ana.

Opal laughed. "There wasn't any point at all, really. It was just an intellectual thing. Just a circle of people who got together occasionally to discuss whether there might be limits to what mankind should know, some sort of point of no return."

Bill McCreary was nodding his head emphatically. *She had just described his life for the past ten years.*

"Ben Fulcher was part of it, too," continued Opal. "At least, he played along at the time."

"Which was when?"

"Late fifties—fifty-seven, fifty-eight, fifty-nine. I left Princeton not long after that. Went back to New York and finished my degree. I eventually got a job designing bomb shelters for the U.S. government, which was a big deal in the sixties. Ten years later, I was living here in this area, in Arlington. My group had just finished construction on the bomb shelter complex beneath the Third Church of Christ, Scientist, in Washington, which I helped design. My career was going great. And then one day, from out of nowhere, Ben Fulcher showed up at my door."

"With a plan to rescue Dr. Holzberg," said Ana.

"Yes. A crazy plan. He explained the time-dilation issue to me. He said that he'd been monitoring the aftereffects in the surrounding areas and that, based on his calculations, the time was perfect to send someone down into the lab to rescue Franz and his team, and to retrieve the stone. We both agreed that the stone had to be protected from any further experimentation. Too dangerous. Too close to disturbing the intricate balance of the clockwork universe. The plan was to lock it away and keep it under the protection of our group, MOSS."

"What happened?" asked Admiral Armstrong.

"Ben had a lot of calculations, none of which I really understood. But he seemed convinced that if someone went in and spent less than ten minutes in the lab, he would lose only five or six days of time, seven at the most. He also explained that, if we waited much longer, as time continued to speed up in the lab, the men inside would soon die of starvation. That's why he said we had to act quickly."

"Why not get the government involved?" Ana asked.

"Ben said that he'd tried. But the government had already washed its hands of the Thurmond lab and written off everyone as dead."

Admiral Armstrong nodded his head. This was true. He'd seen the top-secret reports himself.

Opal continued. "Ben said most of the people at the institute who *should* have known about Thurmond wouldn't even acknowledge its existence. Plus, there was a new administration in office—Nixon. And he had lots of other problems on his hands without having to worry about some carryover from the Eisenhower administration. According to Ben, if we didn't do this thing ourselves, *and soon*, it wasn't going to happen at all."

"So the two of you hatched a plan to go into the lab yourselves," said Ana.

Opal looked down and nodded. "I had access to top-secret topological maps of the area, and it didn't take me long to find a way into the lab through an old coal mine."

"Foster Number Two," said Califano.

"That's right," said Opal.

"And what about Malachi?" Ana asked.

"His name is Daniel." She paused and wiped away a tear. "We had all adopted silly code names—Ben's idea. I was Eve. Ben was Elijah. And Daniel . . . Daniel was Malachi."

"And Malachi—I mean, Daniel—he's the one who actually went down into the lab. Is that right?"

Opal nodded. "He was the youngest and strongest. He insisted that he be the one to go in. I tried to talk him out of it. Too many risks. Too many unknowns. But he insisted." She paused for a moment and sniffled. "I should have tried harder."

"When did he go in?"

"March 14, 1972. The first moonless night in March. We had rehearsed for months, worked out every detail. Ben had told him what to expect in the lab and had walked through dozens of different possible scenarios. I was in charge of the rendezvous. We were to meet at the abandoned coal depot in Thurmond. Ben and I would be there in my car, flashing our lights to signal him. The key to everything was the time. According to Ben's calculations, Daniel was to spend no more than ten minutes in the lab, no matter what. Ben even gave him a special watch to use." She paused and slowly shook her head. "I found out later why he was so insistent about that watch."

"Why was that?"

"Because Ben is a traitor. A selfish, lying, backstabbing traitor . . . and a murderer. He knew all along that Daniel wouldn't be coming out in six days, or anything close to that." Opal let out a bitter laugh. "He was working with the Soviets the entire time."

"*What?*" exclaimed McCreary. "Benjamin Fulcher, the Nobel Prize–winning physicist?"

"Never proven," said Opal without missing a beat. "But there's no doubt in my mind that he was working with the Russians. In fact, why don't you ask British Intelligence what they thought of him? You think it's a coincidence that he left Cambridge in 1980, never to return to Britain? You don't think Cambridge would have loved to keep a Nobel laureate on staff?"

McCreary glanced over at Califano, who was already typing furiously on the keyboard. "Hey!" he barked, realizing what Califano was probably up to. "Don't *hack* into MI6, Michael."

Califano immediately stopped what he was doing.

"We have a cooperative agreement with them." McCreary turned to Goodwin: "Help him out, will you?" Goodwin quickly rose to his feet and joined Califano at the computer.

Two minutes later Califano announced, "She's right. MI6 put Fulcher on their watch list back in 1976. There's just a one-line entry that says 'suspected ties to USSR.'"

Opal arched her eyebrows and nodded knowingly. "Like I said, he's a traitor. And he deserves whatever fate awaits him . . . on earth and in hell."

There was a long period of silence after that, which was finally broken when Califano asked, "How did you know Daniel was going to be at the church today?"

Before Opal could respond, Ana spoke up. "I think I know the answer to that. It was Tom Reynolds, wasn't it?"

Opal nodded.

"I *thought* you looked familiar," said Ana. "Then I remembered seeing you in a picture at Tom Reynolds's house. It was you and his wife, Betty, and two other ladies standing together on a golf course."

"We're close friends," said Opal. "Tom called me and said a young woman had stopped by to ask questions about Franz Holzberg and the book of Jasher. He described her as 'beautiful and wicked smart.'" Opal gave Ana the once-over. "I presume that was you."

Ana nodded and blushed.

"I had a hunch it was about Thurmond," said Opal.

After another stretch of silence, Admiral Armstrong finally spoke up. "I'm sorry, but I still don't know who Malachi—er, Daniel—was." He was apparently the only one in the entire room who hadn't already figured it out.

Opal closed her eyes. "Daniel was my son . . . with Franz. He went down into that lab because he wanted to see his father again. He was only twenty-one years old."

"Ah," said Armstrong, finally getting it. "I'm sorry for your loss."

Ana walked across the room and whispered something in Califano's ear. Moments later, the Madaba map appeared on the large screen at the front of the room. Califano zoomed in on the detail of the building with the twelve circles.

"Opal, do you recognize this?" Ana asked.

Opal studied the picture for a moment and nodded. "Yes. That's from the Madaba map. It marks the location where Joshua created a monument of twelve stones after crossing the Jordan River. At least, that's what the Old Testament says."

Ana suddenly got excited. *Finally, we're getting somewhere.* "Have you ever seen a sketch or modified version of this with German writing on it? Like from an old notebook or something?"

Opal shrugged and shook her head. "No. Not that I can recall."

"You said that Franz Holzberg told you everything. Did he ever tell you where all these stones are located?"

"Other than the two stones he had, you mean?"

Ana nodded.

"No. Franz never mentioned knowing anything about where these other stones are located. As far as I know, that's still a mystery to this day."

"You mean you never heard him mention that ten of these stones are located together in the same place?"

Opal looked genuinely surprised. "No."

Is she telling the truth? Ana wondered. The idea of a lie detector test suddenly came to mind. But Admiral Armstrong beat her to it with a more simplistic approach.

"Ma'am," he said. "Dr. Fulcher knows all about this grouping of ten stones. In fact, that's what he and his men were asking your son about today. So, if these ten stones do in fact exist somewhere, Fulcher is most likely on his way to get them right now."

Opal appeared to be listening intently.

"Now, do you really want *Fulcher* to get his hands on those stones?"

"No. Of course not."

"Then can you tell us *anything* about where they might be?"

Opal shook her head remorsefully. "I'm sorry. I just don't know."

Ana and Armstrong glanced at each other at the same moment and with the same thought. *She was telling the truth.*

47

W HO ORDERED the pepperoni pizza?" asked Steve Goodwin as he entered the DTAI workroom with three take-out bags of Italian and a small pizza box.

"Yo," said Califano, raising his hand.

"Chicken parm for me," said McCreary.

"Caesar salad," said Ana.

Several minutes later, Thorne, Goodwin, and McCreary were all seated at the conference table, unpacking their late dinners. Califano remained at his computer across the room, wolfing down slices of pizza between bursts of keyboard activity.

"I feel like we're missing something," said Ana, poking at her salad. "I was sure Opal would have some information about that sketch and the remaining ten stones."

"I know," said McCreary as he sawed off a huge piece of chicken parm. "I'm worried about those stones, too. There's no telling what kind of havoc Fulcher and his Russian friends might inflict on the world, even if their intentions are perfectly innocent . . . which I doubt."

"Well, what are we missing?" asked Ana. "The spec op guys scrubbed Hillcrest and found nothing of particular interest. Neither of the two Ukrainian knuckleheads they took into custody seemed to have any knowledge about the ten stones or the Madaba map. In fact, all we know for sure from those guys is that Vladamir Krupnov was in charge of their group, and he and Sashko Melnik somehow managed to escape today. Whereabouts unknown."

"Yeah, Fulcher seems to have dropped off the grid, too," said Califano from across the room.

"They know we're on to them now," said McCreary. "They won't be so sloppy anymore. You can count on that. That's why I doubt they're traveling commercial." McCreary gobbled down his slab of chicken parm and then turned toward Califano. "Any luck tracking private aviation?"

"Nope. There's way too many flights, and I can't seem to find any meaningful pattern or connection between any of them. Just random, typical private air traffic."

"Keep working on it," said McCreary glumly. He turned his attention back to his meal.

"What about the stuff Holzberg said before he died?" asked Ana. "Are we sure we've accounted for *everything*?"

"Pretty much," said Califano. "I'm still updating the relevancy engine with the stuff we learned today from Opal and some of the stuff you got from Tom Reynolds. Should be ready for a new data crunch in a few minutes. Maybe it'll point us in the right direction."

McCreary sighed. "Look, even if we can't locate the ten remaining stones, you guys did a hell of a job preventing the Thurmond material from falling into the wrong hands. You should be really proud of that."

Ana wasn't having any part of that consolation prize. "It

won't mean a damn thing if ten *other* pieces of the material fall into Fulcher's hands. I shudder to think what he could do with that much material."

"I know," said McCreary with a heavy sigh.

"Holy shit!" Califano exclaimed.

McCreary swiveled in his seat. "What is it, Michael?"

"I'm an idiot."

"*That's* your big revelation?" said Ana with a dry laugh.

"No, I mean I've been trying to track private flights all over the world by their tail numbers. But then I thought, *what if the tail numbers are changing?* So I wrote a little algorithm to test out that theory, and here's what I got. A Gulfstream 550 took off from Moscow yesterday morning, bound for Almaty, Kazakhstan. Six hours after it arrived, *another* Gulfstream 550 with a different tail number took off from Almaty bound for Lisbon. And then, about five hours ago, *another* Gulfstream 550 with a different tail number left Lisbon en route to Istanbul. That flight touched down in Istanbul about forty-five minutes ago."

"Same plane?" asked McCreary. "Just repainting the tail number each time?"

"Could be. And I bet you anything it's Fulcher. He's on the move."

"But why would he be hopping all over Europe like that?" asked Ana. "And what's in Istanbul?"

"I don't know, but I'm going to find out right now." Califano let loose a torrent of keystrokes and mouse clicks for the better part of a minute until he finally finished with an exaggerated click of the Enter key. "You guys want to watch?"

They all nodded.

Califano pushed a button, and his display suddenly showed up on the large screen at the front of the room. A stream of data was cascading down the screen, so fast that it was impossible to read. "It's crunching now. It'll take a little while."

Several minutes later, the cascading data finally came to an end, and a small window popped up showing the top five paired IIEs that had resulted from this particular data crunch. Califano expanded the window and centered it on the screen.

Everyone in the room stared at the result, which showed two columns labeled IIE 1 and IIE 2, each pair representing two related pieces of data with particular relevance to the information Califano had fed into the system. The first column consisted of the following five items:

Benjamin Fulcher
Vladamir Krupnov
Sashko Melnik
Joshua Stone
Jasher

The second column consisted of a single geographic location, repeated five times.

"Oh my God," whispered Ana, shaking her head in disbelief.

"You two better pack," said McCreary. "Looks like you're going on a trip."

48

"YOU TWO are crazy," said Akeem bin Nayef over his shoulder. He was driving a white Infiniti JX35 SUV with heavily tinted windows, which was inching east toward Mecca on a jammed Highway 40. The sun was just now rising over the horizon.

In the backseat, Mike Califano and Ana Thorne glanced at each other, both thinking the same thing: *He's right.*

"Look at this traffic," said Akeem. "We're in the middle of the hajj. Millions of Muslims from around the world are descending on Mecca this week." He shook his head in frustration. "I've lived here most of my life. I've been a CIA regional coordinator for more than fifteen years. And even *I* don't go anywhere near Mecca during the hajj. I mean, have either of you even *been* to Saudi Arabia before?"

Califano and Thorne both shrugged and shook their heads no.

"Oh my God," groaned Akeem. "Listen to me. People *literally* get trampled to death every year during the hajj.

And God help you if anyone finds out you are not a Muslim. It's a crime in this country to enter Mecca if you are not a Muslim. Five years in prison, followed by deportation. And that's if the crowd doesn't kill you first. Are you guys sure you're up for this?"

Califano shrugged. "Yeah, sounds like fun. I mean, I went to a Springsteen concert at the Meadowlands back in ninety-five. Couldn't be any worse than that, could it?"

Ana rolled her eyes. "Nice mustache," she said.

"Thanks." Califano gently smoothed out the thick black mustache that the CIA disguise people had provided him with just before he and Ana left for their middle-of-the-night flight from Dulles to King Abdulaziz International Airport in Jeddah. In addition to the mustache, Califano was dressed in traditional Ihram attire: a white cloth wrapped around his waist like a skirt, and another white cloth gathered at his shoulder like a tunic. He felt ridiculous. He turned to Ana and sized up her outfit. "Nice burka. Really compliments your figure."

"Hey, at least I don't need sunblock." Indeed, her white burka covered every square inch of her skin except her eyes. And even there, the CIA disguise folks had left nothing to chance. They'd changed her eye color from green to dark brown using tinted contact lenses. They'd tied her hair back and covered it with a black wig to prevent any stray locks of blond hair from suddenly poking out from beneath her veil. And, as with Califano, they'd applied makeup to her face to help her blend in better with the local population. "What are you reading?" she asked.

Califano looked up from the book he'd been flipping through for the past twenty minutes. "Arabic phrase book," he said.

"What, now you're suddenly going to start speaking Arabic?"

"*Ayn al-hammam de mujir?*" Califano replied without missing a beat.

"What did he just say?" Ana asked the CIA driver.

"He said, 'Where is the men's bathroom?' And he has a pretty good accent, too." Akeem caught Califano's eye in the rearview mirror and nodded his head, apparently impressed.

Ana shook her head. *Photographic memory. That's cheating.*

"Actually," said Akeem over his shoulder, "knowing just a few Arabic phrases will probably get you by during the hajj. Muslims make up nearly a quarter of the world's population, and they speak more than sixty different languages. So trust me, you won't be the only ones here who don't speak Arabic. But I wouldn't go around speaking English, either."

Califano's phone suddenly buzzed in his pocket. He checked the incoming text message, which was from Admiral Armstrong. "Fulcher's here," he said quietly. "His plane arrived an hour before ours, and NSA's got a satellite spotlight on his vehicle right now. They're up ahead of us in traffic about two miles."

"You were right about all of this," said Ana, intending to pay Califano a compliment.

"Just lucky. Besides, it was you who figured out the Jasher connection."

Ana smiled beneath her veil. "Okay, so tell me more about this Black Stone. Where exactly is it located in the Kaaba?"

Akeem overheard their conversation. "Are you guys talking about the Black Stone of the Kaaba?"

Ana nodded. "Yeah. Are you familiar with it?"

"*Min-fad-lak,*" said Akeem with wide eyes. "Of course I am. It is the holiest relic in all of Islam. Not that we're supposed to have relics. But if we did . . . *that would be it.*"

"It's got quite a history, huh?" said Califano.

"Indeed. It is said to have formed part of the altar of Adam and Eve. And it is the original cornerstone of the Kaaba in the center of Mecca, the temple where all of these pilgrims are heading right now. In some sense, the Black Stone is the cornerstone of Islam itself. It was placed in its current location by Mohammed, and has only ever been moved once since then."

"That's when it was stolen, right?" asked Califano.

"Correct. Stolen by the Qarmatians in 930. Returned twenty-three years later in a most mysterious manner. It was tossed into the mosque in Kufa during Friday prayers with a note that said 'By God's command we took it, and by God's command we return it.' It is said that the man who stole it suffered a very unusual death. He deteriorated from the inside out, until he was eventually consumed by worms."

Califano and Thorne glanced at each other. They were both thinking about the unusual aging pattern they'd seen with Dr. Holzberg and, to some extent, with his son, Daniel.

"The stone is actually made of several pieces, isn't that right?" asked Califano.

"That's true, although a lot of people don't realize it. The Black Stone actually consists of ten individual stones, which are held together with some type of cement that was made back during the time of Mohammed."

"And I bet no two of them are touching each other," said Califano quietly.

"Huh?"

"Never mind."

"Is it true that the Black Stone predates Islam?" asked Ana.

"Yes, according to historians," said Akeem. "The Black Stone was already an object of worship in Mecca long before Mohammed arrived in the eighth century. No one knows exactly where it came from, other than the myth about it coming from the Garden of Eden. But it was apparently here in Mecca long before Islam."

"And which station is it on the hajj?" asked Califano.

"It's part of the first *tawaf*," said Akeem. "Pilgrims circle the Kaaba seven times. And on each round, they are supposed to kiss the Black Stone."

"*Kiss it?*" said Ana. "Sounds like a lot of germs."

"They do it because Mohammed himself kissed the stone. As I said, the Black Stone is very special to Muslims. It is, without a doubt, the most sacred object in all of Mecca."

Ana turned to Califano. "What do Dr. Fulcher and his goons think they're going to do with it today? I mean, do they actually plan to steal it in broad daylight?"

Akeem laughed aloud from the front seat. "Oh, that would be quite impossible. During the hajj, you are lucky to even *see* the Black Stone, let alone touch it. Most pilgrims are content simply to point in its general direction. The idea that someone could *steal* the Black Stone from the Kaaba is ludicrous. Especially during the hajj."

"Well, they're obviously up to *something*," said Ana.

Califano nodded in agreement. "And unfortunately, they're ahead of us. Hey, Akeem, any chance you could bypass some of this traffic?"

"Impossible," replied Akeem.

Three hours later, the Infiniti SUV pulled into the parking lot of a seedy strip mall and came to a halt.

"Why are we stopping?" asked Ana.

"From here, you walk," said Akeem.

"Where are we?" asked Califano.

"You are just west of Third Ring Road. I can't drive much farther into Mecca without a special permit. Which I don't have. Besides, it will be quicker for you to walk from here anyway. You're only a few miles away. Just follow that parade of white." He pointed out the window at the steady stream of pilgrims just outside the car. It was like a human river of white. "Trust me, they're all going to the same place. Just fall into line with them."

Califano turned to Ana and tapped the Transmit button for his radio. "Can you hear me okay?" he said into his microphone.

"Loud and clear," Ana replied. "How about me?"

Califano nodded. Then he tapped the Transmit button again. "Admiral? You on?"

A second later, the crackly voice of Admiral Armstrong came on the line. "Yes, Michael. I can hear you just fine."

"Still painting their vehicle?" asked Califano.

"Affirmative," Armstrong replied. "It appears to be stopped about a mile east of your location, in a hotel parking lot. Oops, hold on . . ." Armstrong went off-line and returned a few seconds later. "Two men just got out. Both dressed in white. They're joining the crowd. We'll try to paint them both with a beam." He paused for a moment. "Damn, this is going to be a challenge. We've never done this in such a large crowd. And they're all wearing white, too."

"Either of them walking with a cane?" asked Califano.

"Uh, no," replied Armstrong a few seconds later. "They both appear to be fit and able bodied. They're moving along with the crowd now."

"I bet it's Krupnov and Sashko," said Ana quietly.

Califano nodded in agreement. He was still marveling that Armstrong could track two individuals in a huge mob of people using a geosynchronous spy satellite orbiting 22,236 miles above the earth. *Truly incredible.*

Ana tapped Califano on the arm. "Hey, we've got to go. You ready?"

Califano nodded that he was.

"Rendezvous here when you're done," said Akeem. "And good luck."

Moments later, Califano and Thorne were out of the vehicle and were almost immediately swept up by the human river of white that was slowly thronging toward Mecca.

"Stay close," said Califano into his microphone.

"I'm trying," said Ana. She felt herself slowly being wedged away from Califano.

"Here, take my hand." Califano extended his hand, and Ana grabbed it just before she was about to be swept away by the crowd. Califano gripped her hand tightly and pulled her close. "This is our only hope of staying together."

Ana nodded and squeezed his hand tightly.

"Admiral, where are they now?" asked Califano over the radio.

Armstrong's crackly voice came online a couple of seconds later. "Still about a mile ahead of you, heading east with the crowd. You two really need to pick up the pace."

"Easier said than done," Califano muttered. He and Thorne were in a sea of humanity that was moving at its own slow pace. Nevertheless, in an effort to reduce the bad guys' lead, they did what they could to cut and duck through the swarming mass of white.

"How we doing now?" asked Califano over the radio. He and Thorne had been powering their way through the swarming mass of hajji for the past hour, slowly but surely advancing their position in the crowd. It was hot, grueling work. And the stench of body odor was overpowering. Deodorant and perfume were prohibited during the hajj. A true hajji was supposed to enter Mecca "pure." Even if that meant stinking to high heaven.

"They're still a good five hundred yards ahead of you," reported Admiral Armstrong over the radio. "Looks like they just entered the Grand Mosque. You should start seeing it any minute."

"Yeah, I see it now," said Califano. He pointed Ana toward the nine minarets that could just now be seen towering over the crowd in the distance. Ana nodded that she saw it, too.

The Grand Mosque in Mecca was the largest mosque in the world, covering an area of more than eighty-eight acres. The three-story, colonnaded exterior of the mosque enclosed a massive courtyard designed to accommodate more than a *million* pilgrims at once. At the center of this courtyard was the Kaaba, the holiest temple in all of Islam, the exact spot on earth where a quarter of the world's population oriented themselves to pray each day. Facing the *qibla* during Muslim prayers literally meant turning toward the Kaaba.

The Kaaba itself looked like a giant cube that, during the hajj, was draped in a ceremonial black fabric with gold ornamentation and Arabic writing. It was an impressive and incredibly moving sight for devout Muslims, who were required to visit the Kaaba at least once in their lives. For most, seeing the Kaaba for the first time was the most memorable moment in their entire lives.

"We can't move any faster," said Ana. She and Califano were pressed tightly against the thousands of other hajji around them. Shoulder to shoulder, chest to back.

"I know," said Califano. "How are we going to make up five hundred yards?"

Armstrong's voice suddenly crackled over the radio. "You can make it up during the *tawaf*."

"What do you mean?" asked Califano.

"The pilgrims circle the Kaaba seven times, but they do

it in tightening circles. Everyone moves counterclockwise, so as soon as you enter the Grand Mosque, you need to start pushing as hard as you can toward the left. If you can punch through to the faster traffic on the inside, you can still catch these guys."

Several minutes later, Califano and Thorne approached the west entrance of the Grand Mosque. "Check that out," said Califano, pointing to a green neon sign perched high above the west entrance. In Arabic, it said: GO.

"Like a traffic light," said Ana.

A damn good idea, thought Califano. As he watched, the green light suddenly went dark and was replaced with a red neon sign that said STOP in Arabic. *Shit.* "Where are they now, Admiral?" he asked over the radio.

"Inside the Grand Mosque. They've already completed one revolution, and they're just starting their second. You can still catch them before they reach the Black Stone. Remember, push left. Always left."

Five minutes later, the light above the west entrance turned green again, and Califano and Thorne were quickly swept along in the great throng of hajji that were now crushing their way through the west entrance and into the massive courtyard of the Grand Mosque.

As soon as Califano and Thorne entered the courtyard, they understood what Admiral Armstrong had been trying to explain. The entire mass of humanity inside the court-yard was circling counterclockwise. *Everyone. In unison.* And Califano and Thorne were on the very outer radius of that circling motion, practically scraping against the court-yard walls.

"This is incredible," Ana whispered, although nobody could hear her. The noise inside the Grand Mosque court-yard was deafening, as more than a million devoted Muslims shouted out prayers and lamentations over the sustained roar of two million shuffling feet. Above all this, dozens of booming loudspeakers along the perimeter were delivering singsong messages in Arabic.

For more than an hour, Califano and Thorne struggled through the crowd, constantly pushing left, slowly working their way toward the inside of the swirling sea of white circling the Kaaba.

Suddenly, Ana was shoved rudely from behind. She lost her grip on Califano's hand and instantly felt herself being swept away to the right, away from him. "Mike?" she said into her microphone as the jostling and pushing intensified.

"I'm here," Califano replied. "Just keep pushing left. Push *hard*."

"I am," said Ana through gritted teeth. But she wasn't the only one. Everyone, it seemed, was pushing at full strength toward the center of the mosque—toward the Kaaba. Ana dropped her left shoulder and redoubled her effort, finally succeeding in pushing through a trio of fat women in burkas who had tightly linked arms to avoid being separated. This was a common tactic among the hajji, which made punching through to the middle even more difficult.

"You guys are getting close," said Admiral Armstrong over the radio. "They're straight ahead of you, about fifteen yards."

"How close are they to the Black Stone?" asked Califano, screaming to be heard over the tremendous cacophony of grunting and shouting near the Kaaba.

"They're close, Mike." Armstrong's voice suddenly got very tense. "Whatever they've got planned . . . it's about to happen."

Shit. Those words hit Califano like of shot of adrenaline. He immediately lowered his stance, stiffened his shoulders, and barged through the swarm of hajji like a Sevillian bull, pumping his legs in linebacker fashion as he slowly plowed through the sea of sweating bodies.

Behind him, Ana was doing the same but with much less success. "Mike, I think I see you now," she said into her microphone. "I'm about ten feet behind you."

Califano heard nothing. He continued muscling through the crowd using every ounce of his strength. Finally, he looked up.

And there it was. The Black Stone. Just as he'd seen in pictures. It was encased in a silver frame and embedded directly into the eastern corner of the Kaaba. Just as Akeem had described, it was a cornerstone . . . both literally and figuratively.

Califano looked up and noted a guard standing on a platform about six feet above the Black Stone. He was shouting directions to the fervent hajji below, all of whom were desperately jostling for a chance to kiss the stone. Every few seconds, the guard jabbed a long pole into the side of some hajji who dared spend more than half a second with his lips on the Black Stone.

"Mike," said Armstrong over the radio with great urgency. "You're standing right behind one of them! He's directly in front of you!"

Califano glanced all around and quickly spotted a man a few feet in front of him who clearly looked out of place. *And what's that he's holding?* A split second later, Califano realized the man was holding a small chip of black material between his thumb and finger. It was from the Tunis stone that Haroldson had delivered to the Russians, the same one Fulcher had used for his demonstration in the White Sea. Now, the man was extending it outward, straining to touch it to the Black Stone. *Of course*, Califano realized. *He's trying to create a time dilation.*

"No!" Califano shouted. At the same moment, he hurled himself like a human battering ram through the remaining rows of hajji between himself and the other man. As he did, he extended his arms and leaped into the air toward the man. The guard above the stone reacted immediately, shouting angrily in Arabic and attempting to push Califano away with the long pole. But the momentum of Califano's body carried him through the painful jab and straight toward the man with the tiny chip of stone between his fingers.

As Califano fell through the air, he managed to just barely catch the man's forearm and knock it downward with sufficient force that the small chip of stone came dislodged and fell to the ground. It disappeared immediately beneath the thundering crush of feet.

A few yards back, Ana Thorne was watching all of this as if it were happening in slow motion. She recognized the other man as Sashko Melnik, Krupnov's Ukrainian henchman from the Hillcrest estate. As she watched in horror, both men dropped down and disappeared beneath the crowd. *They're going to be trampled to death!*

"Mike!" Ana shouted into her microphone. There was no response. "Mike!" she screamed even louder, no longer caring who might hear her. Suddenly, someone grabbed her roughly by the arm from behind. She craned her neck and found herself staring at the face of Vladamir Krupnov. His cold blue eyes instantly locked onto hers and hardened with rage. A moment later, he pulled a small pistol from his tunic. He aimed it at her head, and . . .

Thwack! The guard with the pole knocked the pistol clear out of Krupnov's hands. In the same instant, there was tremendous shouting in Arabic from above. Then, suddenly, Ana watched in amazement as the crowd itself began turning on Krupnov.

A gun in the Grand Mosque . . . just feet from the Kaaba. Such blasphemy would not be tolerated. Especially during the hajj.

Ana watched as Krupnov struggled futilely against an angry mob of men who had now turned their attention away from the Black Stone and were pummeling Krupnov mercilessly with their fists and elbows. *Street justice in the Grand Mosque.*

Seconds later, Krupnov disappeared completely. Swept away to an unknown fate.

"Mike?" Ana said emphatically into her microphone. *No response.* She felt herself being wedged away by the crowd, and she no longer had the strength to fight it. The Black Stone vanished from her view. "Mike?" she said one more time into her microphone.

Nothing. He was gone.

Two hours later, Akeem bin Nayef greeted Ana at the rendezvous location with a wave. "Did you find what you were looking for?" he asked as she approached.

"Sort of," she mumbled. She was utterly exhausted, sweaty, bruised, rattled, thirsty, and hungry all at once. Yet the only thing she could think of was Mike Califano. *Trampled.* In her mind's eye, she saw him slipping beneath the rampaging feet of a million pilgrims. She couldn't stand that image anymore. Yet it kept coming back, again and again.

"There's water in the car," said Akeem. "You look dehydrated." He opened the door of the SUV for her.

And there he was.

"Why didn't you answer the goddamn radio!" Ana said, seething, as she crawled into the backseat with Califano. Akeem shut the door behind her.

Califano was slumped low in his seat. He slowly pulled

open his tunic and showed her his badly bruised and bloody chest and ribs. "Transmitter broke," he said.

"Jesus," Ana whispered, lightly touching his black-and-blue chest. "That doesn't look good."

"Yeah? You should see the other million guys." Califano tried in vain to laugh at his own stupid joke, but he immediately winced from the pain.

"I'm guessing you have some broken ribs."

"Probably. But look what else I got." He slowly opened his clenched fist to reveal a small black chip of stone—the same chip that had been delivered to the Russians by Stephen Haroldson, which Fulcher had used for the White Sea demonstration. When Califano gently moved his hand away, the tiny object stayed perfectly in place, floating inexplicably in midair.

"My God," Ana whispered, astonished. She stared at the stone for several seconds in silence. Then she said, "Hey, do you think McCreary would let me make a necklace out of this?"

Califano laughed and winced. "I think he might have some concerns about that."

49

OVER THE ATLANTIC OCEAN

IS THERE any booze on this plane?" asked Mike Califano. With effort, he leaned forward in his plush leather seat and scanned all around the sleek cabin of the Gulfstream.

"It's against regulation," Thorne replied. She was seated across from him in the Gulfstream's mahogany-trimmed cabin. Other than the pilot and copilot, they were all alone on the luxury aircraft as it traveled at Mach 0.8 through the lower atmosphere, 35,000 feet above the Atlantic Ocean, en route to Dulles, Virginia.

"Figures," Califano mumbled, slumping back into his seat.

"SOP 20.2.1 prohibits CIA personnel from drinking alcohol while on duty," Thorne explained. "Unless it's directly required by the circumstances of a mission. And if that weren't enough, the director's standing order thirty-seven specifically prohibits drugs and alcohol aboard any CIA vessel, including aircraft."

"Whatever," said Califano with a sigh.

Ana watched him for a few seconds and then smirked. "But . . . I guess some rules were meant to be broken." She rose from her seat and retrieved a bottle of chilled champagne from a cabinet on the port side of the airplane. She placed it on the table between them, along with two flute-style glasses, and then resumed her seat.

"*Now* you're talking," said Califano with a crooked smile.

"Want to do the honors?"

With a wince, Califano leaned forward and unwrapped the foil and wire from the bottle and then quickly popped the cork. He poured two glasses of the bubbly liquid and handed one to Ana.

Ana raised her glass. "Here's to . . ." Her voice trailed off as she tried to figure out who or what to toast.

Califano took over. "Here's to the Office of Disruptive Technology Analysis and Intervention."

Ana laughed. "That's a mouthful." She clinked her glass against Califano's and took a sip. Then they both settled into their seats and relaxed with their drinks.

"So I was wondering," said Califano after a long stretch.

"Hmm?"

"If I came to work for DTAI, would you be my boss?"

"Whoa," said Ana, holding up her hand. "Who said anything about you joining DTAI? First of all, you'd have to be admitted into the CIA." She paused for a moment and considered mentioning the issue of Califano's prison stint, but she decided to let it go. "Then there's a ton of training you'd have to go through. Classroom work, physical training, weapons training, and the whole adventure down at Camp Peary. Then you'd have to *work* your way up to a billet like DTAI. Trust me, there's a lot of grunt work for new recruits." She took a sip of her champagne and shrugged. "But yeah . . . *in theory*, if you came to work at DTAI, I would be your direct supervisor."

"Cool," said Califano, nodding his head slowly. "I think you'd be a good boss to have."

ACKNOWLEDGMENTS

This book would not be complete without an acknowledgment of the many people who helped make it possible. First and foremost, thanks to my beautiful wife, Kelley, for her love, patience, and support. Thanks also to my friend and colleague Andy Holtman for his encouragement and advice on early drafts of this book; to my brothers, Cliff Barney and Jonathan Barney, for their encouragement and support; to my parents, Cliff and Edna Barney, for their comments on early drafts of this book; to Anna Balishina Naydonov, Marcus Luepke, and Dr. Branimir Vojcic for their invaluable assistance in translating Russian, Ukrainian, German, and Croatian phrases; to my in-laws, Debby and David Stoll, for their support and encouragement; to my terrific agent, Mickey Choate; and last but not least, to Jennifer Brehl, Emily Krump, and the rest of the superb team at HarperCollins for making this book a success.

And, of course, I extend a special thanks to everyone who has purchased and read *The Joshua Stone*. I sincerely hope you enjoyed it.

Insights,
Interviews
& More...

Meet James Barney

Dupont Photographers

JAMES BARNEY is the critically acclaimed author of *The Genesis Key*. He is an attorney who lives outside Washington, D.C., with his wife and two children. ∽

Separating Fact from Fiction

I HOPE YOU ENJOYED reading *The Joshua Stone* as much as I enjoyed writing it. If you're anything like me, you're probably now wondering which parts of the story are actually true and which are fictional. Yes, some elements of *The Joshua Stone* are, in fact, true—or at least *true-ish*. But which ones?

For those who like a challenge, I have created a short quiz that measures your skill at separating fact from fiction. (If you don't like quizzes, feel free to skip to the answers at the end.) See if you can identify which statements below are true and which are false.

Questions:

1. True or False: Thurmond, West Virginia, is an abandoned coal-mining town located along the New River Gorge Valley.

2. True or False: Thurmond, West Virginia, was once home to the Thurmond National Laboratory, where the U.S. government conducted secret nuclear experiments in the 1950s.

3. True or False: Fire Creek, West Virginia, is a small town of several hundred residents and has a local diner similar to Thelma's.

4. True or False: The Department of Energy headquarters building in Washington, D.C., is named for a ►

3

former secretary of the Navy who committed suicide in 1949 by jumping from the sixteenth floor of Bethesda Naval Hospital.

5. True or False: Russia has constructed several floating nuclear power stations similar to the Lomonosov-class floating power stations described in the story.

6. True or False: The Great Mosque of Al-Zaytuna in Tunis was constructed of columns and other building materials salvaged from the ancient ruins of Carthage.

7. True or False: During World War II, the Nazis were reportedly interested in a particular stone that was enshrined in the Great Mosque of Al-Zaytuna.

8. True or False: Very small quantities of material have been discovered on earth that do not appear to obey the normal laws of gravity.

9. True or False: The book of Jasher is considered a "lost" book of the Bible. It is mentioned twice in the Old Testament, but no authentic copy of the book of Jasher has ever been found.

10. True or False: U.S. government scientists conducted time-dilation experiments in the late 1950s and were able to generate time dilations of several minutes, as measured by Atomichron clocks.

11. True or False: Project Paperclip was a covert operation conducted by the U.S. government in the aftermath of World War II to entice German scientists to come to the United States.

12. True or False: Dr. Benjamin Fulcher was a Nobel Prize–winning physicist whose most famous work in quantum entanglement was done at the Institute of Advanced Studies in Princeton, New Jersey.

13. True or False: A purported copy of the book of Jasher was published in 1751, claiming to have been "translated into English from the Hebrew by Flaccus Albinus Alcuinus, who

went on a pilgrimage into the Holy Land and Persia, where he discovered this volume in the city of Gazna."

14. True or False: Another purported copy of the book of Jasher was published in Hebrew in Venice in 1625 and translated into English by Mordechai Noah in 1840.

15. True or False: Scholars still dispute the meaning of the word "bow" in the following passage from the second book of Samuel: "teach the children of Judah the use of the bow: behold it is written in the book of Jasher."

16. True or False: The exact cause of gravity is still a mystery to this day.

17. True or False: Experiments have proven one of the basic predictions of quantum entanglement theory, that two particles born in the same quantum event can be separated by a great distance yet still somehow share information nearly instantaneously.

18. True or False: One accepted theory of gravity is that it is a residual force of quantum entanglement originating with the Big Bang.

19. True or False: Time dilation is a real phenomenon, which must be accounted for in GPS satellites.

20. True or False: Physicists are already working on a gravity reactor that can create energy by changing the gravitational state of tiny quantities of matter.

21. True or False: The Third Church of Christ, Scientist, is an octagonal, mostly windowless building of Brutalist design, located three blocks from the White House.

22. True or False: Beneath the Third Church of Christ, Scientist, is a nuclear fallout shelter that is accessible from the West Wing of the White House.

23. True or False: The Madaba mosaic—the oldest known map of the Holy Land—shows the location of the twelve stones ▶

that Joshua commanded be taken up from the Jordan River and "pitched at Gilgal."

24. True or False: The Black Stone is one of the holiest symbols of the Muslim faith and is located in one corner of the Kaaba in Mecca.

25. True or False: The Black Stone of the Kaaba is actually formed from several smaller fragments that have been cemented together.

26. True or False: The Black Stone of the Kaaba is reported to have an unusual physical property: *it floats.*

Answers:

1. **TRUE.** Thurmond, West Virginia, is a former coal-mining town located in Fayette County, near the New River. In 2010, according to the federal census, Thurmond had a population of five. The old railroad depot (described in the story as run-down and partially collapsed) has in fact been restored by the National Park Service, and the entire town is now listed on the National Register of Historic Places.

2. **FALSE.** As far as I know, the Thurmond National Laboratory never existed.

3. **FALSE.** Fire Creek, West Virginia, is a ghost town. For about fifty years, starting in 1880, it was the base of operations for the Fire Creek Coal & Coke Company, which operated a coal mine and several dozen coke ovens there. By the 1930s, however, the population had dwindled, and today only ruins of the town remain.

4. **TRUE.** The Department of Energy headquarters is located in the James V. Forrestal Building at L'Enfant Plaza in Washington, D.C. The building's namesake, James V. Forrestal, served as secretary of the Navy from 1944 to 1947 and secretary of defense from 1947 to 1949. Forrestal was hospitalized in April 1949 for physical exhaustion and depression. On the day he was to be released from the

psychiatric ward of Bethesda Naval Hospital, he was found dead below his window. The official cause of death was determined to be suicide, although assassination theories persist to this day.

5. **TRUE.** Russia commenced construction of the *Akademik Lomonosov* floating nuclear power station in April 2007, and it was launched in July 2010. Several more of these floating power stations are reportedly under construction. Each vessel is a floating barge with two nuclear reactors capable of producing 70 megawatts of electricity, enough to electrify a city of about 200,000 people. Russia reportedly plans to use these floating nuclear power stations in remote regions, for instance to support oil and gas exploration in the Arctic.

6. **TRUE.** The Great Mosque of Al-Zaytuna in Tunis was constructed sometime in the seventh century A.D. and has long been one of the most important mosques in Africa. One of its most distinctive features is its Romanesque appearance, particularly its use of numerous columns to separate the mosque into naves and bays. It is widely believed that these columns, as well as other structural elements of the mosque, were salvaged from the ancient ruins of Carthage, which was sacked and destroyed by the Romans in 146 B.C.

7. **FALSE.** There is no evidence that the Nazis were interested in anything enshrined in the Great Mosque of Al-Zaytuna.

8. **FALSE.** All materials on earth (and as far as we know, in the entire universe) obey the laws of gravity. The floating black stones in this story are purely fictional.

9. **TRUE.** The book of Jasher is mentioned twice in the Old Testament—once in Joshua 10:12–13 and once in 2 Samuel 1:18. However, no authentic copy of the book of Jasher is known to exist. The Hebrew word for "Jasher" has been translated to mean "upright" or "just." Thus, the book of Jasher is sometimes referred to as the "book of the Just" or the "book of the Upright." ▸

10. **FALSE.** As far as I know, the government never conducted time-dilation experiments resulting in time dilations of several minutes. The events described in the story as taking place at the Thurmond National Laboratory in 1959 are purely fictional.

11. **TRUE.** Project Paperclip (or Operation Paperclip) was a covert operation ordered by President Truman in 1945 and carried out by the Office of Strategic Services (OSS), the immediate predecessor of the modern CIA. The purpose of the project was to recruit German scientists to come to the United States to conduct scientific research. One goal of the project was to prevent these scientists from being recruited by the Soviet Union. Among the scientists brought to the United States as part of Project Paperclip were hundreds of rocket scientists, nuclear engineers, chemists, physicists, medical doctors, and aeronautical engineers.

12. **FALSE.** Dr. Benjamin Fulcher and his colleagues are all fictional characters, and any resemblance to any actual persons, living or dead, is purely coincidental.

13. **TRUE.** A purported copy of the book of Jasher was published in 1751, claiming to have been "translated into English from the Hebrew by Flaccus Albinus Alcuinus." This book was reprinted in 1829 in Bristol, England, along with a "preliminary dissertation proving the authenticity of the work." However, from the time it was originally published, this book has been widely considered to be a fraud. You can view a copy of the 1829 version at http://openlibrary.org/books/OL22877553M/The_Book_of_Jasher.

14. **TRUE.** Another purported copy of the book of Jasher was published in Hebrew in Venice in 1625 and was translated into English by Mordechai Noah in 1840. The introduction of the 1625 version mentions an earlier 1552 edition, published in Naples. However, no such earlier text has ever been found. The introduction of the 1625 version also claims that it was originally translated from a book found in the ruins of Jerusalem in A.D. 70 by a Roman officer named Sidrus.

Scholars are split on whether this version of the book of Jasher is a forgery or an actual transcription of an ancient Hebrew document.

15. **TRUE.** Scholars still dispute the meaning of the word "bow" in 2 Samuel 1:18. The Hebrew word is "*Qaset*," but its meaning is unclear in context. The King James Version of the Bible translates this passage as "teach the children of Judah the *use* of the bow," interpreting "bow" as a weapon. In contrast, the New American Standard Version translates this passage as "teach the sons of Judah the *song* of the bow," interpreting "bow" as a song or lamentation. The actual Hebrew text simply says "teach the children of Judah *the bow*," without specifying whether it is a weapon or a song.

16. **TRUE.** Gravity can be measured, and its effects on all things, large and small, can be observed. But as for *why* gravity occurs and what exactly causes it, there are no definitive answers, only theories.

17. **TRUE.** "Quantum entanglement" refers to the relationship between two particles (like photons or electrons) that are forced to interact in a way that causes them to take on certain complementary quantum properties, such as the directions of their spin. Quantum mechanics dictates that, as soon as a quantum state is observed for one such particle (such as a clockwise spin), the other particle will immediately take on the correspondingly appropriate state (such as a counterclockwise spin). Countless experiments have verified this is true. What is perplexing, however, is that this phenomenon occurs even if the particles are physically separated by many miles. Somehow, despite their physical distance, the particles are able to exchange quantum information nearly instantaneously—much faster than the speed of light. Indeed, some scientists have referred to this phenomenon as "quantum teleportation." (See www.nature.com/news/quantum-teleportation-achieved -over-record-distances-1.11163). Albert Einstein was ▶

perplexed and frustrated by this phenomenon, which he referred to as "spooky action at a distance."

18. **FALSE.** As far as I know, there is no mainstream theory of gravity that is based on quantum entanglement originating with the Big Bang. I made this theory up from whole cloth. After I did so, however, I noticed that the topic had already been discussed in various physics forums, so I guess I'm not the only one to have had this thought. It is not an accepted theory of gravity, however.

19. **TRUE.** Time dilation is a real phenomenon, and it occurs precisely as Einstein predicted. In the case of GPS satellites, which are moving through space at a high rate of speed compared to earth's (inertial) frame of reference, the theory of special relativity predicts that clocks on board the satellites will run more slowly than clocks on earth. This, in fact, has been proven. If the GPS clocks weren't adjusted for this phenomenon, they would run about seven microseconds slower per day than clocks on earth due to special relativity. The theory of general relativity, in contrast, predicts that the clocks on the GPS satellites will run faster than clocks on earth because they are farther from earth's gravitational pull. This, too, has been verified and shown to cause an error of about forty-five microseconds per day in GPS satellites. Thus, the offsetting effects of special relativity and general relativity require that the clocks aboard GPS satellites must be adjusted to run about thirty-eight microseconds slower per day than they otherwise would, in order to keep them in sync with time on earth.

20. **FALSE.** As far as I know, there is no such thing as a gravity reactor that can create energy by changing the gravitational state of tiny quantities of matter, and nobody is working on such a device.

21. **TRUE.** The Third Church of Christ, Scientist, is an octagonal, mostly windowless building of Brutalist design, located at 910 Sixteenth Street NW in Washington, D.C., about three blocks from the White House. The congregation of the Third

Church of Christ, Scientist, fought for nearly twenty years for the right to demolish their church and build a new one. Preservation groups opposed this effort and were able to block it by convincing the District of Columbia to designate the Brutalist-inspired church, built in 1971, as a historic landmark. A protracted legal battle ensued. Finally, in October 2012, the congregation won the right to tear down the old church and build a new one on the same site. As of today, the old Brutalist church is still standing, but it is in serious disrepair and is not being used for services.

22. **FALSE.** As far as I know, there is no secret fallout shelter beneath the Third Church of Christ, Scientist, although that would certainly be a logical place for one (and would explain why the government fought so hard to keep the original building intact).

23. **TRUE.** The Madaba mosaic, located on the floor of a Byzantine church in Jordan, is the oldest known map of the Holy Land. It is a fascinating map, which shows, among other things, the location of the twelve stones that Joshua commanded be taken up from the Jordan River and erected as a monument in Gilgal. The map shows a churchlike structure with twelve white circles, annotated in Greek as *Galgala-tokai Dodekalithon*, which means the town of Galgala with twelve stones. You can view the entire Madaba map at www.christusrex.org/www1/ofm/mad/.

24. **TRUE.** The Black Stone is a revered symbol in the Muslim faith and is located in the southeastern corner of the Kaaba in Mecca. Mohammed himself is said to have placed it there in A.D. 605. According to Islamic tradition, the Black Stone was delivered from heaven to show Adam and Eve where to build the first altar. The stone was lost during the Great Flood but was later found by Ibrahim, who was guided to it by the angel Jibrail. Ibrahim instructed his son, Ismael, to build a new temple and to embed the Black Stone into it. That temple was the Kaaba in Mecca. ▶

25. **TRUE.** The Black Stone is not a single stone but, rather, an aggregate of several smaller fragments that have been cemented together. In my story, I suggest that these are ten of the twelve stones that Joshua ordered pulled from the Jordan River after the miracle of the river crossing. But, of course, that is pure fiction.

26. **TRUE.** A famous story about the Black Stone is that it was stolen from Mecca in A.D. 930 by Qarmatians, a group of nonbelievers and bandits who were terrorizing the Arabian Peninsula at that time. According to legend, the Black Stone was returned twenty-three years later, along with a mysterious note that said: "By command we took it, and by command we return it." To verify that the returned stone (which had been broken into several pieces) was actually the Black Stone, it was placed in water and observed to float. This unusual attribute— the ability to float on water—is still associated with the Black Stone, although this has never been scientifically tested in the modern era. ❧

More from
James Barney

THE GENESIS KEY

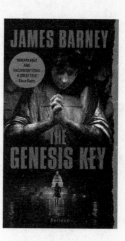

More than three decades ago, Dr. Kathleen Sainsbury's archaeologist parents were murdered at an ancient excavation site in Iraq. Now the gifted biologist stands on the brink of a miraculous breakthrough: the discovery of a gene that could extend a human life by hundreds of years. But at the moment of her greatest triumph, a mysterious phone call reveals a hidden truth that draws chaos and violence once again into Kathleen's world . . . and threatens to irreversibly alter the destiny of humankind.

For somewhere in the shadows, powerful unseen forces are watching . . . and waiting. Suddenly Kathleen is a target of covert government operatives as she races to uncover the mystery behind her parents' secret research and brutal deaths—a mystery locked in the human genome, in the sands of antiquity, and in the book of Genesis. More than survival is at stake for Dr. Kathleen Sainsbury. The future of all humanity hangs in the balance . . . and the prize is the secret of life itself.

"*The Genesis Key* is a solid blend of science, myth, history, and suspense. It's remarkable and unconventional,

Read on

More from James Barney *(continued)*

which together make for a great tale.
There's an intense brand of storytelling
here, utilizing all of the elements I love.
I can't wait for more from James
Barney."   —Steve Berry, *New York Times*
bestselling author of
The Jefferson Key and
The Templar Legacy

on't miss the next
book by your favorite
author. Sign up now for
AuthorTracker by visiting
www.AuthorTracker.com.

BOOKS BY JAMES BARNEY

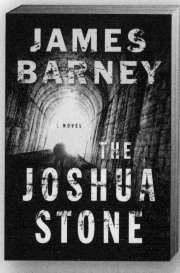

THE JOSHUA STONE

Available in Paperback and eBook

In 1959, in an underground laboratory in a remote region of West Virginia, a secret government experiment went terribly awry. A half dozen scientists mysteriously disappeared, and all subsequent efforts to rescue them failed. In desperation, President Eisenhower ordered the lab sealed shut and all records of its existence destroyed. Now, fifty-four years later, something from the lab has emerged. When mysterious events begin occurring along the New River Valley in West Virginia, government agents Mike Califano and Ana Thorne are sent to investigate. What they discover will shake the foundations of science and religion and put both agents in the crosshairs of a deadly, worldwide conspiracy.

"There's an intense brand of storytelling here. . . . I can't wait for more from James Barney."
—Steve Berry, *New York Times* bestselling author of *The Jefferson Key*

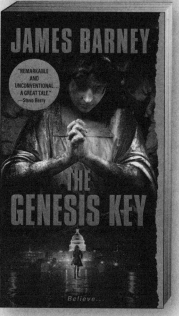

THE GENESIS KEY

Available in Mass Market and eBook

More than three decades ago, Dr. Kathleen Sainsbury's archaeologist parents were murdered at an ancient excavation site in Iraq. Now the gifted biologist stands on the brink of a miraculous breakthrough: the discovery of a gene that could extend a human life by hundreds of years. But at the moment of her greatest triumph, a mysterious phone call reveals a hidden truth that draws chaos and violence once again into Kathleen's world . . . and threatens to irreversibly alter the destiny of humankind. For somewhere in the shadows, powerful unseen forces are watching . . . and waiting. Suddenly Kathleen is a target of covert government operatives as she races to uncover the mystery behind her parents' secret research and brutal deaths—a mystery locked in the human genome, in the sands of antiquity, and in the Book of Genesis.

"Barney's fast-paced debut novel demonstrates his knowledge of ancient history, the bible, and microbiology, as well as his fertile imagination."
—*Publishers Weekly*